"A highly original additio... in turn . . . I thoroughly e... reading more about Zoë M... ...her world."
—Patricia Briggs

"With a quick-witted heroine and truly frightening baddies, Weldon offers a fantastic kickoff to what promises to be a vibrant new series." —*Booklist*

"Launching with a bang, this new detective series/urban fantasy crossover plunges its astral-traveling heroine in the middle of the action. Martinique is strong, resourceful, self-deprecating, and fascinating." —*Library Journal*

"Weldon's lively debut . . . keeps Zoë and her readers off balance with brisk pacing and brain-wrenching plot twists. [She draws] the story to a satisfying close while leaving enough loose ends to set up Zoë's next adventure."
—*Publishers Weekly*

"Interesting, off-kilter characters . . . I can only hope that we will see more of Zoë Martinique and her family."
—*SFRevu*

"This fresh urban fantasy series keeps the action intense with its first-person point of view. Heavy on pop-culture references and quirky dialogue, it features original characters the reader will want to befriend. With a penchant for finding trouble, like Kim Harrison's protagonist [Rachel Morgan], and witty banter akin to that of *Buffy the Vampire Slayer*, Weldon's astral-traveling heroine Zoë makes this series a hit." —*Romantic Times*

"[A] worthwhile debut that bodes well for disembodied adventures to come." —*Kirkus Reviews*

Ace Books by Phaedra Weldon

WRAITH
SPECTRE
PHANTASM

A ZOË MARTINIQUE INVESTIGATION

WRAITH

Phaedra Weldon

ACE BOOKS, NEW YORK

THE BERKLEY PUBLISHING GROUP
Published by the Penguin Group
Penguin Group (USA) Inc.
375 Hudson Street, New York, New York 10014, USA
Penguin Group (Canada), 90 Eglinton Avenue East, Suite 700, Toronto, Ontario M4P 2Y3, Canada
(a division of Pearson Penguin Canada Inc.)
Penguin Books Ltd., 80 Strand, London WC2R 0RL, England
Penguin Group Ireland, 25 St. Stephen's Green, Dublin 2, Ireland (a division of Penguin Books Ltd.)
Penguin Group (Australia), 250 Camberwell Road, Camberwell, Victoria 3124, Australia
(a division of Pearson Australia Group Pty. Ltd.)
Penguin Books India Pvt. Ltd., 11 Community Centre, Panchsheel Park, New Delhi—110 017, India
Penguin Group (NZ), 67 Apollo Drive, Rosedale, North Shore 0632, New Zealand
(a division of Pearson New Zealand Ltd.)
Penguin Books (South Africa) (Pty.) Ltd., 24 Sturdee Avenue, Rosebank, Johannesburg 2196,
South Africa

Penguin Books Ltd., Registered Offices: 80 Strand, London WC2R 0RL, England

This is a work of fiction. Names, characters, places, and incidents either are the product of the author's imagination or are used fictitiously, and any resemblance to actual persons, living or dead, business establishments, events, or locales is entirely coincidental. The publisher does not have any control over and does not assume any responsibility for author or third-party websites or their content.

WRAITH

An Ace Book / published by arrangement with the author

PRINTING HISTORY
Ace trade paperback edition / June 2007
Ace mass-market edition / June 2009

Copyright © 2007 by Phaedra Weldon.
Cover art by Christian McGrath.
Cover design by Judith Lagerman.
Interior text design by Tiffany Estreicher.

ISBN: 978-0-441-01697-6

ACE
Ace Books are published by The Berkley Publishing Group,
a division of Penguin Group (USA) Inc.,
375 Hudson Street, New York, New York 10014.
ACE and the "A" design are trademarks of Penguin Group (USA) Inc.

PRINTED IN THE UNITED STATES OF AMERICA

10   9   8   7   6   5   4   3   2   1

IN APPRECIATION . . .

Much of my gratitude goes out to my parents, DeLois and Leonard Weldon, whose gift of a typewriter when I was twelve definitely set the bar high. And to my siblings Amber, Tara, and Marc, for not making fun of me too much, as well as Sarah Milligan-Weldon, the best sister-in-law a girl could have.

A powerful thank-you goes to Dean Wesley Smith and Kristine Kathryn Rusch, without whose guidance and evil red pen (as well as Dean's "grumpy face"), my plans of becoming a writer would have tanked. Several times. I miss those weeks in Oregon, but I'll never forget the lessons learned.

I owe the following for their support and friendship: Ken "Evilboy" Gunter (Best Friend and First Reader), Dr. Ilsa J. Bick (my voice of reality), Dayle Dermatis (the other half of my brain), Ken Cooper (Mr. Mischievous), "1000 Marietta Blvd" (Ken Gunter, Rachelle Udell, Roy Wilson, Jr., Joe Yost, Blake Sorensen, J. P. Rhea, and Maylon Walker), the Oregon Writers Network—especially the Omega Master Class, Loren L. Coleman and the gang at BattleCorps, Chris and Steven York, and Darren "Dags" McKinty (yes, that's you behind the bar, mate—*skoshi bukimi!*).

A special thanks to my editor, Ginjer Buchanan, for taking a chance on me and a wacky idea and having faith in Zoë. To Jodi

Reamer, for taking on a new writer with a wacky idea and being the best agent ever.

Last but by no means least, Dr. Ernest C. Steele, Jr., husband and accidental supporter, and to my daughter, Indri, for bringing me the happiest moments of my life.

1

THE MENTAL

ONE of the perks of astral travel is the inability to smell, especially when I glide into restaurants that haven't thrown out their raw meat in a day or two.

Now that's an odor that sticks to the back of your tongue like a hairy sock.

My name is Zoë—that's with a long *e*. Not the pronunciation like "toe." Martinique. Irish mother, Latin American father. Which means I have darker than usual skin for an Irish Catholic, a mass of brownish hair, very light brown eyes, a wicked mean temper, and a love of bawdy pub songs.

My mother insists I look like my father, whom I'd always sort of imagined as resembling Antonio Banderas. Okay—so Antonio's not Latin, but Spanish. He's still one beautiful man. But you know how it is, how a daughter always imagines her father as being the most beautiful man in the world. A hero. A legend.

But according to my mom, the only legendary thing my dad did was vanish from my life. As to the whereabouts of one Adiran Martinique, can't help you. Haven't seen him since I was four. Mom refers to his absence as necessary.

Try explaining the word *necessary* to a teenager with raging hormones and the want of a daddy.

As strange as this may sound, I astral travel for a living, gathering up information that people pay good money for. I can't give you the mechanics of *how* I do it, only that I can. I'm not sure there's any real official name for what I am or do. I've sort of self-labeled myself a Traveler for want of a better name. Telling a new client I *travel* to locate the information they pay for is easier than saying "Oh—I go out of body and tootle around in my altogether to snoop on people."

Ever tried explaining the astral plane to any average Joe? They get that whole MEGO look—you know—My Eyes Glaze Over.

Where was I? Oh. Yeah.

Smell.

The smell problem wasn't what brought me into the biggest case of my life—the one that sent me down a road of no return.

It was the sound of a gunshot.

The first step was walking out of the Fox Theatre on a Tuesday night. It was mid-November, one of my favorite months. I'd been hired to look in (okay, snoop—satisfied?) on a meeting between the owners of some dot-com company in Buckhead, one of the more upwardly urban areas of Atlanta, Georgia.

My client had wanted to know if they were discussing his dismissal. Like I was going to find this out while they watched a musical? I mean—who actually *talks* in the middle of *Chicago*? This is Atlanta for crying out loud, the third largest Gay-Mecca in the States.

Talking? Not likely. Singing? Definitely.

These guys hadn't uttered a word in the first half hour,

and I didn't feel like sitting through the show a third time. Not to mention I didn't really have a seat and I felt a bit uncomfortable standing in front of them, waiting, even though no one could see me.

So I left the gig, confident they weren't going to talk about my client during the production. They'd mentioned tentative after-show plans for a coffee at Café Intermezzo over in Buckhead—so I figured I'd step outside and wait for them to leave and resume my snoopiness then.

It was early, and I had time to kill. I'd only been incorporeal for about forty-five minutes (I have a neato-kazeeto watch a friend gave me that actually keeps astral time—I have no idea how it works, but it does). The longest I'd ever remained out of body, without too much physical lethargy later, was four hours. I didn't know if there was some mystical time limit or witching hour for being astral, but there did appear to be various physical reactions to being gone longer. The body did not like having the soul/astral presence/spirit (pick one) away for too long.

It was kinda like having a cat that pushes the plant off of the fireplace mantel when you don't come home and feed it at the preappointed time. Or a dog that piddles on the carpet. Seems the body resents being left alone.

Oh—but don't worry. Nature has a way of getting back what's hers. Trust me. Ever heard of near-death experiences where they mention that silver cord? It's real.

Of course it's a great tether, but as for acting like a bungee cord?

Nada. I haven't had the need to snap back into my body. You can travel back along it, but the end result isn't as peaceful as just stepping back in normally.

But then again, this really isn't normal, is it?

Let's see, I've had an achy back, stiff joints, migraine, loss of vision (that only happened one time and it wasn't my fault though Mom's certain I was faking it), and numbness.

Those are the nasty things that've happened when I've been out of body longer than my personal best of four hours.

I'd been gone much longer. Once. The first time out. It'd been a traumatic experience (one I don't feel like talking about right now). Mom said it was nine hours.

Nine.

My body wouldn't respond to me for nearly six hours after I returned. So for the world, and the doctors at Crawford Long, I lay dormant, in a coma, for fifteen hours.

I never wanted to repeat that again. What if I'd been away longer? Would I have remained like this forever? A ghost? Spook? Spectral entity?

Something for some paranormal society to capture on film?

The feeling when out of body is kind of hard to explain. The closest I can come to is *powerful*. Well, not at first. Takes about five minutes before the powerful part kicks in. In the beginning it's like finding yourself out on a tightwire strung across two buildings with no net. Actually— no wire either. You have no idea what it is you're doing. And all you can think about is becoming a pile of goo on the pavement below.

And then you discover when you fall off that wire (and you *will* fall off) you float in midair instead of crash. There's no goo. There's no real danger (none that I'd seen till that point).

And then you think, this is great! No one can see me. No one can tell me not to do something. The world is my playground. No rules!

Or so you think. Because reality has a posse that does nothing but bring the old smack-down on the young and stupid.

That would be me.

And that would be this night, of all nights.

I stood outside the Fox Theatre, the humming and pulsing bulbs from the marquee above me giving the evening a sort of surreal feel. I was invisible amidst the crowds of night people. I thought about jumping into a cab with someone and taking a ride.

One of the drawbacks of astral traveling is you can't pop here or pop there.

Ghosts, spirits, ethereal bodies—pick a name—don't have teleportation skills. So finding a means to get from point A to point B is still a necessity.

Even ghosts have to take the bus.

And then again, I didn't want to end up in East Suburbia in case my targets for the evening did end up having coffee and I couldn't get back in time.

Atlanta has a unique design in that it's shaped like a huge wagon wheel. The city, with its skyscrapers and mainstream pulse (that whole nexus, center-of-the-universe thing), is the wheel's hub. Roads spin out in all directions, leading to the smaller suburbs like Decatur, Chamblee, Tucker, Doraville—these are the spokes. Then just beyond them is Interstate 285. The "perimeter" as it's called by most natives and residents. It encircles the entire city like the outer tire.

Gobs of people live outside the perimeter, or OTP. Cheaper houses and more land for sale. Worse traffic though, in my opinion. I live inside the perimeter, or ITP. I like the city, the diversity of people, and the convenience of having a Target and a museum in less than a ten-minute drive.

I'd been to several of the large cities, like Boston, Chicago, New York, and Los Angeles. And if there was one thing I enjoyed most about living in Atlanta, it was the trees. All shapes and sizes. I've seen crews knock out areas just to plant trees (and not always peach trees) or divert sidewalks to preserve a long-standing granddaddy of an oak. We are the greenest city I've ever been in.

I moved along the sidewalk with people passing back and forth, bundled in their fall coats. Another good thing about being a Traveler is I don't feel temperature. If anyone could see me, I'd be wearing my usual uniform of a long-sleeved, black spandex cat-suit with my black bunny slippers. They have white nylon whiskers and soft pink noses—and are starting to look a bit frayed, come to think of it. I keep my hair in a long braid that usually truncates at the small of my back.

It's the costume I put on before I go out of body. I found out by accident that if I lay down naked, then I appear outside of my body naked as well, and though technically no one could see me that way, I really didn't want to take any chance I'd run into a kid who saw naked dead people.

Know what I mean?

I didn't have any standard utility belt à la superhero. Couldn't use one. Another of the drawbacks of being incorporeal, other than being sat on, is that I haven't been able to manipulate anything physical. I always figured ghosts who could move things around had something up on me—though maybe it was the upside to really being dead.

If there was an upside.

I knew a few really dead people. And they could move things, albeit not well at times. But as for other people that do what I do?

Nada. I'd been doing this for six years and never met another Traveler. Which is kinda lonely.

After a block or two of walking, I found myself standing in front of one of the more impressive buildings down from the Fox. During the daylight the Bank of America Plaza was made of rust-colored marble and gleamed when the sun shone.

But at night, the polished surface reflected the moon and stars from the November night sky. I liked looking around inside of buildings like this.

Most floors had their cubicle farms. Dozens of feet of blue or gray burlap squares, each containing a snapshot of an individual's life. The concept appealed to the artist in me. Sometimes I would wander through the cubes and look at pictures, mostly of children. Happy families.

Normal families.

Wives and their husbands.

It could get damned depressing too. Especially for a single woman in her late twenties with no prospects for marriage, kids, or normality.

I'd almost talked myself out of heading inside when something touched the edges of my awareness. As a Traveler, I'm a bit sensitive to astral-plane happenings. Stirrings. Much like standing in a quiet meadow and feeling a breeze move the hairs on my arms. Sometimes it was just a shiver, though not from the normal definition of cold but from one that reached deep down inside.

This happens sometimes in my physical body as well. And if I were in my body at that moment, I'd say someone had just walked over my grave.

And that was exactly the feeling I was getting from this building as it loomed in front of me, painted against a comic-book sky. Something pretty oogy was inside. Something, in hindsight, I should have avoided.

Unfortunately I'd worked myself into a rut over the past few weeks and found the prospect of oogy exciting.

Mental note: *oogy is* not *exciting*.

Okay, so I'm not the brightest lightbulb in the sign. But I was in some need for outside stimulation. And since a normal, sexual relationship was out of reach at the moment, adventure seemed the most natural outlet.

The front doors of the building stood seven feet in height. Two urns the size of small horses held mounds of multicolored pansies whose petals moved with the night breeze. The black mat leading up to the building said Bank of America in blue, red, and white lettering. The whole package seemed pretty imposing. Especially for some young gun just out of college and looking for a job. Might even make them turn tail and run.

But not me. I could go anywhere.

Slipping through glass wasn't as easy, or pleasant (not that any type of sieving was pleasant), as going through wood. Wood was more porous, not as taxing on the ethereal goo that comprised my astral body.

Moving through glass was like moving through ice.

Aw-ful. Made my nipples hard. And not in the fun way.

The lobby was nice if not corporate standard. Shiny marble floors, security desk with a dozing, uniformed rent-a-cop in the center chair. And a brief hallway with two walls of elevators.

And since I couldn't push the buttons, I opted for the stairs.

The oogy drew me to it much like cute on a puppy. Though on a few occasions I paused on the steps and wondered if it could sense me the way I sensed it. And I had a very sharp moment of *get the hell out of here*, which I promptly ignored.

The feeling settled around the fifteenth floor. And after climbing fifteen flights of steps, I was tired. I do get tired in this form—mainly I think because I'm still attached to my physical body. And if I got tired in astral form, then I was looking at a real heavy sleep when I got back. I was also going to wake up ravenous.

Guess I'm lucky to have my dad's metabolism too—and not my mom's. I have a sweet tooth that stretches across the entire state of Georgia.

And this little sidebar was going to cost one entire Sara Lee Strawberry Cheesecake.

The fifteenth floor turned out to be a cubicle farm with window offices around the edges. There were no lights on. With only shadows to point my way, I moved cautiously—

the oogy loomed very close, and my stomach twisted into tight knots.

Toward the back of the floor was a long, wide hallway that ran from east to west. There weren't any offices along the opposite wall. Windows brought the city lights inside, illuminating the cubicles. I had a beautiful view of the IBM building, as well as Georgia Power, with its blaring red-and-black logo.

A door framed in yellow capped the end of the hallway. Beside it were two more doors with little stick figures just visible on their fronts in the gloom. Bathrooms maybe?

Voices filtered through the light-framed doorway. I leaned forward to listen but couldn't make out what was said. If I'd had to harbor a guess, I'd say it definitely wasn't English.

Curiosity pulled me closer to the door, and I prepared myself to sieve through just as the gunshot rang out.

I reacted much the same way in astral form as I would in my body. I screamed. Which was bad. Voices carried from the astral to the physical. Or at least mine did. Don't know why. Even though people couldn't *see* me like this, I'd learned they could definitely *hear* me.

So whoever just fired that gun knew some chick just screamed on the other side. I ducked into the closest cubicle and tucked my tail between my legs like any good fraidy-cat would do.

Let me point out—I'm not really a chicken. But I was born with a wicked-mean need to survive. Invisible or not—the sound of the gunshot means pain, death, or bad guy.

Oh—and panic.

So in astral, hiding is good.

I stifled a second horror-movie scream when the door burst open and a dark-haired, dark-suited man barreled out. The lights from the room behind him illuminated his staggered steps. He stumbled to a full stop in front of the cubicle I hid in.

He spun to face the light as he went down on his knees. The light revealed handsome, Asian features. Blood pooled around his knees, pouring like syrup from a gunshot wound in his chest. I could just make out the ripped shirt beneath the suit jacket and saw the dark, cloudy aura of what I assumed was death surrounding him.

This guy was going fast.

I moved back into the shadows, willing myself to be as invisible as possible. I didn't know if it'd work—but I sure as hell didn't want whoever shot him to shoot at me.

Get a grip, Zoë—they can't see you. I told myself this over and over, but somehow I knew I'd really stepped in it this time. I spied on surly types in business suits—insurance fraud mostly. And paranoid bean counters who worried about their jobs—like the guy I was supposed to be working for tonight.

But bullets? Blood? Murder?

This was Court TV in 3-D. This was *America's Most Wanted* in your face. This was *Forensic Files* pre forensicness.

This was *not* where I was supposed to be.

The shooter appeared then—a pretty impressive silhouette in the door. He wore a long trench coat and what I guessed were military camouflage pants tucked inside high, leather boots. I could make out black shades obscuring his features and a smooth scalp—no hair. In his right hand was a gun.

Oh hell.

Big and spooky (I dubbed him Trench-Coat for lack of a better name) ambled closer to the kneeling, shaking man. The bleeding man looked up. Trench-Coat raised the gun and aimed it at the man's forehead.

I shivered and kept a hand over my mouth. *I should*

leave! Now! Run right back down my silver cord to my body and never look back.

Cursed is the one that never listens to the voice of Reason. And when you think about it, if I were Reason in this day and age, I'd pack and leave town. No one ever listens anymore.

"I . . ." The dying man coughed. His hands were now out at his sides in a gesture of surrender. "I do not . . . have it. Please tell your master . . . he is being unreasonable."

Trench-Coat's shoulders rose once, as if to indicate a *tough-shit* shrug as he brought the barrel's end to rest between the man's eyes.

"Please!" The dying man squeezed his eyes shut. He then said something in Japanese and gave a short bow. I committed what he said to memory (one of the cool things about being a Traveler—I can remember everything I see and hear. But one of the bad things was I remembered it with my subconscious mind, and though it was an exact memory—I couldn't always recall it at will) as I watched with wide eyes.

I felt like a guilty rubbernecker passing by the scene of a fatal accident. Didn't want to look, but just couldn't help it. I *had* to look at the trainwreck.

I should do something! But what? Moan? Make Trench-Coat think the building's haunted? Right Zoë, like a guy who shoots people is going to care about a ghost.

Now remember—I'm not a superheroine. I'm not gifted with superpowers, at least not in the Justice League sense of the word. I don't see this kind of thing every day— shooting I mean. Blood. Gore. Downright meanness.

Okay—so maybe the meanness. You haven't met my mom yet.

So I guess most of me hadn't caught on that this was real life—this guy was really bleeding to death kneeling on the floor of this building.

He was *really* pleading for his life.

When the second shot came, I wasn't prepared for it. Not physically, not mentally.

The man's head snapped back as bits of skull and gray matter sprayed the Berber rug behind him, as well as the walls of most of the cubicle I hid in. None of it hit me. Instead, it flew through me and made small splat noises on the computer and desk around me.

Beside the gore-decorated monitor a small, Winnie-the-Pooh frame sat in a pool of viscous blood and bits of bone while a child of perhaps three laughed.

The sound of the bullet entering and exiting the skull was one I'll never forget. Sort of like cracking fresh, wet celery. I won't forget the sound of his body hitting the floor either. A squishy, juicy thud.

I bit my tongue to stop myself from screaming. The logical, sane part of me ordered me to leave. To run. To flee.

But I stood there—paralyzed by a fear so familiar—so dark.

So helpless.

And as I watched, Trench-Coat pocketed the gun and moved toward the body.

He stood over it.

I looked at his feet. That sane part of me, the practical one that wanted me to take the next elevator down somehow, was glad the bastard would leave a telltale shoe print in the bloodied carpet. Ha! They could catch him from his shoes! See? All those sleepless nights watching Court TV weren't wasted!

That's when I noticed he wasn't leaving *any* shoe prints.

I watched him move to the other side of the body, just across from my huddled position behind the cubicle opening. I still couldn't see his face either in the light from the open door. It somehow remained shrouded in shadow.

He raised his right hand and a red light appeared in the center of his palm. It pulsed just as a whitish, wispy cloud rose from the body and spiraled upward. It took on the glassy, transparent appearance of the dead man.

Trench-Coat thrust his red-dotted hand at the spirit (well what else would it be?). Again I watched as the Asian man cringed and tried to move away as his elbow was pulled to a pinpoint and sucked into the red dot, much like a tiny vacuum cleaner.

Was he taking this man's soul? Oh damn. Trench-Coat was a freaking astral sucking Hoover!

That time I did make a noise.

I swore like a sailor.

I wouldn't have been so upset with myself if I'd have screamed, or at least burped. Made the noise worthwhile.

Though I have to admit, I think I used one of my more colorful metaphoric templates at that moment.

Then he looked at me.

He looked *right at me*!

And I could see the windows on the opposite wall *through* him.

"Sonofabitchmotherfucker!"

Now that outburst just had no imagination, but it sure relayed the way I felt.

He lowered his hand, and the ghost of the dead man disappeared. To Heaven or to Hell, I had no idea. Nor did I really give a good goddamn at that moment.

This guy was looking *at* me, and I was looking *through* him! The significance of that moment wasn't lost on me at all.

Part of the light from the windows finally fell over his face, which shouldn't have happened. Only solid objects reflect light, which cause shadows.

I don't make a shadow.

When I looked again, this man did.

What the hell was he? How could he be transparent and still cast shadow?

But I really didn't have the time to worry about the laws of physics right now.

Because Trench-Coat was taking steps *toward* me.

"Stay away," I said. Not exactly a threat. My own voice is sort of gravelly and not something I enjoy listening to.

He didn't speak. But he kept coming toward me.

Mental note: *run you idiot!*

I sieved through the cubicle to the next one—in fact I kept sieving in and out of every cubicle wall until I was at the stair door.

And stopped in my tracks.

Trench-Coat was there ahead of me. And I could see his face now, reflected with the red light of the exit sign overhead.

Bald, nondescript, the face of the ordinary man. Nothing I could remember.

He grinned.

Drool poured from his mouth as he grinned at me; but it never touched the floor.

Oh, gross.

He reached out toward me as I backed away. I tried like hell to sieve through the floor at that moment, drop down a few floors to the lobby, but nothing happened. Not even my feet disappeared into the carpet. What the hell? If I could sieve through a cubicle, why not a floor? I had no idea why I couldn't at that moment.

"I said stay away from me. I saw what you did." Yeah, like that's going to stop him. The thing wasn't even leaving footprints, and I knew he stepped in all that blood!

I asked the creatures of the astral plane: What the fuck was he?

Still he remained silent. I turned to the elevator.

He was there.

I turned back to the staircase door.

Again he was there.

I took several steps backward and turned to slip into the cubicles again—and he was there.

There was only one way out—and it terrified me to try. Not because I hadn't ever used my silver cord to return to my body before—but because I didn't know if this monster could *follow* me *back* to my body!

It would be like showing the stalker where the victim lived.

Trench-Coat had both hands out now, reaching for me.

I had to get back to my body. But returning from a distance took a bit of concentration. Going back isn't a second-nature event for me. I wish it were. Then I wouldn't have to think about it to do it.

It's not something my subconscious wants. And so I have to momentarily fight with it to return home.

I had no choice but to stand still as Trench-Coat advanced on me, that red dot pulsing faster and faster like a small whirlwind in the palm of his hand. I put up my hands to ward him off and closed my eyes, squeezing them shut much as the other guy had done.

Trench-Coat grabbed my left arm, just below my wrist. He was solid all right—and strong. His touch burned as if he'd held my wrist deep into a flame. I cried out.

But I didn't lose my concentration.

Yet even as I thought of my body back in my condo, still and cold on my bed, something tugged softly at me.

Beckoned me not to go. It spoke tenderly of peace, an end to pain.

It promised me happiness.

And love. Never to be lonely again. Something touched me with soft caresses along my cheek, my neck . . . I could almost believe someone kissed my bare flesh.

All I had to do was let go. Just give myself up to it and know endless passion, day upon day of eternal orgasmic ecstasy.

And it appeared on the other side of my eyelids as a red light, pulsating, spinning, whirling.

Come . . . come . . . come . . . give yourself to me . . . be one with me.

No!

I pushed back and saw my body below me just as I fell into it, and the shock of returning was a fire blasting through every finger to every toe. I convulsed as my muscles fought me, and I heard my heart thundering inside of my ears. I gurgled and choked in the quiet room. It was like being given an electric charge while being submerged in ice-cold water.

As my back arched upward, I screamed long and loud until my throat was raw and I was exhausted.

I don't remember how long I lay half-sprawled across the single-sized bed. I remember finally being able to move my arms enough to push myself up. I had to look around the condo—I had to know that thing hadn't followed me.

I didn't want it to know where I lived.

And as I moved, I became aware of the pressure on my arm where the Trench-Coat creepy grabbed me.

The horror of what I'd nearly done—that I'd actually considered letting go forever and accepting the red light's promise of passion and sex—fueled me forward. I stood on shaky legs and stumbled about my home, absently tucking my burning left arm beneath my breast.

I turned on every light I could find as I slowly made my way through the single-story condo. My living room, kitchen, bathroom, spare bathroom and bedroom that housed my office where I'd returned. Last, I went to my bedroom and turned on the lights there.

I smelled blood everywhere, yet there was none in my home or on me. It was ethereal blood.

Death blood.

Each step on my feet was like walking after they went to sleep. Tiny pins and needles stuck into my skin in a ka-billion different places.

I had to turn the wards on. I had to make sure nothing unbidden could get in.

An associate with a penchant for creating the magical out of the mechanical (the one who'd made my neato-watch) had set up a mechanism that created a warding bubble around my home. I have no idea how it works, and I'm sure Rhonda doesn't either—it's just a gift she has.

Like me being a Traveler. She's my Magical MacGyver. If you can imagine it, she can build it.

The throw switch was in the living room, near the door. The clock above my TiVo read 11:33.

The metal of the handle felt good against my palm, and I felt as well as heard the low hum the warding bubble made as it was activated. I'd never really used it before. Never believed in it. Why would I? I'd never seen anything other than myself on the astral plane—nothing like I'd witnessed tonight.

Now I celebrated that I had it. That it worked. According to Rhonda, nothing astral or ethereal, or uninvited, could get past it.

Not even a vampire.

Well . . . not a very big vampire.

I wanted to collapse right there on the spot. Me in my black cat-suit and slippers. I felt beaten—not just physically—but spiritually.

And I was scared shitless.

I did what any normal twentysomething did when she just had a really bad night.

I called Mom.

"You have reached Nona's Botanica and Tea Shop, located in Little Five Points. Our regular store hours are . . ."

I hung up. Mom had the machine on, and I remembered then it was her bridge night. She wasn't home, and she wouldn't have her cell phone on.

I wanted my mommy.

I dialed Rhonda's number and got her voice mail. What did she do on Tuesdays? Clubbing? Gaming? Where was she?

There was no one else I knew to call (not anyone on the physical plane who could actually pick up a phone). No one else who knew about my line of work, about what I did.

There wasn't a man in my life. Hadn't been for nearly three years. There was no one living other than my mother who I kept close ties with.

So I pulled myself up and limped back to my bedroom. I locked the door, leaving all the lights on, ran myself a hot bath. After dumping my clothes on the floor, as well as my neato-watch, I curled up with my knees to my chin in the water, wanting nothing more than to have myself a little pity-party.

That's when I saw the mark on my arm. I moved it out in front of me and turned it to one side, then the other. In stark contrast to my slightly olive skin was a perfect red handprint just beneath the wrist where my watch sat.

God . . . and it felt like the thing was still holding on to me. Putting pressure on it. Squeezing it hard enough to break. I pulled the arm in close and cradled it with my right hand.

I glanced at the floor, at my pile of clothes, and saw the watch. To anyone else, it resembled a clear, pink plastic Powerpuff Girls watch. But the LCD screen was blank, visible only on the astral plane.

I leaned over the side and picked it up.

And there, just below the clasp, on the left band, was a melted area in the shape of a fingertip.

I tossed the watch away, back to the floor.

What if that thing could track me down and kill me? How could I stop it? And what the hell was it?

I felt dirty. Tainted. Much as I had that night, nine years ago, when a man forcibly took my innocence and exchanged it for hell. The first night I left my body, and looked down upon my rape.

2

"ARE you sure it wasn't just a bad dream? You know how you get those bad dreams when you eat ice cream before you go to bed."

I'm sure if I polled every female in just the United States alone, I'd find that 99 percent of them have wanted to strangle their mothers at one point or another.

Probably even more than once.

Which was how I was feeling at that moment. But if I did that, where would I go to mooch a meal, a cup of herbal tea, and the occasional bit of otherworldly gossip?

Of course Mom's comments didn't help the fact I'd found several strands of white hairs all clumped together over my left temple. I had blinked sleep out of my eyes several times and squinted at it. Wasn't a dream—there they were—starting at my part. I'd pulled all of them out.

That's when I caught sight of the mark on my arm again—when I pulled at the long, white strands of hair. Very visible and very real.

It looked more like a big henna tattoo. I'd almost hoped my little adventure the night before had been a nightmare. *Nada*.

The arm hurt in a weird sort of not-really-painful way. Kind of like one of those bruises that remind you it's there with a little pain now and then. I was especially aware of it when I sat at my computer and composed the report e-mail for last night's client and the dot-com company. I explained briefly that the two men in question were more into each other than business. I hit send, and my arm twinged.

Not wanting to draw attention to it till I knew more about what'd happened last night, I wrapped it in one of those ACE bandages and told everyone I'd fallen.

And, of course, Mom was a bit put out when I wouldn't show her my boo-boo.

My mom, Nona Martinique, owned a good-sized business nestled on Euclid off of Moreland in a small community lovingly dubbed Little Five Points, named after an intersection where the five main roads of Atlanta once met.

The house was just past The Junkman's Daughter (a warehouse of vintage clothing and jewelry) and the older location of Sevenanda (formerly an herbal and health food store). They'd long since moved to a bigger location down the street, and the building sort of disguised itself at times as a soon-to-be short-lived business.

Kinda like a dot-com company.

Long known as Atlanta's art community (and gathering place for the unexplainable), Nona had chosen the area after years of working at Delta. I don't know how she did it, but she'd managed to raise me and still save for her dream.

A botanica and tea shop. I never knew she had it in her.

Mom's botanica didn't fit the true definition of the word. Oh, she sold the usual plants, seeds, horticultural information, but that side of the shop also retailed in seven-day candles as well as sachet love potions. The tea side sold preboxed, franchised teas, along with Mom's own special blends. She imported a lot of the dried leaves, then brewed them in the back.

The whole deal made up the lower floor of a Victorian two-story she found six years ago when I took her shopping in the community. I admit we both fell in love with it. I wanted to live in it. Mom saw dollar signs.

Even through the years of neglect we found unique advantages. The house had sturdy, concrete steps leading up from the sidewalk, a nice backyard, and a wraparound porch in surprisingly good shape. The only thing that had marred the view was a honking condemned signpost on the front door.

A bit of investigation on my part (yes, I snooped) revealed the condemned notice wasn't an official one, but something the owner slapped on there in hopes he could raze the building and sell the land to a developer.

But the house was declared a historical landmark, and that prevented him from doing anything destructive to it. He'd been too lazy and pissed off to remove the condemned sign.

So he'd tried selling or leasing it, but all the business owners interested broke their contracts within six months or always dropped the offer.

They all claimed it was haunted.

Which at the time seemed preposterous to me. Even though I was a Traveler, I'd not seen any ghosts during my wanderings. I thought they were figments of too many bad movies and the Sci Fi Channel.

Mom made the owner a purchase offer he couldn't refuse and a promise not to renege on the deal.

She renovated the bathrooms, updated the appliances, painted, refinished the hardwood floors, and then furnished it with antiques she'd been buying and storing through the years.

Needless to say I was impressed with Mom. Most of the time.

It wasn't long before we met Tim and Steve, the former owners of the house on Euclid Avenue, and the reason for the former purchasers' problems.

Longtime companions, the couple had bought the house in the late eighties and been in the process of restoring it to its original splendor when tragedy stuck them down in the middle of an argument over olive green or chartreuse.

Apparently Steve had been on his way down the stairs of the basement to get the chartreuse when one of the wood steps collapsed, and he pitched forward.

The impact on the concrete floor below snapped his neck. Dead.

Tim followed him not long after, calling down to him in the dark. During his fall, Steve had lashed out to grab something and taken the single lightbulb cord with him, yanking it out of its housing in the house frame.

Not so lucky, Tim hit the missing step and fell as well; only he managed to break his back. He didn't die as quickly, but languished in the house beside his decomposing lover for nearly a week before passing away.

Believe me, as gruesome as this story sounds, you hear it over a hundred times, and it just gets to be boring.

They'd been watching what Nona had done to the place and were both pleased. Add to the fact my mom was an avid human-rights activist as well as a dead ringer for Debbie Reynolds, and it was just love at first sight all around.

Mom insisted she'd known they were there the whole time. She says she can see ghosts. Apparently I could too, but the two didn't make their presence known to me till after they discovered I could move out of body.

They became Mom's constant companions in the house—that is, after she set up a few ground rules.

No ghosts in the bathrooms, not corporeal or incorporeal.

No ghosts in the bedroom, the same.

And no ghosts in the shop during business hours.

She threatened that either they mind her or there would be an exorcism of the worst kind.

Because of this, so Mom didn't break her own rules about no ghosts in the shop during working hours, she pushed the shop hours back on Wednesdays to noon. That way we could all sit down on those mornings and have tea and biscuits and homemade butter and discuss our weeks.

We were at the larger, rectangular Tudor-style oak table. Mom had put out biscuits with country ham (that means extra salty—mmmmmm), six different homemade jams (grape, apricot, pear, apple, blackberry, and jalapeño!), three different teas in an assortment of teapots (jasmine, English Breakfast, and Earl Grey—Ick! Stuff tastes like boiled hay), and two cakes, carrot and fennel. Those she'd picked up at the local bakery two blocks away.

After last night, I didn't think I could eat. But once I'd stepped into the shop, my stomach betrayed me. Remember that ravenous thing I mentioned?

Mental note: *mmmmmm . . . biscuits.*

Rhonda joined us late. But that had something to do with staying up till 4 A.M. to work her Magical MacGyver mojo on some mystical whatnot for some wacko customer of Mom's. Her flat black hair was cut short into a Betty Page coif. Her black nails matched the half-moons hanging beneath her eyes.

I'm not sure how old Rhonda is. Sometimes she seems eighteen, and other times she feels forty. I just know she's damned good at her magical mechanics.

And last night, I'd truly appreciated it.

Her greeting this morning included the relinquishing of my astral watch to her. She mumbled something about having a few upgrades ready and proceeded to work her mojo on it while downing three cups of black coffee. I hoped she didn't notice the melted band, or if she did, she'd wait till Mom wasn't about.

"There." She handed it back to me. Evidently she hadn't seen the physical damage. Whew—I think.

I strapped it on my right wrist. "So what does it do now?"

"I installed a gather upgrade, so it'll not only record your time on the astral per little excursion," the side of her mouth twitched. "It'll also give me an accurate reading on total hours."

"You think me going astral has some sort of cumulative effect?"

She shrugged. "Dunno. We still haven't exactly figured out what exactly it is you do, Zoë." Rhonda tore a biscuit in half and dipped one end in some honey. "But I added a little alarm to it too—just to let you know when you're exceeding your daily allotted astral time."

I looked down at the watch. *Alarm? Greeeat.*

So I caught Rhonda up on my night's adventure, of course leaving out the whole he-grabbed-my-arm part. I'd left that out of my telling it to Mom, Steve, and Tim too.

Her usually gloomy façade perked up at the mention of something on the astral plane besides Tim and Steve. "So he wore a trench coat and boots. Kinda like in *The Matrix*?"

I nodded. I was still burned about Nona's ice cream and nightmares comment. "Yea, but he didn't look like Keanu. He looked more like a really scary Vin Diesel." And depending on what movie you watched, that wasn't a hard stretch to imagine.

I vote for *Pitch Black* myself. Same kinda monochromatic look as well.

"Did he have that dreamy voice too?" That was Tim. Apparently he had the hots for the Vin-man.

"No." I took up a biscuit, my third, and slathered rich butter over it. I've always considered Mom's cooking a good remedy for having the shit scared out of me. "He never said a word. Just gave me that evil boogeyman grin."

Rhonda snapped her fingers. "That's it!"

We all paused as she jumped up from the table and ran into the botanica store. A beaded curtain covered the archway that separated the two halves. From a distance the pattern on the beads resembled a sunny meadow.

Up close, it looked like an unpleasant Monet.

"Did that poor man get away?" Nona sipped loudly at her tea.

I shrugged. "I didn't pay much attention to what happened to him. Once I noticed Trench-Coat eyeballing me, I worried about my own bacon."

"So you don't know whether that man's soul ascended or was trapped by this entity? I mean, you did say it looked like he stopped sucking it up into his hand when you blew your wad."

The urge to strangle returned. *Kill, kill!*

But it was a good question. Mom was making me think, and I didn't want to. I was still put off and still frightened. I didn't want to go home. I didn't want to be alone.

But I didn't want to be grilled either.

See, Mom is an avid reader. No, scratch that. Voracious. Goes through words like a vampire goes through blood.

Okay. Ew. Where did I pull *that* analogy from?

Before I got to her shop she'd seen the front page of the *Atlanta Journal and Constitution*, the *AJC*. I hadn't.

Mom had the paper open to the full article, and everyone had taken turns reading it. The guy I'd apparently abandoned, in my mother's opinion, was William Tanaka, vice president of Visitar Incorporated, a gaming and video company based in Atlanta. He was thirty-two years old.

Thirty-two. Shot dead by some creature the poor man had no concept of—

Wait . . .

Tanaka's words came back to me at that moment, the ones he said just before Trench-Coat blew his face out of the back of his head (see? I told you I had no control over the recall).

"Temae mai kihaku temae yuigon iiya." I felt a chill pass over my shoulders and race down over my arms and my spine. And I didn't think it was from the chilly weather outside.

"What?" Steve looked up from the newspaper article. "What did you say?"

"I have no idea." I looked at him. "I think it was something Tanaka said last night, before Trench-Coat killed him."

"Temae mai kihaku?" My mom's housemate frowned. To the natural eye—meaning for anyone that walked in off the street—if Steve wished to be visible to the regular, living populace, he would look normal. I mean, as in you'd never know he was a ghost.

Unless you tried to touch him.

He was solidly built, standing maybe six-foot even, with broad shoulders, thinning red hair, and pale blue eyes.

"Don't change the subject, Steve," Tim said, and pointed to the array of color swatch books that littered their side of the table. "We have to decide on a trim color."

To me, Tim looked more washed-out in comparison to Steve. He was dark-haired, with dark eyes and very pale skin. I think he looked that way because he was depressed all the time. Ghosts apparently reacted to strong emotions, especially their own.

And from what I could gather from the couple's cryptic conversations for most of the morning, they'd been fighting again over whether Mom should paint the house's trim in white or something equally as boring.

"Look." I'd had enough and shoved the rest of the butter-slathered biscuit into my mouth. "Just paint the trim black and be different," I said through the mouthful.

I thought Tim was gonna have a coronary he blanched so white. Steve was looking wide-eyed and horrified.

"Black?" Steve hissed. "*Black?* A Victorian house of this grandeur would never have had black trim. This is a Painted Lady, Zoë. The trim should be white."

I gave him the middle finger of my right hand and swallowed my mouthful, or part of it. "And this is a pissed-off lady, Steve. Drop the trim and tell me about what Tanaka said. Why did you react like that?"

"Zoë, temper." Mom patted the table beside Steve in an attempt to soothe him. She comforted a ghost rather than her own daughter. But that was because she had a crush on him.

Leave it to my mom to have the hots for a dead gay man.

Steve took a deep breath (oh please, ghosts don't actually breathe) and smiled at my mother before raising a fuzzy eyebrow at me. "Well, the man basically declared that the intruder, Trench-Coat, would not take his soul."

I looked at him with surprise. "You can speak Japanese?"

Steve nodded. "International banker, remember? I can speak four languages. Japanese, German, and French."

"You said four. That was only three."

"The fourth is English."

I knew that.

Rhonda came back into the café at that moment holding a massive book. I checked to make sure it wasn't made of human flesh. Hey, with Mom, you never know.

My mom had stranger things in her house than ghosts.

I was more interested in what Steve had said as I took

up another biscuit and my knife. Tanaka had sort of called Trench-Coat a soul thief, which led me to believe he *had* known *what* was about to kill him.

But did Tanaka know *who* he was? Or did spirit thieves have names?

I had a flashback to the brief seconds I'd been trapped in the monster's laser beam (well? Got a better name?). Remembering the contentment I'd begun to feel, the lulling voice in my head, coaxing me to release myself to it. To just let go, and feeling all good and tingly in the right places.

I shuddered when I realized how much I'd *wanted* to do just that. How bad could it be, really? To just shuck this mortal coil and all the day-to-day problems and embrace oblivion?

But that sort of thing scared me—so much so I tried never to leave my body when I was angry. It was too much like running away. And what if someday my body didn't let me back in?

"Zoë?" Nona reached across the table and touched my bandaged wrist. I winced—not that her touch hurt—but it abruptly reminded me of the thing's mark on me. I hadn't realized I'd zoned out while caught in the memory.

I blinked at her. "Yeah Mom?"

"You okay? You were looking into space—and your expression went completely blank. Like there was no one home."

I set my knife and biscuit back on my plate. My stomach twisted again, and I wanted to throw up. I hadn't told anyone that I'd gotten caught in Trench-Coat's snatching-beam.

And I really didn't want to talk about it now. I was almost embarrassed that I'd let that thing get the better of me. And that I was mortally terrified of it.

"Zoë—what's wrong? Is your arm hurting you? Maybe I should call the doctor. I can take you there myself."

Ack. No.

"So what's in the big book, Rhonda?" Tim rested both his elbows on the table as Rhonda started moving things around on the table to make room for the book.

I glanced at Tim, who gave me an almost imperceptible wink. As always, he'd known I wasn't in the mood to talk with Mom and had shifted the subject. Gotta love the wee guy.

I looked over at Rhonda, happy the attention moved away from me. She'd set the bulky thing on the table, shoving her plate and delicate teacup to the table's center. She thumbed to the right, then back to the left in an active search pattern. "I can't find it. But it was a great thing about the bogeyman and the Abysmal plane."

Bogey who and the abysmal what?

"I'm not sure it was the boogeyman, Rhonda," Steve said. "That thing carries away disobedient children."

She didn't glance up but her ruby red painted mouth worked into a smile. Creepy. "Bo-gee-man. Not boo-gee. And you're right, but in that reference I remember seeing something about Symbionts and souls. And—bogeymen and Symbionts seem to appear in most cultures. The bogeyman is synonymous with soul stealing."

"Synonymous," Tim said. "That's a big word. You're doing great with your big words, Rhonda."

"Can it, squirt."

This was a great description of Tim. Squirt. Small. Delicate. Boney. Rhonda, who was not much more than skin and bones at odd angles herself, looked huge compared to his daintiness.

The interchange was also a nice example of their relationship. Tolerant—on good days.

Tim wasn't letting this one go. "Soon you can graduate into contractions, and maybe even conjunctions."

Rhonda looked up from the book. "Tim, if you weren't already dead, it'd be so easy to snap off your—"

"Girls, girls," Steve said calmly, as Nona turned the page of the newspaper for him. He was perfectly capable of manipulating a page in the newspaper (remember when I said I thought ghosts that could manipulate the physical world had an edge up on things? Well, think about how irritated I was sitting there watching him not use that ability)—it was just that Mom liked doing it. "You're both pretty. Now get along."

"Wait, back up a bit." I frowned at Rhonda. "Abysmal plane? Whazzat?"

I saw the joy brighten her face, plump up and actually color her cheeks. She looked like a goth chick high on blood. "It's such a recent theory that not many parapsychologists even know about it yet."

"And?" My arm ached again. I kept it under the table and rubbed it as Rhonda spoke. It felt warm through the bandage.

"Well, we all know about the three bodies. The physical, the mental, and the astral."

I nodded. Yeah, basic metaphysics. Not something that's taught in public school, but if you live with Nona . . .

"The physical is the living anchor to life, it's where the soul sets up house for a period of time to learn. The mental is where the subconscious and conscious connect and where sometimes there's a connection between it and the physical planes. Like with me and Nona. We use thoughts as living things."

Uh-huh. Yeah. Right. I'll get back to you two on that one.

"Then there's the astral, where your"—she nodded to me—"barriers, so to speak, are weakest. Meaning using the mental plane, you can move your astral body from the physical body and move about the physical plane without your physical body. Which is why I first called you a Traveler."

Not true. I first called me a Traveler—after she said I traveled. Hiss.

I nodded. "Okay—review time over. What is the Abysmal?"

"Well, you know where Tim and Steve reside, right? On the Ethereal, outside the astral. That's where ghosts, spirits, Shades, angels, etc., live. Well, the theory is that the Ethereal has a counterpart called the Abysmal. For lack of a better analogy, think of Heaven and Hell. Heaven being the Ethereal and the Abysmal—"

"Being Hell." I arched an eyebrow. Lovely.

"Yeah. Kinda. That's where the darker entities in this form reside. Phantasms, chimeras, Wraiths, bogeymen, phantoms—they stay there." She glanced at each person sitting at the table.

Okay, she had my attention.

Steve spoke. "So why is it that you on the physical, can see us on the Ethereal?"

"Same reason Zoë here can travel back and forth. Weak barriers. Either through strong wills, like yours and Tim's, or small, damaged tears in the fabric."

"So these nasties"—I had a really great image of Trench-Coat in my mind—"are all locked behind barriers. Who set up these barriers?"

Rhonda's shrug did not lighten my mood, or help to re-assure me. "Mother Nature. God. Yahweh. Buddha. Creation. Put a name to it if that helps. They are all separated with tiny leaks where will is used for manipulation. Think about when Tim and Steve move physical objects. That took a long time for them to master. They both chipped away at that barrier separating them from this plane until it thinned. Which might have a lot to do with why they haven't ascended."

"You mean gone to Heaven or Hell," Nona said.

"Maybe. Depends on the individual. What bothers me is this Trench-Coat. Notice he had to kill Tanaka's physical body before he could take the soul. He's broken through the physical completely to manipulate it, but he's still bound by the barriers." She looked at me. "Which is probably why he wasn't able to touch you or take you, even though you were in astral form. Your Traveler capabilities made you visible, but you were still tethered to a living body."

I pursed my lips. "So—what if he *had* touched me? You know—with me still technically stuck to a body?"

Rhonda looked grim. "That could be bad."

Uh-oh. Do I panic? He *did* touch me. And he did nearly take me. But no one knew that. I looked at my buttered biscuit. My stomach twisted as I remembered the feel of his hand on my arm, which now burned beneath the bandage.

Oh hell. It could be bad. What bad? How bad? Oogy bad?

A nice but distracting vibration began in my right jeans pocket. My phone was calling. Or rather, letting me know something was happening in the cyberworld. I have a mighty little phone and PDA combination. I can stay in touch with friends—if I had any living—and keep up with the world.

I get e-mail on the thing as well, and the message flashing on the color screen warned of an incoming client request.

Now, with a business based on information gathering, when it came to gaining clients, I had had to improvise.

I once used "Astral Travel" in the ad. After several months of advertising in small Atlanta papers like *Creative Loafing* and even running ads in the *AJC*, I'd come up with nothing, other than a few scary people who claimed to be Alexander the Great and Charles Manson.

I really didn't have the heart to tell that one girl that Charlie Manson wasn't dead yet, even though she really looked the part, right down to the swastika on her forehead and the beard.

That's when I handed the whole thing over to Rhonda.

She was the genius behind bidding out my services on eBay. The ad ran like a legitimate service for research, and since the means by which I gain information (like snooping on the dot-com guys the night before) aren't legal (not to mention are unbelievable), and sure as hell wouldn't stand up in court, most people wouldn't ask too many questions about my methods.

And the more illegal people think something is, the more willing they are to pay for it.

I hadn't believed that—till Rhonda helped me get things set up online, right down to a PayPal account for immediate payment.

It hadn't worked at first. No one had bid for a month, and I'd nearly decided to keep my job at Target when the first client came through.

I knew them only through the screen name given on eBay. They made their payment and it cleared and I investigated a local insurance company that had supposedly "lost" several claimant's policies and refused to pay out.

Needless to say, there was nothing I could do physically when I discovered the truth—that they had pocketed the money and were planning on closing down shop. I got the account numbers, names, and addresses of those involved and gave back a detailed report on how it was done and what they needed to look for.

The story broke in the *AJC* two days after I handed in my findings to the client (typed up on white paper and no return address).

After that, I had clients on a regular basis, and many of them repeaters.

I checked the message. This one was a repeat client. I'd also had Rhonda set it up to where the bidder could give me a few lines of information on the job. Hey, there were some things I wouldn't do—like snoop on two people making out.

Ew. I have my standards. There are sleazy detectives who do that kind of thing. Go pay them.

And besides, I hadn't had sex in so long, watching that kind of action just brought me closer to my vibrator.

Hrm . . . I said that out loud, didn't I?

"New job?" Nona was being nosey. But she's allowed, being my mom and all. "Make sure to dress warmly—it's getting on toward winter."

It was fall. Sheesh.

"Yeah." I scrolled down to read the text and paused. "That's weird."

"What is it?" Tim asked.

Rhonda had pressed her nose back into the book of everything.

"Repeater. Wants me to snoop in on a meeting between a Mr. Hirokumi and a Lieutenant Daniel Frasier. It's at two this afternoon, downtown. Whoa . . . and it's in the same building."

"Wait." Steve looked up again from the paper, then manipulated the newspaper himself, evidently not willing to wait on Nona.

He turned back two pages, and I watched him scan the text. Steve finally nodded and pointed to the type. "I knew I'd seen that name. That guy you saw murdered? Tanaka? He worked for a Mr. Koba Hirokumi. He's the president of Visitar Inc."

Holy shit.

A longtime repeat customer wanted me to spy on a cop

and a man who was tied to the victim from last night. "Okay, coincidence overload. My spidey-sense is not happy with this one."

Nona pulled the paper toward her and scanned the article. "Zoë, you said this is a repeat client?"

"Yeah, this one's been with me since I started this information-gathering gig two years ago." Which was another factor that was raising hair on my arms, as well as clenching my stomach even tighter.

I'd never refused a client before (other than Alex and Charlotte Manson) but I was seriously considering at least questioning this one. And if I'd not witnessed Tanaka's murder the night before, nothing about the request would have seemed amiss to me.

I felt the mark on my arm, could even imagine the outline of his handprint on my skin. With a slight intake of breath, I held my bandaged left arm beneath my right and debated whether to tell everyone—especially Mom—everything that happened.

I wanted to scream that he'd touched me. That'd he'd left a mark. That it hurt and I was scared and just not sure what to do.

I'm not sure, but I think at that moment I came closer to crying for my mommy than I had in fifteen years.

Too bad she was busy turning Steve's pages for him.

3

MOM hadn't been exaggerating about the weather. It'd been chilly when I'd driven to her house around nine. But the sun had been shining then, and it looked like it would be a fairly nice day for November.

Since then gray clouds conjugated overhead, spreading their monochromatic joy over the city. The people I saw on the streets on the way to my condo huddled beneath thin jackets and sweaters as the wind made tiny twisters of brown, yellow, gold, and red leaves.

I lived in a building near the Midtown Eight movie theater on Monroe Drive. I chose it because of the spectacular view of Piedmont Park (add in the hot bods—though all gay—in the Atlanta summers) and the Atlanta skyline. Midtown itself rests as a halfway point between downtown Atlanta and the northern upper-class area of Buckhead.

But still on the hub.

When I moved to Atlanta, no one lived in Midtown— scary place. Run-down, vacant, graffiti-splashed buildings and a high crime rate kept the prices low. Then there was this incredible influx of the homosexual community. They started buying houses, fixed them up, and decided to stay. Some sold and moved into Grant Park, a few miles southeast.

Now we have nice restaurants, shopping, and more traffic than the old roads can handle. Crime is still a problem, but we've got the Atlanta PD nearby.

It was close to twelve thirty when I pulled my car into my parking space. Since taking MARTA would make me late for my assignment, Mom eagerly volunteered herself and one of her housemates to drive me to the Bank of America building.

Originally she'd wanted either Tim or Steve to go with me to snoop on me snooping on this meeting. But they were *housebound*, as Nona liked to say. They died tragically in that house, and their existence as ghosts depended on the structure.

Don't ask, I don't know why.

Their dependence on the house was part of the limits the two had tested since discovering they were dead. I had always thought of *Beetle Juice* and the Maitlands' imprisonment—only without the giant sandworms part.

In order for them to travel more than a hundred meters from the house, I'd have to carry with me some physical part of the house itself. Tim preferred it if Nona carried a piece of the brick. Steve was more partial to one of the old skeleton keys.

The problem with this was that after I jumped, what then? I couldn't carry the damned thing physically, so they'd be stuck in my condo with my apparently comatose body.

Steve's suggestion of me jumping from my car was out of the question. I wasn't going to leave my body that vulnerable in a car, in a parking garage, with my mom hanging about.

Nasty things happen in multidecked parking garages. I read about it in the papers all the time. People get robbed in garages. And their cars are broken into and things are stolen. Not that I really thought that someone would steal my body (except maybe in one of those organ extraction stories), but what if they thought I was dead and dumped me out and stole my car?

And besides, what if some nice neighbor saw my unmoving body and freaked? What then? What if I woke up on a morgue table after they did an autopsy?

Talk about waking up dead.

So as a compromise, Nona agreed to pick me up in astral form and take me there and hang out in the parking lot. Rhonda would mind the store, and Nona bent the rules a little so Tim could help. On the promise he wouldn't abruptly disappear and spook the customers.

Steve, of course, would be with Mom.

So alone I went upstairs to my place, saying hello to Jimmy the doorboy (the kid's gotta be eighteen at most).

I lived on the eighth floor, facing the park. The layout was simple and open. A marble foyer greeted me after coming through the door, then into a large living area with a gas fireplace and sliding-glass doors to a balcony.

To the left was the kitchen, complete with a gas-stove island in the center and a cutaway in the separating wall so I could cook and still watch *Oprah* on my big-screen television.

I really wanted one of those plasma wall-mounted deals. I make okay money, but I'm also a budgeter. I've gone two months at a time with no bids, so I have to make my pay—when I get it—last. Mortgage and food take precedence. Oh, and Häagen-Dazs.

I'd furnished the place in antiques, thanks to my mom and her nose for finding bargains. The couch was the only modern-style piece that I'd given myself for Christmas last year. A dark brown suede seven-footer with lots of forest green and wine red pillows. It sat between the television and the kitchen. It did wonders for the dark oak of most everything else.

The walls I'd painted in olive green with off-white trim. Everything sort of complemented everything else. Or so I thought. I'm sure my framed Waterhouse prints weren't the "in" thing in design, but they were my favorite.

Especially the one called *The Magic Circle*. That one hung over my fireplace. Just looking at it gave me goose pimples.

I also had a few of my ceramic dragons about the living room. Here and there.

To the right were the two bedrooms. The master was mine, of course, complete with both shower and garden tub. I had a nice sleigh bed I'd refinished myself, along with a few antique pieces here and there, including an armoire I'd converted into an entertainment center and put a television in.

I'd always thought it'd be nice to wake up next to someone and have fruit and cheese and some Le Madeleine's strawberries Romanoff and French roast coffee in bed and watch the morning news together.

Of course that had never happened. The only guests I'd had since I moved in were . . . well . . . Mom and Rhonda and the boys.

That was a sad and sobering realization.

I'd cry about it later.

The spare bedroom, which was the first one to the right of the living room, was my office. I'd had the doors reinforced (and the walls) of this room, a cozy twelve-by-twelve with two Mac computers, two twenty-inch flatscreens, a scanner, and a PC, which I kept in the corner for any emergencies.

On occasion I did get the weird, superencrypted file, and that's when I knew the client was young and had more money than sense. I really knew that when I'd open up the doc file and he wanted me to off his little sister or she her little brother.

Those were the ones where I returned money and refused.

I had never offed anyone in my life.

At least not yet.

Facing the computers sat a small, single bed. Something from my childhood. I barely fit on it, but it was comfortable enough for me to rest on while I traveled out of body. I'd gone astral once or twice in a standing position— which in hindsight seemed kinda silly—and my body, of course, with no pilot on board, fell over. On one occasion I'd needed stitches.

I didn't do that anymore if I could help it.

Before heading into the office I moved to the control switch beside the door and threw the warding shield to protect the entire condo. My imagination had sort of worked itself up into believing Trench-Coat watched me now and was waiting for the opportunity to find my body and catch me.

Even thinking about that made my arm twitch where he'd touched me.

Sometimes having an imagination was a real bitch.

After checking the fax machine to read the entire eBay transaction, I went to the bedroom to get my cat-suit. Since I was still freaked by Trench-Coat, I took it into my office and sealed the door.

The client, known to me for two years as maharba@maharba.com, had deposited the money directly into my PayPal account.

With extras.

I checked my account online. Extras meaning besides the standard fee for a snoop at five thousand, they'd put in an additional ten thousand.

That much money alone would carry me through several months without another job, as well as get my medical and dental insurance caught up.

Hey, I get cavities too.

I think it's all that late-night Java Mocha ice cream and Sara Lee cheesecake.

Whatever might happen between this Hirokumi and Lieutenant Frasier was damned important to this client.

I toyed with the idea of not changing into my cat-suit. I hadn't washed it yet after last night's little scare, and I imagined it had Trench-Coat cooties on it.

I could go naked. Wouldn't matter. There wouldn't be any ghost-seeing kids in a corporate headquarters, right?

After thinking about my recent run of luck, I changed into the suit and sat in front of the computer and did something I'd never done.

I tried finding out *who* Maharba was.

Of course my limited search capability turned up zilch. I could call Rhonda and have her look it up, but I was sure she was still toting that book of everything around the shop looking for whatever it was that had caught her attention that morning.

But it was getting late and Mom would be here with the car.

I turned off the lights and settled onto the bed, flat on my back. I closed my eyes and went through the three deep breaths I'd always used to calm my nerves.

Moving out of body was the easy part—almost too easy at times. So much so that when I was working in the public arena, like at Target, and an irate customer started berating me, my inclination was to astral out of that situation and strangle her—that is if I could affect physical objects.

I mean, who'd know? Anyone astral traveling wouldn't show up on a security camera. It'd look like the woman was like—choking on a chicken bone. Right?

That's how I learned to travel in the first place.

Turning away from a situation too horrible to face.

I stood and heard again the weird tearing sound that always followed my separation of astral and physical. It reminded me of the sound of Velcro. And in a way, my astral body was attached with Velcro.

But like Velcro, I hoped my jumping out and jumping in didn't wear down the attachment after a while to where it wouldn't stick anymore.

That would suck.

It wasn't two seconds in this form I noticed my arm still ached. I noticed it because "Ouch" the pain and because I normally didn't feel anything when astral. The ache was much more pronounced in this form. I looked at it—the handprint was still there—a garish burgundy beneath my watch. Usually any physical ailments didn't follow me into this realm, so what made this one different?

Might be because it was made by someone of this realm yah dufus?

Don't you hate the voice of common sense?

Though it did make me look around the room for any sign of Trench-Coat. There was none, and there shouldn't be. Not with the ward up.

The great thing about the warding Rhonda set up is that it allowed things *out* of the condo but not in. Except me. I don't know how it does that. It was something I'd always wanted to ask Rhonda. If it didn't let me pass back and forth, I'd never be able to get back to my body—especially quickly.

Mental note: *Ask Rhonda about the mechanics. Don't want to get caught out and slam into an invisible wall.*

That would suck worse.

And I say suck worse because I have no idea what would happen to my body if I didn't go back to it. Or what would happen to *me* for that matter. I mean, I'm pretty sure I'm not supposed to be able to do what I do. I don't think moving in and out of the physical was one of the loopholes the great creator of the universe intended.

So—if I got caught out of the house and the house burned down—what then? Would Daddy, so to speak, disown me?

Pphhtt.

I checked the watch—it was zeroed at 237 minutes. I'd been astral three minutes.

I rode the elevator down with old Miss Petra. I stood behind her hunched and blue-haired self. She lived on the same floor as me. Her condo smelled of cats and cinnamon, a bad combo of the cat box and air freshener.

Usually the smell traveled with her. Fortunately, I couldn't smell it in this state.

Go me.

Nona was outside in her Volvo wagon. She got out and opened the door for me. This wasn't really necessary—I could sieve through a car door as easily (metal—yuck!) as I could most things—but Mom thought it was charming being the batty old bird. Sometimes it was good if people thought you were crazy on a regular basis.

Then again, maybe not. This was Midtown. Crazy old ladies were a dime a dozen. Weirder things I'm sure have happened.

"Ready?" Mom said as she got back in and backed out.

"Yeah." I wasn't, and my stomach turned in knots again. Wow, the arm was gonna be a liability if it didn't stop throbbing. It would definitely put a crimp in my feeling of omnipotence.

What is up with the handprint? And should I tell Mom and Rhonda? No—Mom would see it as some omen and find a way to keep me from doing this job. And I needed the money.

"What's the plan if things go sour?"

"I run like hell back to the car. And if I can't get to the car, I shoot down the cord back to my body directly." Of course, I still wasn't clear how Mom would know if things went south—or if I'd jumped back to my body.

So I asked her that.

"I'm thinking that not returning to the car would be the first hint," she said, turning onto Monroe Drive, past Ru San's, my favorite sushi restaurant, just across from Ansley Mall.

Well duh.

I looked out the window. The day just got grayer, and I was glad I couldn't feel the cold through the glass. Steve looked out the passenger window like a big Labrador who'd never been allowed out. Then again, I guess it would be awful to have to live in the same house and not go anywhere, year after year, decade after decade.

Imagine never going out to eat, to see movies, to have drinks, or to play in the park.

That was another kind of suck.

4

ARRIVAL went without a hitch—except for the "no parking available" situation in a nonexistent parking garage.

I don't know why Mom thought there was a parking garage. There wasn't one. Luckily there was no sign of Trench-Coat either. And I thought he might not look or seem so scary in the daylight.

Not that I wanted to find out.

The sky kept darkening. Bring on the gloom. Radio voice said it'd dropped to forty-three. I watched the pedestrian traffic surround me as I walked toward the building, which at the moment didn't have any of the same oogy as last night. Everyone looked miserable, but was it from their jobs or the weather?

Wow, it looked really cold outside.

Neener-nee.

I followed a couple of suits in through the front glass doors after leaving my mom's car, still chuckling at the honking horns when Debbie Reynolds stepped out of a Volvo and opened the door for . . . no one.

The foyer looked pretty much the same as it had before, only there was a larger police presence. And more people. Different security officer—this one not snoring. Hadn't noticed the chemically treated ficus trees near the elevators last night—the kind that never dropped leaves.

I slipped into the elevator with about six other people. It was a risk as the closer they got to my astral form, the harder it would be to keep myself focused.

See, there's a little problem of physicality that I have when in this form, and being this close to people—there's always the chance they'll move *into* me.

Literally. I'll get an elbow in my astral form, or else a foot. Sometimes the whole person displaces me. Even in this form I take up space and exist in time—that whole spatial thing Rhonda talks about. But when there's no room, I sort of mold around to fit, and that has in the past sort of caused blank spots in my memory.

Kinda like being jam spread too thin on toast.

Or did I just completely lose the point here? Just understand that it's no fun on my part. For the person, it's more like a feeling of being in a freezer with no skin.

Luckily the people entering stopped, and since there were plenty of bodies surrounding me, no one blinked an eye when I said, "Hit twenty-eight please."

The suit closest to the panel pushed the number. The woman in front of me (I'd scooted to the back of the elevator) looked around. When she couldn't find the source of the voice (being the only other female but me in there) she gave herself a mental shrug and faced front again.

Isn't it weird how everyone in an elevator faces the same way?

Visitar Incorporated took up most of the twenty-seventh

and twenty-eighth floors. Their front door, visible right off the elevator, was impressive. Huge V superimposed over a globe exposing North America appeared to be their logo. The whole thing decorated the wall behind the front desk.

I moved around that desk and stood beside the receptionist. A petite African-American woman in a firecracker red dress with a hairdo that could pass for an ice sculpture. She was busy with someone on her headset.

"Can you tell me where Mr. Hirokumi's office is?"

The woman never looked up from her computer screen. "Down the hall, turn to the right. Big doors. Can't miss it."

She didn't even ask me if I had an appointment. Then again, if she'd looked up, she'd have been talking to herself.

The basic décor of the place is what I'd call corporate generic. Beige Berber carpet covered every inch of the floor that I could see. The walls were all painted a color very similar to Michael Jackson's skin tone. Somewhere between neutral flesh and apartment blah. Framed pictures of mundane scenes decorated the walls. A boat here, a forest meadow there.

Boring.

The office was right where she said it would be. I started to move through the door—

—and slammed into a solid wall.

Nose first.

I found myself on my ass looking up at the door. My ears rang.

Okay—this was new.

What the fuck? I stood and dusted myself off, then reached out with my right hand. There it was. An invisible wall a few inches in front of the door.

I heard something and turned to look back the way I'd come. A statuesque brunette in a stunning jade green dress suit came down the hall. She had blue-black hair down to the hem of her high skirt.

But that was where the stunning ended.

This woman had no face.

I should explain something here a minute—as I think I neglected it before. People don't normally see me when I'm out of body—except for Tim, Steve, and Rhonda and Mom (and I honestly haven't figured out their weirdness to this point). Yet I'm there.

Which sort of lends to the myth of things existing around us all the time and we're not aware of them. Like what Rhonda had said earlier, with ghosts and such on the ethereal.

I'm on that plane of existence before Ethereal. Astral. That "other side" we see on the Sci Fi Channel.

You know like Tom Edward. Or is it Bob? John?

And while I'm on the astral plane, seeing is subjective. When I look at people, sometimes I see strange things. Wispy, smoky things. Like when I saw the darkness around Tanaka last night as he knelt there dying. And sometimes I just see colors. Not all the time. Normal people don't seem to have those weird wispy things around them. Mom doesn't.

Whoa—I can't believe I just called Mom normal.

Around Mom I see wispy butterflies. With Rhonda I see colors. Pinks and purples, with hints of green. She can see me. And the color isn't like some weird force field aura outlining their bodies (which is what I know you were thinking), but more like a two-year-old coloring parts of her body with crayon. A purple arm or a green leg.

But with my six years at mastering what I *could* do, that'd been the extent of my senses. Until that moment.

This woman didn't have just colors—freaky enough, this woman had no face. I couldn't see it. Best I can describe it—ever noticed something out of the corner of your eye but when you looked directly at it—it disappeared?

That's the way her face was for me. If I looked at her

from the side, I could see she had one—a face that is. But I couldn't make out her features. When I looked directly at her—nothing. Blank void.

Creeped me the hell out. Which of course should have been the first clue I was on the right track but in the wrong place.

The second clue was when she stopped in front of me and actually faced me (or I assumed her face was facing me). I couldn't see her eyes, but I sort of knew she sensed me. Somehow. But not visually. When she put her hand up, I moved back.

It took a few seconds for her either to lose interest or tell herself that cold feeling (that would be me) was nothing.

I watched as she knocked on the door before opening it.

When she opened it, I *saw* something part like the flaps of a tent. The air seemed to fold in on itself. Ah-ha! So there *was* something solid there.

I moved in right behind her.

And through whatever the hell it was that'd smacked me back on my butt. It was like moving through soured beer, thick and hard to swallow. Not that you'd want to.

I didn't have time to wonder too hard about what kind of ward this guy had up or why he had it in place (mental note: *clue phone ringing!*) because my jaw hit the floor when I looked into the office.

Niiiiiiice.

The deep forest green carpet alone must have cost the company close to $150 a yard. The décor was Japanese urban American. Simple. Elegant. Lots of carved wood. To the right of the desk was a two-foot-by-six-foot Zen garden. A sand and rock garden actually built into the floor.

A rich cat's sandbox, complete with huge-ass boulders. I didn't see the rake used to move the sand in patterns though. It probably tucked into a neato secret panel in the wall.

Bamboo trees grew everywhere—from big terra-cotta pots to small, flat glass bowls with clear beads.

Water sheeted down the sides of a six-foot glass panel mounted in the center of a recessed pool in the floor. This piece of art separated guests from the rest of the office. Kind of like a small waiting room complete with two chairs and a low coffee table made of cherrywood covered in a fan of business magazines.

Something was as wrong with the magazines as there was with the woman's missing face. I recognized the titles. *Newsweek*, *Business Week*, *Atlanta Magazine*, *Time*, etc. I sort of flipped through them sometimes, like while waiting on my oil change when I hadn't brought a book to read.

But that was the only thing identifiable about the covers. Someone had mutilated the ones I could see, left the upper mastheads for the magazines there but cut out the lower halves where the feature picture and stories would be listed.

I only wished I could move the magazines around and see if the entire stack was done that way. I knew in doctors' offices they usually took a black marker and blocked out the mailing address to protect whoever left the magazines or donated them. But to remove the lower front page?

Weird.

The door opened behind me, and I stepped back, not wanting anyone to walk *through* me. This might be the cop.

Or it could be Trench-Coat, though I doubt that thing needed to open doors any more than I did . . . yet I wondered if that invisible wall would give him the same pause as it did me.

I glanced at the new arrival—then looked again. Astral double take.

Well helllooooo, beautiful. . . .

If there is one thing television cop shows do, it's give false impressions of our peacekeepers. Because if this was the cop I was supposed to watch, I was going to have a hard time keeping my attention on the conversation.

I had somehow concocted in my head that a lieutenant was a balding, short, uniformed, roundish man with a penchant for donuts and coffee who spoke with a New York accent.

I didn't know how this man was going to talk, but the visual was stunning enough for me. I just stood beside the gushing water and did a bit of staring.

He was a good height, probably around six-foot-one or so. I'm five-foot-eight barefooted and was sure my head would tuck perfectly under his chin.

The space between his eyebrows crinkled as he looked around the area with blue eyes. Wireless, round glasses perched on a nicely sloped nose. His lips were pulled tight as if he were tense. His hair was brown and cut close along the back and sides, though the top had a bit of length. Strands of hair turned and curled over his forehead.

And he had sideburns. They added a nice touch.

He was dressed in a gray suit and tie, with a tan trench coat draped over one arm.

"Lieutenant Frasier?"

I turned as he looked past me at the woman I'd followed in.

"Yes ma'am. I'm here to see Mr. Hirokumi?" Not a New York accent. Definitely Southern gentleman. Great smile. I could already feel an egg releasing just looking at him.

Bootiful.

I followed them past the gushing water into a spacious room of floor-to-ceiling windows. In the corner were a simple oak desk, credenza, and high-backed leather chair.

There were more plants scattered about but none as impressive as the one to the right of Hirokumi's desk, complete with waterfall and lava rocks. I was thinking I could probably make me one of those to put in my own living room.

Though the sound of trickling water might make for frequent bathroom breaks.

Hirokumi sat in his pilot's chair. A formidable-looking man. Kind of like a sumo wrestler, only without all the blubber. In fact, from what I could tell from the tailored suit the man wore, there wasn't an ounce of fat on him. Shouldn't he be stroking a white cat?

He made the cop look small when he stood.

"Lieutenant Daniel Frasier," Hirokumi said as he moved from behind his desk. He bowed, stiff and formal.

"Koba Hirokumi," Daniel said, and returned the bow. "I'm honored that you would agree to see me on such short notice."

"Cut the crap, Lieutenant." Hirokumi moved away from Daniel and stopped in front of one of those windows. I could sort of see his reflection in it. A transparent ghost overlooking gloomy Atlanta. "You're hoping my agreeing to see you personally will give you an in as to why Tanaka was here last night." He gave a half turn in Daniel's direction, but not giving him his full attention. "I'd hate to disappoint you. My intention was to look you in the eye and tell you I have no idea."

Daniel took a step to one of the chairs facing the desk and dropped his coat into it. "You haven't looked me in the eye yet."

I liked this guy.

Bold, cute, tall—single?

Wanted to check for a ring, but the lieutenant slipped his hands into the pockets of his pants. Damn.

Hirokumi nodded once, and I thought I glimpsed just the hint of a smile on his stalwart face. What was happening here? Was this man saying he knew why Tanaka was there—and if so—did he know about Trench-Coat's existence?

And if something happened to the nice-looking cop,

would it reflect badly on Hirokumi? One of those honor things?

The Japanese could be a very strange bunch. Now we Southerners—we definitely believed in an eye for an eye.

Daniel moved to stand to the man's right, between him and the desk. "We want Tanaka's murderer, sir. Don't you?"

"Yes." Hirokumi continued to look out over the city. Through the gathering gloom I could see the World of Coca-Cola if I stared hard enough, as well as the Georgia Dome and Turner Field. I moved to the opposite side, in the area of the office where two windows formed a corner. It was kinda dizzying looking out—especially when I found my apartment building.

How do people work way the hell up here on a daily basis and not get vertigo? Or at least get a god complex.

I turned and looked around this man's stunning office. Hrm . . . maybe they do.

I noticed Daniel avoided looking out the window. In fact, he kept his back to it and his attention focused on Hirokumi.

"Take some advice from me," the businessman said. His voice had softened, which of course piqued my curiosity as well as Daniel's. "Stay away from him."

"Who? The murderer?"

One nod.

"Then you *know* who the murderer is."

One shake of his head, slow and deliberate. "No one knows *who* he is, Lieutenant. Much less what."

Shit. What he is? Trench-Coat? I hate it when people speak in riddles. I wanted to blurt out my own questions. But I didn't. I suspected Hirokumi knew what killed his employee. I also wondered why Maharba wanted to know about this particular conversation. Was it because of Trench-Coat? Did Maharba know about the spook? I was sure Hirokumi did.

And I think he was afraid of it.

"Lieutenant Frasier, the man you seek is a myth, a ghost, nothing more. My advice—turn away. Before you, or someone you love, gets hurt."

I looked around the room and wondered where Faceless got off to. I don't trust someone when I can't see her eyes.

Literally.

Daniel clasped his hands together in front of him and frowned. Score, no ring! "Was that a threat, Koba?"

"No, Lieutenant Frasier." Hirokumi turned then. It was a poignant movement, made all the more important because of the dramatic pause the man made before answering. "Only a warning. The man who destroyed Tanaka is a myth because in the world you and I live in, he doesn't exist. But in the world around us, the unseen one, he is the servant of a greater evil."

I'm sure at that moment every hair on my physical body stood on end. I was getting astral goose bumps. Picking Hirokumi's brain for more information would answer my fondest wish at that moment.

"I'm not here to discuss mysticism, Mr. Hirokumi. I'm here to find out what enemies Tanaka would have who would turn on him so brutally."

"William had no enemies."

"So his death wasn't his fault."

"No," Hirokumi said, and turned his attention back to the window.

I could almost hear his mental admission, *It is my fault.*

"So let me understand this." Daniel took in a deep breath and focused his gaze on Hirokumi. "You can't look me in the eye and say you don't know the killer, because you do. Or rather you know who he is, but he's a myth. But the killer didn't have a personal vendetta with Mr. Tanaka—he had it with you." He cocked his head sideways as he looked at the businessman. "Am I right?"

One nod.

"Mr. Hirokumi, I could have you arrested right now for obstruction of justice, as well as harboring a criminal. If you know who killed Tanaka and why, you have to say."

"You can try to put me in jail, Lieutenant Frasier, but that will not stop evil. Even when it is cloaked in good."

Ack. Riddles again. Evil cloaked in good was basically a wolf in sheep's clothing. Even I knew that. But would Daniel get it?

And what the hell did it mean?

I felt something at that moment—a cold presence behind me. Much like someone had opened a door and let in the winter chill.

I turned.

Faceless stood directly behind me. And even though I couldn't see her eyes, I knew she was looking right at me, or at least in my general direction.

"Mitsuri?" Hirokumi said as he turned and looked at us. But he only saw her.

I looked over at the window and saw the woman's reflection in it. In there I could see her face. Asian. Very Lucy Liu.

And she was squinting at me.

She said something in Japanese. The color drained from Hirokumi's face.

I took a few steps back. Daniel was looking from his suspect to the female.

"Mr. Hirokumi? Is there a problem?"

The man nodded several times. "Mitsuri is a Japanese seer. She can sense the presence of spirits. She'd thought she'd sensed one outside the barrier earlier, before you arrived. But somehow it made its way here. In my office." He shook his head. "But that's impossible."

Mitsuri said something else and glanced at Hirokumi.

He gave her a slight nod, and the woman left the office at a dead run. And in heels. Impressive.

So, Faceless sensed a presence—that would be me.

I was worried about what Faceless had planned. I don't speak Japanese, but it sure as hell sounded like she said, "Hey boss, should I go get the gun?"

"Where did your assistant go?"

"To retrieve a few items." Hirokumi moved back toward the waterfall. "I'm afraid we have to end this discussion, Lieutenant. I had believed my office a safe place."

"Safe from what?"

I was following close to Daniel. If that nasty wall at the door had been thrown up as Hirokumi's "safe" measure, I sure as hell didn't want to be caught inside the freak'n office when Faceless returned.

My thoughts were I could ride the wave behind Daniel out the same way I got in.

We were in that little space at the door.

"This talk isn't finished, Hirokumi," Daniel was saying in his best cop voice. "We still have that other matter to discuss."

Huh? What other matter?

"We are done for now, Lieutenant Frasier. I'm afraid we were spied on, and the enemy knows we've spoken. Neither of us is safe at the moment. I didn't want you involved, Daniel. But now it's seen your face."

Spied on? Damn. I looked around the office. There were surveillance cameras galore, but did he mean some other form of snooping?

Like astral projection?

"What's seen my face?" Daniel wasn't having any of it. "What the hell are you talking about?"

I got right behind him and stuck to him. His emotion level was a bit high, and I could almost feel his frustration and panic. But I wasn't going to let that stop me from getting out of there. Trench-Coat's mark throbbed again, and I tucked my arm beneath my right arm.

"Evil, Lieutenant Frasier." Hirokumi opened the door just as Mitsuri stepped back in. She held a small jade statue in the shape of a dragon.

Very nice piece actually. Too bad I wasn't staying to find out what it was.

Daniel squinted at Hirokumi. "You're serious, aren't you? You're afraid we've been spied on by evil?"

Evil? Me? Never. Sure I cheated on a few tests in high school, and maybe I forgot to file taxes a few times, but evil?

"Good-bye, Lieutenant."

Daniel stepped through the door, and I saw the air shimmer as he passed.

I jumped right in there behind him—

And smashed into the barrier again. This time I'd sort of built up speed and the crash back made me a bit dizzy. Or was it the barrier itself? I felt tired as I fell back on the floor beside the coffee table.

I heard the door shut and looked up to see the curtain close back together seamlessly.

Not one to give up without a fight, I stood and put my hands out to the door and felt again the invisible wall. The sleeve of my astral cat-suit slid up on my left arm, and I saw Trench-Coat's handprint. So vividly red on my monochromatic astral self.

Crap. I tried a shoulder slam against the barrier. When all other intelligent options don't present themselves, brute force is the most obvious option.

Ouch.

I paused and tried returning to my body through my silver cord.

Nothing. I couldn't even "sense" my body. I was cut off from it. Time, time. I looked at my watch. One hundred fifty minutes remaining. An hour and a half out. Okay—I had some time.

I ran to the windows. Even there I could feel the barrier I'd not noticed before.

I heard the door open again, but I was too far away to try to dive through the opening. Faceless was back.

"Is it still here?" Hirokumi asked.

"Yes but it is trying to get out. It tried to leave with Lieutenant Frasier but he closed the door before it could make its escape."

Rats.

"But this will trap it inside so that I can torture it and discover what its purpose is." She turned her blank face to Hirokumi. "I told you the ward was a good idea."

Trap it? Torture it? They meant trapping and torturing me!

"Can you see it?"

"No, but I can sense it. It is still now, and perhaps watching and listening to us."

I did not want to be tortured. I thought being bodiless meant no torture if I was ever caught.

My arm chose that moment to throb with an electrifying pain, as if reminding me that being incorporeal did not mean painless. I held my arm with my other hand as I watched and listened.

I'd never been caught on any job—

Wait . . .

Hirokumi! Was he maharba@maharba.com? Or was Mitsuri? Was this a setup? To lure me here, then capture me?

No . . . that seemed unlikely. Faceless and her Big Cheese seemed honestly surprised I was there.

"Is it the one that killed William?"

Mitsuri shook her head. "No. It is something—else. But do not worry, once it is trapped inside the dragon for a while, I will know its purpose, then I will exorcise it."

Trapped for a while? How long is a while? I thought of my body. Right now it was like an old car sitting in the front yard with no motor. Up on blocks.

Useless. No soul inside.

An empty house.

The dragon Mitsuri mentioned turned out to be that nine-inch-high statue she'd brought in earlier. Looked like something I could buy at the Phoenix and Dragon over off of Roswell Road. Couldn't tell if it was wood or marble. It thunked when she set it on Hirokumi's desk. She struck a match and lit the sculpture's extended tongue.

A large orange flame burst outward, then snuffed immediately into a winding tendril of green smoke. I watched with my mouth open as the smoke morphed and changed into the dragon's image—extending its neck and then its tongue and showing several rows of smoky teeth.

I watched in fascination as it undulated through the air much like a sea serpent would in the water. Up and down and up and down. It moved past Mitsuri toward the door, then turned and looked at me.

The eyes glowed red like two pinpoints within the mist.

I wondered if Hirokumi could see it too. Or was he just seeing smoke and fire from what looked like an overdecorated incense burner?

"It's found it," Mitsuri said in a low voice.

The thing bared its teeth and hissed as it turned and came right at me.

"Oh shit," I muttered out loud.

5

ONE day I'm going to learn to keep my mouth shut. A thief is silent and invisible. And even if a thief isn't, a snoop sure as hell is.

And until now, I thought I had at least one of those requirements nailed down.

The moment I swore, both of them turned and looked in my direction. Well, I'm assuming Mitsuri did—she still didn't have a face as far as I could tell.

What I did know was that I'd given away my location. And the truth of my presence.

"Did you hear that?" Hirokumi's expression twisted. He looked as if he couldn't believe what he'd heard. Wide-eyed, pale complexion (well he was pale before—but he graduated to pasty white) and very tense. "It sounded like a woman."

"Demons can take on many shapes and forms."

And again my mouth slipped past my control. "Who you calling a demon? At least I have a face."

The businessman stepped back as if struck, but Mitsuri didn't. She folded her arms over her chest. I sooooo wished I could see her face.

I hadn't forgotten that snaky, dragonlike smoke thing either. It was hanging about in the air just over Mitsuri's head. It looked as if it was going to strike at me—which it kinda surprised me that it hadn't already. It looked as if it was waiting on some secret, silent command.

Not that I was complaining or anything.

Would it hurt? Would it kill me? Would it go through me and out the window behind me? Or would it bump into the barrier as well?

"Speak, demon." Mitsuri had a very commanding, as well as annoying, tone.

And it pissed me off. Speak? Like a dog? "Woof."

That actually produced a slight smile from Hirokumi.

And that touched off my wicked curiosity at the situation. "Mr. Hirokumi, can you see the smoke dragon coming out of that statue thing-a-ma-boojie?"

I could have sworn the man's color went from pasty white to bone white when I said his name. Who knew there were so many shades of scared? I caught myself rubbing my left arm again. The ache was now a full-on fire.

Pain in the astral. This was new.

"I—I s-see only smoke."

I looked up at the dragon. Still there. Hanging in the air above Mitsuri. Glaring at me. Mouth open. Shiny teeth. Drool.

Ew.

"Uh-huh—but Mitsubishi here sees it, I'll bet."

Mitsuri turned her body to face me. No hesitation, as if she could actually see my astral form. "Do not speak names, demon. You believe you have power over him—but we will avenge Tanaka's death. Your master will not succeed in terrorizing the honorable Hirokumi. He will not give him what he wants."

Say *what*? This was all beginning to sound like a really bad Japanese movie—you know with power and honor and all that. Only the English dub was done much better.

At least it matched the movement of the lips.

"This is silly," I said, and moved away from the window, intent on getting past these two nutcases and back to the door. Someone had to walk in at some point, and that's when I was going to get out. I'd been paid to listen in on the conversation between Frasier (Yummy!) and Hirokumi (Boo!). That was done.

I heard the thing before I saw it coming. A wet, gurgling hiss as I turned and looked up. The dragon had tripled in size as its mouth extended much like a snake's, ready to strike.

The damned thing was going to eat me!

My first instinct was to duck and run—forward. So I did. I screamed like a girl and ran right into—and through—Mitsuri.

Her scream joined my own.

I'd passed through people during my early experiments as an astral Traveler. I mean, think about it. Standing on the city's sidewalk, looking up all wide-eyed and thinking "What the hell . . ." and you're bound to have a passerby walk through you.

They can't see you.

And you're not paying any attention. I sure wasn't.

And when they passed through me, I'd catch glimpses of whatever was on their minds at that moment. Usually I see their pets. Fish, birds, dogs, cats. And if the person doesn't have a pet, I usually see the next closest thing to their heart.

Their car. Their money. Their . . . well let's say it is true what men think *about* and *with* all the time.

The first "walk-through" was the most memorable. It'd been a man in a suit ten-hutting at a brisk pace down Peachtree N.E., just outside the Starbucks on the corner.

His most dominating thought at that moment had been the black, lacy women's underwear he'd been wearing, and how good it felt against his balls.

Surprised? I sure as hell was.

But this . . .

This wasn't right. Usually there's *some* sort of thought. Some hint of the person's soul as I brush by it. Some glimmer of the personality formed through that person's experiences in life. It was always in flashes, images. Sometimes feelings. Warmth. Cold. Trees.

Mitsuri had none of this inside. It felt like passing through a hollow container filled with ice.

Gave new meaning to the phrase "frosty bitch."

I can only imagine what it'd felt like to her with me passing through. I think I thawed a few things on my way out.

I pitched forward, probably from my momentum as well as her own soul's unique ability to shove me out. Never had that happened before.

Landing beside the tall, flat panel of cascading water, I lay on the green carpet shivering. I usually don't feel things like temperature while traveling. But first the ache in my hand, and now this cold? The cold had crept into my soul.

Mitsuri wasn't standing either. She writhed on the floor as if something pretty nasty and slimy had gotten up her dress. Her hands flailed around, and she was wailing something at the top of her lungs. "Wraith! Wraith! He has sent a Wraith!"

Heh?

Wraith? I pulled myself up to a sitting position and looked around. Where was a Wraith? I remembered that being one of the creatures Rhonda mentioned that morning as living in the abisol plane. Ambisol?

Christ. Pox on my memory!

"A Wraith? He has shown us our death." Hirokumi looked really upset. Let's say to the point of keeling over. Which would be weird because he was on his knees in front of his desk beside the less-than-calm secretary.

Wait a minute. I blinked at the two of them. They were calling *me* a Wraith?

"Now wait just one damned minute," I said as I started to get up. "I am not a Wraith here, people. And that's just mean calling me names like that."

"Kill it! Destroy it!" Mitsuri commanded. "Before it returns to its master."

I almost didn't see the smoky dragon's head till it was on top of me. I used a few of my more colorful phrases on this one, hoping their evil design—the promise of Hell my mother used to spout at me for having a foul mouth— would warm me up enough to move faster.

I was getting tired. But why? I still had an hour or more to go, didn't I? Before the lethargy of out-of-body fatigue set in? It was like pushing my body through peanut butter. I'd never experienced anything like this before—not after passing through someone—but then I suspected Mitsuri wasn't in any way a *normal* someone. I could hear Hirokumi from somewhere in the room, speaking to Mitsuri. It was all in Japanese, and I figured I'd file it away for later.

If there was a later. I might be embracing my own mortality.

Luckily, I managed to move myself into the receiving area with the chairs and magazines before the dragon's head came crashing down a few inches from my bunny slipper.

I watched in abject horror (*abject* . . . what a fun word) as the snout, tongue, glowing eyes, horns, and scales plunged into the carpet and through it.

The snakelike body followed it down until it disappeared.

I sat very still.

Was it gone? Did the invisible barrier keeping me there not extend below? Hrm . . . could I try and sieve down through the floor? As an astral being, I'd always concentrated on staying *above* the floor—no practice at sinking. And I hadn't had any luck at it last night while facing Trench-Coat.

Or what if it came up from beneath me—trapping me in its mouth?

I'd just pulled myself up onto my knees when I heard it. Not in the sense of hearing a sound, but *hearing* it with astral hearing.

The thing crashed back up through the floor, its maw open, swallowing the panel-fountain without really touching it. The thing was made of smoke after all.

I screamed.

Mitsuri screamed.

I think Hirokumi screamed too. I can't be sure.

Because at that moment the office door came open and Lieutenant Hottie-McHot burst in, gun drawn. "Freeze! Police!"

He stopped just inside the door, legs spread wide, his face a beautiful mask of concentration.

The smoky dragon disappeared.

Poof. It was gone. And Lieutenant Frasier frowned as he looked around, his gun still drawn. "What's going on here? I heard screaming."

I can only imagine what it looked like to the detective. Me? I was pushing myself up to a standing position, intent on making my way to the door with the cop.

Mitsuri was on the floor in front of Hirokumi's desk. Her dress was hiked up above her knees, just showing a pair of hot red lacy panties (ooh, Victoria's Secret, no doubt). Hirokumi was hunched over her on all fours.

Now, I knew what'd happened. Something had passed

through her and she'd probably fainted like any decent secretary would, and Mr. Hirokumi, like the good, decent man he was, had bent down to make sure she was okay.

But for the detective—well—I just watched as his imagination stole the words from his mouth. He stepped into the office and returned his gun to a belt holster.

He pursed his lips as he neared the two of them, grabbed his coat from the back of the chair where he'd left it. "I see you're handling the danger quite well, Mr. Hirokumi. I'll make sure to put that in my report." With a sneer, he turned and moved back to the door.

"Detective." Mr. Hirokumi was on his feet in an instant.

"Don't let it escape!" Mitsuri yelled out. "A Wraith! A Wraith!"

But I was way ahead of her. I had no idea what had happened to the dragon, and I didn't care. I was taking my one ticket out of Visitar's offices on the coattails of a handsome detective.

And I still had no idea who'd hired me, or why. Or why the hell this faceless nutcase was calling me a Wraith.

Wraith.

That did have a sexy ring to it though.

Nuts.

6

I could tell from the way Frasier snuggled down into his coat once we were outside that the temperature had dropped even further. I checked my watch—a little under two hours out. I had two hours and some change to go before I reached my no-hurt-the-body-on-return limit.

Two choices loomed in front of me once I was out of the building, close on the detective's trench coattails (and a nice tail it was). I could run like hell to see if Mom's car was parked nearby and have a small nervous breakdown while she drove me home, or I could jump down my cord now and do the same, only in the safety of my own place.

Remember what I said before about Reason? Well, she wasn't on my side that time either. But on this one, I think it was good she was out taking a pill. Because Reason would have wanted me to get back into my body and keep safe (and ask Rhonda about what the hell Mitsuri was and why she was calling me names) away from smoky dragons (yikes!) and doom-spouting Japanese businessmen (weird).

But—there was a really cute cop beside me, so I chose option three and followed Lieutenant Frasier into a cab.

Why was a cop taking a cab?

"Fadó's, Buckhead." Lieutenant Frasier shut the door and leaned back into the seat as I scrambled in ahead of him. I watched him remove a small flip phone from his trench coat pocket and hit a speed dial button. The ache in my arm flared, and I rubbed at it again.

"Ken? It's me." He paused and gave the passing traffic a scowl. "No, it was a total waste of time. Asshole blew me off so he could hump his secretary. Real piece of work."

I noticed how he avoided telling whoever was on the other side about Hirokumi's warning of bad juju. I'm not so sure I'd have mentioned the warnings of bad spirits myself. Bring up stories of ghosts and goblins to the police, and you'll see a whole new level of MEGO.

I guarantee it.

Sitting on the backseat with him, I had a chance to watch him close-up. He was indeed one of the prettiest men I'd seen in a long time. But he was attractive in an almost geeky sort of way.

I liked the way he ran his fingers through his hair while he spoke. "No, I'll be back in after lunch. My car's not going to be ready till two, so I'm gonna take an hour or so at Fadó's. No . . . no . . . I want an hour or so alone on this one. I've got a few ideas, but I want to sort it out for a bit."

Well, that explained where the cop's car was.

He nodded (as if this Ken could see him), then closed the phone. Lieutenant Frasier stuck the forefinger and thumb of his left hand under his glasses and rubbed at the bridge of his nose.

I was so gone with a schoolgirl crush at that moment

that butterflies—no make that 747s—circled in my stomach. Watching him was enough therapy to take my mind off of my near capture by a faceless Charlie's Angel double-armed with a *Mortal Kombat* prop.

Wow. Hello pop culture.

Buckhead is a slightly triangular area of North Atlanta that extends from around Piedmont Circle and toward East Paces Ferry Road. From the west it starts around Northside Drive to Cheshire Bridge. Four major interstates run north to south, south to north through it: Interstates 85, 19, 400, and 75.

Most visitors to Atlanta travel to Buckhead because of its elegant homes, legendary shops, and nightclubs.

For me it was the food.

All manner of food can be found in Buckhead. Want something to just wet the whistle—maybe a good tapas restaurant? Try Café Tu Tu Tango. Got a sweet tooth just aching for a variety of desserts? Settle on in at the Cheesecake Factory. All you can eat Brazilian? Hey, try the enormous slabs of meat at Fogo de Chao.

Or if you're like me and love seafood, there's always the Atlanta Fish Market—well-known for the sixty-five-foot copper-and-steel fish sculpture in front of the door. Rocking seafood—freaky outside décor. I don't think I've ever passed by that place when there wasn't some goofy family or couple taking their picture at its feet.

Or should I say flippers.

And then there are the more subtle places like the Buckhead Diner for a variety of Greek favorites and for a little Cajun there's Voodoo.

There are shops too, for those who can afford it. I'm not one of them. I might cruise around on Sunday afternoon after a meal of appetizers, but to actually buy something?

Uh-uh.

But don't think this area's residents are entirely happy

about their predicament. Most of those who live in Buck-head are from old money, yet it's the young money that keeps the bars open way past midnight on weekends.

Rowdy. Young. Rich.

There's always some story on the news, some distur-bance, some nasty thing that happened over the weekend in one of the Buckhead clubs. And the images shown on the late-night news are always streets crowded with young people.

No one drives in Buckhead on a Friday or Saturday night. Mainly because the streets are parking lots.

Fadó's is an Irish pub that sits on the corner of Peachtree Road and Buckhead Avenue. A beige, rustic-looking build-ing that boasts live music on some weekends and profes-sionally drawn pints of Guinness beer. I liked the place for brunch on Sundays—meeting up with Rhonda there for a feast of fish 'n' chips and a black-and-tan after a night of too many beers.

Today was the quietist I'd seen the place, being a week-end patron myself. I scooted out of the cab behind Frasier and followed him inside. The place is usually dark, giving privacy to cozy nooks and crannies all throughout the building, unless a soccer game was the preference. And then there was always a crowd of young men and a few women in the bar, pints in hand, their attention riveted to the oversized projection television.

Fadó's kept up with all the soccer games and tourna-ments year-round.

Today there wasn't a game, and the bar had been deco-rated with a garland of silver, draped in large waves be-neath the outside front. A small tree twinkled on top of one end of the bar, standing perhaps as tall as a portable poker machine. It was decorated in tiny little mugs of Guinness beer.

Aw, how cute.

The detective took a seat at the bar near the tree and removed his coat. He set it on the empty stool to his right, so I took up a position on the stool to his left. Quick check of my watch. Two hours left on the nose.

"Hey, Danny-boy," the bartender said as he set a round cardboard coaster advertising Bass Ale on the bar in front of him. "Coffee?"

"Yeah." Lieutenant Frasier nodded as he placed his elbows on the surface. "And just black."

"Rough morning?" The bartender was nice on the eyes, and not one I remembered seeing there before. He was average height—or at least as far as I could tell from his position behind the dark wood bar. He had long dark hair, pulled neatly back into a silver band, and dark eyes that matched the mischievous dimple that appeared when he smiled.

He wore a simple green-and-white-striped, long-sleeved tee and had a ring on his right hand.

"Oh, you could say that," Lieutenant Frasier said. "How was it over the weekend?"

"Oh." The bartender turned and poured up a steaming mug of coffee from a set of perking carafes behind him. "Here? I don't know. Had an early Christmas party to work up at the Public House." He set the cup in front of the detective.

"See any ghosts, Dags? Or evil spirits?"

Okay. First off—Dags? What kind of name is that?

Sounded like something I'd name my—well—what *would* you name Dags?

Second—evil spirits. Got my attention. I raised an eyebrow at the bartender. The Public House was one of a chain of nice, five-star restaurants in the Atlanta area. The interesting tidbit I knew about the Public House was its former occupation as a mortuary, and a general store before that during the Civil War.

Allegedly two ghosts haunted the loft of the restaurant, where guests were served drinks and desserts. I'd always wanted to try out the place but never made the time.

There was a slight hesitation, and—did he just glance at me? "Nah." Dags shook his head and braced his hands, palms down, on the bar's surface. I noticed the ring again—silver with a simple light blue stone. "But I've only been doing the weekend gig here and there. Some of the staff insist they've had a few run-ins with ghosts." He lifted his hands shoulder height and wiggled his fingers.

I grinned. The detective grinned. I liked this bartender. I'd never taken the time to get know a server of tasty beverages before. Might need to make a start with this one.

That is, when he could see me.

He's probably gay.

Dags leaned forward, his hands again on the bar. "I'm willing to bet the long face you're pulling is from that killing downtown last night." He turned and produced an *Atlanta Journal and Constitution* from beneath the bar.

It was the same one Steve had been reading earlier. Only I'd not seen the actual front-page header. LOCAL BUSINESSMAN SHOT; POLICE CLUELESS.

"Ouch," I said, and quickly covered my mouth. The outburst wasn't exactly for the headline as much as the sharp pain that came from the handprint on my arm. I looked down and pulled my black sleeve away.

Trench-Coat's handprint was darkening like black ink on my white skin. Red and then black. It was red when I was being attacked—and black when I wasn't. What did this mean? And if it didn't go away, maybe I could say it was a tattoo?

I'd swear the bartender glared at me before nodding to the lieutenant. "Yeah, ouch is right. Looks like Heather Noir, Brenda Starr of the South, is still holding that grudge against the APD. Or is she still holding it against you?"

Frowning, Lieutenant Frasier looked to his left—right through me—then behind him. He'd heard me say ouch. And I was beginning to suspect there was more to this bartender than met the eye. His astral colors all seemed normal, though there were lots of purple spots around his head. Either way, I have got to learn to keep my mouth shut, or I'm going to get myself in some deep kaka one day.

The detective continued to look a bit confused but didn't comment on the disembodied *ouch*.

What sucked more than me not keeping my mouth shut was that I knew who—uh—what—no—I'd *seen* the murder. I knew what the murderer looked like. I didn't know what it was, but I could point him out in a lineup. Though I doubted this detective, much less anyone else on Atlanta's Finest, was going to find Trench-Coat and haul his ass downtown.

I gave an uncontrolled shudder as I had a flash of Lieutenant Frasier caught in Trench-Coat's red beam.

"I don't want to talk about Heather. That's long-dead history."

Oooh. Gossip? Old lover? Ex-wife?

The lieutenant grabbed up his coat and pulled a rolled magazine from the inside pocket (Isn't it kinda a mystery as to the measurable space inside a trench coat? I mean, the things are mysteries of quantum physics. I've seen movies where they've kept entire swords in those things—and no one's noticed!). I watched him unroll it and spread it flat on top of the bar.

It was the same issue of *Atlanta Magazine* I'd seen in Hirokumi's office. Only this one still had its cover intact.

Lieutenant Frasier pinned the magazine to the bar with the index finger of his left hand. "This guy's the key, Dags. And Hirokumi didn't even mention him. I never said a word about him either—not wanting to color anything he said."

I wanted to inch closer and get a good look at the cover, but the bartender reached out and spun the magazine around so he could see it. But I did manage to catch a glimpse at the pic and the name in bold white-and-black type. "Reverend Rollins?" The incredulousness was so very present in my now-loud voice.

"Damnit!"

Both men looked at each other, and then around their immediate area.

Keep your mouth, shut, Zoë!

"Did you say . . ."

That time I was sure Dags looked at me with a dark eyebrow raised in that same face my mother gave me when she was getting annoyed with me. Then he looked away, and his face cracked into a foot-wide grin as he looked at Lieutenant Frasier. "How in the hell are you going to connect a televangelist to the shooting of a corporate vice president?"

I was glad Dags asked that question because that was what I was burning to know. I knew who Reverend Theodore Rollins was—top Southern televangelist. He had ratings that would make any of the top three networks drool with envy. Popular on the religious channels (the ones I skipped over on my TV) and on some of those early-morning church services from Mount Paran.

But that's about as far as my knowledge reached.

I had to agree with the bartender here. How were the two related? And so I turned where I sat to face the cute detective and leaned on the bar.

Lieutenant Frasier smiled. It was one of those knowing kinds of smiles. He had the answer. And he was about to say it when—

"Hey, Dags!"

The bartender turned to his right. A woman in a white shirt and black pants waved a red-and-white-checkered towel at him. "Yeah?"

"Need you and your muscles in the back." She wiggled her eyebrows up and down before disappearing into the bowels of the bar.

Dags put up a finger at Lieutenant Frasier. "Hold that thought. I'll be right back." And he was gone, quickly replaced by a female bartender. Though adequate with a new coffee for the detective, not as good-looking.

Damnit, damnit, damnit. I wanted to know the connection. Mainly because I knew who killed Tanaka and wondered how this detective, a man who is paid to find the unfindable, was going to link up a televangelist to the bald überspook in the trench coat.

Ow, ow, ow. The arm burned. I set it on the bar and stared at it, wishing it to just stop. What was happening? Was my physical arm going to fall off? Why did it hurt?

Maybe I *should* get back to my body. I checked my watch. Two and a half hours out or so. One and a half left.

Lieutenant Frasier pursed his lips (full lips I noticed) and lowered his head to the magazine. He opened the cover and began flipping through.

I sighed. My curiosity is a dangerous thing—in case you hadn't already noticed that. It's what kept me glued to that hard wooden stool. I knew he could hear me, and I toyed with the idea of asking him outright about the connection. But then he'd probably freak out or think the lady bartender had asked.

For the first time since my learning how to astral project, I wanted more than anything to be visible, for him to see me. But wishing this was hopeless. In the six years I'd been at this, I'd never learned how to become corporeal. If it could even be done. Tim and Steve could do it but only for very short bursts. But they were ghosts.

I wasn't.

Frustration pressed down on my shoulders, as if someone were standing on them. The stool beneath me seemed even harder and colder. My back ached, and I wanted more than anything to talk to this man.

I also wanted to touch him, run my fingers over those pouty lips as well as through his thick, brown hair. Wow . . . things were getting warm in here.

"Would you like something to drink?"

I could always pop back to my body, deal with the lethargy I knew would come from back-traveling, and maybe get back here in my car in my physical body before the lieutenant left.

"Miss?"

I shifted on the stool. The smell of fried food made my stomach growl.

"Miss," Lieutenant Frasier said, and put a hand on my right arm. Warm. Gentle. "Would you like to order a drink?"

It was all I could do not to let out the girlie scream of the century at that moment.

Not only had the pretty detective *touched* me, physically, but he was looking at me.

He was looking right at me!

So was the girl bartender.

And I felt the stool.

I smelled food.

I gave him a weak smile. "Guess it's a good thing I wore clothes after all."

7

"I recommend the Irish coffee," Lieutenant Frasier said, and moved his stool back a few inches. It scraped against the scuffed hardwood floor.

I nodded, unsure what else to say.

Yeah, I know. Me. Speechless. Take a picture.

But everything had abruptly turned surreal. I know what being solid means—hell—that's my natural state. But something about this seemed . . . wrong. I just couldn't put my finger on it.

The bartender waited patiently on me. I looked at her and nodded. My thoughts bounced around in an erratic way. Was my hair still braided? Was I going to go invisible again if I moved? Did I put on makeup that morning? Could I go invisible if I wanted to? *Wow, it's chilly in here. Could I get back into my body like this? Does my breath smell?*

Does astral breath *have* a smell?

The full weight of what just happened hadn't really

crashed into me yet—that was for later when I could have a full, running-around-the-apartment conniption fit.

I was visible!

The lieutenant offered me his left hand.

What did . . . oh! He wanted to shake my hand. Me being right-handed, I didn't quite know what to do. And I hesitated again—I was visible—but was I *really* solid?

He was looking at me with those melt-in-your-mouth eyes.

I managed a smile, though I'm sure I looked goofy as hell, and slid my left hand into his. I glanced down at my arm, where I'd rolled my sleeve up. The handprint was there, no longer dark, but more of a light, bruised purple, yet the ache was gone.

Daniel's skin was smooth, warm.

The contact made me feel nice in all the right places.

"Lieutenant Daniel Frasier. And you are . . . ?"

I blinked—I was still thinking with my goodie parts. "Zoë Martinique."

He squeezed my hand before letting go. "I didn't see you come in, Zoë. Are you okay? You look a little pale."

Pale? I'm an astral projection of myself! I'm supposed to be pale! "I'm fine. Really. Thank you for asking."

With a smile (what a great smile—all straight white teeth) the lieutenant did a quick, detective-take-it-all-in of my attire. "You dressed for catburglaring?"

I laughed. It was a stupid sound. Kinda reminded me of chalk squeaking on a just-washed chalkboard. Nervous laughter. I cringed inwardly. "Oh. No. No. I just find this more comfortable."

"You must." His right eyebrow arched. "It's very flattering. Not very warm though. And I like your bunny slippers."

Aw shit.

The bartender brought me the coffee. I could smell the

warm, buttery rum mingled with the bitter bite of strong coffee. I had another instant of panic. Could I actually *lift* a solid object? I felt Daniel's hand. And I could feel the stool beneath me.

Then another harrowing thought followed on the heels of that one. Could I drink it? Would it actually go into my physical stomach or would it pool on the stool and dribble down the sides to the floor, making me look like a young candidate for Depends?

I decided to tackle the actual lifting first. I'd worry about drinking it later. Though an Irish coffee sounded really good right now. So did whiskey, vodka, or a gigantic shot of tequila. Anything to relieve the stress running up my spine.

He was watching me. I could feel his eyes boring holes into my profile. Mr. Detective was doing his investigator thing—studying me, sizing me up, checking me out.

And this kind of scrutiny wouldn't be so bad if I were actually out looking for it.

I reached out to the steaming white Fadó's mug. There was no telling how full the mug was as the whipped cream floating on top obscured the rim. I think I expected my hand to pass through the ceramic.

I gasped when my fingers actually made contact. I hissed and pulled back—damn that was hot.

Mental note: *hot was hot, no matter if you were dead, living, or in between.*

Wait . . . was that it? Had I died? And now I was a ghost like Tim and Steve?

"It helps if you take it up by the handle."

Had Trench-Coat found a way into my condo and killed me?

"Zoë, are you sure you're okay?"

Should I try to go invisible now and get back into my body, just to make sure I wasn't dead?

His touch on my right arm startled me. "Wha . . ."

He leaned in closer, his eyes bright behind his glasses. "Are you okay? You seem a bit—distracted."

I knew I should engage him in conversation, but I was still a bit flustered. Hell, I was confused. So I experimented a few times with the mug. I touched it with my right hand, then my left. It was solid. I was solid.

"Yeah . . . I'm a bit upset. Just came in for a bit of company." Not that I could tell him why I was upset or that I wanted *his* company. "So—humor me, Lieutenant. What case are you working on? Is this a business lunch or a moment of regrouping?"

He looked like my words had relaxed him a bit. Wish they could relax me. I was still gaping over my new condition.

How had this happened? Had I wished it to happen?
Nah—that was silly.

"Call me Daniel." The detective pointed to the newspaper on the bar and the glaring headline. "And I'm the clueless part of that."

I pulled the paper close across the bar's surface—still a bit surprised that I could actually touch it. "Nah—you just haven't caught the bastard yet. But you will."

He turned his beautiful face to me. I could see his blue eyes through the glasses. "You sound very sure, Zoë Martinique. Wish I had that kind of confidence." He shook his head. Daniel opened his mouth, paused, then turned to face the magazine in front of him. It looked to me as if he'd been all ready to tell me his suspicion—spill it!—but then decided against it.

After all, I was a stranger in a bar wearing bunny slippers.

"Do you have any leads?" Keep him talking, keep him talking. I figured at this point I should use simple questions, direct and to the point. I wanted to know why he thought the Reverend had something to do with Tanaka's murder. And I'm not really patient when I'm in an unfamiliar situation.

And being astral—and physical—was as unfamiliar as it gets for me. Little did I know it was gonna get a whole lot more so.

He appeared to come to a decision by lowering his shoulders. Lieutenant Frasier closed the magazine and turned it my way. I could finally see the headline. REVEREND ROLLINS FIGHTS FOR PRIVACY AGAINST CORPORATE AMERICA.

The picture was one of the more flattering ones I'd seen of old Preacher Teddy. He was a tall man, reported to stand close to six-foot-three. Big guy, with broad shoulders. I'd read once he'd played football in college at Florida State.

He was in his midforties and his blond trophy hair had thinned in all the wrong places. A pronounced widow's peak pointed down to a high forehead above thick, arched yellow eyebrows.

His nose was straight, and his mouth was a thin cut beneath handlebar mustaches.

He was one unattractive man. Or at least so to me, anyway, in comparison to the man at the bar beside me. Reverend Rollins looked like a freak'n Muppet if you asked me.

Again I was a bit surprised I could open the magazine, and I flipped to the article. It didn't take long before I saw the printed type spelling out Visitar Incorporated in the first paragraph.

Visitar. Koba Hirokumi.

William Tanaka.

I pointed to the newspaper, indicating the murder. "You think the Reverend had something to do with that?"

Daniel nodded and took a sip of his coffee. "No one else thinks so, but I do. I haven't got a damned bit of evidence to prove it. All I know is what's in that article—that Visitar bought the rights to something Rollins allegedly lost in the early eighties. Doesn't say what it was—but I'm sure it's important."

I had to ask. "Have you spoken to the Reverend?"

Daniel shook his head. "He's not speaking to anyone unless they're a reporter. And if he talks to the police, he's sure not talking to me."

"Why not?"

"Zoë." Daniel gave me a slight smile, punctuated by furrowed brows. "You ask a lot of questions."

"Yeah, and? I'm a stranger. You don't know me. I'm here for lunch. You're here for lunch. Talk to me. What's the harm?" I had no idea who said those words. Wasn't me.

I'm usually not that Rico Sauvé.

He was looking at me, sizing me up. I smiled back at him and locked his gaze in mine. I don't know how long we sat like that, looking at each other.

And it was making me nervous. Why was he staring at me? Was I going invisible again? Could he see through me?

"So why won't he talk to you? Because you're not lead detective? Isn't that how it works?"

Daniel blinked, as if coming out of a light sleep. He smiled. I really liked the smile. Brightened his whole face. "No, I'm not the lead—not really. Well, yes I am. Just not in the way you might be thinking. It's kinda complicated."

And I thought *I* was confused.

"Daniel—start over. But wait till my eyes roll back around and catch up. You made me dizzy with that statement."

He laughed.

I liked that.

"Sorry." He pushed his stool farther away from the bar so he could face me. "To answer the second question, I'm partnerless at the moment and my captain would rather I play desk jockey till they find someone else to work with me."

"What happened to your partner?"

Daniel looked away from me then, and his eyes glazed, but not in the MEGO sense. More like in the remembering something he'd rather not way. "He was killed about a month ago. Walked in on a holdup at the 7-Eleven over off of Ponce de Leon and Monroe."

I felt my own eyes widen in surprise. That wasn't that far from my condo building on Virginia Avenue.

He rubbed at his eyes with the index finger and thumb of his right hand. I wasn't sure if it was from frustration from the failed interview with Hirokumi or from fatigue.

At that particular moment I noticed a small, methodical pounding at the base of my skull. Damn—that was usually my first signal that I'd been out of my body too long. But that was impossible. I still had about an hour or so. I wanted to check my watch, but didn't want to bring attention to the handprint on my forearm.

Daniel continued. "Apparently not many other officers are interested in working with me. I should have had another partner by now."

"Were you close to the one that was killed?"

"Not really. We'd only been partners for a year—and he had a family. Three kids. I went to the funeral." He rested his chin on his right fist, his right elbow on the bar. "I'd never really thought about the danger of my work till then—mainly because there's never been anyone as important as a family in my background. But that afternoon . . ." He sighed and refocused his incredible eyes back on me. So sad. "That was tough to see those kids as they realized Daddy wasn't ever coming home."

I really hated that he was getting bummed. And I hated that such a nasty thing had happened to him. I also hated that this here train of thought was going to get us nowhere but further away from the topic of Visitar and Reverend Rollins.

Now, I'm not a heartless bitch—not really. But the pounding in my head increased in volume, and hearing was at a premium. I glanced quickly at my watch. Forty-five minutes. I still had forty-five minutes—so why was I getting the initial headache of a gone-too-long hangover? "And the answer to why the Reverend won't talk to you is . . ."

Daniel's focus shifted back to me. He looked serious. "No great mystery there. I'm not six o'clock news material. No one knows me in this city—except as the one that keeps losing partners. I guess I'm sort of a joke in that respect." He gestured to the paper. "I'm more the one that'll garner that kind of bad press. Reverend Rollins always wants to smell like a rose." He smiled to himself and took up his coffee. "With me he'd smell more like his true self." He wiggled his eyes up and down. "Ass."

I laughed. I'd not expected that sort of line out of this nice, soft-spoken man. He didn't strike me as the typical detective either. But my knowledge of police procedures depended largely on my addiction to the "doink, doink" on *Law & Order.*

I'm a huge Orbach fan. I miss him.

"I take it you don't care much for the good Reverend?" I gave him my best smile.

"I don't like any form of legalized proselytization."

Ooh. School word. Was that like prostitution?

"And I just find it interesting that a week after this magazine is published"—he picked up the *Atlanta Magazine* and held it out where I could see it—"Tanaka is dead."

The pictures and words blurred. Yow . . .

He dropped the magazine back to the bar. "Rollins killed Tanaka. And soon, he's going to come after Hirokumi.

And I suspect Hirokumi knows this." Daniel's jaw worked back and forth for a few seconds. The light from the windows reflected from his glasses again, the glare blocking my view of his eyes. "And he's not going to cooperate with police."

Well, first off, I knew Rollins hadn't killed Tanaka—not unless he moonlighted as a bald-demon-ghosty-guy. Or hired one—which wasn't such a far-out idea when I thought about my own situation.

I mean, I'm an astral Traveler, and I pretty much rent myself out to learn things for other people. I thought again of Mitsuri—did Hirokumi know his little Japanese seer combo secretary was more than meets the eyes? And what was up with her accusing me of being a Wraith? What the hell did that mean?

So maybe the Reverend did the same—as in astral traveled? Only on the astral plane he looked like Vin Diesel?

Nahhhhh. . . . That was just wrong.

"Zoë, is something wrong with your arm? You keep rubbing it."

I hadn't realized I'd been doing that, so I nearly protested, until I looked down and the mark was deep red again. The shape of the handprint was even more visible against my very pale skin.

That's when several things clicked (including the stress of the wooden stool beneath me). For six years I'd traveled in the astral and never managed to become corporeal. Now, less than twenty-four hours after I'm astrally touched by some überspook with dark shades, I'm visible in a bar in Buckhead.

And as I looked at Daniel, then at the bar and bartender, at my cooling coffee, and finally when I turned to look at the other patrons scattered about the room, I realized what had been niggling at me since I realized I was solid.

There were shadows everywhere. Misty, dark, slight

wisps of something like the smoke that curls up after snuffing a candle. I knew this look, I saw it when I was out of body. But never when I was physical.

Christ. What did Trench-Coat do to me?

I should go home, drink a lot of Coke, burp, and call Rhonda. For some reason I'd reached my usual out-of-body limit quicker. Had he mucked with that as well?

Better not waste time and find out.

"No, no. I'm fine."

But he reached out and caught my wrist just above the very visible mark.

He turned a serious (but cute!) look to me. "Zoë, are you being abused? Who did this to you? That's a very nasty bruise. Christ—it's a handprint."

I managed to pull my arm back. "Uh, no one. Really. I'm fine."

The pounding at the back of my head moved forward, crawled through my brain, and settled behind my eyes. The beautiful—if not misled—lieutenant was losing sharpness for me.

I also became aware of a weight pressing down not only on my shoulders, but on my chest.

I didn't know what was happening—and there sure as hell wasn't anyone in the bar I could ask. Oh, excuse me. Can you help me a moment? I seem to have gone all corporeal, but I'm not sure if this is good for my body, which, of course, I left back at my condo.

I blinked several times at Daniel, trying to bring him into sharper focus—but my body—what there was of it—wasn't cooperating.

"What . . ." I shook my head, and as I looked down at my hand, I found I could see the bar through it. Oh hell! "Let's get back to Rollins and Hirokumi . . ." An ocean crested in my ears.

Oh damn . . . I felt the tug of my body calling. This

wasn't going to be pretty. I was gonna be sucked back whether I wanted to be or not. And by the hazy dial on my watch, I still had forty minutes!

Luckily, Daniel had looked inside his suit jacket and pulled out a card. He wasn't looking at me. "Zoë, I work with battered women and volunteer at one of the shelters downtown. If you'd like, we could continue this discussion tonight over dinner, and maybe I could introduce you to the shelter's—" But it was too late. Daniel looked up from his coffee to look at me—and stopped. His eyes widened, and I felt my heart sink when he looked *through* me.

He stood, the stool scraping the wood floor, and looked around the bar. If I spoke, he'd hear me. He was going to ask me out! I have got to be Murphy's Bitch, you know? A man finally asks me out, and I go all invisible.

Shit.

Argh! I wanted to say yes. I wanted to tell him I'd meet him over at the Red Chair! But I also knew it wouldn't be a good thing for him to hear my disembodied voice.

Not everyone likes hearing voices, you know? Not a good sign in our culture.

"Miss"—he leaned forward to get the bartender's attention—"did you see where Zoë went?"

"No." She looked around. "She was sitting right here." With a glance at my untouched coffee, she scooped it up. "And she never drank her coffee."

Daniel fished a few dollars from his pocket. "I'll get it. Just put it on my tab. I'm going to go check the ladies' room. She was looking a bit pale, and I might have upset her. Maybe she's sick." He pulled a card from his back pocket. "And give her this if you see her, okay?" Daniel handed it to the bartender.

He was getting ready to leave. I didn't want to leave him. I almost had a date with Hottie Detective!

Within seconds I was traveling through the bar, into the street. Everything was a blur, and I was inexplicably pulled away from the detective . . .

. . . and back into my body to find my mother giving me mouth-to-mouth.

8

"I told her not to do that," Steve said, as I scrubbed the enamel off of my teeth. I was standing—well, more like leaning—against the sink in my bathroom and on my third teeth-cleaning since coming home. "But you know how Nona can be."

Yeah. I know. She tastes like Old Lady.

Ewwwwww.

The toothpaste numbed my tongue, and my gums were bleeding. It really didn't help. I still had the image of my mom's lips plastered to my own burned on the hard drive of my mind.

As for how I felt physically. *Drained* wasn't even close to a good description. I needed a harsher word.

Sucked?

No, that just led to some real nasty gutter translations.

To look in the mirror, *sucked* worked though. I was paler than I'd ever remembered being. My Latino genes looked to be on vacation, and my Irish was hanging about. I could actually see the freckles on my nose.

And—were those more white hairs? There were more there than before—like ten?

"Is that gray hair?"

I turned and glared at Steve where he stood in the bathroom door before looking back at my reflection.

Half-moons hung beneath my eyes.

Speaking of eyes, mine looked wrong—darker than usual. Still amber in an off sort of color, but more of a caramel. I looked tired.

And I was. If Mom and Don Juan De-Ghosty here weren't still in my condo, I'd be asleep. After a good pint of vanilla ice cream. I was famished.

I rinsed. Used some mouthwash. Minty-fresh. Hissed as the antiseptic stung my tender gums, then wiped my mouth on a towel hanging on my shower door. The bathroom smelled like soap and shampoo. Watermelon scent. "Yeah, I know my mom."

"Well, it was pretty scary for her. She's seen your silver cord before, like that first time you moved out of body. Only this time it was really faint, like it was disappearing. So she panicked and gave you CPR."

I cocked an eyebrow at him and motioned for him to move out of my way. As an astral entity, I didn't like people passing through me. So as a corporeal being, I sure as hell didn't want Steve's ectoplasmic goo on me. I wasn't sure what it felt like to a real dead person to have someone walk through them.

Wasn't sure I wanted to know. As far as I was concerned being dead wasn't the same thing as astral traveling. Dead meant no body.

I didn't want dead. I enjoyed my body and all its feminine parts.

Once back in my bedroom, I changed into jeans and a black sweatshirt with a yellow Wonder Woman insignia on the front. A gift from Rhonda.

Speaking of which . . . "Steve, did Rhonda ever figure out what it was she was looking for in that book? And do you by chance know exactly what a Wraith is?"

He had moved to my bed and was lounging back Cleopatra-style, with both legs on my nice, clean white divan. Good thing ghosts don't track dirt. "Well, first answer is you'd have to ask Tim. He stayed behind with Rhonda at the shop, remember? On that second one . . ." He frowned at me and sat up, swinging his legs off of my bed. "Why do you want to know about Wraiths?"

"Honey?" Mom knocked on my door. I'm not sure she'd recovered from my glass-shattering shriek upon waking. "Can I come in? I've made you a hot toddy."

A what?

"Come in," I pulled on my bear-claw slippers when she opened the door. They made my inner child feel happy and protected. Grrr . . . I'm a bear. Watch out.

"You still look awful." She still wore the navy blue sweatpants and sweatshirt, topped off by a red-and-gold scarf tied around her neck in true Boy Scout fashion.

She looked ridiculous. I'd much rather have preferred her usual caftan and slippers. Store attire.

"And you really need to talk to your hairdresser about that gray."

Bite me.

"I feel awful."

Mom held a steaming cup of something in front of me. I sneered at it. "What is it?"

"A hot toddy. Great comfort for when you're sick."

"Mom, I'm not sick. I'm tired, which I think has a lot to do with me somehow going corporeal." I looked at her.

She frowned at me.

"You don't get it, do you, Mom? I became solid. The detective, the one I was sent to watch, he *saw* me. So did the bartender." Not to mention the cute bartender with the ponytail—I was sure he'd seen me astrally.

"Maybe he's just one of those sensitives. You know, like me."

"Mom." I stood and put my hands to the sides of my head. Frustration is not a favorite emotion I like to visit. I think that's because during my years with Mom, I've set up house with it. "I'm not sick."

"Well, you look sick."

"Gee. Thanks."

"Now, Zoë, you know I didn't mean it like that. I'm just worried. We came in and I found you on that bed and you looked dead."

"I was still breathing."

She looked pained. "I couldn't tell."

Apparently when I didn't come out of the Bank of America building, Mom and Steve had gone to my condo only to discover Mom didn't have her key or her code. So they'd driven all the way back to Euclid to her house to retrieve her set and the pass code I'd written down for her.

And apparently Rhonda had closed up the shop, and she and Tim were missing.

"Well, you blew any chance I had of getting a date with a cop, Mom. He was going to ask me out, but then your revival yanked me right back. I still had time on my clock!"

She set the cup on the nightstand beside my bed and stood, both hands on her hips. "Did it even occur to you that making yourself physical like that was sucking the life out of your body? Look at you, Zoë. Have you looked in the mirror? You were pale, and it didn't look like you were breathing . . ." She turned, and I thought I saw a tear fall gently from her left eye.

Crap. I hated it when Mom went all Scarlett O'Hara on

me. "Mom—it's just that—I think Trench-Coat changed me." She'd already seen the glaring, ugly red mark while I lay unconscious and of course demanded an explanation before allowing me to brush my teeth. Though it had been a relief finally to get it off my chest. "When he tried to take me and failed. There are things happening." I touched my chest above my breasts as Mom turned and looked at me. "Things that I don't understand yet."

"You have to tell Rhonda these things. You should have told us he touched you, Zoë. There might have been something we could have done." A sniff.

The doorbell rang.

"I'll get it." Mom turned.

Gone was the sob. Dried up were the tears. She was up and ready to do battle with the next adventure.

Well, that's Mom. I think one day I'll shoot her and have her mounted to my wall.

I let Mom and Steve answer it—I was tired. What my granddaddy called "bone tired," when you felt it all the way to the marrow. I lay back on my pillows and closed my eyes. Geez . . . I could just drift off and sleep for days.

I still didn't know who or really what Trench-Coat was. Nor did I feel anywhere near up to tackling him. I planned on driving over to Fadó's to retrieve that business card Daniel had given the bartender ASAP.

I didn't have much of a clue as to what Mitsuri was either. I sort of wanted to go back there in body to see if I could see her the same way. Most of the time the ability to see auras and such didn't manifest through to my physical body.

No, I saw icky, wispy, shadowy things.

In this skinny, bony, worn-out shell I was just Zoë—out-of-work midnight-checkout-convenience-store queen.

But when out of body—I was special. I was invincible. Yeah. Sure.

I just didn't realize at that time exactly how *special* I was going to get.

I could go incorporeal. And there was a nice-looking detective out there that apparently liked me well enough to want to ask me out.

If I took all those things and set them up behind me three-dimensionally, then looked back—I'd probably run screaming.

Steve came to my door and knocked. I kept my eyes closed. It was just too damned hard to open them. "It's Rhonda and Tim. Rhonda says she's got some new information. And, she's got a new toy."

I smiled. Yay. I liked Rhonda's toys.

Wonder what she'd conjured up this time.

"Who's watching the store?"

But Steve didn't answer. I sensed he'd moved away. I opened my eyes and glanced at the clock. It was after five. It really didn't matter.

I stood, abruptly aware of the sore stiffness in my joints. I felt the way one normally would the day after a tough workout. Definitely a side effect of something. Shaky.

Who knew? And there really wasn't any sort of Ask Abby in the local paper for people who did what I do. Maybe I should start a column in the *National Enquirer.*

Ah well.

I moved slowly out of my bedroom and into the short hallway past my office. My bed was a mess, and I'd have to clean it up soon. I'm not a neat freak or anything, but I do enjoy a nice, clean condo. That always leaves me my spare time for fun things and not housework.

Everyone was huddled around my dining table. The intoxicating aroma of Starbucks French roast permeated the air, and I took in a deep breath. Mmmm . . . coffee.

"What exactly does it do?" I heard my mom say. It was

her standard operating question when Rhonda brought home some new toy.

"The guy I fenced it from said it's supposed to cage bogeymen—which is why I got it for Zoë. You know, just in case Trench-Coat shows up."

I shuffled closer as Mom stepped away. Tim did too, giving me his usual scowl. Rhonda stood on the opposite side of the table and looked up at me.

Her eyes widened, the kohl around them having faded a bit. She took a step backward. "Damn, Zoë—what the hell is wrong with you? And what's with the hair?"

I cringed. Leave it to Rhonda to notice the gray strands.

"I mean"—Rhonda made a pained face—"if you're gonna do a Rogue, at least do the whole front and not a piece of it."

I frowned at her. A what?

"Rogue," Mom said as she put a hand to her chin, narrowing her eyes at me. "You know. *X-Men*. The little girl that can't touch people?" She paused. "You didn't have that little streak this morning, did you?"

I reached up and touched my left temple where the discolored hair started. "Oh—yeah. It—it was the hairdresser's idea. Yesterday. Afternoon. Before I traveled." I said in the best it's-not-because-of-anything-stupid voice I could muster. I didn't have any clue as to why my hair turned white in one concentrated spot. Or how. But I definitely wanted to kick any attention to it away. "I had my hair up in a ponytail this morning—probably didn't notice it."

Mom puckered her red lips into a tight bow.

"Well," Rhonda said. "You still look like hammered shit."

"Nice to see you too, Pinky."

She moved from around the table and took two hesitant steps toward me. After narrowing her eyes, she turned to Mom. "Don't you see it?"

Mom nodded. "I wanted to see what you saw first."

Okay, I was not liking being talked about with me *in* the room. "That's it—I'm going to bed." I turned and took two steps toward my bedroom, away from rude people.

"Zoë, wait," Rhonda said. I turned back to her. "You know your mom and I can see auras and things, right?"

I nodded.

"Yours . . . it's changed. Not a lot, and it's a subtle change. You're suddenly more purple than red."

"Is that good?"

Rhonda grinned. "Don't know. I'll have to read up on it. But I hear you actually went physical in the astral?"

I laughed. It was a cool phrase. Physical in the astral. Sounded kinky.

Wonder if I could make a bumper sticker out of it.

"Yeah." I nodded to her and moved past them right on to the kitchen counter and my coffeemaker. Java. I needed java.

I pulled a brown coffee mug from my white cabinet and poured myself a steaming-hot cup. One sip and I felt as if my strength and stamina would return.

That is, until I turned and caught sight through the cutaway of what the others were ogling over on my dining room table.

I dropped the coffee cup. The hot beverage splashed over my slippers and beige tile floor. The crash of the ceramic on the tile turned everyone around. They stared at me wide-eyed as I pointed to my table and screamed.

"That's Lucy Liu's oogy dragon!"

9

I'M afraid my declaration garnered nothing more than a few confused expressions from my houseguests. But my reaction lowered the boom right where it needed to be.

"Honey"—Mom stepped forward, her hands reaching out to touch me—"are you okay? You're even whiter now than before."

"That . . ." I pointed at the dragon statue. It wasn't lit, not like in Hirokumi's office. But I kept imagining the smoke-made dragon-thingie opening up its jaws and swallowing me whole. "Why is that in here? Where did it come from? Get it out of here immediately."

Rhonda shifted her position and stood in front of it, blocking my view. I did calm down.

A little.

"Hey, Zoë, relax." The goth chick had her own hands up, palms down. "This isn't going to hurt you."

"Like hell!" I'd not meant to scream quite so loud, but that damned thing in my dining room was making my skin crawl. "That nasty thing nearly ate me today in Hirokumi's office. It's some kind of soul eater."

Rhonda looked bug-eyed. "You know about these things?"

I forced myself to look away from it. Part of me was afraid it was the same one from this afternoon—though the more rational part (yes I have one of those—it's ignored a lot though) of me said it couldn't be. I yanked open a drawer and pulled out a few clean blue-and-green kitchen towels. "I want it out of my house."

"I brought it in here to protect you."

I whirled around and fixed Rhonda with something . . . something that scared her. She took a step away from me as I spoke. "That . . . thing . . . or something identical to it nearly ate me today, Rhonda. I want it out of my house."

"What the hell . . ." Tim said softly as he moved from his perch on one of the stools behind the counter. He glided around to stand beside Rhonda, who was still looking at me as if I'd sprouted a second head.

Then Mom joined the two and all three stood in the entrance of my kitchen staring at me.

Steve remained beside the dragon statue, intently looking at it.

"You two do see it, don't you? Do you feel it?" Tim said.

Mom nodded. "I sort of noticed it at breakfast, but it was really bad after she came back."

Rhonda had her hand to her mouth. "You know, I thought it was because she was tired from her OOB"—Rhonda tended to use those initial things all the time. Took me forever to figure out what she meant sometimes. OOB was out of body. And I really didn't care at that moment—"but just now, when she got angry . . ."

Tim nodded. "I saw it." He looked at Rhonda. "Remember what we talked about in the car? What Steve and I've seen over the years? Well." He pointed at me. "That was sort of it."

Oh this was insufferable. "WHAT?!"

Mom held up her hands. "Calm down, Zoë. Don't make me call someone."

That doused my anger real fast. Call someone? "Call who?"

"You need to calm down." Mom wasn't really looking at me. "You don't think it was because he touched her, do you?"

Rhonda whirled on Mom. "Touched her? Who touched her?"

"Trench-Coat," Mom blabbed.

"Trench-Coat *touched* her?"

"That's what she said. Didn't tell us anything till I gave her mouth-to-mouth."

"Why did you give her that? Was she convulsing? You know I've always wondered if that could happen if she stayed away too long."

"I wasn't convulsing," I finally said, though I was still lingering on Mom's threat to call someone. "Who are you going to call and why?"

"Her cord was very light."

Rhonda pursed her lips. "Light? As in faint?"

"Yes."

"I can't believe he actually *touched* you." Rhonda looked like she wanted to step closer to me, but hesitated. "Where?"

I held up my arm so everyone could see. It really did look like a faded tattoo now. I nearly laughed when all three of them did an "Aaahhhhh" together.

"It's still there. This could be bad."

I ignored Rhonda. I was sick of things being bad. Seemed "bad" was the soup du jour since I'd walked into that building. "Mom, who you gonna call? For what?"

But Mom was looking at Rhonda. "You think it's a brand?"

"I won't know till I figure out what Trench-Coat is."

"I thought you said he was a soul thief," Tim said.

"No, that was your assumption. Tanaka just said that Trench-Coat wouldn't steal his soul," I said. "Mom, answer me."

"Calm down, Zoë. You're not well."

"You're not gonna be well if you don't start telling me what you three are talking about." I was getting dizzy, standing in front of my sink, in my kitchen, in my bathrobe, bear-claw slippers, and holding two towels with coffee painting the floor a light chocolate.

I was also incredibly thirsty.

Rhonda tapped her lower lip with a black-painted nail. "I think I need to find out more about what Trench-Coat is before I know what he's done to Zoë."

Done to me? Was I right in thinking something had changed? *Well duh, girl. You went all corporeal while out of body. I'd call that changed.*

I stared at the floor as I recalled last night. He'd been corporeal. He'd cast a shadow. He'd held a real gun and shot Tanaka. And then he'd been insubstantial again as he'd chased me in that building.

Oh damn. Damn, damn, damn.

"The secretary called her a Wraith," Steve said, glancing up from the statue.

Rhonda held up her right hand. "Okay—whoa. What secretary? Wraith? Called Zoë?" She looked at me. "I think I need to be brought up to speed here."

Mom took the towels and cleaned up the mess as I gave Rhonda and Tim a blow-by-blow of my afternoon in Hirokumi's office. No one spoke. Not even Tim.

When I was done, Rhonda took the dragon and moved it into the living room. It was still in the house, but at least

I couldn't see it anymore as I tried to enjoy another cup of coffee.

"I'm sorry, Zoë," she said as she came back into the kitchen. "I didn't know you'd gone through that. But you should have told us Trench-Coat touched you. I'm going on the assumption that he's housed or anchored in the Abysmal plane. You were astral. He should not have touched you. That's breaking the rules. Those are two separate planes of existence."

I looked at my arm. "Well, he did." I leaned back against the counter and rubbed my eyes with the heels of my palms. Tired. It was dark outside, moving on toward seven o'clock.

Tim shook his head. He'd moved to stand near the counter again. "Well, that theory about the planes being separated doesn't really stand very well. Steve and I live on the Ethereal, if your theory is right. And yet you see us. I can manipulate physical things if I wish."

Rhonda nodded. "Right." She held out her hand. "Touch me then."

So Tim reached out and his hand passed through Rhonda's. "Ah—okay, need a little enlightenment here."

"I'm housed, or my spirit is anchored, in the physical plane. Your spirit is in the Ethereal. The two may see one another. And even interact, as we do. We can both expend energy to manipulate physical, inanimate objects, but that's the limit. You ever tried picking up a cat?" She shook her head. "The cat wouldn't let you. That breaks the rules."

"So Trench-Coat broke the rules." I sipped my coffee. It really wasn't what I wanted. I was craving something sweet. Like orange juice.

"Yes, I'd say he did. And somehow that's changed you." She narrowed her eyes at me. "And you didn't sense or hear anything when you passed through this Mitsuri?"

"Blanko. Ice bitch. *Nada*." Orange juice was really sounding good about now. Or maybe a liter of Coke?

"And she called Zoë a Wraith." Tim shrugged. "I'm not sure I've ever met a Wraith before. You think it had something to do with that buildup of power we saw a minute ago?"

I moved my attention from the door of the refrigerator to look at Tim. "Is that what you three were ogling over?"

He nodded. "Just like you can see auras and things when you travel astrally, Steve and I see them all the time, because we live on the plane within which they exist. Normally you're all oranges and reds (go figure). But this morning you seemed to be more . . ."

I leaned forward. He was going to say black. I knew he was gonna say black.

"Shadowy."

Ooh. I was close. "Shadowy?"

"And earlier when you got angry, your colors all flared, and then dimmed. Sort of like a vacuum just sucked all the color out of you." Rhonda looked around the kitchen, then stepped out toward the living room. "I need to get my laptop and do a bit of research. I have to find out what Trench-Coat is, and what Mitsuri is before I can really put pieces together."

"Well." I moved past Tim and into the living room too. "Look up that article on Rollins and Visitar too. See what you can dig up. Oh, and what the hell *is* a Wraith?"

"Where did you get it?" Steve asked, so I never got my question answered. He pointed at the statue.

"A friend over at the Phoenix and Dragon bookstore," Rhonda said. "I have little pockets of informers all over the city. They let me know when something odd's been happening. Said some Asian chick came in the other day asking if they had one. Even called it by the proper name. They had two of them and sold her one. My friend bought the other one."

"And she just called to tell you out of the blue that some Asian woman bought one?"

"No, it was odd that right after she put the second one away for herself two men came in the store and asked about the same item. When she told them they were sold out, they demanded the names of the buyers."

"And?" I asked. My interest was piqued, though my initial terror at seeing that thing had hardly disappeared. I eyeballed the fridge again. Did I have some juice in there?

And why was the living room tilted?

"She didn't give it. Against policy. So they left."

I shook my head—to make a point but also to clear the cobwebs. Rhonda's image was blurring. "I'm still unclear why she felt it was important to call you and tell you about it."

"She didn't. I called her to see if they'd gotten my *Runix de Soul* tome." Rhonda took in a deep breath and looked me in the eye. "She told me two guys had come in. One looked like Vin Diesel in a black trench coat."

Oh. Hell.

I dropped the second cup just before I hit the floor.

MY head hurt. I couldn't sleep—as exhausted as I was—so I took a shower while Nona made dinner.

I could smell the aroma of pork chops, fried potatoes, and green beans through the perfumy smell of my shampoo. Of course I didn't actually have those things in my fridge—she'd gone out and picked them up.

My stomach echoed against the tiled walls.

After a healthy sampling of dinner and three full glasses

of orange Tang, I curled up with my SpongeBob slippers and my fuzzy blanket on the couch for a night of *Ghost Hunters* on Sci Fi with a towel over the statue.

I'm afraid I didn't make it past the opening credits.

I found Rhonda still in my condo the next morning. She'd curled up on the couch. I had no idea how I'd gotten into my bed, unless Mom put me there. Didn't matter. I felt better, but I was sore.

Over a breakfast of fried eggs, toast, butter, and grape jelly, and bacon, Rhonda gave me her theory about my physical symptoms as she pounded away on her laptop.

"It's proven you get pretty darn tired when you've been AFB for a while."

I swallowed some juice. "AFB?"

"Away from Body. You know, like AFK?" She grinned. "Away from Keyboard?"

Oh good grief. "Go on."

"Well, I'm thinking your astral body, AB, draws power from your physical body, PB, much like a battery. And you have to recharge that battery with food and sleep."

I nodded. Though I wasn't sure I was liking or getting the text message abbreviations. "That's proven, yeah. The longer I'm away from my body, the harder it is to get back in as well. Or I mean, the more painful."

"And there's that lethargic aftertaste."

Uh. Yeah. I nodded.

"I'm figuring in order to make your astral body physical, it has to draw more power. So the battery burns out faster, using up your time quicker. I've made some charts to give you a visual representation of your power consumption based on your experience yesterday, calculating for time spent astral prior to going solid. I took this all from the watch upgrade I added yesterday."

She turned her laptop to face me. My head was still

dizzy from the explanation, let alone understanding what I was looking at. "So . . . bottom line is what?"

"I'd say your endurance went down forty percent." She turned the laptop back around. "For right now, I'd try not to go corporeal. You were physical for approximately twenty minutes?"

"Yeah." I knew this because I'd kept looking at my watch.

"You started feeling bad about forty minutes earlier than you should have. See, that's where we're fuzzy again. I'm not sure how long you would have lasted if Nona hadn't of jerked you back in."

True. Well, I'd experiment later. I agreed and sipped my juice. It was my third glass.

It was really good.

Rhonda scratched at her head. Her stiff, moussed black-and-blue tresses sort of stood on end. On her it looked cute in a just-woke-up sort of way. On me? My bunny slippers would run and hide.

"I'm wondering if that white streak you've got going is some sort of physical reflection—like Trench-Coat's hand-print."

I put my hand up to my forehead. "Is it whiter?"

"Not so much whiter—there just seems to be a few more. I'd say you've got about ten or twenty white hairs all in that one spot. It's kinda weird."

Hrm. Did I have a bottle of hair color around here somewhere?

Rhonda was staring at me—but not really seeing me. I decided to draw her attention back to the corporeal thing.

"So if I want to be physical when I jump, then I need to pace myself. Not do it in long stretches like I did with Daniel." Now I just have to figure out how I did it. Was it thought? Desire?

A sneeze?

Rhonda grinned, then looked all shy.

"What?" I finished off my juice and poured another glass. That finished up the pitcher. "What was that look for?"

"Oh." The goth chick shrugged and toyed with her own glass, rubbing her index finger over the rim. "I can't remember the last time you talked about a guy this much."

"That's because I spent a lot of time with him yesterday. And for some reason somebody *wanted* me to spy on his conversation with Hirokumi." I hadn't forgotten that small bit. I still had a report to write up and e-mail. That client had paid me in spades.

But do I tell him the truth of what I'd seen? Do I tell him about the faceless secretary? Or Hirokumi's apparent belief that he knew who had killed Tanaka?

I thought again about what Hirokumi told Daniel. In hindsight it sounded to me as if the man had warned the detective. That he had been protecting him. Telling him to be careful when looking for who had killed Tanaka.

"That bad, huh?"

I blinked and looked at Rhonda. "Not bad. Just all a bit confusing. I saw Tanaka killed by a . . . well, Trench-Coat for lack of a better description. Hirokumi seemed to know what it was and tried to warn the lieutenant. But the lieutenant thinks it was the Reverend Rollins that killed Tanaka, and he did this because Visitar bought something he wants."

"Oh." She held up her finger. "I almost forgot." She stood and retrieved her black book bag from the couch. It was decorated in hand-painted skulls and arcane symbols. I had no idea if the symbols meant or did anything. They did look kinda cool.

She fished out an *Atlanta Magazine* and handed it to me. It was the same issue Lieutenant Frasier had had. "Your mom had this. I read the article." Rhonda returned to her chair, her book bag now occupying one of the empty chairs. The larger of the skulls stared at me over the table.

I thought about offering it toast.

Checking the table of contents, I flipped to the cover article.

Not that I needed to. Rhonda had every intention of filling me in on what she'd found.

"Apparently there is *something*—the *what* is not exactly given in that article—that Rollins is furious about Visitar buying. Actually, the article says Visitar *acquired* the rights to whatever it is, not purchased. So I'm thinking it's like an intellectual property or something."

I skimmed the article, making plans to read it better later. Rhonda was right. It was almost as if the reporter skirted around revealing what it was, or just didn't know himself. My bet was that the Reverend didn't *want* anyone to know. Which, of course, just hooked that old curiosity problem of mine.

Daniel obviously didn't know what it was either. Or so I suspected. If he did, I believed he would have mentioned it. But he was convinced of Rollins's guilt.

Me? I wasn't sure. I knew Rollins himself hadn't killed Tanaka. But had he hired someone to do it, and that someone had sent in the bald spook?

I stared at the article's lead picture of Rollins. The camera angle was sort of warped, as if the photographer had been lying on the ground aiming up, which only made the man look taller. Behind him was his church, a monstrosity rebuilt out of an old Target building. I'd never been inside it, but I'd seen it. Couldn't miss the neon signs off of 85 North just outside the city's perimeter. OTP.

The Word, he called it. And that's all there was of the name, except for a neon red cross above and between the *e* and the *w*. Made the thing look like it was on fire.

Rollins wore his usual tailored suit with his trademark blue shirt and white collar and cuffs. The cuff links were tiny crosses (oh how gauche) and his tie was red. Not the bright red of his church's "flaming cross," but red enough to make me think of blood.

I thought about this man hiring a killer. I could see it. Though I wasn't so sure I was ready to believe the good Reverend would hire a demonic one.

Rhonda's friend claimed she'd seen Trench-Coat, which made him corporeal. And if I'd not done the trick yesterday, I'm not really sure I'd believe it myself. But the friend reported there was someone else. Unfortunately, Rhonda's friend couldn't describe the other guy.

She was a Vin Diesel fan. Couldn't see anything else.

I'd have noticed. Unless the other guy looked like Brad Pitt, then I'd have been in trouble. With the state of my underworked libido, I might have jumped over the counter at him.

I preferred cute little blue-eyed detectives with hair.

Thinking of Rhonda's friend brought the memory of the artifact back to me. I sat up and looked around the room. "Where's that thing? Did you smash it up like I asked?"

"No, I didn't." Rhonda took the magazine from me and started leafing through it. "I brought it here to protect you from Trench-Coat, just as I said."

"Uh-uh." I stood and picked up my plate. "I want it gone. What if I'm out of body, and that thing tries to eat me like its cousin did?"

"Zoë." Rhonda put down the magazine and stood. She grabbed a few plates herself. "It's unofficially called a soul cage. It won't eat you. And it's triggered to the person lighting its tongue. If you told it to protect you and lit it, then it would. Even if you went OOB. It wouldn't see your own astral self as a threat. Even a Wraith can use it."

I stopped in the middle of the kitchen and walked back to the edge of my dining area. "So you found out what a Wraith is? Am I it?"

She nodded, holding up plates. She looked very calm. Calm is good, right? "By all the definitions I found of Wraiths, I'd say so. But that's a generalization. Not all astral Travelers are considered Wraiths."

"But I'm different?"

"You are now. People who astral travel, or bilocate, do *only* that. You're a Traveler that can become visible to the living, Zoë. That makes you a candidate for Wraithdom."

I heard it then, the slight catch in her voice. There was something she wasn't telling me. Something oogy. "Rhonda . . ."

"That's all I know for now, Zoë. Mitsuri was right in pegging you. For now. You're a Wraith. Which if you think about it, is kinda cool in a dark and sexy way." She smiled. "So, don't worry about the soul cage. It won't eat you, unless someone sets one on you like Mitsuri did."

Right. "You didn't see what it could do." I set the dishes in the sink. *Wraith. I'm a Wraith.* Well, it did sort of have that sexy, superhero sound to it. I yawned. Yeah, me the mighty Wraith, who wanted nothing more than to go back to bed and pull the covers over my head.

I eyed the refrigerator. Did I have any juice left?

"No, but I'd love to!" Rhonda moved to the sink and started scraping off the remaining food into the garbage disposal. "I mean, I'd love to see what it does to the actual intruder, you know? I mean, I'm glad you didn't get caged, but . . ." She paused, and I heard the *clink* of utensils on ceramic as I opened the refrigerator and took out a pitcher of grape Kool-Aid I'd made the day before.

"But," I started up as I set the pitcher on the table, "if I had, then I could have given you a firsthand description of what happened." There weren't any clean glasses on the table, so I just tilted the pitcher and drank from the spout.

"Well I'm not saying I'd want anything icky to happen to you, but if you'd have been . . . ZOË!"

Her yell startled me and I choked. Grape Kool-Aid dribbled down the sides of my mouth and onto my tee shirt. I coughed, set the pitcher on the table, and grabbed a paper towel to wipe the spill. "What the hell was that for? You scared the pooh out of me."

"My mom would have killed me for doing what you just did. That's gross." She stood in front of the sink, her eyes wide again. In fact, I'm not sure I liked the way she was looking at me. "Zoë, why are you drinking so much?"

After tossing the wet paper towel in the trash, I shrugged. "I don't know. I'm just thirsty."

"Maybe you should go to a doctor about that. It's not normal."

"Neither is being a *Wraith*, but what the hey." I held up my hands. "Since when has my life been normal?"

"And your voice is huskier than usual." She smiled. "It's kinda sexy."

I shot her a bird.

I wanted to say more. Rhonda's observation about my thirst hadn't gone unnoticed by me, just unchecked. I was always hungry and tired after a long OOB. I just didn't remember being this thirsty.

"Ride of the Valkyries" chimed from somewhere in my condo. I had no idea what it was from, but Rhonda apparently did. Her face lit up, and she wiggled her dark eyebrows up and down. "Ah-ha! I think I got a hit."

I followed her into my office, the pitcher in tow (I was still thirsty), and she sat down at my computer. Rhonda had been the one to set it all up for me, and she was always ready with the latest software or update. I figured she'd been at her job and had installed something.

So she'd installed a musical alarm?

I stood behind her and carefully put down a few more gulps of grape.

"Would you go get a glass?"

I poked out my bottom lip. "No, it's my house. I'll do what I want."

"Kids." She shook her head, and at that moment, I had another of those really oogy feelings that Rhonda was a lot older than she looked.

I hated that.

Mental note: *spy on Rhonda*.

She pulled up Entourage mail. There were three messages in her in-box (and two in mine, I noticed with mild interest). Two of those had attachments.

Rhonda seemed very excited. "My friend in Missouri came through."

"Came through?" I downed a few more gulps of grape and set the pitcher down. It was nearly empty. "On what?"

"Our Reverend friend." She tapped a few keys. "I tried Googling Reverend Rollins last night to find anything of interest. *Nada*. Seems most of the search engines just pegged on his religious works. And I found nothing on any kind of item or property that he might have had—lots of speculation in chat rooms and on message boards. Then"— she held up her index finger—"I found a small bit about his former career on one of those boards. Seems he worked in the porn industry for a while, not just behind the camera but in front of it. So I contacted my friend in New Orleans—remember the guy I dated last year?"

I narrowed my eyes at her. Yeah, I sort of remembered a tall, dark-haired guy with rings in his nose. Come to think of it, Tim had commented he looked like he'd rolled around in a tackle box. "Yeah . . . Bruno?"

"Hey, good for you, Zoë. He e-mailed me these." She moved the mouse and an extremely odd-looking picture plastered itself over my flat-screen monitor.

"Oh . . . my," Rhonda said, and leaned forward.

I did the same over her shoulder.

Bare in the buff, lounged on his side to expose his working mechanics, was a very young, very well hung, Theodore Rollins.

I slapped my hand to my mouth. *Oh Jesus! How clichéd is this?*

The title read *Fair Play*, starring the Tremendous Teddy Rollover.

"He was a porn actor!" Rhonda blurted out, and started laughing.

Oh, it was worse than that. I leaned forward and read a bit more of the fine print. Well, if this was the "intellectual property" that Visitar had gotten their hands on, it was certainly enough motive for me.

"Rhonda, honey. He wasn't just a porn actor." I reached over her shoulder and pointed to one of the smaller group shots. "He was a *gay* porn *star*."

10

THE ASTRAL

MOMS are sneaky creatures.

And they love you unconditionally.

Mine coerced her minion Rhonda to keep an eye on me for the day, and Rhonda was no schmooze. With the temptation of digging up more information on Wraiths, as well as a free lunch of Shrimp Portafino at Macaroni Grill (mmmmmm buttery, lemony goodness and al dente pasta!), I was a willing captive.

We visited her friend at the Phoenix and Dragon and grilled her about the guy with Trench-Coat who wanted one of the dragon statues. *Nada.* Both women remembered there being a second person, but neither of them could describe him.

They couldn't even say for certain it was a man or a woman. But they definitely remembered Trench-Coat. Vin Diesel lookalike. One interesting note was that he never spoke. The other guy did.

Rhonda bought a few books on folklore and hustled me out of there when the store's cat started hissing at me. That was new too. Usually cats loved me, pressed their fur all over me.

Not this minitiger. She was ready to take my head off.

What I hadn't expected was for Rhonda to drive her purple Volkswagen Beetle to my doctor's office. I evidently had an appointment with the family physician, set up earlier that morning by one Nona Martinique.

And I had to face it—something *was* wrong. That morning I'd consumed several gallons of juice, water, and tea, then downed two Evian bottles of water in Rhonda's car, not to mention gone through her entire stash of Little Debbie Brownies.

Dr. Melvin Maddox was my family doctor. A tall, Grand Moff Tarkin sort of guy (à la Peter Cushing) who looked scary as hell, but had a bedside manner that would make Mother Teresa seem cruel.

He'd watched me grow from the age of eight to twenty-eight—and he was the only person in my life who ever openly discussed my father with me.

Dr. Maddox was also good about delivering bad news. Up front. Intense stare. And full of suggestions. He examined me, took blood samples, pushed and poked the skin around the mark left by Trench-Coat (we neglected to tell him about the bald überspook), then had me drink this foul, thick, orange overly sweet juice.

Killed my thirst instantly, as well as the craving for a candy bar I'd had since entering the office. And nausea. In spades. Ugh. After an hour he took my blood again, then pulled Rhonda and me into his office (she'd adopted him as her doctor as well).

"Zoë." Dr. Maddox sat behind his organized desk in his high-backed black chair. The office had seemed so big when I was a child. Now I saw it as a square, twelve-by-twelve-foot room, with its walls covered in framed certificates, diplomas, and scads of pictures of Maddox's family.

A family he'd lost in a tragic car accident three years ago. His wife of twenty-eight years, his two sons, Robert and Joseph, and their dog, Butchy.

That had been my first funeral, and the worst.

Parts of Maddox's office were a shrine to them. And to his happiness while they lived.

I sat to the left, near the door, ready to make a break for it like I always had. Rhonda stood and looked at the pictures. There were hundreds of them.

Literally.

"Give it to me straight, Doc," I always said.

"I have no idea."

I'd never heard those words out of Maddox before. "Whut?"

"That mark on your arm appears to be a part of the melanin in your skin, much like a birthmark. And, there have been documented cases of birthmarks appearing as late as a person's seventies. I admit it's odd that it's in the shape of a hand, but there have been other accounts of birthmarks in the shape of animals or even faces. I think I read once where a woman had one in the shape of Elvis."

Snort.

"But as for your other symptoms, they all fit someone with diabetes. Incredible thirst, hunger, fatigue, inability to concentrate (though you've always had that according to Nona), and irritability—"

I put my hand up before he could comment on *that* symptom too. I knew Mom thought I was irritable most of the time. I preferred the word *cranky.* Or *colorful.*

"But?"

"I'm willing to bet your glucose tolerance test comes back negative."

"Was that that nasty stuff I drank?"

Maddox nodded. "Healthy, as always. But I'll give you a call and let you know the results."

"Great. Are we done?"

"I'm going to prescribe you a mild sedative." He reached to his right and retrieved a small pad and started scribbling. "Nona said you'd been having trouble getting a good night's sleep, which might have something to do with these symptoms, but I doubt it."

I did not need sleeping pills, and I'd been about to tell the good doctor those were probably for my mother's benefit when I saw Joseph Maddox step out of the shadows behind his father's desk.

Shiiiiit.

"I'll let Nona know you passed the physical with all As, and once I have the results . . . Zoë?"

I hadn't noticed him there before, standing in the shadows. I'd known the doctor's kids. I went to high school with Joseph. We weren't all that close in social positions. I was poor, he was rich. He was on the football team, and I was a geek who never went to a game.

But he knew me, and I knew him, the moment he appeared. He looked just like he had the last time I saw him, two days before the accident. Tall, like his father, and extremely pale.

In fact, he was black-and-white. All monochromatic. An old silent movie.

Silent because he was talking and I couldn't hear a word.

Rhonda snapped her fingers in front of my face. "Hey, snap out of it."

Maddox ripped the prescription for the sedative off of his pad. He started writing something else and handed it to

Rhonda. "This is for Nona, and tell her to call me for the instructions." He looked at me. "Zoë . . . are you sick? All the color's drained from your face."

I'll bet. And it should. I was sitting here in my doctor's office staring at his dead son. Argh. How more confusing could my life get?

Mental note: *never ask that question of the universe; it has a sick sense of humor.*

"Maybe you should take her home and get her to bed?" Maddox was saying to Rhonda. "That syrup might be upsetting her stomach."

Oh yeah—my stomach was upset all right. I was looking at a ghost. A ghost I couldn't hear. But he was sure talking to me as if he knew I knew what was happening.

I stood with some pulling on my arm and gave Joseph another stare as Rhonda pulled me out of the doctor's office.

The sky had turned a bit overcast and the wind cut through my sweater and jeans. Rhonda dragged me into her car, got in, and backed out of the parking lot quickly. Once out on Roswell Road, she slowed and pulled into the parking lot of the Starbucks Coffee across from the Hammond Square Shopping Center.

She cut the engine but left her radio on softly as she twisted in her seat and looked at me. "What was it? Was it Trench-Coat? Did he show up in the office?"

I shook my head and watched a small finch, perhaps one of the last remaining in the city before winter really moved in, bounce around on the grooved and pitted asphalt beside the car. A Dumpster sat to the right and I looked at it, read the red-and-white graffiti that read "He's Coming."

And then it hit me as I turned and stared at Rhonda. "*You* didn't see it?"

"See what?"

"That ghost. There was a ghost standing right beside Maddox. It was Joseph, his dead son."

Rhonda looked as shocked as I felt. She stared at the Beetle's center brake before giving me a stricken face. "Oh nuts, Zoë. I didn't see anything. I just assumed it was Trench-Coat because I *couldn't* see anything. I *should* have seen a ghost. I always see ghosts—or at least sense them."

Nona and Rhonda always saw the same things I saw, except while I was astral. I'd tried to describe the colors and the afterimages, like vapors on a hot Southern night, trails of light that followed the living. I think they got it, or at least got what I meant. But in these past six years of tripping the astral plane, I'd never seen any other ghosts except for Tim and Steve.

None.

Until today.

Oh there was Trench-Coat, but we still didn't know where the hell he fit into this mess. "Joseph was there, Rhonda. But he was different. All black-and-white. And I couldn't hear him. Not one word."

I looked at her when she didn't respond for a few seconds. Her kohl-rimmed eyes narrowed, and she chewed on her lower lip. That meant she was thinking. "Well—it would make sense. Wraiths can see through all the planes, Zoë. And there are parts of the Astral and Ethereal that I just can't see—and now you can."

"So." I rubbed at my head. Too much. Way too much information. "Joseph Maddox is caught in an area of death that you can't see, but that I can, because I'm a Wraith? Is this what you wouldn't tell me before? The part you left out?"

"A little. And you're *becoming* a Wraith. I don't think you're fully there yet. Sort of like what a person goes through when they transgender. It's in stages."

I glared at Rhonda. "That analogy so sucked ass."

"Sorry—best I can do on limited knowledge. Wraiths—by old-world standards—are the harbingers of death. It makes sense that you see all the levels of dead." She shivered. "And I just creeped myself out. Knowing there are so many states of death. Oh man . . . I need to read some more."

My PDA cell chimed before I could choke a sensible answer out of her. I habitually twisted in the narrow seat and pulled the phone from its leather hip holder. "Hello."

"Zoë Martinique?"

Oh. I knew this voice. Soft. Sexy. A bit of a Southern accent.

"Hello there, Detective Frasier." I glanced over at Rhonda, but she'd grabbed up one of the books she'd bought at the Phoenix and Dragon and was thumbing through the table of contents. "How did you get this number?"

"Well, first off, I'm a detective. Second, do you know how many Zoë Martiniques there are in Atlanta?"

Touché. "So—what can I do for you?"

"Well"—there was a pause—"I was hoping I could do something for you."

Uh-oh.

"I was worried yesterday, when you disappeared like that. So I decided to do a little snooping of my own."

And then I knew it. He'd found my file.

My rape file.

I knew it from the inflection in his voice. The slight lowering of an octave and the now-present sound of concern in his voice. Captain Do-gooder. I wasn't in the mood.

"Look, Lieutenant. What happened six years ago was a one-time thing."

"They never caught your attacker."

True. "My attacker didn't cause the mark on my arm. I'm not in any trouble." Well, none that the good men and women of the Atlanta Police Department could comprehend. "So, if you don't mind, I'd like to get on with my life. *Ciao.*"

I disconnected.

I mean . . . I literally hung up on Hottie-Mc-Copper. I couldn't believe I'd done that. But then again, I was pissed. Pissed because my mom had set up a doctor's appointment without even bothering to consult me. Pissed because her little minion here beside me had taken me there, no questions asked. I was pissed because I saw a ghost that she didn't see, and I couldn't hear the bastard.

Pissed because some spooky Vin-man had grabbed me and done something to me, only we didn't have any sort of answer book of any kind to know what the hell it was we were doing. Pissed because some faceless ice bitch had called me a Wraith (though I kinda liked it).

And now I had a cop snooping about me in my file. How dare he? And he'd made me remember that damned rape. Asshole.

And I had gray hairs!

The phone rang again. Same number.

Of course I answered it.

"Don't hang up."

Uh-huh.

"Look, I'm sorry. It's just that mark on your arm—"

"It's a birthmark, Frasier. Nothing more." Well, so it wasn't the whole truth. Maddox did say it had all the indications of being a natural occurrence.

Not. Natural as far as being grabbed by some muscled guy in a trench coat who killed people, then apparently sucked their souls.

"I'm sorry. I'm out of line, but I just wanted to help a beautiful woman."

Okay, so it was a hokey line. But it was a hokey line used on *me*. That was different. And now I felt bad. I'm such a wuss. He wanted to help me. Well, maybe there was a way I could help him? "Hey, what do you say to an early dinner? I found some stuff out on your reverend."

Pause. "You did?"

"Oh now don't go all suspicious. You snooped on me. Why can't I snoop on him?"

He laughed. I liked the laugh. Had a nice ring to it. "Okay, I just doubt you've found out anything I haven't already. How about Fadó's in about half an hour?"

I checked my phone's clock. It was a little after four. "How about we meet at five? Fadó's huh? Do you ever go anywhere else?"

"Sometimes I go home, but I figured that might be a bit forward."

Uh. Right. Did the cop just come on to me? Nice. "Five." I disconnected.

Rhonda was still moving pages. I wanted water. Lots of water. Cold. I was nervous, and when I get nervous, I get really, really sweaty. "Take me home, Rhonda. I got a date with the detective."

"You think that's a good idea?" She didn't look up from the book under her nose. "I mean, we're still not sure what's wrong with you."

"Being less a few hairs when I pull it will be wrong with you if you don't get me home in time to brush my teeth, comb this hair, and change my clothes."

Rhonda tossed the book in the back. "Okay. But don't call me when you do something all Wraithy and frighten the good cop who knows nothing about your little secret."

I think my response was perfect. "Tthhhppptt."

11

I managed to brush my teeth, braid my hair (I started to yank out all the white hairs but figured I'd do more damage than good), and change into a nice pair of jeans, my fake-fur-lined camel boots, and a blue turtleneck sweater, and grabbed the folder of Rhonda's Rollins research before setting out in my silver Mustang.

The car was my pride and joy, and the bane of my budget. I'd always wanted the classic lines of a '69 Mach One fastback, but desired the interior comfort of one of the late models. So, when Ford came out with the new Mustang with its classic front end and irresistible lines, well, I *had* to have one.

I admitted to myself as I pulled off of Virginia Avenue and onto Monroe Drive—I looked good.

As I passed the park my thoughts turned dark for the second time that day. Everyone has bad events in their lives. An embarrassing situation in school, maybe a humiliating public assault on their character. They might have even been mugged or fired from a job.

A rape . . . that's something that never heals. Oh, the scars aren't so visible, sometimes. And the physical ones mend. But nothing mends the mind, or the memories. I'd managed for years to simply put those memories away, file them in a secret locked place.

But every now and then they bounced to the surface, like a buoy held beneath the ocean too long. For months after I dealt with those moments alone. I knew groups were the in thing. The way to combat all manner of horrors was to share those experiences with others who would understand.

But you see, not many people *see* their own rape. They feel it, remember the hurt, the pain and humiliation. But me . . . I saw everything.

I was twenty-two and had just left a dinner play at the Shakespeare Tavern on Peachtree. *The Tempest*—my all-time favorite of Bill's masterpieces. And there'd been a new guy with our clique.

His name was Barry Stephens.

Cute. Smart. A friend of one of the girls in my business class at Georgia State. We'd flirted just a bit during the play, and he was charming. Polite. He offered to take me home.

A small voice inside my head warned me this wasn't a good idea. I barely knew him. But I never listened to that voice. Still don't.

How many times in my life had I known regret in never paying attention to my instincts? It wasn't that I sensed imminent danger in Barry himself—but there was something wrong—somewhere.

On the way to my mom's house he wanted to go by Piedmont Park. There was something he wanted to show me there. Something special. I said no at first—it was late, and I couldn't shake that ominous feeling that something dark waited around the corner.

The air had just turned cold and windy, like now. It was November six years ago. He'd given me his coat, and I remember the smell of Drakaar cologne and minty Speed Stick deodorant. It'd been months since I'd been kissed, much less touched, even casually.

I'd suspected he'd been having the same impure thoughts as I, and maybe there was some place in the park he liked to take advantage of. I'd never been in the park at night, which made the whole exercise a bit thrilling.

As we neared the pool, he pointed up at the sky. The lights from the city stole most of the night. No stars twinkled, though I knew it'd been cloudless all day. But if I looked closely to the north, I could see the moon. It was full, a mere shade of its true beauty, but there.

I felt his arms slip beneath mine, behind me, my back to his front. Barry pulled me to him and I melted backward. He rested his chin on my right shoulder and I could hear his breathing, almost taste the breath mint he'd slipped in when he thought I wasn't looking.

"This is the only place in the city where I've found you can see the full moon." His voice was a whisper. Deep. Soothing. "What's even more special is how it reflects in the pool." He chuckled. "That is, when it's full of water."

I smiled and turned in his arms. I kissed him. Miss Bold, that's me. He tasted minty-fresh, and his lips were warm against mine. I wanted to be held, to be touched tenderly.

Barry made a noise then, gurgling deep in his throat.

Something warm and coppery tasting filled my mouth. It came from Barry's lips.

I pulled away, only a few steps. He stood there, the lights from the city illuminating only one side of him; the other was cast in shadow. His eyes were wide. His mouth was open, and something pooled out like dark, chocolate syrup.

The front of his shirt was also dark.

I saw the clean slice along his neck as he fell to my right, all the while making moist, wet, gurgling sounds as he tried to bring air into his severed throat.

I managed a good-sized scream before something struck me from behind. I remember seeing stars and falling to the cold, hard ground. Hard because I cracked my skull on it when I landed. Something heavy pressed on my chest, pinning me down, my arms at my sides. It smelled of vomit and dog piss, the way my great-aunt's house did when they found her six days after she'd died, locked in the house with her two poodles.

The same hard blows happened several times against my face, over and over when I tried to cry out. I'd never been hit so hard before—to the point of being aware of what was happening but unable to do anything about it. My body refused to move.

How many times had I seen this happen in the movies, on television, and become so disgusted because the women didn't just kick the rapist in the balls?

But fear is a funny thing. It can motivate you to do strange things, like lift a car from a child, or it can make you do terrible things, like murder, or it can rob you of all movement and make you meek as a kitten.

I was a kitten, unable to move or defend myself, afraid he would slit my throat as he had Barry's. I was only coherent enough to whimper as my jeans were unfastened and pulled down to my knees. I closed my eyes, and I could hear Barry's rasping breaths to my right as he gasped for life.

I could hear my attacker's excited breaths hovering over me even as I tried to open my swelling eyes and see him. And I did see him illuminated in the same light that had shown me Barry's wounds. Matted blond hair, wild blue eyes. His lips were chapped. Round, red sores dotted one corner.

As he bent down to me, I tried to cry out again. Something was shoved into my mouth and my lips stung as they were smashed against my teeth. I felt his breath on my face, telling me to shut up or he'd kill me.

And when it started—when he shoved his penis roughly inside of me—I cried into the gag, unable to comprehend what was happening. He held my wrists out to my sides, jamming them into the ground over and over as he thrust himself deeper and deeper inside.

I wanted to die.

I wanted a hero to rescue me.

I heard Barry's final, strangled, dying breath.

I wanted to be . . . *away*.

Even as I listened to my rapist's rhythmic grunting, I heard something else.

It was the sound of tearing cloth. I recalled that noise from a childhood memory. Listening to it when my mom would tear the hem from one of my shirts to restitch it.

And with it came a searing pain that spread into every muscle, toe, finger, nook and cranny of my body. The sensation overwhelmed the horror of what was being done physically to me. I screamed into the cloth as I felt myself lifted up, wrenched from the ground.

He paused and hit me again, only harder this time.

The final blow.

The pain ceased. All pain. Gone. I was nearly taken with the abrupt end to the agony of his thrusts, of the fire that had spread throughout every inch of my body.

The only sound was that of his breathing. His grunting thrusts.

I stood in the moonlight, looking down at my hands. At my feet.

Barry stood beside me and smiled. He'd reached out for my hand, but I couldn't touch him. He was insubstantial. He wasn't bleeding either. And he looked sad as I watched him fade away to little more than a group of twinkling lights that spiraled upward into the city sky.

The sounds of the night returned. Traffic. Someone yelled out across the park. And there was panting. It echoed inside of my head. Slow. Deliberate. Sated.

I turned and looked down.

I saw his white ass in the light, thrusting over and over and over again. I was frozen where I stood as he continued to have his way with me, oblivious to the fact I no longer struggled.

And then I saw my own face.

I saw my eyes open. Staring.

I saw the cloth forcing my jaws wide apart.

Was I dead?

How—how could I be standing, watching, *and* lying on the ground? WTF?

And when he'd finished with one orifice, I staggered back as he removed the rag and shoved himself into my mouth.

I ran. I ran as far as I could away from my body. It was broken. Defiled.

Dead.

I tried to get the attention of two cops sitting in a black-and-white near the park's entrance on Piedmont. They heard me, which made me happy.

But they couldn't see me. I told them I was being raped. A boy was dead! I yelled at them to go to the pool and shoot the motherfucker! I shouted at them over and over.

They stood outside their car and looked into the darkness, guns drawn, looking for the source of the disembodied voice.

Was this death? Was this Hell? I'd seen Barry disappear. Why wasn't I disappearing? Was I not going to Heaven? My old Catholic upbringing surged forward, and I started reciting my "Hail Marys" over and over again.

What had I done . . .

WHAT HAD I DONE?

I was the one being raped! I'd never harmed a single soul! Why was I still here? Why? Why? Why?

No one I passed could see me.

But they could all hear me!

I wandered around like a lost soul for a while, freaking out passersby as I asked them to help me. And when they heard a disembodied ghost, many of them ran the other way.

And the whole time I wondered why I wasn't going to Heaven.

I'd never done anything wrong!

Finally, I found my home, where I lived with my mother on Chandler Street near Little Five Points. I wasn't cold. But I was shivering. I was breathing, but I didn't see any breath in the light outside the house.

Mom was asleep, and I tried to wake her. I wanted her to call the police and tell them I was being raped. That my body was in the park.

My hands passed through her.

I couldn't wake her. As many times as I was forced to remember that moment, I don't know why I never called out her name. I think I was afraid she *wouldn't* hear me.

And I was damned.

I went to my room and into my closet. There I kept my old stuffed animals. My old white panda sat in the corner on top of a pile of shoes and old clothes. I wanted to grab him up and hold him tight, to bury my face and my tears into his soft, worn fur. I wanted to smell his mustiness, so comforting. So familiar.

But my hands passed completely through him.

I wailed. I cried. I sat in that closet, too terrified to move or step out again. I had no idea what was happening to me. If this was Heaven or Hell.

Before the phone rang.

They'd found Nona's daughter in the park, beside the body of a young man. His throat had been slit, and she'd been raped and stabbed.

Stabbed. The bastard had stabbed me.

I followed Mom into the car and went to Grady Hospital. It was the best place in Atlanta for trauma. I kept quiet, unsure of what to say as I listened to the doctor talk to my mom.

She was crying. She wanted to see her baby.

I was in a coma. Head trauma, they said. The knife just missed my heart, but had pierced my lung. I was in ICU.

I wasn't dead?

But I wasn't expected to live.

I'd moved past them all to the room where my body was.

I'll never forget that moment, seeing myself hooked up to machines and tubes. My face was bruised, my lips black-and-blue. A tube rested between my teeth, taped there. My eyes were closed now.

Wires from my chest trailed from beneath the hospital gown. My arms were bandaged and taped with more tubes.

I looked like a thing, something from a horrible science-fiction movie. Me the victim keeping the world alive.

My mom came in and burst into tears. I'd never seen her cry like that before.

Mom had always said I'd taken more after my father and his personality. Sarcastic. Easy to bounce back after any situation. Not this one.

I'd been at a loss for words.

They gave her a chair, got her some coffee.

And she sat by my side.

I stood beside her, watching her watching me.

I knew then she really loved me. My mom. So strong. So impervious to the world's hurts.

And then I noticed the cord. It ran from my navel to the navel of my body. And it was fading. Disappearing. And when it disappeared completely, I *knew* instinctively I would be officially dead.

I don't know how I knew it, I just did. The clock on the wall said six thirty in the morning. I'd been like this for nine hours.

I wasn't dead—I was dying.

And when the doctors left, my mom spoke out loud. "Well? Are you getting back in? (sniff) Or am I going to have to spend my savings on a funeral?"

It had taken a second before I realized my mother was looking at me as I stood beside my body.

"You can see me?" My voice echoed in the room.

She sniffed. Blew her nose. "I can see things. Always have. When I noticed you in the backseat, I thought you were already dead. But since you're in a coma"—she pointed to the bed—"there's a chance you can survive. If you stay out like this, then you *will* die. Your body will. You going to let this asshole get away with this? Or are you going to get back in and fight? Put him away?"

I blinked at her. "Aren't you just a little freaked out by this?" I'd pointed to myself and glared at her. "This isn't normal."

"Neither was your father. You need to make a choice soon, or your body's going to make it for you. The living body can't exist without the soul for very long before it starts to break down."

What? "My father? Did my father do this shit?"

"Get back in, and I'll tell you, Zoë."

I hadn't thought about it like that. If I died, they really wouldn't know who did this. Oh, I'd shouted to Adam-12 by the park, but I doubted they'd actually listened.

"Mom, I don't know how I got out. I'm not sure how to get back in."

"You see the cord?"

I looked at my stomach. "Yeah."

"Follow it back in."

I looked at her. "And that's it?"

"Well"—she dabbed at her eyes—"it's not going to be easy. I'm sure you're going to hurt like hell. The bastard did a number on you."

She looked away from me then. "Don't leave me, Zoë." She looked back at me. "Don't leave me alone."

I melted then. I could never leave this strong, fierce woman alone. Though I'd never seen her like this before.

I took a step to my body. Would it work? Would I be able to get back in?

I did, and the world disappeared.

But I knew nothing for three days. I didn't know if it was from the damage from the blows to my head, the stabbing, or if it was from the drugs they'd given me. The world just went blank as I slept.

And healed.

And when I did wake up, I screamed from the pain. It reached from my toes to my hair. I couldn't move—couldn't talk. Well, who can with a tube down their throat?

In private my mom assured me I would be fine. My soul and my body were getting reacquainted. That was the burning sensation.

Riiiight. And exactly how did she know all this?

Eventually I could form words again. Slurred, but coherent. I gave them a description of my attacker, Barry's murderer. But it was really too late. It'd been three weeks since that night.

Three weeks of my life. Stolen.

And as the detective mentioned, they never caught my attacker, Barry's murderer. But when I do find him, I plan on finishing the job myself.

12

I was shaking by the time I reached Fadó's. I didn't like thinking about that night, or the weeks afterward. I didn't like being reminded that sometimes, when I was alone at night, I searched the shadows for *him*.

And I sniffed the air for his foul scent.

I parked the Mustang in the lot. Business was slow for a Thursday evening. I grabbed up my phone, shoved the hook onto the edge of my jeans, got the folder, and locked up the car, and hurried inside. The air was crisp and smelled of rain. The wind had grown stronger. A few crusty, brown leaves blew past me as I stepped inside.

It was dark as usual, which I liked, then didn't. I went to the bar immediately. Daniel was there, seated on the same stool as yesterday. The aroma of fried fish and beer was heavy, and my stomach lurched.

Ignoring Daniel, who stood when I approached, his stool scraping noisily against the wood floor, I turned to the bartender. It wasn't Dags, and I felt a slight bit of disappointment. This guy was shorter, with a shaved head and dark soul patch beneath his lower lip. "Whiskey. No ice."

He nodded, and I remained fixed on what he was doing. Daniel stayed quiet, and I felt him watching me, scrutinizing my actions, and at that moment, it didn't matter.

The bartender set the shot glass of whiskey on the table. I scooped it up, took a deep breath, and downed the firewater in a single gulp.

And fire it was—igniting my entire esophagus on its way to an explosion in my stomach.

Oi! I knew the stuff killed brain cells, but at that moment, I wanted it to deaden emotions.

I nodded to the bartender and croaked out, "Irish coffee" before taking up the barstool I'd had the day before.

"Can I ask . . ." Daniel nodded to the empty shot glass.

I kept my gaze locked on the bar. Most of my concentration was kept busy by my will not to throw up. "No. And yes. I don't like to be . . . reminded of bad things."

"I'm sorry." He sighed. "The file, right? Please, forgive me. Can I start the evening over?"

I swallowed bile. "Sure," I managed to croak and turned on the stool. "Hi." I waved, then immediately felt twelve.

"What, no bunny slippers?" Lieutenant Frasier looked even nicer now than he had yesterday. He still wore a nice suit, though he'd shed the suit jacket. His shirt was white and wrinkled, and his tie was pulled loose from his neck.

He wasn't wearing his glasses, and his eyes were a brilliant blue. "I thought maybe you were a figment of my imagination. The way you disappeared like that yesterday."

"Sorry about that." I blushed. GAH! I blushed! "I got a little sick and needed to leave." Though not as sick as I was gonna get if I didn't get rid of this whiskey. What the hell was I thinking? I realized then I was holding the folder in my arms in a Klingon Death Grip.

(Don't argue with me on whether it's Vulcan or Klingon—at that moment, only a Klingon could have wrestled it from me.)

I paused. Come to think of it, I don't believe there is a Vulcan Death Grip, is there?

"Are you okay now?" He finally sat back down on his stool. He had a half-full beer in front of him.

I nodded. "Fine." I paused. "I'm not sure that whiskey's going to stay down—so if I disappear again—it's because I need to hurl. I was thinking about what you'd said yesterday—about Reverend Rollins."

"Oh?" He sat forward. I really liked his sideburns. "Well, I'd like to see what you discovered, but it's probably the same stuff I uncovered." He frowned. "How exactly did you do your investigation?"

Okay, Zoë—how do you break the news that you too were now sort of investigating Tanaka's death, only you weren't a cop or even a private investigator, or even using legal or believable methods of search?

Breathe.

"Yes?"

I smiled. Big, guilty smile. "Lieutenant Frasier—"

"Daniel."

"Daniel. I have a friend who can find things, and I was curious—do you know what it was that Visitar bought of the Reverend's?"

"Intellectual properties." Daniel leaned back in the chair. The stool gave a horrendously loud squeak in the bar. You know, that fingernails-on-chalkboard kinda screech. "Or that's still all I've been able to uncover. I'm not exactly welcome on the case, seeing as how no one believes there's a connection between Tanaka and Rollins."

"Yeah . . ." I felt this was the perfect opening to investigate Detective Hottie myself. "Are you not welcome because you think there *is* a connection?"

He lowered his shoulders and rested his elbows on the bar. "I told you about losing my partner, right?"

I nodded. Uh-oh. "In that convenience store."

"Yeah. He died . . ." Daniel paused. "He died *because* of me. Because I didn't follow procedure. I was there with him. I was foolish. Reckless. And I made a wrong decision. And he was shot. We both were, only his was fatal." He rubbed at his face. "I'm lucky they didn't take my badge from me permanently."

"Is that why you haven't found a partner yet?"

"Sort of. No one really wants to work with me. And I'm still technically on probation."

Probation? Was this why my client wanted this particular detective spied on? Wait—I got it. "You weren't supposed to go interview Hirokumi yesterday, were you?"

He shook his head, stopped, then turned very wide blue eyes at me. "How did you know I interviewed Koba Hirokumi?"

Oops. Shit. Big. Mouth.

Think. Think. Did he tell that bartender guy? "I overheard you talking to the bartender—the one with the ponytail—before I came over."

I didn't breathe as he thought about this. Luckily, either I was right or his memory was a bit off, but he relaxed and nodded.

Big. Freak'n. Mouth. It was going to get me in soooo much trouble one day.

"Well, no. I mean, yes. See, he agreed to see me when I called. And then he got all mysterious and started talking about protection and told me to leave." He shook his head and picked up his beer. "Then I went back and found him poking it to his secretary. Dick."

Well, I knew the truth, but I didn't think Daniel here

was ready to hear it. I also thought again about Rhonda finding that dragon artifact and wondered what she'd done with it.

I looked down at the folder in my hands. "Well, like I said, I have a friend who finds things. She's good at it too. And she found these this morning. I'm not sure if it's what Visitar bought, but I think if it was, it might give your killer motive."

He looked dubious (and it looked good on him) as he took the folder. I waited patiently as he set it on the bar in front of him and opened it.

I expected his reaction to be as mine and Rhonda's had been. Shock and some sort of humor.

Daniel Frasier only nodded as he thumbed through the printouts of the jpegs. He closed the folder and handed it back to me. "I've seen these."

At that moment I wanted to strangle him. How dare he not be impressed with what we found. "You have?"

"Yeah . . ." He nodded. "And I thought the same thing as you. Only the actual tapes don't seem to exist. Someone proved a year ago those covers were faked, made up by some religion-hating college art kid. Rollins even gave a statement on them."

I looked at the pictures again. These were faked? Well, they were good fakes. "Wow . . . I mean, I've seen porno covers before, and if an art student did these, then either they were really bad, or they nailed the authenticity."

Daniel laughed. Nice sound. *Okay. I won't strangle him. Just kick him.*

"Zoë—can I call you Zoë?"

I nodded. *You can call me anything you want.*

"I think the kid was prosecuted, then Rollins did some saving thing, and now the artist works for him."

"You're kidding."

"Nope." He rubbed at his chin. "Look, I'm sorry you came all this way down here for me to tell you it won't help. I do appreciate your trying."

"Oh, no problem." Oh, none at all. I really wanted to be humiliated in front of a sexy cop. Go me. I stood.

He did too and offered his hand. Real touching this time—not the fake astral physical touch. I felt the vibration of his skin on mine rock my world. I wondered if it did his too. "Zoë, we can still have dinner?"

I paused. I was embarrassed, and my stomach felt reeeeeally upset. I needed to throw up.

"Zoë, I also hope you know that all men aren't like that. That there are some men that find that kind of behavior more than disgusting."

"You mean like cops?" I gave him a coy smile. Or at least I hoped it was coy and not leering.

He blushed. Oh he was so cute! "Yeah. Let's just say that because of that, what you went through, I'm doubly appreciative that you tried to help me."

"Too bad it wasn't helpful." I opened the folder again and looked at the images. "They *are* very well done, though. And I did get a chuckle at the Reverend being a gay porn actor." I smiled at him. I needed to back out of this one. Not because I didn't want to have dinner with Daniel, but because I was really starting to feel awful from the whiskey.

Time to retreat nicely and find that pint of Rocky Road in my freezer. "I'd like to have dinner with you, Detective Frasier—but after you understand that I'm not abused. Not now. And"—I gave him a crooked smile—"after I don't stomp in here and order a shot." I shook his hand. "Thanks, Frasier. Hope to see you again."

But after a few steps away, he called my name. I turned and he was beside me, his eyes wide.

"You said, gay porn star?"

I nodded.

He took the folder again and moved back to the bar. This time he turned the printed page toward the light and narrowed his eyes. After examining the pictures, he held up his hand, and said, "Wait right here."

I did, though I did watch him move his little cute self out the door. He was back by the time I returned to my stool. My coffee was there, and I sipped it, still not sure I was combining the right stuff for my quivering stomach. Bailey's and Dewars? Oook.

Daniel had a folder in his hands, twice as thick as my own. I assumed he'd stepped outside to his car to get it. He removed printouts of the covers and put them side by side. He looked from one to the other.

He turned, abruptly grabbed my shoulders, and kissed me. Yow! Red alert! All hands on deck, and on the cop! Crank up the juices and let the manhandling begin! "Zoë, this might be it! I've gone over this case again and again, and I'm sure the pictures on the Web are the ones the artist allegedly fixed. But these . . ." He pointed to mine. "These are different. I've never seen these before."

I blinked.

And I blinked again. My knees were still shaking. "Uh . . . what's the catch? You're seeing something I'm not."

Mental note: *kiss from cute cop fries the hard drive.*

"Actually, *you* saw it, and *I* didn't." He pointed to the nearest one. "You nailed it. The ones on the left are faked. The ones on the right might just be real." He fixed me with those incredibly blue eyes. Were his knees shaking too? "I'd always wondered why the Reverend's legal team would prosecute that artist so heatedly if they were simple fakes. You know—just debunk the guy. I always suspected there was more to it, and the whole time there was never any mention of the tapes being listed as gay porn. The difference is the gay part, Zoë. I think the ones you found are legitimate."

Yeah, yeah, yeah. Big freak'n deal.

Could you kiss me again?

13

OUR excitement at the find on the Rollins covers was short-lived.

Very short-lived.

Having this new bit of information, Daniel wanted to get back to work on the case. No dinner. Which was fine, as my stomach was in foul shape. He did promise me a rain check, exclaiming he'd never met anyone quite like me.

Well, that much was true. How many girlfriend candidates did anyone have who could move out of body and see dead kids in doctors' offices?

I left and headed over to Mom's shop for a cup of tea and a remedy for whiskey-burdened stupidity.

Clouds continued to breeze in from Alabama and covered the city in a canopy of dirty cotton balls. The temperature had dropped again, and I dug out my mom's hand-knitted, six-foot burgundy-and-gold scarf from the back of my car.

My cell rang—chirped, made some strange noise—and

I checked the number as I got out of the car after parking in the lot behind Mom's shop. Didn't recognize it. The gloom that had settled with the clouds hung in the wind and lowered its already-biting cold. Chunks of hair escaped my braid and whipped about my face. I caught sight of the white hairs—they seemed to glow in the dark. I patted at them irritably, knowing that the whole thing would become a tangled mess as I said "Hello?"

"They shut me down."

Uhm. Nice. And you would be?

Click.

Oh! Daniel.

I didn't miss a beat. "What do you mean? They didn't believe your theory after seeing those photos?"

"I think the captain does believe me, but there's nothing they can do. The photos, whether real or not really, don't have anything to do with the murder. There's no evidence they're the property that Visitar bought, and buying intellectual property isn't illegal. And there's absolutely no evidence of Rollins at the crime scene. Nothing physical. And as for forensics—" He made a snuff noise. I think he snorted. "Well, we all know how long they take."

Uhm. "Thirty seconds in a sixty-minute television show?"

I took it from the thick frustration in his voice that it was a lot longer than that.

"Anyway, I've been ordered to drop it. Tanaka's murder is pretty much now in the hands of other detectives." He sighed. "I wanted to call you and thank you again for your interest. And I—"

I stood in the cold, beside my excellent car, my hair tangling in the ever-increasing wind velocity, and waited for him to finish the statement. It was a pure movie moment. I even believed the sun broke through the clouds and shone on me alone.

Of course in a matter of seconds I'd already imagined what he would say:

And I—I'd like to see you again.

And I—I'd like to take you out, Zoë.

And I—I'd like to make sweet, hot, passionate love to you in front of a roaring fire while we do things declared illegal in forty states—

"—I was wondering if you could give me the name of your source—the one that found those pictures."

Uh. Oh. Fantasy gone. Crash.

Crap. I was sure Rhonda's friend Bruno wouldn't appreciate me giving over his name to an Atlanta detective. I had a suspicion the boy's means of info gathering were as "unique" as my own. Though I doubted Bruno left his body to do it—except with recreational pharmaceuticals. "I'm not sure. I'll have to ask. Client privilege and all that."

"Client privilege? Are you a shrink or something? Is that what you do for a living? You know you didn't tell me."

Big mouth, big mouth, big freak'n mouth.

"I didn't? Oh, I'm sorry. Look, I'm in the middle of something. I'll get back to you, okay?" I disconnected and shoved the phone into my bag before running up the steps and into the shop.

Roses warred with gardenias in my nose as I paused inside. Two customers were near the far wall, examining the seven-day candles for love, war, and restarting a period.

Rhonda stood behind the counter, the book from yesterday closed and propping up a sample tray of brownies. I shivered, brushing off the cold, and moved forward over the creaking floor.

"Hey, Zoë." Rhonda frowned at me. She wore a black turtleneck, black jeans, and black driving gloves. She looked like a paintbrush dipped in black paint. "Whoa—your hair's sticking out everywhere. What happened?" She narrowed her eyes. "Okay—I'm reading both good and bad here. He kiss you?"

I nodded quickly as I went behind the counter and stuffed my purse into one of the cabinets. "Yeah, it was a quick one, but it still messed with all the right parts."

"And—you're here and he's not because those parts didn't like to be messed with?"

"No, I—" I could go into our conversation at Fadó's, and I could go into what Daniel just told me in the parking lot, and I could go into how he wanted Bruno's number. But right now, I was hungry and thirsty. "Never mind. I'll tell you later." I snatched up a brownie. "Where's Mom?"

"Out with that Shultz woman."

I caught the slight acid in Rhonda's tone. Jemmy Shultz was the owner of one of the smaller junk shops along Euclid in Little Five Points. A stout woman of African-American and Hispanic descent, she was the scariest broad I knew. Next to Mom.

Jemmy kept her salt-and-pepper hair braided and wound around her head beneath a wide-brimmed floppy hat that she wore night and day, winter and summer. She and Mom had formed a fast friendship—Jemmy being the only other person I knew who could see Tim or Steve.

Jemmy offered tea-leaf reading, tarot card reading, and astrological chart printouts. When the two women got together, something weird always happened. I was a little worried about them being together now.

Rhonda thought the woman was a fraud and a bamboozler. And, of course, Rhonda was the only person I knew who could use that word with a straight face. So what if she could see ghosts? I didn't know if Mom had ever told her about my unique ability. Didn't really care. Nona knew her assistant disliked Jemmy, and I sometimes thought the old bat (Mom, not Jemmy) kept her friendship with the boozler just to grate on Rhonda's nerves.

I popped the brownie in my mouth. It immediately turned to cardboard.

Rhonda gave me a lopsided grin and pointed to the trash. "Now you know why the tray's still full."

With a loud *p'tooey*, I spit the nasty slice of corrugated board and chocolate into the small lined basket behind the counter. "Oh. Foul. Foul. Mom trying to poison her customers?"

"A new recipe from Jemmy your mom tried. I've been warning customers not to eat it."

"You didn't warn me." I spit into the trash can again.

"Since when do you listen?"

I arched my eyebrows and noticed Rhonda's gaze lingering on my hair. What? I patted it down with my hands. "I'm wondering if I should call Daniel back, you know? Maybe set up a real date?"

She crossed her arms over her chest. "You asking me for advice? Not unless you do something about that gray—though my first inclination is to say no. Something weird's happening to you, and I don't think you should put yourself at risk for exposure. What if you go OOB and then become all Wraithy?"

"There's a difference?"

"Maybe. I found two very interesting things while you were flirting with the detective."

One of the customers neared the counter and once again I was nearly knocked over by the smell of roses and gardenias. I realized then it wasn't from some incense in the shop, but from her.

I sneezed from the overpowering scents in my nose. Man, forget sulfur. I think exorcisms should be carried out using cheap perfume.

Stinky Lady bought two bars of soap (egh—go wash off

that perfume) and a Love Charm candle. Rhonda rang her up and smiled. "Please come back."

After the door closed she pulled the *Book of Everything* toward her over the counter and opened it to a dog-eared page. I pointed to the bent page. "Does Mom know you're doing that to her book pages?"

"Here it is."

"Here is what?" I moved closer and leaned down to see whatever it was she'd jabbed her finger at.

The pages were yellowed, though I'm not sure it was from actual age or from the printer. I'd not checked to see what the publishing date was on the book. The type was easy to read, though the context made little sense.

Her finger pointed to what looked like an old wood engraving of a woman on the ground as a brighter image of the woman sprang forth out of her chest. Several men in armor stood to the side, all of them cowering and pointing. One of them had a cross around his neck, and he seemed to be the focus of the brighter image's attention. "I think I'm not getting what you're pointing at."

"Read the fine print—under the picture." Steve appeared behind Rhonda. He looked serious—but again— Steve always looked serious.

"Aren't you supposed to NOT be in here during business hours?"

"It's after six. That was the last customer. Zoë, read it."

I sighed and looked down and read the single line of type. "A sixteenth-century woodcut of a Wraith being cast out of a . . ." I blinked, then looked harder at the woodcut.

A Wraith.

I looked at Rhonda, who arched a dark eyebrow at me. "Found the reference in one of those books I bought today. I was looking at a Wraith in the usual definition of the word, as a harbinger, or disembodied spirit. Never occurred to me to look at one in the demonic realm."

"Demonic?" I straightened up. "I am *not* demonic."

"No, but I think Trench-Coat might be—or at least he's Abysmal-plane goo—and if he's sort of given you this new ability, then it could have tainted you. Especially if he's a Symbiont."

Okay, I'd heard that word before. It'd been in biology in college. Symbionts were organisms that lived on or with another in a mutually beneficial relationship. But I doubted Rhonda was talking in a biological sense. "Want to eh-ja-ma-cate me on this?"

"I'm not sure if I can explain this better than your mom. Remember the different planes, thinking of them as concentric circles? Center is physical, then mental, then astral, and then we have the Ethereal and Abysmal? Symbionts are created on the Ethereal plane, made up of scattered thoughts and emotions, mostly of those that were exorcised on the astral or even the Ethereal."

Ew. Mixed parts. "Do they make themselves or are they made?"

Steve spoke up. "They're created, conjured if you want a more brash term. Phantasms are well-known for using Symbionts as servants in the physical world."

"Servants? As in do its bidding sort of thing?"

"In a manner of speaking. The ones created for symbiosis, living within a host, are less physical and are made to be dependent on their hosts. Phantasms sometimes use the Symbionts as either channels for gaining more power in the physical plane or they use them as windows. The Symbiont grants the host all manner of things, from long life to health and sometimes wealth, but the Phantasm that created the Symbiont exacts a price."

Rhonda spoke up. "But sometimes they create Symbionts to use as trackers."

"Trackers? Like in they're used to track something?"

"Yes." Steve pursed his lips as he shrugged. "As to what

that something is, only the Phantasm that controls the Symbiont knows. It could be a bogey, sprite, willow, ghost, Shade, spook, spectre." He looked at me. "Even a living being."

I caught myself staring at Steve as I stood in Mom's shop. I also felt a chill come from behind and wrap itself around my shoulders. My arm burned where Trench-Coat had touched it, and I cradled it closer to my chest. "You think this Trench-Coat was trying to take me as a host for some Phantasm?" I frowned. "What's a Phantasm?"

Rhonda shook her head. "Not a host for a Phantasm— though that would be a fascinating piece of research. I think he was trying to—well—eat you."

Gah. That's gross.

"Phantasms are the kings of the Abysmal plane. Made up of nightmares and the things that scare us. They rarely leave their plane of existence because that's their place of power. But sometimes they take a walk on the wild side, to lend aid to their own." She sighed. "Or sometimes to recall a misbehaving servant."

"And you think Trench-Coat is a Symbiont sent or created by a Phantasm? And he's after me?"

She thumbed pages in the large book and stopped several sections to the left of the Wraith image. "I don't think you're his main goal, or his target. I do think you interrupted something, and that's why he noticed you. You saw him taking a soul. Phantasms don't take or feed on souls directly, they do it through their Symbionts. Symbionts *can* take souls for their own needs when their masters are sated. Those Symbionts without hosts, which I suspect TC is, can sometimes flourish in the Abysmal, and the astral, and sometimes the physical, though that's rare. They have to be given power by their Phantasmic creator, and those are the ones used as trackers."

I shuffled my feet. I was getting uncomfortable, and my

toes were cold in my boots. "Trench-Coat could be a tracker. He's one of these rare buggers."

"I think so. And he took Tanaka's soul either because he was instructed to do so by a master, or because he's building power."

"Well, Tanaka did tell him to tell his master he didn't have whatever it was he was looking for. So, that master could be a Phantasm?" And if so, what the hell had Tanaka gotten into?

Rhonda nodded, though absently as she'd pushed her face into the book again.

I rubbed my nose. "So I interrupted something, kinda like a witness at a murder, and TC tried to take me out?" I wasn't sure I really wanted to know.

Rhonda looked up. "Yes. Following the rules of the planes, he had to kill Tanaka in order to take his soul. Take him out of his physical body," Rhonda said. Her voice lowered, as did the room's temperature. I wanted to start a fire in the fireplace in the tea shop. "A Symbiont cannot touch the living without the host's permission. And of course Tanaka wasn't going to give permission, so TC killed him. When the soul tried to flee, he snatched it. But when he touched you . . ."

Rhonda's words lingered in the air—when he touched you . . . I looked wide-eyed at both of them. "I wasn't dead. I was an astral image of myself."

Steve nodded. "You were still attached to your body. So when he touched you, something happened. Even though TC's been given a certain level of independence from a host, he's still at his roots a Symbiont. So by touching you, we think he instigated a *sort* of Symbiosis. A sharing of power."

"Sharing of power?" I pulled off my coat, hung it over my arm, and pulled down the sleeve of my sweater. The mark was still there, a dark pink against my skin. Henna.

Was it possible? I mean, I'd seen Trench-Coat as half-physical. He'd cast a shadow that night, but he'd left no footprint. And now . . .

And now I could become solid. Had I taken that power from him? Was it permanent? And more importantly, what had he taken from me?

I said this last out loud.

Rhonda looked worried. "I think at that moment, your mind was filled with the need to be solid and run like hell. And he had been in the middle of feeding, so to speak. I have a sneaky suspicion you got his ability to become corporeal, and he took your health."

The thirst. My hunger. Maddox's sugar findings. Oh son of a bitch.

Steve moved forward. "Hey, Zoë, sit down before you fall down. Have you eaten this evening?"

I shook my head and moved to one of the tables in the botanica. Rhonda turned on the gas fireplace and made me a cup of tea. Steve actually brought me a plate with a piece of lemon cake on it. He was getting really good at physical manipulation. But then again, we were in his house.

"Where's Tim?"

"With Nona and Jemmy." Rhonda and Steve sat down at the table. "Look, your mom and I sort of came up with this theory yesterday, and after the doctor's appointment, and you seeing the doctor's dead son, she went over to Jemmy's for more research. We're not really sure of all this yet. This is all theory."

Steve snorted. "Like Jemmy Shultz is an expert in the afterlife?"

I gave the ghost a half smile. Steve didn't particularly care for Miss Shultz any more than Rhonda did. Which explained to me why Steve was here and Tim was with Mom.

I'd forgotten about Joseph Maddox. Standing there beside

his oblivious father. I asked Steve about what I'd seen. What did it mean?

Steve clasped his hands together on the table. "It sounds like he's trapped. If his father has set up a shrine in his office like she described, my guess is Joseph is stuck between worlds because his father is holding him there. I'm pretty sure if you hadn't been in your body at that moment, you would have heard him."

"He seemed really anxious to tell me something." I chewed on my upper lip. "Maybe I need to travel over there and see what he wants?"

"Uh"—Rhonda moved away from her book—"maybe—but not right now. I honestly don't know how far you're going to change."

I sipped at the tea. It was sweet and a bit spicy. "So you think I'm being changed, by something from the Abysmal plane."

Both of them nodded.

Shit.

Damn. I'd been called twisted before—but now it seemed more poignant. "So—Mitsuri had sensed this about me and she'd lit the dragon's tongue. She was protecting Hirokumi because of what happened to Tanaka."

"I think maybe Mitsuri is a good guy." Rhonda shifted where she sat.

"Good guys have faces, Rhonda. This chick was one of those blurred sponsor ads on MTV."

"True"—Rhonda crossed her arms over her chest—"but good guys don't always wear white."

I gave her my own version of sardonic as I looked at her all-black getup. "Yah think?" I sighed. I had to concentrate on what I'd seen, on the dead Tanaka, and on Trench-Coat. Mainly because if I thought about what might or might not be happening to me, I might go screaming into the night naked.

Okay, maybe not so dramatic. But I'd at least hide in the closet again.

I took a deep breath. "It's a safe bet that Hirokumi is refusing to help Lieutenant Frasier capture Tanaka's killer because he knows the killer isn't capture-able in any known sense. And maybe he's protecting Daniel in that way." I was losing ground here on the reality check. I snapped my fingers.

Rhonda nodded. "The lieutenant could really get hurt if Trench-Coat noticed him. As a Symbiont, he couldn't touch him. But apparently he *could* kill him."

Ooh. Not good. Didn't want something oogy to happen to Daniel.

Mental note: *protect Daniel.*

Right.

Somehow I just knew I was going to end up rescuing his cute ass before this was all over with.

I set my tea on the table. "Then I'm a little backed up on how Trench-Coat fits in with Reverend Rollins."

"Ah . . ." Rhonda nodded. "Did you talk to Lieutenant Frasier?"

That made me think of Daniel's phone call, and I gave her and Steve the skinny on what had happened that afternoon.

Mom's little helper shook her head. "Thanks for not giving Bruno's name away, Zoë."

I nodded. "No problem. But this puts us back to square one. If the police aren't going to check into Rollins, then Tanaka's death will probably go unsolved. I mean, they're right. There really isn't any good, solid, hard evidence."

It was a few minutes before I realized I was being stared at by Steve and Rhonda.

I straightened up and wondered if I had cake on my face or something. "What?"

"I'm not believing this." Rhonda opened her arms wide,

her palms facing up. "If the police can't investigate Rollins, the case is done? You're giving up? Hello?"

Okay. I was feeling a bit out of step here. Usually I'm really good at keeping up on conversations, jokes, trends, that sort of thing. But from the looks on their faces I'd missed something. "I'm not sure I—"

"Zoë." Steve set his clasped hands on the table. He looked so solid, so alive, he looked touchable. "Why don't *you* investigate the good Reverend? Who's to stop you?"

Indeed.

I *had* missed something. I'd missed my brain somewhere back at the bar. Left it there. Or maybe I'd misplaced it in my car? "But Rhonda keeps saying I need to be cautious because we don't know what's happening to me."

"Yeah, she's right." Rhonda nodded. She grinned. "But you normally don't listen to me or Nona anyway."

It was a brilliant idea that should have come to me. Why not go spy on the old Reverend myself? I could travel, and no one would see me. Of course, I'm not sure that if I found anything out, Daniel could use it.

But—he might know of a way to exploit it.

Mom came in the back door just then, followed by Jemmy Shultz. She stopped when she saw us gathered around the counter. Tim phased in behind her, saw me, and started motioning at me to do . . . something.

I frowned at him. Dance? Jig? Run?

"It's here!" hissed Miss Shultz.

After that things happened fast. I stood up to greet Mom. Tim yelled at Steve to stop her. Mom yelled at me to stand still. Rhonda let out a stream of very colorful metaphors. And Miss Shultz pulled something from her carpetbag as she took three steps toward me.

Within seconds my one summer of martial arts training snapped to the forefront. I grabbed Miss Shultz's arm, ducked low, twisted it around and came up behind her with it, kicked out the back of her knees, and had Jemmy Shultz on her face on the floor.

Not a bad piece of work if I do say so myself.

That's when I saw the large silver cross she had clasped in her hand.

"Let her go, Zoë."

A cross? The woman had come at me with a cross? Crap—I thought she'd had a gun. Mom was going to be pissed.

"Let. Her. Go."

Yep. Mom sounded pissed. I let go of Miss Shultz and stood. And I would have offered to help the cross-wielding nut up—except when I turned I beheld my mother aiming her Colt .45 level with my chest.

"Mom?"

"Move, demon, or I'll blow a hole through you and my shop."

Gulp.

14

"MOM . . ."

"Hush!"

"This is stupid. I'm not a demon."

"If you don't be quiet, there's a roll of duct tape behind the counter."

I waited. Sat still. What else could I do? I had a gun pressed against my neck.

Miss Shultz, her dignity—which I'd obviously robbed her of when I tossed her on her ass—restored, continued her kneeling prayers in front of me. She wore one of her usual blue flower print housedresses, which billowed up around her middle. I had a great view of her braided, polished steel hair.

I sat completely still in one of the wooden chairs. I had a cross around my neck that felt as if it were made of lead. It was getting hard to breathe, with it pressing against my chest.

I'd already been doused with holy water from a small flask Miss Shultz kept in her carpetbag. I felt ridiculous. And the gun was just way over the top.

"Nona—there's no need for the gun. Zoë's fine. She's not possessed *by* a Wraith." Rhonda sounded as exasperated as I felt.

"No, I apparently *am* a Wraith."

Mom whacked me with the gun barrel. "YOW!"

"My daughter is *not* a Wraith," she hissed.

I wanted to rub my head where she'd knocked it, but I was too afraid she'd shoot me. The woman was upset.

Insane.

Mental note: *clear Mom's house of all guns.*

Finally, Miss Shultz struggled to her feet. I saw that the dress barely covered her knees, which themselves were covered by knee-high hose. Yuck. At least she wore real shoes and not slippers. She motioned to my mom with a wave of her hand. I thought I caught a whiff of Ben-Gay. "She's fine. No possession."

Mom moved the gun away. I removed the lead-weight cross, handed it to Mom (okay, more like shoved it at her), then reached up and rubbed the sore spot on my head. "I told you that."

"So she's not a Wraith?" Mom seemed anxious as she moved away and handed the cross back.

"That I don't know." Miss Shultz moved to her bag where it sat on the counter. Steve and Tim sat on stools behind the register. They'd been oddly quiet ever since Mom and Priestess Shultzie came in. She dropped the cross inside the bag, and in my imagination I heard a cat scream from inside.

Well . . . it was a really big bag.

"All I can say is that she doesn't possess a spirit inside that isn't her own."

I glanced over at Rhonda, who arched her eyebrows at me. Could crazy lady be talking about possessing a Symbiont? I really hadn't given her that much credit in the knowledge department.

"What should we do?"

"Well." Miss Shultz shot me a scary look. I knew it. She hated me. Always had. Didn't know why—it was just a feeling. "My suggestion is you keep her locked up till the next full moon. Drugged preferably. And if you see any more of these spirits you saw about her, then call me. I have a priest friend—lives in Biloxi—and he'd be here within a day for a good old-fashioned exorcism."

I blinked at her, then looked at Mom, willing her to turn and look at me. Locked up? Drugged? Till the next full moon? Are these people insane?

I looked at the door and tried to guesstimate how quickly I could clear the distance and get to my car. I was hungry. Well, actually ravenous. And überthirsty.

And very pissed off.

Mom thanked Miss Shultz profusely and showed her out the front door and down the steps. We all sat in stunned silence for a few beats—it felt as if the past half hour had been some weird, trippy mushroom-induced dream.

When Mom came back in, everyone tried to speak at once. Except me. I stood, moved around the counter, retrieved my purse, and headed for the door.

Mom moved in front of me. Everyone else's voice stopped. "Where do you think you're going?"

"You are not locking me up, and if you come near me with a drug, I'll report you to somebody. I have a job to do."

"You should stay here, Zoë."

"Here?" I pointed to the floor with my right index finger. "With you? Do you realize how humiliated I feel? To have had my mother hold me at gunpoint while some crazed woman with a cross and pond water did her stupid mojo over me?"

"Yes, I do. And if you . . ." She paused and looked at everyone in the shop. "All of you, will listen two seconds, I can explain."

I pulled my bag over my shoulder and crossed my arms over my chest. "You got one."

"As nutty as that woman is, she's well-read. And she knows the lore of the dead better than anyone." She looked over at Rhonda. "No offense, love, but she does." Mom looked back up at me. "I had to question her—pick her brain. And in order to do that I had to give her some story. I told her you were possessed and had been throwing things about the shop. And that you spit pea soup."

My jaw dropped. Took a second to pull it off the floor. "You told her I spit pea soup?"

"Look, it worked." Mom moved away from me and started doing that weird once-over she always did at the end of the day, going from shelf to shelf, examining the merchandise and straightening it when she saw something out of position. Mom always swore she knew if something was missing.

The woman had eyes in the back of her head too. Of that I was sure.

"The price for her insight was to let her do a blessing on you. I know you're not possessed. And now she feels satisfied, and the door's open for me to ask her more questions."

"I was the price? You could have shot me with that gun." That's when I noticed she didn't have it anymore. "Where is it?"

"Put away. Safe. And yes, Zoë, you were the price."

"Did you get something, Nona?" Rhonda asked.

"Yeah . . ." She sighed as she moved away from the shelves to the table and sat down slowly in the chair I'd been in. I figured it was probably still warm.

What Mom said next struck a chord somewhere deep inside of me. "We all believe that Trench-Coat's touch has changed you. I'm afraid it's done more than that. A seer called you Wraith. In the usual sense of the word it means ghost, spirit, spectre, and so on. Zoë, the word *Wraith* is related to *writhe*, which means to twist. I think your spirit, your astral self, has been twisted in some way—maybe in a way that could affect your physical life as well as your astral."

Twisted. "This is bad."

No one commented.

My appetite disappeared. I looked at Mom, at Rhonda, at Tim and Steve, and back to Mom. "Can I reverse it?"

"I don't know." Mom shrugged. "I'm not sure I'm right. Or any of this is right. I just think you need to stay indoors and away from this case—look what it's already done."

Stay indoors? Was she kidding? "Mom . . . a man was murdered. I saw who—erm, what—did it. Now it's going to be craziness trying to prove it, but I can't just sit here while it might kill someone else."

"And what if that someone else is you?"

There was a ferocity to Mom's voice I hadn't heard well . . . ever. Oh, she'd yelled at me through the years. Lots. But this tone was close to panic.

"Mom, I need to help. I need to do something. Daniel suspects Reverend Rollins, but the police can't touch him without evidence. Maybe I can find that evidence. I just go and listen in on Rollins for a while. See if I can find out if there's any truth to the connection between him and Hiro-kumi and Tanaka's death."

Mom went to the counter, retrieved a worn, rooster-feathered duster, and started whacking at things. Including Rhonda, who moved as quickly out of Mom's way as possible. "Zoë, this discussion is over. You're not spying on that man."

I narrowed my eyes at her. Something was different. Had been since she walked in the door. Earlier she'd thought Trench-Coat was the aftermath of some ice-cream binge, now she looked honestly worried.

And when Mom worried, so did I.

"What is it you're not telling me, Mom?" I tried softening my voice. Using that old "gee Mom you're right but you have to tell me the secrets" voice.

I wished I'd not done that.

Sometimes I just don't know when to shut up.

She kept whacking those feathers at things. The longer she stayed silent, the faster she whacked. I was glad I wasn't in the way of that insane duster.

Abruptly she turned and pinned me to the back wall with her eyes. Ever seen Debbie Reynolds mad? I have. Not a pretty picture. And me being the daughter—well—I'd done it more than I care to admit.

"Since the morning I saw you in the back of my car, that morning the police called me, I'd accepted the fact that you could die before me. And a parent never wishes or believes they could outlive their children. Especially not a mother and her daughter.

"But you—you weren't dead. And somehow you'd gained this ability to bypass death. Instead of destroying you, that rape changed you. Made you stronger. And I was glad of that. But now something just as threatening has happened again. Trench-Coat changed you, but into what? A Wraith? Something twisted—so bent it may never completely rest in Heaven? I don't know. You don't know. We can only assume this faceless bitch was right." She paused and closed her eyes, feather duster on her hip. One breath. Two breaths. She opened her eyes. "In all these years, did you ever stop to wonder *why* you've never seen another astral Traveler, Zoë?"

Uh, er, nope. Not lately anyway. I shook my head. I'd

not seen this level of passion in Mom since she spoke at the gay pride rally in Piedmont Park back in June.

"Well, Zoë, *I've* wondered. That's all I've wondered about since you finally showed me that mark on your arm. Since I realized you *weren't* invincible, and my baby *could* indeed die. What happens if it takes you? Do you die? Or does it take your body as it becomes one with you?" She was sobbing by the time she said the last. "Or does it leave you as nothing more than a living husk of the one and only bright thing in my life?"

She put the duster down and finally moved past me into the tea shop. A hot pot of water was always ready, and she poured some over a spiced lemon bag in a plain white mug. Her hands were shaking and she spilled hot water on the table.

I went to her then and took the pot away from her. In the movies, this would be the moment I'd take her in my arms and kiss her deeply.

Uh . . . wait. No. Not my mom. That would make a whole different kind of movie, in a genre I just didn't feel like getting into right now. "Mom, what did you find out today? What's got you so scared?"

"I'm not scared."

Oh, of course not. You're shaking and you're telling me, your twenty-eight-year-old daughter, you weren't going to allow her to do this.

Like you can stop me?

"Mom."

She looked up at me then, and I'd not realized how much taller I was than my mother till that moment. Was she shrinking? "You don't know what's out there, Zoë. On that plane—the Abysmal. Things that thrive on fear and the innocent. You don't belong there. And they know it. Now that he knows you're there, it won't be long before the darkest things of all do."

The hairs on my arms stood on end at that moment. I forced a smile, but the truth was she'd just creeped me out. Reeeeally bad.

I saw fear in her eyes. She knew something—something terrible. Something she wasn't going to share with me—not yet. I could see that much in her eyes.

And maybe . . . maybe it was best I didn't know. Because I thought of Daniel at that moment. And of Tanaka. William Tanaka deserved to have his killer brought to justice, and I believed Daniel was the man to do it.

With my help. And if I knew what really waited for me out there, on a plane the average man or woman never saw, I might not be up to being the best I could be. I might just hide in my closet and chew on my boots.

And if my libido was going to lead the way, then so be it. At least I could do something here, something constructive with my gift.

I said these things aloud to Mom, and watched the worry in her eyes just get deeper. Tim and Steve seemed to have vanished, though that didn't mean they weren't somewhere nearby.

"Please, Mom. I'm just going to eavesdrop—just long enough to see if there is a connection between Rollins and Tanaka's death. I won't actually do anything—that's up to Daniel and the police."

She didn't say anything at first, just looked at me. A few seconds of this, and Mom took the cup of tea and moved to the tea-shop counter, where she grabbed up a wooden stir stick from a yellow-and-green tin.

"Zoë, this isn't your job."

"I know that." I smiled and walked in closer. "And you've never acted like this before. Care to let me in on your paranoia?"

Please?

She stirred the tea. "Reverend Rollins is a powerful

man, Zoë. And he's not the pure-souled man so many believe he is."

"Hello—televangelist." How much more crooked a word did she need here?

"That's not the reason. There are several men of God that truly follow the Good Book, and they reach thousands on television. Those that are sick and can't attend church, or those who may not live close enough to a church to hear the words of peace and love."

"Okay—now you're sounding like a Born Again, and that's creeping me out more."

"I don't dismiss Christianity, Zoë. I don't dismiss any religion, not if it helps people come to grips with whatever it is in their life they feel destroys them. It may not be my path, but it sure as hell isn't the absolute wrong path. Have I not taught you this?"

She had. And I'd listened. "I just have this problem with big showy preachers on television, that's all."

"And with Rollins you should. He's evil. He's dangerous. And I don't want you near him."

Isn't it amazing how moms have that uncanny ability to switch gears like that?

I shook my head and blew at a stray strand of hair. Apparently a lot had come loose from my braid. "Wait. First you were spouting oogies about what was on the Abysmal plane like you'd been there and had the shit scared out of you. And now you're tooting the righteous horn by declaring Reverend Rollins a sinner but not because he's a preacher?"

Mom shook her head and then motioned me to sit at one of the chairs behind the counter. I did, and she grabbed up a brush from somewhere (moms have that teleportation ability to produce objects out of thin air, ever noticed?) and started yanking at my hair. I was happy she unbraided it first.

"I know it's hard for you to take me seriously most of

the time. You feel you're always right about things, but this time I need you to shut up and listen to what I'm saying."

I did, and winced as she pulled hair from the crown of my head. I shouldn't let her do this—my scalp was going to be bloodied in a few seconds. But I needed to know what it was she was afraid of. And if fixing my hair was going to loosen her tongue, then bloody away.

"I'm no hairdresser—but these white hairs are odd. They're not wiry like normal gray hairs"—she paused in her brushing and I could feel her pulling at the hairs sprouting from my left temple—"and they don't feel bleached. Did you mean for your hairdresser to do so few?"

"Yes. Move past the hair, Mom."

She continued. "Men like Rollins attract the wrong kind of people, dead or alive. They believe in money and power and will stop at nothing to achieve them." Mom paused. "Or protect them."

I moved away from her, leaning forward, and turned to look up into her face. "You act as if you know him."

Mom's expression was a little frightening. She looked cold and calculating herself, but then again, I'd seen that look before when she was contemplating the last slice of cheesecake. "No. I just know people like him. Something awful could happen to you."

I let her brush my hair a bit more. Then she wove it into a single french braid down my back.

Neither of us spoke.

"Got it," Rhonda said from the shop, and appeared in the archway between the two rooms. I'd been so intent on Mom's speech I hadn't even noticed she'd slipped away. She held a scrap of paper in her hand. "Got that address. And let me tell yah, this guy doesn't take any chances. He's guarded to the teeth."

I went to Rhonda and retrieved the address—1313 Mockingbird Lane.

With my best scolding look I wadded the slip of paper up. "The real address, thank you?"

"Oh, I thought it was sort of appropriate."

I had to agree, even though snooping on the Munsters might have been less exciting, and probably less dangerous.

Rhonda produced another piece of paper. This address put the house on Northside Drive, closer to the governor's mansion, as well as a few infamous Falcons football team members.

I turned to Mom. "You going to give me a lift?"

"No."

Shock. Amazement. Anger.

Oh, I ran several emotions at that moment. "No?"

I think in all of my years on this earth she'd never actually said no to me. Not even as a teenager had she said no. It'd always been "I'd prefer you didn't," or "You might want to rethink that," or even "Are you really sure that's what you want?"

All of those responses had elicited in me the proper decisions—mostly because all of them dredged up doubt and guilt in some fashion.

But not the word *no*.

Mom stood very still behind the tea-shop counter, the stool I'd sat on still in front of her, her hands clasped under her breast.

I watched her for a few seconds to see if there was some glimmer of humor in her expression. Nothing.

After getting my bag, I gave Rhonda a glance and walked to the front door. Steve abruptly appeared beside it.

"Don't do this, Zoë. Your mother has a bad feeling about this. She's certain something bad will happen to you."

I nodded. "She also had a feeling about Anna Nicole being a man, Steve."

Didn't even glance back at Mom, though I could feel her watching me.

The sun had set when I stepped outside. The wind whipped around my ears, cold and relentless.

Mom was scared.

And when Mom was scared, I was terrified.

But I wanted to help Daniel, and I was letting my libido lead the way. And I knew if I stayed here, or even in my condo, I'd only spiral myself into a lumpy depression over what might or might not be happening to me. I had to get out and at least do something.

You know . . . daughters really should listen to their mothers.

15

THE whole place just screamed, "I'm up to something."

Kinda up there with "Neener nee!"

Rollins's spread was a palace better suited to Miami. Or California. It sprawled in an L-shape in the center of three acres in a stucco-and-palm-tree sort of style. A twelve-foot matching wall fence surrounded the entire property except for the black iron gate at the entrance.

Forty minutes after I left Mom's I stood outside of the property, facing that gate. Two stone gargoyles watched me. I watched them. And the hairs on my body, resting safely back at my condo, stood on end. I'd swear those things moved.

Gargoyles. Big bats with humongous teeth.

Rhonda came through on the transportation. She drove me out here in her Beetle and was now exiting the road at the farthest end. Mom's attitude had creeped her out too.

Most of the time we sort of tolerated my mom's eccentricities for their cuteness. But she'd rarely gotten so scary.

The last time was the night I went out with friends, that night in college.

The night my life changed.

Okay, Zoë, keep thinking like that, and you'll talk yourself out of this.

Another voice piped up from somewhere behind my ears, *Not a bad idea. You could always just go home and eat ice cream.*

Growl.

"Now don't wear yourself out too quickly," Rhonda had said on the trip here. "Don't go all solid and such. One, they'll see you, and two, you'll deplete your energy reserves. I mean, what happens if you run out of power while being Wraithy? I'm hoping the outcome's not something like being a wandering soul. You know, like your body dying and not letting you back in."

"Geez, Ro," I'd said. "Thanks for the pep talk."

"Sorry. I think I'm a little more worried about this than I wanted to let on. We don't really know where the Symbiont—"

"Trench-Coat."

"—Trench-Coat comes from; Ethereal or Abysmal, or who summoned it. Who was the other person my friend saw with him? And it's been right around twenty-four hours since your first corporeal trip." The red LCD from her Beetle's dash gave her a rather undead appearance, which I think she would have liked. "What about fuel? When was the last time you ate?"

"Uhm . . ."

"Oh hell, Zoë. Was it this morning?"

"I was supposed to have pasta and shrimp, remember? But you took me to the doctor instead."

"We were going to go afterward, but you went all Wraithlike and saw a ghost. Then it was you that ran off after your libido for the detective . . ."

Yeah, yeah, yeah. Blame the Wraith.

We'd both given each other a moment of silence. Rhonda spoke first. "If you run into *him* . . ."

"I know. Shoot back home. But you'd better have a ton of aspirin ready. The headaches after I do that are getting a bit more intense."

"Not to mention that really freaky thirst thing you got going on. How many containers of Sunny Delight did you guzzle before we left your place?"

"How many did we pick up at Kroger?" I'd actually put away only one.

I'd often wondered what would happen if I had to pee really bad while out of body. In a usual sleep, hydraulic pressure forced me up and into the bathroom. But when it came to being astral, my body was pretty much tied to it. It wasn't going anywhere unless I returned to it.

And vice versa.

All of these variables didn't sway my good old Irish stubbornness. Or my Latino romanticism of me finding the answers and having Daniel Frasier fall hopelessly in love with me.

Barf.

Anyway, back to my present predicament. I sieved through the gate, shivering just a bit at the iron. Glad I wasn't a fairy—that was real iron back there. The taste of it lingered oddly in my mouth.

Hadn't had *that* happen before.

The lawn stretched out before me like smooth, dew-laced hills. The inside of the wall was well groomed with flowering plants, many of which slept for the winter. Fruit trees stood in intervals, and I could see their sparkling auras even without the aid of the moon overhead.

The full moon would be visible once the clouds parted.

The house sat several hundred yards ahead of me. Lights

were on in the main building, the front entrance illuminated around a parked white limo. Nice ride.

I was looking for something in particular. A menace I suspected lived on these grounds. Hell, anyone with this much property always had two or three of them.

Dogs.

And if I could smell in this form, I'd be able to know easier.

Why dogs? One thing about the astrally traveled—animals seemed to *know*. Or they could see. Either way, if a dog were around, it'd sense me and start barking.

Not that it could really hurt me or anything. But it could make the inhabitants inside nervous. And I needed them relaxed so they'd feel at ease and say something naughty.

Not worry about something in the yard all night.

I waited a good five minutes or so, moving slowly over the grass and around the occasional pine tree. When no dogs appeared to be present, I started jogging to the house.

Along the way, I started wishing again there was some way to like pop in and out of places.

Mental note: *need astral Vespa.*

I reached the house with no barking dogs and snuck around to the front door. I don't know why I was all hunched over and playing in the shadows—who was going to see me?

God, I hate it when I'm wrong.

So I stood and faced the house, standing beneath what I called the front drive. It looked like the front of a hotel, where guests pulled their cars to step in and make reservations. Above me was a huge-ass chandelier with a crystal cross hanging in its center.

And standing in front of the door were three men in suits, each of them wearing one of those curly-fry wires in his ear.

Impressive. Anyone'd think the president of the United States was inside.

Reverend Rollins had pots with pansies set out to either side. That seemed appropriate. I tested my invisibility (since yesterday, with Daniel actually seeing me, I'd been a bit concerned about that) by standing in front of them and lifting up my shirt.

No response.

Either I was invisible, or they were gay.

Or dead. I mean, I'm not like overly well endowed, but I know my boobs have a nice shape. I usually get a response to them.

I also tested the house for oogy.

It was full of it.

Not the same kind of oogy I'd detected the other night when Tanaka was killed. This was something smoother, darker. The entire place seemed shrouded in the wispy shadows that flitted and ducked here and there. I didn't like them, and I feared they were a new part of my astral sight. Had they always been there before, and I'd never seen them?

Nasty.

Breathe, Zoë. Relax.

Think of the cute detective who could use your help. Think of his cute nose and sexy sideburns. Think of that knee-watering kiss.

I never said my priorities were in the right place.

I moved forward between two of the pro-wrestler types, through the oak doors (or it tasted of oak—kinda woody) and into a spacious, Beverly Hillbilly kinda foyer, complete with black-and-white-checkerboard tiling.

Double doors to my right, double doors to my left, and *Beauty and the Beast* staircase before me. The kind that ascended about ten steps with a landing, and then split in two different directions. What was it Beast had said—don't go into the West Wing?

Can't say I'd ever seen the television show *West Wing* either. Glancing about, I caught sight of another burly security person moving from beneath the stairs. He was mumbling into a walkie-talkie, giving a report of all clear.

Cool.

I avoided the stairs for the moment. There appeared to be several rooms on the lower floor. I'm sure a smarter snoop would have had a floor plan or something like that. I just sort of worked on gut instinct.

Standing before the staircase, I sensed something to my right. There was something here, something that really wasn't part of the physical world.

If it was Trench-Coat, then I had my proof that Rollins was making deals with the spirit world. And I knew I could use my silver cord to get home protected, like before. But if it wasn't Trench-Coat—and it was something I'd never encountered . . .

Well, let's not think about that right now.

I looked from the left to the right. There didn't seem to be any movement to my left, and the lights were either dimmed or off, but I did see a security guy move about to the right.

And the lights were on, though I couldn't see much from my vantage point.

The right it is. I figured the Reverend would have security. I moved away from the stairs and down a hallway off the main foyer. The sense of oogy increased, as did the number of wispy shadows. I couldn't see any eyes watching me, but I felt them.

The lighting was interesting—small, desktoplike lamps stuck out from the wall at regular intervals, illuminating pictures on display. Oh, so it was like a hall of fame kinda thing.

A set of double doors waited at the end of the hall, and standing outside were two more of the pro-wrestler types.

I checked my watch. An hour left. It'd taken longer to get here than I thought. Not much time. As long as I didn't go corporeal, I should be fine. I'd already prearranged my return to body along my silver cord.

The pictures were all framed the same, about the same size, width, and height. They were all of Rollins—from his college days in football to pictures of him with former president Jimmy Carter (we *are* in Georgia). There were also pics of him with famous football stars (look it's Deion Saunders!) and actors (is that Brad Pitt? Mmmmmmmm . . .).

As I neared the doors I noticed Rollins's aging process as well. And as he got older, the pictures changed from stars to men of religion. There was old Oral Roberts (is there not something freaky about a guy claiming to give the word of God through a porn name like Oral?) and Jim Bakker (you gotta be kidding me).

I finally stood at the door, having had my fill of Rollins's never-changing cheese smile. I needed a bath. *Ick.* Two of the suited men stood to either side of the double doors. With a glance at these guys, I sieved between them.

Only this time there was something else—something felt rough. Not rough as in sandpaper texture, but rough as in tougher to move through. It wasn't like that weird sci-fi force-field ward thing I'd slammed into in Hirokumi's office. This was more like . . . static?

When I got to the other side I turned and looked back at the door. I couldn't *see* anything different about it—not on the astral plane at least.

I turned back to the sound of an angry voice.

"What the fuck do I pay you people for, anyway? To stand around here and do nothing?"

My, my, my, Mr. Preacher man. What a potty mouth you have.

The room I stood in was as spacious as the foyer downstairs. Potted palm trees decorated most of the corners in front of floor-to-ceiling windows. Little knots of chairs and coffee tables filled two spaces where a few of the goons sat while having their asses chewed.

In the center of the room was the desk to end all desks. Mongo desk. Heck, Beast from *X-Men* would be swallowed by this desk. It was made of a dark wood. Solid frame. In the front, carved directly into the wood, was the Reverend's trademark—a cross combo sword slicing into a globe of the world.

Nice. Violent. But nice. Sort of had that Crusades feel to it.

Two more comfy chairs sat facing that desk, but I gathered from their slightly tense shoulders that the guys sitting in those chairs weren't comfy. Ah, but it's never comfy when you get chewed a new asshole.

I couldn't actually see Rollins from where I stood. There were too many men in black suits and black leather standing around him. When I did see him, he was the glowing figure in white.

Glowing because of the bright white suit, white shirt, white tie, and white Dr. Strange streaks along his temples. And there was a light trained on him from above. Kinda giving him that ethereal look.

And there were shadows surrounding him, like gauzy wisps of torn clothing that hung from his body, superimposed on his actual clothing.

Ooooooooogy.

Behind the blaring Reverend sat another set of windows. Only these were stained glass and represented the crucifixion in bloody, gory detail.

Sick. This guy was just sick. I felt vindicated that I'd chosen the right bad guy.

One of the standing guys, dressed in a short-waisted leather jacket, held up his hands. He talked like he would have the name Vinnie. "Hey, boss—we was watching him like we always do. But he was with this hot chick this morning, and then we were watching her and they started fighting, and he just disappeared . . ."

I looked to the Reverend. The way Rollins stared at this guy—he should have burst into flames on the spot. Whoosh. Reverend Firestarter.

"You were supposed to get rid of him. Is that so hard? The man's known to be accident-prone. Just make it look like an accident. We don't need any cop snooping around me, or my network. Especially not now. And if you can't make him disappear—I'm going to take the spin out on all of you!"

Get rid of him. A cop. Daniel? He was the only one I knew that'd been snooping around the good Reverend. Had he been with a hot chick this morning? They had a fight? Crap . . . I'd assumed Daniel didn't have a girlfriend—that he'd been showing interest in me.

But I'd never actually asked him.

And they argued. Hrm.

All the standing guys nodded, and somehow knew they'd been dismissed. I stepped out of their way as they nearly stampeded out of the room.

The two guys in the chairs remained. They were the ones in suits.

Rollins gracefully set his elbows on his desk, which I could see more of now. It was pretty much empty, save for a desk calendar and some sort of devotional daily flip thing to the Reverend's right.

He looked from one to the other. "Well?"

I moved around the room to stand beside the desk. That way I could see Rollins and the faces of the guys in the chairs. One was slimmer than the other (by about a hundred pounds), with a black, greased-back ponytail and a soul patch. His pockmarked skin reminded me of Edward James Olmos.

But not as good-looking.

The other guy was stout. Hell—this guy was fat. Two chins, bald head, and a handlebar mustache.

That was how they looked physically.

Astrally, both men had voids on them. They honestly looked like refugees from *101 Dalmations*.

By that I mean darker spots. Kinda like looking at them through a spotted veil. Their auras moved and encircled them so that the spots shifted and changed. Right now I was noticing a definite shift from fight to flight with both of them.

Looked to me as if they should stand and say "Eet mor chikin."

When it came to looking at the Reverend, besides the clinging, wispy Spanish moss, I saw purple. Which surprised me. All of those New Age chakra books I'd thumbed through at Mom's insistence had said that purple was more of the head chakra, and that was supposed to mean . . .

. . . oh bugger. I forgot.

I really should pay more attention to this stuff. But honestly, all I'd ever done was snoop to get information, and that'd always been on corporate or business owners. Rarely had I ever spied on well-known televangelists with houses bigger than the governor's mansion and half of the WWE in patrolling suits.

Either way, it wasn't what I'd expected to see.

The two cow-men glanced at each other. Ponytail answered first. "Well, we ain't had no luck in finding him. He's usually surrounded by people."

The Reverend pursed his thin lips. He looked at Fatso. "And I supposed Tiny here agrees with you?"

I giggled. Tiny. The fat one was called Tiny.

The Reverend immediately looked in my direction.

Damnit! I have got to learn to keep my mouth shut! No giggling aloud.

When Rollins continued staring in my direction, the

two thugs started shifting in their seats. "Boss?" the pony-tail one said. I noticed he was looking nervously about the room himself. "Is *he* here?"

"No," Rollins said distractedly. He continued looking in my direction. When he didn't see anything (I'd gone rigid as a board—just in case this guy was as weird as my mom) he looked back at his minions. "He's not here. Even you'd know if he was here."

Both minions looked relieved.

"But the question is still on the table, gentlemen." Rollins pushed his chair back and stood. Man this guy's suit just glowed all warm and angelic-y.

This image just didn't jibe with the pictures on those videos we'd seen in the e-mail. And of course I almost commented on this.

I slapped my hand over my mouth. *Maybe I should just gag myself before I step out of my body. Sheesh.*

"I'm telling yah, boss, Tanaka's death hasn't fazed Koba." Ponytail definitely seemed to be the one with the balls.

"You saw him then?"

Ponytail nodded. "He believes you sent the Archer, but that wasn't going to frighten him. He's not budging."

Rollins crossed his arms over his chest. The suit jacket sleeves pulled away from the shirt's cuffs, revealing diamond-studded crosses for cuff links.

Oh how tacky can we be?

"Then perhaps I should send the Archer back to make a stronger statement. That is, if I can trust it not to kill again. It was supposed to threaten Tanaka—not kill him. If any-one should have died, I'd have preferred Hirokumi."

Pay dirt! Yay! Wahoo! The Reverend really was in-volved! Daniel's cop instincts were right.

Whoa. Wait a minute.

I blinked. The Archer?

Was that Trench-Coat? And if so, what did it mean, the Archer?

Ponytail spoke up. "Boss, yah can't exactly control it. It does what it wants."

"*I* control him, Beckett. And I did not want a prominent businessman shot in cold blood." Rollins leaned forward and pressed his hands palms down on his desk. "I wanted his soul destroyed, leaving his death a mystery. There would have been no police involved. And now I've got some cop calling me, wanting an interview. He's already been in to see Hirokumi." Rollins stood and smiled. "Luckily, the man told him nothing."

"How do you know that?" Tiny squeaked.

I blinked. Wait—he controls the Archer—urm, TC? I took a longer, harder look at the Reverend. Was this a Phantasm? Didn't Rhonda say they don't leave their places of power?

Why *the Archer*?

"I have faith in the old man to keep his quiet. But as an added insurance, I wanted the cop to disappear. But I also have sources."

Sources. The only other person in that room had been invisible me. Sent there to spy on Hirokumi and Frasier. No—it couldn't be. Was the Reverend actually marharba@ marharba.com?

I was going to be sick. Thinking about the e-mail addy again, I thought of the moniker. Maharba. Where would that word come from? In code, first breakdown was to try the word backwards. Abraham.

First of God.

Oh Christ on a cross. I wanted to find something really hard and bang my head against it. I'd just turned in my lame-ass report to him this morning. I'd avoided all the spook stuff.

"Can I trust either of you to at least lean on the cop to back off?"

That perked me up. I didn't want anyone to lean on Detective Hottie.

Except me.

Beckett smiled. "I don't think you'll need to worry about him. Apparently he's not exactly a cop in good standing. Even if he found anything out—I doubt his boss would listen to him."

"I can't depend on that. And I can't wait on Hirokumi's damned sense of honor. I need that document back. And since Tanaka's death seems to have had little effect—we might have to put on a different kind of pressure." He rubbed at his chin. "We could arrange an accident with the cop and frame Hirokumi."

Daniel! That's twice I'd heard them threaten my cutie-cop. Nothing had been said in a direct confession, but I'd gotten the proof I'd needed, and I wanted to warn Daniel.

"A document" didn't sound like porn tapes. But it did sound more like "intellectual property." Either way, Hirokumi did have something that Rollins would kill for. *Had* killed for.

But what was the point of this? Surely Koba Hirokumi wasn't in the game of extortion. He was rich. He was powerful. What would he need with threatening some two-bit televangelist?

This wasn't making any sense.

And if I'd been on the ball, I might have put something together just then.

But nooooooo.

I had the information I needed—though of course inadmissible in court. In fact, I wasn't even sure I knew if Daniel would believe me.

I had to reevaluate. I now knew that a powerful businessman had acquired some valuable document belonging to a famous televangelist, who had hired a supernatural creature to threaten him.

Sounded like bad television to me.

I checked my watch. A little over half an hour. I'd used up more than I'd thought in getting to Rollins's house. Hunger plucked at me, like the echo of my physical stomach growling. There was half a pint of Java Chocolate Chip in the freezer and a pair of warm, fuzzy SpongeBob slippers with my name on them.

That's when I realized my feet were cold.

I looked down at myself. I wasn't supposed to feel like that—unless I'd somehow made myself visible?

No. No one saw me. So why the cold feet?

The doors to the office burst open at that moment. Both thugs were on their feet, guns drawn (where did those come from—and so fast!) and aimed, their bodies shielding the Reverend.

In fact, three more of the suited wrestlers stepped in after the intruder, their own guns drawn.

It was then I saw her.

Or rather didn't see her.

Her face, that is.

"Theodore," came the smooth voice from the void. "There is a problem. I'm detecting a presence . . ."

Mitsuri.

Hirokumi's secretary/seer in the Reverend's house.

I almost swore—but didn't. Good for me!

Instead my watch alarm went off. Ack! Rhonda and her thirty-minute warning!

She turned and looked at me.

Looked *at me. This wasn't my fault! I hadn't said a word!*

And this time I saw her face and nearly lost my appetite.

It was as if during her time in Hirokumi's office she'd worn a mask. Ew! And right now I wanted her to put that mask back on!

There was a face now—but not any normal face. This thing had pale, bone-white skin, smooth as baby powder. There were no eyebrows below a high forehead. The nose was little more than a rise, a small bump with two holes. Its mouth was a thin line, and its eyes . . .

Its eyes were dark, hollow pits like the empty sockets of a skull.

What the fuck was Mitsuri? Okay, so the missing face should have been clue once she wasn't human!

"The Wraith!" She pointed to me. "The Wraith is here!"

Everyone turned and pointed their guns and gazes at me. Well—in my general direction. Evidently Mitsuri-the-damned-ugly was the only one that could see me. And why now? Why not yesterday? What was the difference?

"The same one you detected in Hirokumi's office?" Rollins said, even as he started climbing up on his desk (Where the hell is he going? I'm not a mouse!).

Now I knew who the informant was. And it wasn't me! Maharba wasn't Rollins.

I figured I'd do my happy dance later. Right now I just wanted to cuss.

A lot.

"Yes, it's the same one." Mitsuri took a couple of steps toward me. I took a couple of steps back. "But who summoned such a creature?" She cocked her head to the right. "And for whom does your presence spell doom, Wraith?"

"Fuck that," Rollins said. I arched an eyebrow at him. "I don't care. Kill it."

"Shame on you! Do you kiss your mother with that mouth?"

The Reverend's eyes widened.

I have GOT to stop doing that. I have a very distinctive voice.

Rollins started jumping up and down. "I heard it! Stop it. It's been listening to us."

My cue to motor.

Mitsuri lunged at me then. Not the familiar run, jump, and pounce lunge. But more like this weird spring into the air, float there, and *then* pounce on me kind of thing. In *Swan Lake*—primo move.

After me, scary as shit.

I hissed and sidestepped her, running around behind the Reverend's desk. I needed to get out of her line of sight long enough to give my silver cord a bit of concentration. Times like this I reeeeally wish'd I could just teleport.

Oh, I think I've said that already.

Don't let my witty banter fool you—I was scared shit-less. Oh, maybe not as afraid as I was with Trench-Coat. There was something about him that frightened me down to my . . . well my soul I guess.

This creature was somehow a lesser thing in compari-son. Like the two thugs Beckett and Tiny, who were now swinging their guns around the room and shouting. The Reverend jumped from his desk and ducked behind it a few times when his minions' aim threatened him.

As I came around the back side of the room, Mitsuri closed in from my left, its arms out wide as if to give me a really, nice cozy hug.

No way José. I ducked. It flew by overhead, missing me by an inch. As odd as it sounds, I could *feel* it. And it was cold. Freezing, frostbite, immobilizing cold. Ice bitch.

With a grunt, I did a tumble a four-year-old would be proud of and came up running again. Thank God for all those katas that evil sensei made me do! (The only reason I took karate was because it was supposed to make my butt look like J-Lo's.) A jumble of palm trees in huge terra-cotta pots gave me a bit of protection as I paused and looked around for the flying ugly.

Gunfire like rapid popping flared in the room. It whizzed by me and pinged against the windows, shattering one of them into a bazillion pieces. Other bullets slammed into the window frames and sent bits of wood and plaster dust everywhere.

This put me a bit on the sketchy side of fear. First thought was that a bullet really couldn't do much damage to me—I'm astral—urh . . . as long as I don't do that insto-flesho thing I did before with Daniel. Or could it? If I went corporeal, then got shot with a bullet, would it have any effect on my physical body? I really didn't think now was the time for experimentation.

But how did they know where to shoot?

The second thought was immediately answered when I came up from my instinctual duck and saw the minions actually firing all over the place. One or two had gotten a lucky shot in my direction.

"Stop firing, you idiots!"

Well at least Rollins was sane. Firing at invisible Wraiths? That was just silly.

Or he wasn't happy about having his palace shot all to hell.

My vote's on the décor.

Flying oogy was somewhere around the room's ceiling. I grew still and concentrated on my body.

There was my cord, silver and pretty darned strong as compared to the other night when Trench-Coat was chasing me.

I felt the pull of my body and surrendered to it. In a few seconds I'd be home, slamming most painfully back inside.

I should have opened my eyes then.

I'm such a fool.

Just because one spooky oogy didn't follow me back didn't mean it couldn't be done. It never occurred to me that Trench-Coat might have *chosen* not to hitch a ride back (still not sure at the time if something like that was possible) but actually could.

The pain was all too familiar but a comfort as I traveled the cord and slammed back into my body from sheer momentum. My chest arched up, pretty much looking like I'd been zapped with those paddles in the hospital. I gasped, opened my eyes.

And saw Mitsuri hovering above me. She grinned death at me with her lipless smile and empty eyes. My office was cold.

Freezer cold. I could see my breath.

Movement in my physical body was always a bit sluggish after a jump back like that. Have I mentioned this?

And it was even more exaggerated now than ever.

I screamed my freak'n head off as I tried to scramble off the bed. But Mitsuri was solid again now, and as I fell to the floor, she jerked up a handful of my hair and wrenched me nearly off my feet.

I was tossed into the opposite wall much the way someone tosses dirty laundry.

My scalp ached, as did those angles of my body that'd hit the wall and put dents into the drywall as I slammed on the floor. My radio came to life then with Enomine's "Das Omen."

She was in front of me, and I was shoving myself as far into the wall as possible. I was still seeing stars twirling about my head, but nothing will ever erase her ugly face.

Empty eyes peered at me and she cocked her head to her shoulder as if examining a bug. Her white-and-black-streaked hair, which now looked more like an affectation than reality, floated out above her head as if she were underwater.

Her powder white, thin, fuck'n ugly fingers reached out toward me.

"You bear the taint of the Archer. He has claimed you, yes."

I gave her my best *oh get a grip* look. "What the fuck are *you*? And how'd you get in my house?" I was pressing myself farther back into the wall as she was coming closer. Of course I was going to lose if I didn't do something because the wall wasn't going to give.

And if it did, I was going to be in my bedroom.

So I did what any red-blooded, defense-trained straight white Latino female did when backed into a wall.

I punched her. I also gave her a string of really colorful metaphors when I did it.

I didn't really expect to hit anything except cold air. Imagine my surprise when my fist connected with a sheet of ice.

I howled.

She howled.

But she moved back. I think it was the momentum from my own fear, squished into the size of my fist. I moved as quickly as I could and stood on wobbly legs.

I made it to the door and into the hallway toward the living room.

And then I felt her behind me. She tackled me from behind and sent me sprawling on my hardwood floors. My cat-suit made it feel and look as if I were on a Slip 'n Slide as I put my arms out in front of me to stop myself.

I turned onto my back and saw her angling about in the air for another pass. What the hell was I supposed to do to get this bitch out of my house? Why weren't the wards working?

And where the hell was Rhonda? She was supposed to be here when I got back!

Not that I was sure she could do anything against this thing.

I was sure there was some weirdo incantation or something, but I sure as hell didn't know it.

I lifted myself up again and turned as she made another pass. With a scream I reached up and grabbed her hair and yanked back. *There! How you like that, you screaming oogy bitch!*

You know, I had to wonder at that point if someone outside of these walls could hear both of us, or just me?

I pulled her to my right as I spun to the left. She went into, and then through, my couch, and I took off toward the front door. Mitsuri came blasting out of my couch and tore through the air to block my path.

Fine.

I turned and ran to the kitchen.

It was then I noticed an odd rumble from somewhere. I thought at first it was thunder, especially when old Mitsuri came at me again from behind and whacked me in the back with something unmistakably solid.

The blow knocked the wind out of me, as well as took my balance, and I pitched forward into the kitchen on the tiles. I twisted as I slid and this time slammed my head into the nearest cabinet.

Oh, there were stars again, as before. And this time I'd hit it pretty damned hard. Things around me started to fade to black.

The rumbling came again and it sounded a lot like—

She was on me then, pulling me by my shoulders and hoisting me onto my back. I tried to hit at her again but my hand went through her. She'd somehow learned to duck back into the incorporeal at will.

There was ghastly pressure on my chest. She pressed bony knees into my ribs, making it harder to breathe. I glanced down and saw her actually melting *inside* of me!

"In flesh, you will be mine . . ."

Christ!

I screamed out again and fought—but there was nothing solid to grab hold of. Her fingers were on my neck, and I couldn't breathe. My lungs, my chest, all were turning to ice, and I fought the urge to travel out of my body.

I wanted more than anything to escape my body. But I couldn't concentrate. I was transported back to that night, into the cold, at the park, and the rapist was over me once again.

And as I felt the upper half of my body wrench free of my physical, Mitsuri's shape changed again. There was nothing human about this creature! Those dark holes glowed with pinpoints of fire that flickered as smoke the color of midnight moved about her head in some garish semblance of human hair.

"Yes . . . come out of that flesh and play," she said in a slithering, oily voice. It smelled like rotting meat left in the Southern August sun. Odd that I could smell and not breathe, eh?

I started to lose consciousness with the loss of oxygen and abruptly smelled sulfur.

Wow—I'm being choked to death and it smells like rotten eggs.

I managed to get my hands around her wrists, which had to be solid in order to strangle me. But it was no use. I was in an awkward position, on the floor, shoved into the corner between my stove and my sink. I yanked and I pulled and I kicked, until I couldn't anymore.

I felt myself slipping away, though into unconsciousness or death, I didn't know. I heard her voice inside my head. "Diiiiiieeeeeee . . . ."

That message was swiftly accompanied by a really loud roar.

Now—either I'd gotten a very large zoo-kitty at some point in my house—or that familiar noise was none other than . . .

. . . Mitsuri screamed.

The pressure around my neck vanished. I was no longer being choked.

I opened my eyes to see Red Eyes Big Fucking Dragon in my kitchen. It wasn't quite the same wispy, smoky dragon that had tried to eat me the day before, but it was similar—in that it had really big teeth. And it had Mitsuri in its mouth. The bitch was kicking like crazy, her entire top half inside the thing's jaws.

As I gasped for air, Mitsuri became a late-night snack. The screams were terrible. That thing was actually *chewing* her. I tried to move, to get out of its way. Would it eat me too? I was flesh, wasn't I? I tried to turn to my side and succeeded, sort of. I think I was still flesh.

My head hurt. And I was tired. Fatigue overran my fight-or-flight instinct at that moment, and I lay back on my kitchen floor. Oh, this was under protest, let me tell you. My subconscious was not happy and was trying to push me up and out the freak'n front door.

I mean, come on, there was an eight-foot smoky dragon in my kitchen, eating a really ugly Lucy Liu. Did my physical self not see all the wrongs of this scene?

"Ho-lee-shit!"

Ah. I knew that voice.

Rhonda.

"Kid—I told you to wait at the door. Fuck—looks like she was attacked. Now get back and let me check the house."

Okay—that voice I didn't quite recognize. Male. Sounded nice.

Man in the house! Alert the media.

And I was in no condition to thank the libido gods.

With effort, I opened my eyes, lifted up and onto my elbows.

Rhonda was bent over me, the dragon behind her enjoying his snacky-poo. He could've been eating Cap'n Crunch for all I could see. *Crunch, crunch.*

Except for the shoe stuck between his teeth. Ew.

Rhonda's eyes were wide. "Zoë, you realize you're half-in, half-out of your body?" She whispered this.

I looked down. Ack! She was right. My body lay on its back, but my Wraith self was now halfway out, leaning up from the waist. Oh how weird was that?

I caught sight of a familiar, beautiful sideburned profile as it moved through the chomping dragon, gun extended.

Daniel.

Rhonda smiled. "Told you that artifact would come in handy."

"Bitch."

"Snot-nose punk."

Dizziness replaced the fatigue. I felt disoriented and a bit out of control, as if I were being pulled back inside.

"Zoë . . . what's happening? You're fading," Rhonda said as she took my physical hand.

I couldn't answer her then. Both worlds, my physical and my astral, grew dark. I was falling backward through a very dark tunnel, and there was nothing for me to grab hold of.

16

"THERE . . . I think I saw her eyes flutter."

"No, no—that's REM sleep. She's dreaming."

"No, she didn't go to sleep—she passed out. She's unconscious."

"So—what's the difference? Asleep or unconscious?"

You know, even I didn't know the answer to that. If you go to sleep, you're in a state of slumber, relaxation. So, if you passed out or were choked into unconsciousness—are you not sleeping?

In a sense?

What I did realize at that moment, through the rather silly interchange going on somewhere outside the world of my eyelids, was that my throat *hurt*. Someone had shoved some of those sticky, sweet-gum tree burrs down my throat as I slept—er, lay unconscious. No fair.

I tried to swallow.

Oh. Bad idea.

". . . shit . . ." Oh, now saying that hurt even worse.

"Oh, now see? She's awake. I don't think unconscious people swear."

No. But they bite if you don't stop talking so freak'n loud. Chomp.

I also heard something else—a really annoying beeping noise. Had one of these faceless boobs turned on my alarm? Couldn't they turn it off?

". . . water . . ." Oh! A word! And not a swear one.

Mom would be proud.

"Water. Rhonda, get me that water—and a straw."

Now let's work on prying the eyes open. Something was pressed against my lips. I opened my mouth and recognized the straw. I swallowed. The water was cool and felt really good.

And I was incredibly thirsty. Like this was news over the past two days?

I reached up and took hold of the glass and did not stop drinking.

"Okay, out of her way. She's up."

And I was. I realized I'd sort of sat up to drink when I did open my eyes. The fuzzy images of Mom and Rhonda came into focus. They were standing to my right, just past this really weird-looking silver bar.

"Zoë honey," Mom said, and she neared. "Let me prop the bed up. That'll make it easier." She tried to take my glass away.

Uh-uh. Not having none of that. I grunted at her.

She did prop the bed up—she turned on the motor and my body bent at my waist.

That was when I realized I wasn't in Kansas anymore, and certainly not in my bed. I was in a hospital bed, in a beige room, and there was a heart monitor just to the right of my head. Ah, the beeping thing.

There was also a tube in my right arm. IV?

WTF?

I ran out of water with a rude sucking noise at the end of my straw. Mom took the glass and I let her.

Sheet. Hospital gown. No underwear. "Wha . . ." —owch—"Where . . . are my clothes?" Wow, my voice had been scratchy before, now I really could give Stevie Nicks a run for her money.

"Maybe you shouldn't talk," Rhonda said. I wasn't really happy with the expression on her face either. It looked like she'd seen a plate of brains.

Uncooked.

I put a hand to my throat. I was going to ask what happened—you know—jog the old noodle.

That's when that damned memory of mine came back like a two-by-four to my head. I blinked as I flashed on Mitsuri's eyeless face and her hands around my throat. Red pinpoints of flickering death.

"Zoë?" Mom was there again. She'd pushed Rhonda aside and had a hand on mine. I squeezed tightly as all the fear I hadn't had time to express during the attack came careening back.

In spades.

I started shaking. Really bad. And Mom did the best thing she could have done. She hugged me. She put that damned bed guard down and got in bed with me and held me.

Okay. So maybe I'm too big for this kind of shit.

But have you ever been chased by a flying ugly bitch before? Nay, nay I say.

Mental note: *get hugs from Mom more often.*

"Well, well—I see our patient is awake now."

I turned just as Mom did to see Dr. Maddox glide through the door. He wore one of those unflattering long white coats over a white shirt and bad tie.

Mom started to get out of the bed, but he put up a hand. "No—it's okay, Nona. Zoë's had a bad scare."

"How long"—*ow, ow, ow*—"before my throat doesn't . . . *hurt?*"

"Time will tell. You've got some nasty bruising."

"Hell," Rhonda piped up. "She's got a red-and-purple choke collar going there." She smiled. "It's kinda cool. Sort of goes with the white hairs up there."

Sheesh. I still had the white hair?

Dr. Maddox nodded. "The bruising will go away in a few days. Take it easy on speaking. Okay, Zoë? Though I know that's going to be difficult for you."

Oh screw you. I do not talk that much.

Well. Maybe I do. "Anything else?"

"You've got a slight concussion, nothing I'm worried about. You've been unconscious for nearly six hours and—"

Six hours?

"—your blood work isn't very promising."

I looked over at Mom. I noticed her perfume then. Ode to Elizabeth Taylor. I couldn't remember the name of it, only that it usually gave me a headache. "Six hours?"

She nodded. "We'll talk."

Code for "I'm going to ream you a new asshole after we fill you in."

Maddox picked up a clipboard from the end of my bed and thumbed through it. "Remember what we talked about during your appointment yesterday?"

Uh-oh. I sort of did. Life was a motion blur at the moment.

He set the clipboard against his chest. "Zoë—when I learned you were here, I checked on the tolerance test and compared it to your recent test."

Mom looked sharply at him. "You think she's diabetic?"

I sat forward. "What? You said you . . . you didn't think I was." *Ow.* I put a hand to my throat.

With his hand up, and one of those oh-don't-go-second-guessing-the-superior-doctor looks, he said, "Nona, calm down. Zoë, this morning, or rather yesterday morning, I wasn't sure. I'm still not. But your blood came back from the lab here with elevated sugar levels, and according to what Rhonda said, you hadn't really eaten anything in nearly fifteen hours. So I checked with the results from the test. Nearly the same level. That's not good and is a sign of diabetes. Which might explain your fatigue and why you were unconscious so long. I want you to come back in later in the week with an empty stomach and let's do a stepped glucose test."

I didn't really get most of that. All I heard was diabetes. Me?

That was a cruel, evil word. I'd had a friend growing up who'd been diabetic. Sharon Crumpton.

Sharon had never eaten a chocolate cake. Or tasted double mocha mint ice cream. She'd never had a Hershey bar!

Diabetic meant no Java Mocha Chip ice cream.

No double-chocolate fudge brownies.

No Sara Lee cheesecake.

No Häagen-Dazs ice cream of any flavor.

I looked wide-eyed at the doctor. "I—I can't be diabetic."

He came forward then and sat on the edge of the bed. "Zoë, I don't know that for certain, and if you are, I'm sure it's Type II, which we can regulate with diet. It could be something we can control."

Diet?

He thought I was afraid of insulin shots!

I was more afraid of the loss of sweets.

He patted my hand. "I'll have a nurse come in and remove the IV. I'd say you're good to go home." He looked at Mom. "But keep an eye on her. She's got several nasty bruises besides the ones on her neck. I want her to get bed rest for at least a full day."

Mom nodded and got out of bed. I felt a bit sad. And a bit cold. Mom was a great heating pad. I nodded. "I'll be . . . fine. So . . ." I looked around. Swallowed. *OUCH.* "Clothes?"

He turned then. "Oh—before you leave—there are a couple of officers outside who need to speak with you."

I paused. Daniel? He was in my condo wasn't he? Or at least I remembered seeing him. "For?"

"You were attacked in your condo, Zoë. That's very serious. And we need to catch the person who did this." He smiled. "Remember, I expect to see you in my office in a few days."

He left the room. I turned to Mom. "I don't want to be diabetic."

She put her hand in the air. "Oh posh. Those symptoms are just you being OOB for too long. Trust me. You'll be fine." She moved to a small closet I'd not seen before set into the wall by the door and pulled out my black gym bag.

Either she was ignoring what Maddox said, or she'd entered that Scarlett O'Hara "I'll deal with it tomorrow" phase. This was serious, and for once, I needed her to be serious.

"Mom." I rubbed at my forehead. My throat still hurt, and my head throbbed. I wanted to go home and curl up on my couch and eat brownies. "Rhonda thought maybe Trench-Coat and I might have done a bit of a symbiotic switch."

"We've already discussed this, Zoë. And I refuse to believe that. You are not connected to a Symbiont. It's just not possible."

"Why is it not possible?"

But she turned away. And that was the end of that discussion with Nona Martinique. I was her daughter, and I knew the signs. This woman was upset. Had something happened while I'd been in unconscious-land?

"You're not still mad at me, are you?"

Mom set the gym bag on the bed and pulled out my gray sweatpants, purple socks, tee shirt, and a pair of bright, canary yellow slippers with orange beaks on them. She'd bought those for me a year ago, thinking they were cute chicks.

I thought they were hideously deformed ducks.

I blinked at the miasma of colors as it attacked my frontal lobe through my eyes. "Yow—who packed this stuff?"

When she didn't answer, I glanced over at Rhonda. She chewed on her lower lip but didn't say anything. Well, she tried telling me something by pulling her index finger across her neck.

I took that to mean cease and desist. It was then I noticed my mom's red-rimmed eyes.

All my life I'd thought of myself as being average. Average height. Average weight. Average looks (hey, brown hair and brown eyes—not exactly anything unique there). Average intelligence.

But I knew from early on I had a knack for reading people. Reading their actions. I watched her movements, jerky and hasty.

Her head was bent. Her shoulders rounded.

And she'd crawled into a high-set hospital bed while ignoring her own back troubles just to be next to me.

Mom was scared.

I'd scared her. Much like the night of my rape.

And I'd done this to her by acting against her wishes. Just as I had that night I'd gone out with friends.

I reached out and took her hand. "Mom . . ."

The door to my room opened then and Daniel walked in. He looked pale and a bit drawn, dressed in a dark blue shirt, khakis, and suit jacket.

And he wasn't alone.

A taller man, dressed in an expensive gray suit, followed

him in. His hair was short-cropped and graying at the temples, and his face was a mixture of wisdom and youth.

Mom caught my eyes and winked before moving away. When she and Rhonda left the room, I pulled the bed's blankets back up to my waist. I hadn't had time to get dressed in Mom's rainbow choices. Thank God.

Daniel was beside me first. I could tell he was holding back, and I think if the other guy hadn't been in there, he'd have hugged me.

"Zoë, this is Captain Ken Cooper, my boss. He's the one I showed the pictures to." He turned and pulled the chair Mom had been sitting in closer. "We need to ask you some questions about the attack."

I had to blink several times to release my libido from the man's incredibly blue eyes. I'd also noticed for the first time that his lower lip was a bit larger than his upper, giving him an almost pouty look. "S-sure. Sir, can you hand me that pitcher there? The one next to the mug?"

Captain Cooper did as I asked and stood beside Daniel. "Miss Martinique, can you give us an account of what happened? When did you notice the attacker in your home?"

Uh-oh. Now how did I work with this one? I couldn't say I saw her in my face after jumping back into my body. I took several long gulps out of the pitcher of water, hoping it would ease the burn in my throat. "Sorry. Very thirsty. Well, I—I'd been napping. When I woke up, she was there, hovering over me." This was the literal truth.

"She?" Daniel said. "Did you recognize her?"

I started to tell him it was the same woman from Hirokumi's office, that afternoon, the one from the meeting.

But he didn't know I was there.

Crap.

But you know, even with a bruised throat and knocked head, I can usually think on my feet.

I glanced down at my seated position. Er . . . make that

my butt. "I thought"—*owch*—damn this throat—"thought she looked a lot like . . . that Asian actress. You know . . . Lucy Liu? She had some really great karate moves." There, use that to explain my injuries, instead of saying I'd been tossed around by a pissed-off incorporeal ice bitch.

My point hit home with Daniel. His eyes widened. He knew whom I was talking about—but how much of his meeting had he told Cooper? I could see he was getting excited.

Gee—I wonder if he'd look that cute when *sexually* excited? I drank more water, hoping to at least put a damper on my overreacting private parts.

Cute, cute, cute.

I wanted to tell Daniel what I'd learned at Rollins's home. But saying this in front of the big guy probably wasn't a good idea.

"Miss Martinique, do you know why this woman would attack you?" Cooper asked this question. He seemed interested as well as skeptical.

"No." I shook my head. I probably wouldn't have passed a polygraph, but on the outside, I think I was pretty convincing.

Daniel glanced to his right, where Cooper stood. "Zoë, there was a break-in at Reverend Rollins's estate last night. Gunfire was reported. The Reverend insists it was nothing."

I gave him a shocked look, complete with girly wide eyes and open mouth. "Really? The good Reverend? That's terrible."

"Yeah," Cooper said. He sounded less than enthused. "Look, do you know any reason why this woman would be in your apartment? We saw no signs of a break-in, and Detective Frasier here said he arrived within minutes of a neighbor's complaint of loud noises. Now, no one saw this woman leave."

I thought of the dragon artifact and wanted desperately to talk to Rhonda. Was Mitsuri *in* the bowels of an ethereal dragon? Or was she *in* the actual stone statue? Or was she ethereal mush?

"I'm sorry, sir. She chased me around my home. I was yelling, screaming, anything to get help. Once she started choking me, I don't remember anything after that."

Cooper nodded. "Well, I'm sorry this happened to you, Miss Martinique." He reached inside his jacket and pulled out a card. I took it from him. "If you remember anything else or need anything, please feel free to call me or Detective Frasier."

I watched him turn and take several steps to the door. He paused and turned. "Frasier?"

"I'd like to stay, Captain." Daniel continued looking at me. If he used those eyes to interrogate me, I would blab anything he wanted. "Make sure Miss Martinique gets home safe."

"Her family's here, Frasier. I expect to see you downstairs in the car in ten minutes." With a nod to me, he left.

"Pushy," I muttered.

When I turned, Daniel moved in front of me, his hands on my face, his lips pressing into mine again.

Oh sweet Jesus! Nirvana! Heaven! Summerlands! And whatever other paradise there was in the universe!

It was a moment before I kissed back, and then all those nasty thoughts that pass by most of us girls strayed into my brain. You know the ones: do I taste like garlic, does my breath smell? I haven't brushed my teeth!

And I probably looked like hell if I thought about how bruised and sore I felt.

He pulled away, and I took a deep breath. And you know me—big mouth and all. "Well." I cleared my throat and that just hurt like hell. "I didn't realize our relationship had progressed to that yet."

"Oh." He looked embarrassed, turned a beet red, and backed away.

No! Get back over here! Damn mouth.

"I'm sorry Zoë, I just wasn't—I mean, when I saw you there—in your kitchen—"

I gave him a smile as he ran his hand through his thick brown hair. Oh I reeeeeally wanted to do that myself. "Hey, I'm fine. Care to tell me though, what you were doing there? Or how you got there so fast?"

"Oh, I can answer that," Rhonda said, as she and Mom stepped back into the room.

Daniel nodded to Rhonda, then offered his hand to Mom. "Detective Lieutenant Daniel Frasier, APD."

I gaped as I watched my mother blush when she took Daniel's hand. "Oh, it's so nice to meet you, Detective. And I'm Nona Martinique, botanica and tea-shop owner."

And then she did it—that damned thing I always hate. She took his hand in both of hers and flipped it over so she could look at his palm.

Oh puh-lease.

"Oh dear, Detective, you have a cold brewing in your future. I see sickness. Perhaps you should come to my shop and enjoy a bit of yarrow tea. I also have several charms in sachets that could help with that dark cloud you have about your shoulders."

"Mom."

Daniel took a step back. "Uh . . . thanks." He did manage to wrangle his hand free.

I sighed and finished off the water before looking at Rhonda. "You were saying?"

"Oh yeah." She grinned. "I was coming back up the drive after running down to Brewster's—you know you're out of ice cream? That's a crime in your place. Anyway, I saw this guy sitting in his car outside the condo building. He looked a bit odd, and he was talking to himself."

"I was not talking to myself," Daniel said. "I was sort of—trying to make up my mind." He looked at me. "I wanted to come see you—felt a bit like a rude son of a bitch earlier, especially after you helped me with those photos. You believed in me, and I cut you out."

"Well." My voice was crackling a bit, more throaty than usual. I wanted more water. "Oh . . . geez this hurts. But it's not your fault the case is closed."

"I'm not sure it is." He looked from me to Mom to Rhonda.

I held up my hand. "It's okay—they're in on it—so to speak."

He appeared to relax. "The woman you described— I've seen her. She was at Visitar Inc., the other day when I had my meeting with Hirokumi. Kept saying she felt a presence in the room, when really I thought she was just sticking it to Koba."

"So this intruder works for Visitar?" Mom shook her head. "Now that doesn't make any sense. Why attack my daughter?"

I looked at her. "Because I saw her at Rollins's house."

Oops.

Curse my mouth!

Daniel was on his feet. "You *were* there. Was that you that broke in?"

Uh. I—well—uh—

Damn.

Teleport, teleport, teleport . . . crap.

17

RHONDA moved closer. "She *saw* you?"

I understood her emphasis on *saw*. No one was supposed to have *seen* me. I nodded at Rhonda but then cut my eyes over at Daniel. This was not the place to have this conversation.

"Saw you . . . wait." He shook his head. "That couldn't have been you. Rollins lives across town, and you were already on the way to the hospital before I heard about the break-in. Rhonda said you were in your condo while I was there. I saw your car. You couldn't have been in Rollins's house."

Mom came to the rescue. She reached out and put a hand on Daniel's arm. "Honey, relax. You're going to pop an artery."

"Ma'am, what Zoë's saying is impossible. She couldn't have been there."

What do I do now? Daniel—being the incredible detective I suspected he was—was not going to let this go. And how could I tell him I was an astral Traveler on the fast track to becoming a Wraith (one of the twisted)? He'd never believe me.

Unless . . .

"I wasn't, Daniel." Well, not physically anyway. "But like I told my mom earlier . . ." I gave Nona a meaningful stare, hoping she'd go along with me as I made this up. "I drove by Rollins's place yesterday, after you called. And I saw this Asian woman coming out of his estate."

There. It was a whopper of a little white lie. But I sure as heck wasn't ready to explain my little condition to the future father of my children.

He seemed to relax a little and took a step back to me. "And she saw you, watching her?"

I nodded. He seemed to be buying it. "I'm sure that's it. And I figure maybe she followed me, and she maybe saw me with you." Under my breath I was reciting my Hail Marys at record speed.

"Well"—Daniel shook his head—"I guess that makes sense. I just—when I heard about the shooting out at the Rollinses' house—I somehow believed you'd been there." He gave me an endearing smile. "I guess that's impossible, huh?"

A circus tune played in the room from somewhere, and I thought for an instant I was hearing the wrong kind of music—especially since I disliked circuses. They have clowns.

I hate clowns. Well not so much hate them—I'm damned scared of them.

Tacky things give me the creeps. Especially harlequins. Evil creatures.

Daniel reached inside his jacket pocket and pulled out a small phone and looked at the screen. "It's Cooper. He wants me downstairs." He tucked the phone back in his pocket. "I'll look into this woman, check out her background. And I'm going to have an officer outside your building."

I started to open my mouth, but he put a finger to my lips. I resisted the urge to pull that finger in my mouth and suck it.

Hey, a near-death experience makes some people very horny. I wasn't sure sex was an option in the afterlife. Might as well grab the gusto while it stood in front of me, right?

Daniel smiled and leaned over to kiss my cheek. "Can I see you tonight? Maybe stop by?"

"Sure." I felt all giddy inside, kinda like the first time Bob Ryerson asked me to a basketball game. Of course, my mom was the coach, and I was playing, so I got him in free and he sat with Paula Woods while I beat sweat on the court.

Hrm. Well—maybe not like *that*.

"You come on by, and I'll have a nice dinner fixed," Mom said, and she took Daniel's hand and squeezed it.

"You'll make sure she takes it easy?" He glanced at me. I blushed.

Mom beamed. "Even if I have to chain her to the bed."

Uh . . . Now that was a bit scary. Mom might really have chains somewhere. And she'd use 'em. Hell, the woman had pulled a gun on me!

Once he was gone, the nurse came in and removed the IV and handed me a little cup of pills and a fresh glass of water.

I looked at the pills, then looked at Mom. She gestured for me to take them. I got dressed in the clown suit and was glad Rhonda had brought my long trench coat.

I rode the wheelchair out of the hospital and we piled in Mom's car. It was pitch-black outside, being somewhere between 5:00 A.M. and 6:00 A.M., and it was damned cold. A few stars shone overhead, glitter abandoned on a black velvet cloth. The wind cut through my coat, and my teeth chattered. Once tucked inside the passenger's side, Mom made sure I was well secured in a blanket and the seat belt snuggly fitted over me.

I dozed on the way home, unable to keep my eyes open. I found out later those pills were Mom's insurance I wouldn't take an astral walk while she got me home and tucked back into bed. That was just sneaky.

When I woke up again I was in my own bed. I was warm. Dulled sunlight streamed in my bedroom windows through the slats of the tightly closed blinds. The house smelled of Mom's incredible rosemary chicken. My throat felt a little better—not as scratchy or raw—and the clock on my nightstand read 4:37 P.M.

I'd slept all day?

Curse that woman. And now I felt all woozy when I got up. I paused, making sure I didn't sense anything ugly and uninvited in my house. I could *hear* the wards, a slight humming in the back of my head, something I intended asking Rhonda about as soon as I had a shower.

I felt greasy, and I had socks on my teeth.

Another good toothbrushing was in order. Only when I staggered to the bathroom and flipped on the light I clapped my hands over my mouth to stifle a scream.

The little clump of white hairs at my left temple had multiplied into a larger clump of white hairs—making them even more visible from a distance. And not just a little start at the roots—like when a dye job grows out. Hell no—the white traveled from the root all the way down to the frazzled split ends.

Careful not to fall over in my enthusiasm to raid the cabinet under my sink, I found a coloring kit I'd bought a month or two ago when I'd seen my first gray hair (*but these are white!*) and proceeded to bypass the instructions and douse the errant spot with foul-smelling chemicals.

Die you evil white hair. Grrr . . .

After a hot shower and a thorough toothbrushing, I pulled on some gray sweats, a VAST tee shirt, and my bear-claw slippers before meandering into my living room. Rhonda was there, as well as Tim. Steve was busy helping Mom in the kitchen. He was solid, which meant he was able to lift small things—basically he could toss spices and set the table.

Tim and Rhonda were at the dining table looking at—

Shit. The dragon thingie was still in my house!

"You look much better, honey." Mom looked through the opening from the kitchen to the dining area. I could see she wore an apron around her waist. Her hair was pulled back, but several strands had pulled loose. Kinda gave her a more feminine Debbie Einstein look.

Kinda like a crazy mom.

I shuffled past the table and the dragon statue and she took me in her arms. I pointed to the table. "What is that doing here?"

"Oh, you've got to see this, Zoë," Rhonda called out, and I could see her motioning me over through the look-through.

I went, cautiously, terrified that thing was going to come to life and suck me inside and I'd be strangled all over again in its bowels.

The statue bounced just slightly, as if it had those little bugs in it like Mexican jumping beans. Only this wasn't a cute little bug—this was a nasty evil killing ugly bitch inside of it.

Or was that the dragon with indigestion? Hey, if I'd eaten something that ugly, I'd have stomach problems too. I wondered if it needed to go potty.

"I guess after last night you're glad I left this here, and activated?" She beamed at me, and looked all of twelve years old. "If it hadn't of detected that thing's presence, you might be done for."

Tim was less impressed. "And if you'd have turned the ward back on when you left to get ice cream Zoë'd never have been in danger because that thing couldn't have gotten into this condo."

I sat down at the table next to Tim, my stare still riveted to the silent, slightly bouncing dragon in the center of the table. "I think it came back *with* me. Back along my cord. It was there in Rollins's house, then it was hovering over me when I opened my eyes here." I looked at each of them.

"Zoë, tell us what happened last night. And leave nothing out." Mom came to stand by the table. She carried a glass of juice and several white pills with her and set them in front of me. "Antibiotics."

Antibiotics my ass. Those little white ditties were the same things I'd taken in the hospital, and probably Mom's insurance policy that I wasn't going anywhere anytime soon. I just nodded and drank all the juice while palming the pills.

But I did tell them everything, from the moment Rhonda dropped me off till I was being strangled on the kitchen floor.

"That's when I came in," Rhonda said. "I was leading supercop up in the elevator, and he got a call on his radio. Disturbance reported right in this building, and as we got to the door, we could hear you screaming and things being thrown about.

"Lieutenant Frasier went into *Adam-12* mode with his gun and told me to stay behind him. But while he went left I went right. I could smell that thing." She pointed to the artifact.

"You smelled the dragon?" I asked.

Rhonda nodded. "Smells like sulfur. Rotten eggs. That's when I saw it"—she nodded to the dragon—"eat that lady. I saw her legs kicking out of its mouth. And then I saw you, half-in and half-out of your body. I thought maybe you'd tried to go all Wraithy and were just too tired. Then you passed out, and I thought you'd stopped breathing."

Well, that was news to me. I thought I'd kept breathing the whole time. Interesting how things look from the other side of the room, isn't it?

"Could we not use that *Wraith* word?" Mom said.

I glanced at her but didn't comment. I kinda liked the word. Had a better ring than anything else I'd tried.

Traveler. Wraith.

Hrm. Wraith. Traveler sounded like an insurance company.

"Lieutenant Frasier called an ambulance and started CPR. Didn't take much, and you sucked in air, coughed, and that's when you sort of sat up, *out* of your body. Then you went limp again. Your neck looks better." Rhonda grinned. "Not as radical as before. Makes a great accessory."

Sick puppy.

She frowned at me. "You dyed your hair."

Hesh up.

I looked at each of them, Tim and Rhonda seated at the table and Mom standing. "That's it. End of story. What's for eats?"

"That's it?" Ooh—Mom sounded upset. "Zoë, I warned you not to go there. There's no telling what that man had lurking about that house. He's evil."

Well yeah. That much I understood now. I smelled the buttery aroma of Mom's cooking and took a deep breath. My stomach growled. Maddox had said I hadn't eaten in fifteen hours. Well, add in my sleepy time and that added up to—twenty-seven hours!

And I wanted more juice.

Standing, I moved past Mom and into the kitchen. Steve saw me coming and opened the refrigerator door. I pulled out the entire carton of Sunny Delight someone had bought.

With a single wrench, I twisted off the cap and turned the container up and gulped down as much as I could stand before the pain of too much cold against the roof of my mouth caused the all-too-familiar ache.

I lowered the container and put my fingers to the space in between my eyebrows. "Oh. Brain freeze."

"So let's get this straight before supercop gets here," Rhonda said, and she moved to the kitchen. Tim faded away and then reappeared beside Steve near the stove. "Visitar has something of Rollins's that Rollins wants back—which we're no longer assuming is porn tapes, but a document. Rollins hired this Archer, which I have to look up, whom we call Trench-Coat, to soul suck Tanaka, but instead he used a gun, which caused problems, questions. And this Mitsuri, who's stuck in the dragon's belly, works for Rollins and was supposedly spying on Hirokumi."

I nodded. Sounded right.

It was a good *Reader's Digest* version. Bravo.

"I wonder if there's a way to interrogate her." Rhonda looked closer at the sometimes-wiggling dragon.

"So she's inside the statue thing—I saw her being eaten."

"It was metaphorical, really. Just a fancy end to a spiritual vacuum cleaner." Rhonda beamed.

"Well, don't get too close," I cautioned. I was still a bit jumpy—and who wouldn't be? After having their windpipe nearly crushed? "And find out why Rollins called TC the Archer."

"I will tonight. I'll do a little more searching on this little gem." She nodded to the dragon statue. "Nona's going to do a bit more investigative work on the Archer as well."

Oh great. Mom was going to gather Miss Shultz and the rest of the geriatric Scooby gang. That could reeeeally spell trouble. As long as they didn't douse me with pond water again and hold a gun to my head—fine by me.

The doorbell rang. I stood. "Who . . ."

"The detective, remember?" Mom smiled as she stepped closer to me. "Luckily you took a shower."

Steve vanished, but Tim remained in his chair. Steve's voice came in from somewhere nearby. "Tim—we're going home. It wouldn't be a good idea for the nice policeman to see you."

"And why not? I want to see him." The ghost gave me a wicked smile and a wink. "I'd like to see the guy that has Zoë so messed up."

"Tim," Steve hissed. "Now!"

"Oh all right." He stuck out his tongue and vanished as well.

That's when I realized the table was already set for two on the other end. Only two.

I sat there as Mom went to the door, and I heard Daniel's voice. I looked up to see him come in, a bouquet of colorful, fresh-cut flowers in one hand. He was dressed nice, and casual, in a soft white cable-knit sweater and jeans. Mom took his long coat and held the flowers out to me. "Vase. Water."

She knew me well enough that the sight of such a good-looking man was enough to wipe my most basic brain functions. Giving me simple instructions was best.

Mental note: *daaammmnnnnn* . . .

He immediately came to me, his eyes wide and full of concern behind his glasses. Daniel smelled of soap and Halston. His hand was warm on my cheek. "You look better. Throat still hurt?"

I nodded. "It will for a while."

"I see it's made that voice of yours sexier than ever."

I blushed. And of course I heard an "Awwww" from Rhonda and Mom.

Kill. Kill. Kill.

Mom finished setting the table for us. There were pink-eyed purple-hull peas, pressure-cooked just under firm and salty sitting just beside the steaming rosemary chicken. Homemade mashed potatoes smashed with evaporated milk and butter. Sweet corn, crescent rolls, and fresh-made sweet tea.

Mom had gone all out. I guess it was good that she liked Detective Frasier.

"Miz Martinique, this looks incredible," Daniel gushed. "I didn't realize how hungry I was till I smelled it."

"You eat till you're full, honey." She turned to me, placed a hand on my forehead, and checked my neck. "Please—no going out. Stay home and get a bit more sleep. Take those pills I gave you that you slipped into your pocket."

I nodded. *Rats! See? Eyes in the back of her head.* I also knew what she meant by no going out. Phhhtt.

"You're not staying?" Daniel looked almost panicked as Rhonda and Mom gathered their coats and moved to the door. I noticed Rhonda had also taken the artifact. I wondered if it was a one-shot deal—one-spook-at-a-time thing.

As much as I was afraid of it, I was also a bit afraid to be without it.

I assumed Rhonda planned on studying it. Yay go her and not me.

Mom gave me a kiss and a hug, and they left. I could only assume Mom had the physical items from her house in her purse so that Tim and Steve traveled with her.

Well—their absence was followed by a very awkward moment between us.

Uh . . . Hmmm. Jump him now or later? "Well, sit down. I'll get ice in the glasses."

That seemed to break the moment. "I'll help."

My kitchen isn't very big, but it's not small either. Two people can move fairly easily in it, as long as they suck in their guts and know what they're doing and where things are.

Daniel was clueless. Twice he bumped into me, but I didn't complain. I finally had two large glasses full of ice and poured the tea. The ice clicked as it cracked when the hot liquid melted it a bit.

But before I brought them to the table, I couldn't help but swallow an entire glassful before replenishing it.

I noticed Daniel watching me with a half smile, and a bit of worry. "Zoë—I'm not sure that's normal. I mean, you drinking so much. You were downing that water this morning as if you'd not had any for a week."

"It's nothing." I brought both glasses to the table, then returned for the pitcher. I felt I was going to need it.

"Did the doctor find anything weird about it?"

Nope. Not a word. Might need to go in for tests though. I couldn't bring myself to say those things out loud.

We sat looking at the food a few seconds. The awkward thing had to go. This was my house, and I was famished. "Look, Daniel. Let's call it now. I like you—a lot. If I wasn't recovering from an attack, I'd jump you where you sat. But, I'm hungry. You're hungry. Let's dig in?"

He grinned. "I'd jump you too."

Not another word was spoken for a good five minutes while we sliced and hacked at the chicken, dumped heaps of potatoes on our plates, ladled peas and corn, then covered everything with my mom's spicy gravy.

Then we dug in with smiles. Well, he smiled. I winced as I slowly worked food past my still-sore throat.

"Okay—now—" Daniel said as he took a big sip of tea. "Let's be honest here. You saw this woman leaving Rollins's house?"

I shook my head. "No talky about business while we

eat. First up—you tell me about you. You know about me—far more than I'd ever wanted you to."

He knew I hinted at the rape and looked almost crestfallen. *Poor widdle copper.* Serves him right—shouldn't be snooping. He took a drink of tea and cleared his throat. "Well, you know about my partner problem. Uhm let's see. I was born just outside of New Orleans, moved to Savannah when I was twelve, and I lived there with my parents until my mom died when I turned fifteen."

"Oh, I'm sorry to hear that."

"It's okay." He smiled. "Breast cancer. She'd been sick for a while. And I think in a way Dad was okay with it. But, I stayed there, finished high school, went into the academy and became a cop." He looked at me. "Just like my dad."

"So he's a cop in Savannah?"

"He's retired now. Fishes mostly. I go see him on holidays." Daniel took up his fork and toyed with his potatoes. "Let's see, other than fish with my dad I like to draw and paint, I tinker with motorcycles. I have one locked up in my garage I haven't messed with in over a year. And I—" He stopped.

I leaned in when he stopped. "You what?"

"Oh it's silly."

"No it's not. Tell me." *Or I'll strangle it out of you. We're having a moment here.*

"Okay." Daniel smiled at me. "I love old horror movies. Vampires, werewolves, Frankenstein, mummies. I have a whole collection of them, and I love to sit up late on the weekends, eat popcorn with Tabasco sauce, and watch them."

I frowned at him. Didn't sound too bad, or too wiggy. "But you don't believe in them?"

"Monsters?" He shoved a happy mouthful of potatoes in and swallowed. After that he shook his head. "Of course not. No such thing. Ghosts and goblins. Makes a great tourist trade in Savannah. Ever been?"

I shook my head.

"I'll take you sometime. Now, if your mom makes me more of these potatoes, I'll tell you how I became a detective. It's a lot shorter and more boring."

Huh. Didn't believe in ghosts. Kinda a shame, 'cause little did Mr. Detective realize he was sitting beside a Wraith. *Boo! Bwahahaha!*

"Now, about this Mitsuri woman. You think she saw you leave Rollins's?"

Ah, back to business. At least I knew to ply him with potatoes to make him my slave. I nodded and poured my third glass of tea. "Sure did." *She left with me. Heh.*

Mmmm . . . rosemary chicken. With the ache in my throat I was glad it wasn't barbecue.

"I'm just not sure about this attack. Even Rhonda says she saw this woman, but she ducked around to the living room as I came in the kitchen. We've not found anything on her either. And Hirokumi isn't returning my phone calls."

I nodded and wiped my fingers on a paper napkin. I'm sure Mom would have set out cloth ones if I'd had any. I wanted to tell him what I'd overheard, that I knew Rollins was guilty of Tanaka's murder and that he'd hired something Rhonda and Mom thought was a Symbiont, but I also knew I didn't want to spend the night in a padded room.

So how did I go about helping him without coming off as a nutcase? "What kind of evidence do you need to prove Rollins killed Tanaka? Or at least hired someone to do it?"

Daniel narrowed his eyes. "You believe he hired someone?"

"Oh—just think about it. Rollins actually muddy his hands?" I took a nice small portion of potatoes.

Mmmmmm . . . potatoes. And the potatoes didn't hurt my throat. *Yay!*

Daniel nodded, his fork poised above his plate and full of buttery fluffiness. "I think you're right. And if so, then I'd either have to have witnesses to the exchange willing to testify. The testimony of the actual hit man. Or, some sort of proof of payment." He sighed and lowered his fork. "I'd also have to find out who the hit man was. I can put out some feelers, do a little digging as to his or her identity."

I nodded, though I was sure he wasn't going to get the answers he wanted on that one. I doubt old Trench-Coat was listed in the yellow pages.

The detective dropped his fork with a clank on his plate. "What if it's the same woman who attacked you? This Mitsuri woman? *She's* the assassin."

I looked up at him. It was a logical leap. Not the right one, but logical.

"She was in Hirokumi's office, apparently spying on him, and she obviously didn't want me in there—which now makes sense with all that mumbo jumbo about evil spirits. She sees you, and probably had me under surveillance, then sees me with you, so attacks you—nearly kills you— because you see her leaving Rollins's place." He beamed. He looked so good when he beamed like that. "I already put out an APB on this woman—hopefully it'll turn up something. And don't forget—there's an officer watching your building."

Yay.

Once we'd finished, I went to the refrigerator and pulled out a pint of Brewster's Praline. Not exactly the chocolatey goodness of Java Chocolate Chip—but its sugary-sweet caramel would hit the spot.

"You sure you should eat that?"

I eyeballed him over the two bowls and my just-purchased Ronco Ice Cream Scooper (guaranteed not to stick to the ice cream). "You gonna stop me?"

Daniel stood, his chair scraping against my hardwood.

Any other time I might have protested his rough treatment of my chair and my floor. But I liked the look in his eyes as he neared me.

I sort of forgot the scoop as the detective (oh I love it when they're taller than me!) moved around the counter. He stood close, facing me. I looked up at him—and the look in those beautiful eyes made all the right places grow warm and tingly.

Oh yes, yes, yes. I sighed as he reached up and stroked my cheek softly with his hand. It was warm and full of electricity. If I really stepped back and thought about it, this sort of behavior was a bit fast.

We'd only met a few days ago, and that'd been happenstance in a pub (and I'd technically been a ghost and something he didn't believe in).

But he'd been outside my condo last night—that much he'd admitted since Rhonda had seen him.

He liked me. He really liked me!

His hand moved from my cheek to my throat, and he gingerly touched the rough, red bruises there. It hurt just a little and I couldn't squelch the flinch.

"I'm sorry." He removed his hand.

My heart and hopes crashed to the floor, and I grabbed his hand and brought it back up to my face. "Please—it's okay."

"Does it still hurt?"

"You saw me eat my weight in chicken and potatoes."

He grinned. Beautiful, straight white teeth. "Yeah . . . you have quite an appetite." His hand dropped from my face to my shoulder and ran down my arm to the front of my waist to my hips. Oohhhhhh . . . don't stop!

Daniel's expression grew serious. "You have a way about you, Zoë Martinique—something that attracts me. From the moment I saw you in Fadó's. I'm—I'm not sure I know what it is. I barely know you."

Kiss me, kiss me, kiss me . . .

"We barely know each other," I said, and I noticed the breathlessness to my voice. Oh—I was a goner, and if he didn't kiss me soon or put his hand in special places, it was gonna be Mr. Vibrator tonight.

I was reeeeeeally tired of Mr. Vibrator.

He came closer, lowering his face to mine. "I'm not usually this forward . . ." His voice was breathless too, and his eyelids were lazy.

"Daniel . . ."

He moved his beautifully shaped upturned nose over my forehead, then down the side of my face to my cheek. "If this is too fast . . . I shouldn't get involved with a potential witness . . ."

"Daniel . . ."

Oh. Oh. Oh. I found my own hands doing their thing along his hips. They snaked their way up and around his lean, strong back.

"Zoë . . . I'm not sure this is . . ."

"Shut up and kiss me." And I didn't give him another opportunity to answer. My libido—long denied the pleasures of man-flesh—dove right into my carnal needs. I pressed my lips over his, delighting in his smells and tastes.

His tongue danced along with mine as our hands roamed over each other's body. We were a perfect fit and I felt the incredible hardness of his mighty sword against my pelvic bone and pressed my hips into him.

Unless that was his gun.

He moaned and leaned down over me, almost lifting me up off my feet. Nope. Not a gun, but definitely loaded.

He kissed my lips, my cheeks, my chin, then pressed his lips and teeth to my neck.

I gasped at the pain from the bruising there, and he pulled back abruptly.

"Oh God—Zoë, I'm so sorry. I'm sorry—I forgot." His

expression just melted my wee-little heart! He looked crushed, like a child who'd hurt the bug he'd been playing with. Torn off the leg and—

Oh bad analogy. Geezuz Zoë.

Scratch that. He looked cute. And I pulled him back to me, pressing my lips into his and erasing his fear of hurting me.

Passion, lust, desire, yearning, thirst . . .

Oh those were definitely the words rotating around in my head. And if we didn't move to my bedroom to my nice, soft, warm sheets, I was going to take him here—in the middle of my kitchen.

I nibbled on his full lower lip and traced my tongue down his throat to that sexy dip at the base of his neck between his collarbones. He moaned again, and I swear I orgasmed right then.

"Are . . ." he said softly. "Are you . . . sure?"

Sure? Was he *kidding*?

To make my point that I wanted sex now, I grabbed hold of the zipper on his jeans and slowly pulled it down. He gasped.

Oh, I was sure.

Now if I could just . . .

A phone rang.

Ah! Murphy—you suck!

It was his phone—that cursed circus tune. Which immediately turned my stomach. I searched his body looking for the damned thing so I could drown it.

But Daniel grabbed my hands and pulled away, taking his warmth with him. I felt my lower lip do that large boo-boo lip thing. He squeezed my hands. "Let me shut it off." He grinned. "Christ, you're beautiful. Your eyes aren't really brown—they're glowing topaz—and they're so turned on right now. Hold that thought . . ."

Hurry! My engines are overheating!

If the tune wasn't that infernal circus one, I'd have said ignore the damned phone.

Daniel half jogged to the living room and grabbed at his suit jacket. He pulled out his phone and looked at the face. His expression sharpened, and he frowned. "Zoë, I gotta take this. It's Cooper."

Motherfuckerdamnshitfire.

Ooh. I got a worse potty mouth than the Reverend—but at least I didn't say things like that out loud.

I looked at the opened pint of ice cream and decided I'd better put it in the freezer. No need to let any kind of sweet goodness go to waste. Unless I drizzled it over his naked body later.

Daniel spoke in a low voice and moved even farther away.

Uh-oh.

I knew from his body language something was wrong. And not just the red flags that announced our steamy little night had just abruptly ended.

Something had happened, bad or serious enough for the captain to call Daniel.

I watched him hang up and put the jacket on.

I pouted. Daniel turned a very serious face to me and was beside me in three steps. He had his hands on my shoulders, his body close. "I have to go—something's come up. But I'll be back, okay?"

I nodded. "Is it the Tanaka case?"

He hesitated and set his phone on the counter. I frowned at him. "Daniel Frasier—don't you cut me out of this."

"I just can't say right now. But what I do suspect is that your life is still in danger, as long as this woman is still out there. Promise me when I leave you'll lock the doors and set the alarms. Maybe call your mom to come back over and stay with you?"

I shook my head. Uh, no. "I'll be fine. But you'll be back?"

"Maybe—it depends on what I find. I have to go."

I grabbed his hand. He took me into his arms and buried his face in my hair and my neck, careful this time not to hurt me. "Just please, stay here tonight. And don't let anyone in you don't know."

Like I would do that? I nodded, and he kissed me again.

My thighs swelled.

I cursed Cooper for calling, hoping his penis would swell to the size of a deformed zucchini. All rough and lumpy too. Phhht.

Daniel grabbed his coat and was out the door. "Lock it!" he called back.

I did and turned. I had a mess to clean in the kitchen, and I didn't feel like touching a thing. I was still hot and bothered, and more awake now than I'd been in two days. I thought of Mr. Vibrator and my now-wet sweats.

Nah—I was gonna save myself for when he came back. If he came back.

But what to do in the meantime? I thought about the phone call and its fracked-up timing—

And that's when I remembered more of Rollins's conversation. He'd threatened Daniel. Even mentioned setting Hirokumi up with the detective's death.

I stopped in place. *And now he gets a mysterious phone call he doesn't tell me about. Crap! I need to tell him. Warn him!*

It was then I saw his phone on the counter.

Damn!

My mind played out all sorts of nasty scenarios, from Daniel ending up under a truck to Daniel being found in Lake Lanier.

Or worse . . . at the hand end of Trench-Coat. Rollins

had to be planning something, and I had no idea how to warn Daniel.

Unless . . .

I spied on Rollins again.

No, no, no . . . it was stupid. I knew I wasn't in the best health physically. I'd just slept for fifteen hours, and before that I'd been unconscious for six.

But if I just watched the Reverend, and didn't exert myself, then maybe I could follow Rollins or find out what he wanted Beckett and Tiny to do to Daniel Frasier.

Mom would kill me. But what about Daniel? Damn . . . after that little almost-fuck I wanted him back here. I just couldn't sit here and not do anything!

But how to get there? I didn't dare call Rhonda—not after what had just happened. And if Mom got word, she'd drug me or something. She'd done it once.

I made sure the pills Mom gave me were still in my pocket.

I could always drive myself, and park nearby. I'd only gone astral outside of my condo a few times, but Mom or Tim or someone had always watched my body. If someone came along and found me, they'd think I was dead.

But if I left my body here, I'd have to take the bus or hitch a ride, and there was no guarantee I'd get to where I wanted to go—and definitely not in a speedy way.

As I watched the chicken sit there, I came up with a plan. I'd jump from my car, but I'd put my body in the trunk. There was an emergency release, and as long as the car was parked in a safe location, no one would bother it. There was a MARTA Park 'n' Ride near Rollins's estate, and the cars there were patrolled by the MARTA police.

Yeah, they were more rent-a-cops than real police, but it was less likely someone would steal the Mustang from there, with me in it.

I'd take my phone too, and Daniel's. I could maybe call Cooper if something awful happened.

I had a plan. In hindsight, it was a stupid one, but I needed to watch Daniel. I needed to know Rollins's goons weren't going to use him as leverage against Hirokumi.

And it all seemed like such a good idea at the time. I only wish in hindsight I'd taken my pills and stayed in bed.

18

SINCE I didn't want my body to be found in a cat-burglar suit (not that I expected it to be found—but just to be cautious) I wore regular clothes.

And I realized how not well I was when I nearly collapsed onto the bed just from putting on thick wool socks (I might not get cold in astral form, but my body sure as hell could—especially jammed in the trunk of a car), my black sneakers, red turtleneck, black fleece pullover, and gloves. After lying on the bed for a good ten minutes, I figured my sweats would do. Screw the jeans.

On that same note, I decided against a braid this time, as my hair was a bit warmer on the ears if I left it down. And I wasn't sure I could keep my arms up that long to braid it.

Traffic sucked.

But it was a Friday night and I should have expected that. I had my cell with me in the pocket of the shirt, Daniel's in the other pocket, and a gallon of orange juice stashed in the trunk.

Hey . . . I was still thirsty.

It was also colder than I thought it'd be. I smelled rain when I stepped outside, and I used a few words in frustration for my lack of checking out the Weather Channel.

Not that I'd have learned Atlanta's weather right away—but I'd have known the temperature of California.

I parked the Mustang in the Park 'n' Ride as planned. Unfortunately several boys in their early teens were gathered several feet away near a trash can in which someone had started a fire. I wasn't about to climb into my trunk with a bunch of kids around—that would make things too curious. I'd have to wait till they left.

Which took them about fifteen minutes. I'm not sure if it was me in my car that made them nervous, but eventually they moved as a group out of the parking lot and disappeared into the night air.

There were several other cars, including another late-model 'Stang, so I didn't feel so conspicuous.

Now getting into the car's trunk—that was probably going to look weird. Shivering, I popped the top, looked around for a MARTA cop. When I didn't see any, I jumped in and slammed it shut.

Odd—was that what a coffin lid sounded like? 'Cause it sure as hell had the impression of finality to it.

Mental note: *Ew. Must be Rhonda rubbing off on me.*

I pulled the blanket and Granny's quilt over me, checked to make sure I knew where the emergency release was, then closed my eyes.

Going astral, or Wraithing out, or whatever I was doing, took a bit longer than expected—and I chalked it up to being a bit tired.

Duh—yah think?

But finally I separated from my body and found myself just outside the car. Passing through the metal of the car was a lot like passing through glass, only not as cold. I did keep a sort of tin taste in my mouth though.

Now I had a three-mile hike to the house.

Go me.

There were a few dogs that barked at me—remember that animal thing? I growled back at them, and they ran off squealing like pigs. Okay, that was new.

Cool. I'm spooky!

Though I couldn't feel it in this form, I could see the wind bowing the trees around. Dead leaves of brown, orange, and yellow twisted and fluttered like nighttime butterflies under the streetlights.

Yeah, it was gonna rain all right. And it was going to be nasty.

I finally made it to Rollins's house about a half hour later. The whole place was lit up, a bit more intensely than the night before. I realized then that I'd lost an entire day thanks to creepy Mitsuri. I'd slept it all away—and that's a day I wasn't going to get back.

Mental note: *grab dragon artifact and shake it* really *hard.*

I sieved through the gate and started across the yard again when this time I heard the dogs. They were near the house and barking loudly.

Shit.

I hunched down and moved as quietly as I could (not to attract the pooch factor) around the wall. There was something happening in the driveway at the front door. Two limousines were parked outside and several of Rollins's WWE stooges stood around, guns drawn.

Guns?

What the hell was going on? I didn't see Daniel, and I hoped he wasn't stuffed in a trunk.

I moved around the edges of the house's light, noting the dogs—really big black Dobermans—moving about the guards. I had to admit a bit of surprise when a guard here or there petted one of the ferocious beasties on the head.

I guess like attracts like, huh?

Rollins stepped outside, flanked by Beckett and Tiny (heh-heh), and they both had guns in their hands. I had to wonder what had happened to incite such a show of force.

They stepped inside the nearest limo. I needed to make sure Daniel, or someone else, wasn't in one of those trunks.

Two of the trunks were opened and I looked in each. Nothing. Actually—they were all very clean for trunks. Not even a fast-food bag.

The limo nearest Rollins was closed. Keeping an eye on the poochies, I sieved into the trunk. Oh. Yuck. It was like sucking on a nail.

It was a spacious area, and being astral, I could see better back here. There were several lengths of rope, duct tape, and two pillowcases.

Okay—I'm not criminally minded—but even I saw these items as kidnap paraphernalia. Bingo. I knew I'd been right to head out to Rollins's at that instant.

They were on their way to somehow kidnap my cop. And just think how cool it'd be if I tagged along and foiled them all by warning him? I checked my watch. Forty minutes out, tops. I had over three hours left. If I paid attention, I could maybe even go corporeal to help him whip out a can of whup-ass.

Heh. Ow. Headache.

The limo started forward. I could hear Rollins talking but not well enough to understand what he was saying. I guessed from his cadence and the lack of another voice responding that he was on the phone.

I wanted to sieve through and sit inside to watch—but I

didn't want to risk there being another Mitsuri creature lurking about.

We drove for a while. I was surprised how smooth the shocks were, even in the trunk. *I need to get me one of these.*

The irony of me riding astrally inside a trunk while my body lay inside the trunk of my own car wasn't lost on me. Rhonda would think it was cool. Mom would think it was a sign. A sign of me going crazy.

My opinion?

I was starting to get creeped out.

When the limo stopped, I checked my watch. We'd been on the road half an hour. That left . . . just under three hours. I waited till I heard the same number of doors close that opened. Voices again.

And then the trunk was opened.

Yikes!

Beckett bent in, shoved his hand through my stomach and grabbed some rope and a roll of duct tape.

For the brief instance his skin connected with my astral form, I saw what he was thinking of—

Steak. Medium well. And a tall Sam Adams beer.

Pretty benign actually. He was hungry.

Oohh . . . steak.

My astral stomach rumbled, and I moved out before he shut the trunk. What was up with that? I just ate a full dinner!

I honestly couldn't tell you where the hell we were.

The wind had definitely reached the point of monsoon. There were no stars, and the few streetlights I could see didn't work. I had to rely on their flashlights (they being Beckett, Tiny, Rollins, and two more of the WWE work'n part-time for the gov'ner) and what my spirit-eyes could see.

Oogy.

All oogy. Hell—it was downright fucked up.

I actually shivered in this form, though not from the cold. This place was wrong. I thought I saw movement in nearly every shadow. Faces that appeared and vanished. Voices whispering on the wind. Sets of tiny red pinpoint eyes, blinking at me from the darkest shadows, like ethereal hounds of hell.

Mommy.

They'd parked the limo on the curb of an old-neighborhood street. The asphalt was littered with old clothing, refuse scattered over the patchy grass to the left. I could make out buildings on either side of the street. They looked like brick barracks—long, with tiny wood separators between backyards.

A kid's Big Wheel lay on its side nearby. The wind blew an empty soda can along the pavement, the sound catching everyone's attention.

The boys were on edge.

And so was I—but I'm sure it was for entirely different reasons.

There were things here they couldn't see. But I could. And I knew those things could see me. And they were watching me, whispering about me, following me in the shadows.

I was scared shitless. I felt naked and very vulnerable. I had no way to protect myself in this state, at least none that I knew of. I'd never really had to until a few days ago. I never knew such a place existed in Atlanta, whether physical or the one I walked in. I was in two worlds at that moment, and for the first time, I was *really* aware of it. The astral world was just as scary as the physical in this area of town.

And I didn't know where it was or why Rollins would come here.

I needed to call Daniel. I was getting a very bad feeling.

The men—six in all—spread out to flank the Reverend.

Rollins had dressed down for the occasion, all in black, down to the trench coat and gloves.

I followed behind as they moved between two of the buildings. I could see them better now and see inside to sliding glass doors. Some places had card tables for furniture while others had little to nothing. Secondhand, broken toys littered most of the tiny concrete slabs at the rear of each place.

I'd been right to believe these were places where people lived. These were housing development projects. We were somewhere in west Atlanta. Probably out on Hollowell Parkway.

Ooh . . . I was a long way from my car. And my body.

Lightning flashed across the sky, quickly followed by the sound of distant thunder. Rain was on its way.

We stopped halfway down in front of an empty slab. Light from within illuminated a sheet-covered glass door.

I'd done that with my first apartment when I couldn't afford curtains. They'd been gingham with little blue flowers, and Mom had been horrified. She'd gone home that night and made me a whole set for the place.

Beckett pulled a walkie-talkie from his bulky coat and muttered into it.

A movement inside and another of the WWE opened the door.

We all piled in.

I'm sure if I could smell in this state I'd have had a noseful of stale Chinese. Empty boxes littered a card table in the kitchen. Several half-empty liters of Coke and Sprite were on the counter. All the cabinets were open and empty.

I could hear the hum of the refrigerator just under the sound of Final Jeopardy.

"Hey, boss," someone with a throaty voice and Savannah drawl spoke from the other room as Rollins stepped in.

"McGee," Rollins said.

I moved past them all to stand in the corner of the living room. This room wasn't much better decorated than the kitchen. A couple of collapsible chairs, thirteen-inch television, and lots of beer cans.

There was an ashtray near one of the chairs, and a cigarette smoldered in it. Glad I couldn't smell. *Ick.*

I was beginning to wonder why we were here. Was Daniel already kidnapped?

"What's up?" one of the residents asked. He'd been sitting closest to the television and now stood, proudly displaying his gun holster. He was a grizzled-looking man, with baggy black slacks and a soiled white shirt that looked as if the buttons were going to explode at any second.

Deadly weapons for anyone caught in the blast of those things.

"I came to see her."

Wait . . . *her?*

Rollins kept his hands in his pockets. "And to congratulate you on your stealth in apprehension. There's been no word on the local news."

The man nodded and smiled, exposing perfect white teeth. "I do my job well. A few of my men claimed they saw that contract dude you mentioned."

Rollins's expression darkened for a second. "Where? Here?"

"No, near the school where we swiped her. Barnard said the guy was just standing there, watching. When he looked back, the guy was gone. All spooky-like."

"You don't realize how spooky. But it means we need to move her now." He nodded to a door on the wall opposite the kitchen. "She in there?"

"Snug as a bug."

She. Her. No Daniel? Damn. I'd been prepared to rescue Daniel, be the heroine and all. I moved through the door before they did.

It was a bedroom, with another door on the opposing wall that was either a closet or bathroom (I was thinking bathroom since I'd not seen one out there—and with the amount of beer these guys were drinking—*ew*).

A single lamp on a pressboard nightstand illuminated the room. A single bed had been set up in the center beside the nightstand.

And on that bed struggled a small girl. No older than maybe ten. She wore the white shirt and plaid, pleated skirt of a private school uniform. Her hands were bound together, then pulled over her head and fastened to the bed somehow—probably the frame.

Her feet were also securely bound, and her mouth was covered in duct tape.

I blinked a few times as the vision of this girl mingled with the vision I'd had of my own body. Held helpless. Gagged. Unable to move. Were these assholes going to rape this little girl?

A shiver attacked my spine. Or had they already?

Christ . . . I needed to get her out of there!

Remember how I said sometimes kids could see me? Which is why I prefer to have clothes on? Well, this kid wasn't one of them. I waved and said "Psssst" over and over as low as I could.

Nada.

She was trying so very hard to get free and crying hard, if a bit muffled.

I wanted to let her know I was there—that I wasn't going to let this keep happening, even though I really wasn't sure what my plan was. Rollins and his goons were on the other side of that door—and I was just an astral presence.

There really wasn't much I could do physically—

Wait. Ah—I must have hit my head harder than I thought last night. I *can* become physical. Oh duh. I'd only done it once, so there was that little worried moment where I wasn't sure if I could do that again.

I heard a key in the lock.

And right now wasn't the right time to experiment. Being physical in front of these guys wasn't my first choice. Since I didn't know what being physical meant—I sure as hell didn't want to end up like her.

Or shot.

Okay, now I had to really consider this. If I were physical, and then shot, would it affect my physical body? Or would the bullet just pass through? Wait—hadn't I wondered that before?

Beckett stepped across the threshold.

Now wasn't the time to really worry about that. I backed up into the farthest corner, hoping to become as invisible as possible.

Tiny came in, as well as the grizzly one called McGee. The little girl tried harder to get free.

Rollins came in then, and I went ice-cold at the predatory smile on his face. *Oh God ew.* Was the Reverend a pedophile as well? Had these goons grabbed him some poor child for his personal amusement?

Why was it that as a spirit like this, I couldn't open an astral can of whup-ass like in the movie *Poltergeist* and do some damage?

Of course, there were some other things in that movie that were just too gross, even for me. I'd not been able to eat steak for a long time after it crawled across the counter and spewed maggots.

I guess I couldn't be a superhero because those were the movies, not real life. Guess that sort of said something about my state of real life, huh?

Rollins immediately went to the little girl and put a hand on her leg. *Pervert!*

A vibration traveled through my body and I paused. Okay, that was new. Was that a tremor? Some signal that was new that I'd been out of my body too long? I checked my watch. No, I'd been out an hour and a half, almost two. And I hadn't been solid. So I still had over two hours to go.

Right? Or had that changed too?

"There, there. Stop struggling. I'll have you free of those ropes soon, and you'll have a room to play in with lots and lots of toys. Would you like that?"

Even in this dim light I could see the indecision on the child's face. Free and lots of toys? That sort of outweighed the scariness of being all cooped up in this room. And tied up I guess. Or it did for a child. For me, I was thinking of toys as torture devices. I had no idea what this pervert was planning on doing with this child, but this was beyond hiring an astral hit man in my opinion. He needed to be arrested and put in a cell with a man who would sodomize him!

She shook her head and tried to say something. I'd thought he'd pull the tape from her mouth.

No. Instead he rose, a smile still glued to that sick face. This guy was an A-plus menace. With this kind of knowledge, Daniel could put him away for life.

So I figured what I needed to do was hang around, see what would happen, and then follow them and report back to the detective. I could catch a cross sign outside, get a street name, travel back through my cord, and call Daniel. Then he could rescue the little girl and book'em, Danno.

That is, if I left this little girl in this monster's hands.

I wasn't sure I could do that. Having been raped in my early twenties, I wasn't sure I'd have survived as easily if I hadn't have been able to escape my body. But I knew not everyone could do that. I didn't want to see her ruined or her childhood taken away from her. It wasn't this little girl's fault she'd been snatched.

Now her parents—where were they?

Rollins nodded to Beckett. "Get her ready—I want her moved tonight. We'll send a message to her father in the morning." He gave a slow smile, and I swear his perfect, white, even teeth glowed in the dim light. "Let Hirokumi suffer tonight—just as I've suffered."

Hirokumi?

I looked back at the girl again—at her beautiful Asian features. She was Koba's daughter! I wanted to punch a duck. Of course—this was one of those "more drastic measures" the asshole had spoken about when I'd been in his office, before all hell broke loose.

So this guy wasn't such a pervert—well he was but not a pedophile—he'd kidnapped the kid to get to Hirokumi. And they were moving her.

I had to stick around and find out where. I also needed to watch my time.

I looked around as they filed out of the room. I should head outside and find the street signs and do my great plan.

The little girl had stopped struggling and was now just sobbing into the gag.

Oh I couldn't stand this. I needed to comfort her—tell her it was going to be all right. But to do that I'd need to go solid, and that would indeed decrease my astral time. But as I watched her, I knew I had no choice. I had to help her.

I'm so stupid. Especially looking back on things.

I closed my eyes and tried to do as I'd done before. Wishing I could talk to this little girl—that she could see me—and that I could touch her. I expected the arm to start burning as it had before, but it didn't.

It didn't work.

Damnit. Was there some secret password that I'd had before and didn't have now? I closed my eyes and tried again, trying to remember what it was I'd done in Fadó's that afternoon. I'd wanted to talk with Daniel.

No, in truth, I'd wanted to kiss Daniel. Really bad. And thinking of kissing Daniel made all the right parts stand at attention, including every astral hair on my body.

The mark on my arm turned to fire.

And in seconds I was corporeal. I knew this because the little girl started talking into her gag. And she was looking at me. I turned to her and put a finger to my lips, trying to get her to be quiet.

Her eyes widened even more and she started mumbling something into the gag again. Actually, it sounded more like she was screaming "look out."

Curse me and my dim-wittedness.

I straightened and turned around, intent on heading outside and getting an exact bead on where we were.

I found myself face-to-face with Trench-Coat.

Blind terror. I'd always yelled at the ditsy heroines on-screen—the ones who hesitated and were captured by the bad guys, because you know, they just shoulda seen that one coming. I'm smarter than that—I always knew I'd be more careful.

Well, I was feeling pretty sympathetic with those ditsy heroines at that point.

I hesitated. Shocked. I hadn't heard him. Sensed him. I should have been able to sense him, shouldn't I have? But there he was, in his black leather coat and black shades.

I started to back up—to say something—but his movements were faster than a cat's and he had his meaty paw wrapped around my throat, cutting off any hope of a scream.

I was solid.

And so was he.

And it hurt! Bruises on bruises.

I couldn't breathe, and I tried to hit him with my fist. I also tried some of those neat defense moves I'd learned during defense class—with the kung fu punch and the twist. But I had no balance, no means of leverage with his hand clamped firmly around my throat.

I also had no air, which was odd because I was technically astral and had no need to breathe—was it my body that struggled for air in the trunk of my car?

The sleeve of his coat melted as fleshy, bloody, snake-like appendages shot out and grabbed at my wrists, my shoulders, and my legs. In seconds I was wrapped in shreds of flesh, blood, and what looked like veins.

I was gonna puke.

Then he raised his arm, lifting me up and into the air. I tried to become ethereal again—tried to concentrate on my cord. I didn't know if my panicked state prevented me from concentrating, or Trench-Coat's chummy embrace did.

I started gasping for air.

I still fought, struggled to get free. I was certain my physical body was choking as well, convulsing as I did to get free—and breathe.

My body! I tried to find my cord, but I couldn't see it. Couldn't sense it. I couldn't relax long enough to let my body pull me back. Was I too far from it?

He was going to kill me—and there wasn't a damned thing I could do about it.

Trench-Coat raised his left hand and I saw the swirling red light (evidently he was ambidextrous on the soul-sucking ability), and I closed my eyes.

No! This was not how things were supposed to go!

Damn it! Goddamnit!

Being this close to death I probably should tidy up my language, but I was also fucking scared. If it took my soul, that meant God wouldn't get it, or Yahweh, or whoever the hell was in charge these days. Would it somehow get trapped inside of baldy here? Would I simply cease to think and feel?

And have pleasant dreams about my cute cop?

Trench-Coat never made a sound. Not even heavy breathing. He did cock his head then, and for the first time I noticed he was still wearing those black shades. I had never seen his eyes. He lowered his left hand, the swirling-eye-of-death disappearing away with it. He smiled, showing perfect white teeth (what is this with the teeth in this story?).

Then something flickered out from between those perfect dentures.

I blinked. *What the hell* . . .

His grin widened—and it flickered again.

Holymotherfucker—it was a forked tongue. A little, bitty, black forked tongue. Just like a snake! He had a forked tongue!

And then he did the ultimate—he pulled me closer to him as he turned his head to the side.

Our noses touched. Smells abruptly poured in from all sides. I smelled the day-old-chicken smell of decay in the house, the earthy scent of mildew in the bathroom nearby, and I smelled *him*.

And he smelled of death. Of mold and earth, bloated flesh.

He kissed me.

I pressed my lips tight against the tongue as it pushed harder and harder to get into my mouth. What horrified me more was my body's betrayal. I was actually excited to have him so near me. I felt warm, overheated. Flushed. My thighs swelled, and I felt a familiar, cloying need to have him closer to me. A part of me.

Inside of me.

Oh God no!

When I resisted my body's urges, one of the fleshy appendages slid over my nose, successful in cutting off my breath.

I saw stars and tried to scream.

I opened my mouth for air as I felt him relax his hold on my throat.

He slid his tongue in deep. I screamed.

And all the world fell silent in a single instant.

19

THE ETHEREAL

EVERYBODY has one of those dissecting stories. You know, it's against my religion to chop this seven-year-dead testosterone-enhanced frog (enhanced because I refuse to believe those things can grow that big in nature—ugh!) ones.

I had mine too. Didn't do it. Got a C+ though. But it wasn't because of the actual cutting part—I'm not that girlie.

It was the smell of the formaldehyde. Twisted my stomach up something terrible. So I got a doctor's excuse—one of the doctors my mom was seeing at the time wrote it out for me. I really didn't care about the grade, just getting out of that room and away from that smell before I hurled was all that mattered.

That smell lingered with me for a while, too.

And it was *that* smell that surrounded my first conscious thoughts as my body convulsed when I slammed back into it.

My second thought was closer to *mygodthisfucking-hurts*.

Or something along those lines. I thought I'd said it out loud, then realized I hadn't heard myself yet.

Knives carved away chunks of flesh as I moved, and it felt as if my bones had somehow broken and snapped and ripped my skin to shreds.

My knees, elbows, and ankles banged painfully into something hard. The sound of pounding metal rang in my ears.

And there was that smell.

Cold. Freezing cold. Naked cold. There was a cold that reached from the top of my head to my toes. I shook so violently I was close to vibrating. Not even the fire searing my joints could warm me up.

I opened my eyes to darkness. Had the temperature dropped outside my car? I reached out to feel the sides. Smooth. Polished. Metallic. Don't remember my trunk feeling like that.

I continued moving my arms up, then to the sides. Fire ignited my joints, my muscles burned as if I'd fiercely exercised the day before. No—this wasn't my trunk.

I was in a box.

I screamed.

Nothing came out. I opened my mouth again and called out for someone, hoping like all hell I wasn't in a coffin.

No. No. Coffins were all satin and cushion, weren't they?

Still nothing came out of my mouth. What the hell?

I banged and banged on the sides—and that's when I realized I was naked.

Butt-naked.

Bare on a metal slab. With only a stiff sheet to cover me. In a metal box.

And the smell of formaldehyde . . .

Oh Jesus . . .

I was in the freak'n morgue!

Oh that did it. Hysteria, thy name is goddess. And I was feel'n the need to lay down some serious power to get the hell out of this box.

First order of business—was there already an autopsy? 'Cause if there was, and I was back in my body—

The name *ghoul* came to mind.

I felt myself up—well—I ran my hands along my chest, over my breasts. No stitches. No cuts. No autopsy yet.

I had to get out of this box.

Drawer. You're in a drawer, girl, not a box. Well what makes a drawer better than a bloody box?

And why wasn't my voice working? Maybe I just couldn't hear it in the box.

Drawer.

Whatever.

I felt around above my head. Bodies were usually put in feet first, right? Or at least that's what I remember from watching *CSI*. That way you could look at their faces when you pulled them out.

So that meant the opener was above my head. Somewhere. Surely they'd have like—a catch or something? An emergency release in case someone gets trapped in one of these things?

Then again, alive people aren't supposed to be *in one of these things.*

I'm not sure if it was my quick finger searching, my constant pounding, or that maybe the medical examiner's assistant didn't close the door all the way, but the drawer abruptly opened.

The formaldehyde smell flooded the interior of my cell, but I didn't care. I hadn't realized how stale the air had been inside the box.

Drawer.

Box-drawer.

Shaking, I reached out through the crack and grabbed at the upper edge, pressing down to push the drawer forward, sliding naked me out into the open.

Only a few fluorescent lights pulsed slightly above me, but they were bright enough to make me blink repeatedly. I assumed it was still night—and everyone was home and tucked in their beds. But oh no—not me. I'm in a drawer!

Box.

I'd never been in a morgue before. It was perhaps the length of three of the larger SUVs on the market, at least from my half-prone perspective. I felt exposed as I pushed myself up into a sitting position and gripped the single, flimsy, starched sheet. I was on a slab extended from the wall, in the middle of three columns with three rows that made up one wall of the room.

Not all of the wall. If I leaned out a little. I saw a sink with a high-arched faucet. Two bare examination tables—the kinds with hoses on one end and big octopus lights overhead—sat in the center. I saw several gurneys over to the right against a wall of shelves. The gurneys were occupied with sheet-shrouded bodies.

This was nuts.

I called out for someone as I looked down to see my bare feet dangle over the drawer's edge.

Nothing came out of my mouth again. I put a hand to my throat and winced. It was still sore and raw. Had Mitsuri done more damage than we thought and somehow damaged my voice? Or had being stuffed in the cold in my car's trunk made me catch a major case of laryngitis?

I opened my mouth and just yelled. Nothing. I heard air passing through, but no sound. Well—I didn't have time for this. I was cold, hungry, damp (had they had me on one of those tables and hosed me off just before I woke up?), scared, hungry, thirsty—

I heard voices and looked in front of me, finally seeing the double doors leading in and out of the morgue. Smoked glass revealed shapes as they passed back and forth.

Yelling out again (*what's with my voice?*), I carefully, if a bit unsteadily, eased myself off the table. My legs refused to support me, and I immediately collapsed onto the floor. Kerplunk.

Well, more like a plop. Me and the sheet. Bare flesh on shiny, cold tile floor. Ow.

Okay—major problems here. Voice was on the fritz as well as my legs. What the hell did the doctors do to me? I checked again to make sure I wasn't cut open in some way. I didn't see the big Y-shaped accessory down my chest. So what the hell was going on?

"Whoa, easy there. You've been out of body too long."

Okay—*that* wasn't me.

I covered my nakedness with my hand—about as well as a fig leaf—and looked around for the voice. It'd been a male voice.

The medical examiner?

I tried to say "hello?" but that didn't come out either.

He seemed to appear from behind me and moved to my right to the rows of cabinets. He was dark-haired and wore a red flannel shirt and jeans. He pulled a dark blue fleece blanket out of the first door he opened, then came directly at me.

I stared up at him as he wrapped the blanket around me. Beautiful, in a sort of outdoorsy way. Long face, short black hair that sort of had that spiked look in front and at the crown.

"There," he said in his nice voice. He smelled of soap and antiseptic. "Getting warm?"

I said yes, but again nothing came out of my mouth, so I nodded. I still shivered, and I still ached. Mr. Mystery-Hero put his arms around me, around the blanket, and helped me to my feet. With a quick glance at the door, he practically carried me to a desk and sat me upright in the chair.

After rearranging the blanket around me, he grabbed a stethoscope from the desk, shoved it into his ears, and placed the ice-cold end on my chest. "Hold still and breathe."

I did as he asked, though I hadn't been able to stop shivering. My teeth chattered.

He listened a few seconds, then pulled a penlight from his back pocket. He shined it in my left eye, then my right. "Okay, pupils are dilated and fixed, which is normal, at least for you as of now." He looked directly at me as he pushed a strand of hair out of my face. "I'm sorry about you waking up *in* the drawer. I'd intended on having you out of it when I restarted your heart, but I had unexpected company and had to hide." He smiled, and it only improved his looks. "It's a good thing you didn't return when the ME was in the room. I'm afraid having a corpse pound on the drawer might have sent the old geezer into cardiac arrest."

I tried to ask him who he was. I tried asking him where I was. I demanded to know why I couldn't talk. In the end, I only managed to sob. And even that was quiet.

What the hell was happening?

"Hey, hey, shhhh." He folded me in his arms again, and though he was warm and alive, I was still cold, and damned scared. "That's one hell of a wacky tattoo you've got on your arm there, girl."

As he pulled me away, he touched my neck with soft hands, gently moving my head to the right so he could shine his penlight. "But that bruise necklace you've got there isn't a tattoo, is it? But that's not why you're in here."

I sniffed and shook my head. I tried speaking again. I could feel the air moving through my vocal cords, but there was no sound. Not even a squeak.

After I tried to sign to him that I needed a pen and

paper, his eyebrows arched up. "Wow, are you deaf?" He licked his lips, then said in slow loud words. "You. Are. Deaf?"

Why is it when people think you're deaf they believe shouting will break through the physical challenge? Duh.

I shook my head and tried again to ask him who and what he was. Nothing. Not even a squeak. AHHHHH!

And what was with this headache?

"Can. You. Write?!"

I nodded, and if I could have bitch-slapped his pretty face, I would have. He leaned to my right and picked up a pharmaceutical pad and pen from the desk. With the worst, shakiest penmanship I'd ever seen at my own hand, I wrote, I AM NOT DEAF. STOP FUCKING SHOUTING!!

He smiled at me without even a trace of resentment or anger. "Feisty. That's good. You're gonna need it. You're Zoë Martinique? I found your driver's license in your purse."

I nodded. AND YOU? WHAT ARE YOU?

Another smile. "Call me Joe. I don't actually work here at the hospital. I sort of work—tangentially—with the morgue. During my off-hours." He looked away and sort of muttered to himself. "I was expecting one of the newcomers to wake and give me at least some clue on who popped him."

What? Huh?

HOW DID U KNOW I WASN'T DEAD?

He shrugged. "Let's just say I know these things. I'll tell you about it sometime. I mainly try and help kids, junkies, who end up taking a walk on the astral due to drugs or something." Joe narrowed his eyes at me. "But you didn't do this with drugs. You're the real thing, aren't you?"

I frowned as the ache in the back of my head shot into the back of my eyes. THE REAL WHAT?

"My grandma used to talk about people like you. But

the way she described your kind, you're much prettier in the flesh. I'm disappointed I didn't get to see you out of that flesh." He grinned. "Though you do have nice flesh, if a bit goose-pimply."

I had no idea what this man was talking about. I set the pad and paper in my lap and put my hands to my head.

"Headache. Unfortunate side effect, I'm afraid. Not exactly from the cocktail I shot you with, but from being out of your body. I'm guessing from the muscle lethargy— meaning your inability to stand up or walk at the moment— you've been out a long time—long enough for them to wheel you down here with a toe tag. I've seen it before, Zoë. You're lucky I was in the ER when you were brought in. Otherwise, you'd have one hell of a Y incision right now."

Yay. You want a freak'n medal? Tiny gnomes with pick-axes mined the interior of my skull. I reached for the pad and pen again. COCKTAIL? WHAT HAPPENED? WHY CAN'T I TALK?

He shifted onto his knees as he stayed at eye level with me, though I'm sure it had to be killing his calves. "The cocktail is my own special recipe. Helps kick the junkies back into their bodies. Usually they hop off the gurneys in the hallway before they're identified and processed. As for what happened." He stood and went to the still-open drawer where I'd woken. Joe pulled a clipboard from the outside and scanned it.

"Well, seems your car was found near 285 at Roswell Road. It'd been vandalized. Police received an anonymous call about a dead body in the trunk." He smiled as he set the clipboard back and returned to me. He knelt. "Apparently the thugs that messed up your car had a conscience and called it in."

My car. Oh shit. Vandalized. I guessed it was those kids I'd seen before getting in the trunk. Had they hot-wired it and taken it to Sandy Springs? I could only imagine it was missing everything from the CD player to the tires and hubcaps. Greeeeat.

"As for your voice"—he frowned—"that I'm not sure of. I don't think it's from whoever choked you. The fatigue you're going to feel, if it hasn't already hit you, is because of the physical stress you put on your body by being away from it."

He wasn't kidding about the fatigue. It'd been building, accumulating like weight placed on my shoulders by small increments as I sat there, in the morgue, somewhere in Atlanta.

That's when I noticed them. Gauzy shadows at first, lingering here and there. Until a few of them took on more solid shapes. They stood by the double doors, the morgue drawers, and one of them looked over Joe's shoulder at the clipboard.

Men, women, some old, some very young. Monochromatic shadows whose features melted and re-formed as if made of smoke, blown by an unseen wind.

Joe moved beside me, disturbing one of the shadows. A tiny girl, perhaps no more than six, with large eyes, pigtails. She clutched a bear in her left arm. They looked like Joseph Maddox had. Simply shadows.

My rescuer reached up to my face with both hands and forced me to look at him. "You see them, don't you?" He pulled his hands away.

I nodded, aware of the increasing number of them. They started filling the room.

"Zoë, they're nothing more than Shades, do you understand me? They're being drawn to you—they're how I knew you were different earlier. They can't hurt you."

I scribbled. ARE THEY SOULS?

He nodded. "Only Shades of souls, of people who died here either violently, or unprepared."

THEY'RE LOOKING AT ME.

"I know. I don't know why. You're—different—somehow." Joe put a hand to my cheek. Warm. Calloused. He was a laborer. Protector. "God you're pretty, even with those dark circles under your eyes. When did you leave your body?"

I scribbled it down. ABOUT 7:40 P.M.

His eyes widened. "Seven forty *Friday* night? Holy shit—you've been gone nearly twenty-four hours, did you know that?"

I blinked. Say what?

"It's after eight on Saturday night, Miss Martinique. That's more than twenty-four hours. That's just not possible—most astral walkers stay away from their bodies only three to five hours, max."

Twenty-four hours? That wasn't possible, was it? Hell, no wonder I couldn't stand, and every movement took my full concentration. The pain waking in my muscles and joints made the little needle pain from before seem like a minor paper cut.

The Shades continued to increase in number. They pressed closer, merged around Joe. He said they couldn't hurt me, but did they know that?

I only vaguely wondered why or how this guy knew I'd astral traveled (I like how he called me an astral walker). My thoughts concentrated on why I'd been OOB for so long—what had I been doing? I remembered the trunk of my car, and the teenagers, then the trunk of a limo and—

That insane memory of mine brought it all back. All of it. *He'd* been there. In the little girl's room.

Hirokumi's daughter! They were going to move her. Probably already had. And Trench-Coat had stopped me from seeing where they'd move her to. I remembered his face, his hand on my neck, and the twisting, almost sensual snakes that moved from his hands.

I remembered his lips on mine, and his tongue sliding between my lips and into my soul . . .

The Shades reached out to me. Hundreds of gray shadows wanting to touch me.

"Zoë!" Joe hissed.

I was shaking even worse now as I pushed myself back into the chair, my gaze tracking the Shades as my mind refused to believe what I remembered. The pad and pencil clattered to the tiled floor. The memories . . . they were too much. This thing, this Symbiont, had obviously taken me—*and I'd enjoyed it.* I had flashes of being caressed, of rough hands touching my breasts, squeezing my nipples.

And I smelled death. Decay.

They were touching me. They were *touching* me!

I started to scream, but Joe put a hand over my mouth. He had his arms around me, his mouth close to my ear. "Miss Martinique, you're going to have to calm down. Listen to me. The doctor's on his way here with family, probably yours. They won't find my compound in your body, but they *are* going to examine you, because you were clinically dead. I'm going to be around to keep an eye on you. Do you understand me?"

I did, and I didn't. My mind kept mixing his face with Trench-Coat's. And then with Daniel. And all of these people packed into one room. My God . . . how many of the dead lingered in this morgue?

We both heard a voice near the door and turned to look, but I couldn't see past the crowds of Shades. I heard a man's voice, and a woman's.

Mom?

Joe released me and sat back into the closest of the Shades. "It's showtime, Zoë. You're going to be okay, but it's going to hurt like nothing you've ever experienced before. But it'll go away. The longer you sleep, the more you eat, the faster your soul and body will mend. Do you understand?"

What was he? How had I survived for that long? Where had I been?

I think I knew the answer to that last question, but I didn't want to think about it. Oh God, I couldn't think about that . . . even as the sensations of fingertips over my skin returned as a dark, pleasant memory. Of my hands roaming over smooth, hard muscles—ice-cold flesh.

I'd been with him!

Two elderly men with white hair and white coats preceded my mom into the morgue, moving through the Shades. The crowds of shadows swirled like mist and moved away. The two men stopped in their tracks as they saw me, looked at the open drawer, then looked back at me.

Dead girl sitting up.

Mom rushed in and knelt on the floor beside me before I could take a breath. The pounding behind my eyes pounded harder, and I was squinting. And shaking. I never stopped shaking.

The crowd of Shades moved in again. Closer. Hands out. Begging—begging for what?

Fire. It started behind my eyes. I blinked, and blinked. It spread to my hips. Shaking. Trembling.

She was kissing me, hugging me. Then she thumped me on the back of the head. *OW!*

"They said you were dead—they found you *dead*."

Yes and no . . . but if you don't stop squeezing me so hard, I will be.

I opened my mouth and tried to tell her, but again, there was nothing. She frowned at me, her eyes searching mine, just as a few more people in scrubs and white coats stepped into the morgue.

I noticed the pad and pen on the floor and motioned for Mom to give it to me. Shades' hands tried to take my own, and I batted them away as I scribbled down the information for Daniel and pressed the note into her hands. My joints scraped, bone on bone, as if the cartilage had been sucked out from between them. But I wrote the note. I gave her as pleading a look as I could. I mouthed the words "give this to Daniel" as best as I could.

Then for added effect I took the paper and scribbled Daniel's name on the other side and the word *hurry!*

And so like my mommy dearest, Nona shoved the note into the front of her blouse, over her left boob. Those two endowments had always served Mom well—especially when it came to hiding things. Who was going to go in there after something?

Not me.

One of the men took one look at me, saw the tag on my toe, and turned to the door. He hit a red button beside the door, and a bell sounded from somewhere.

What? Was that the oops-they're-not-dead-yet alarm?

My back lurched, and I was thrown from the chair, the blanket the only cushion beneath me. The shaking took on a frantic pace as my body woke. I could only imagine these were the throes of my soul fitting itself back into its suit.

My suit.

"Honey . . . Zoë . . . what's wrong?" Mom's voice was in my ear.

And I was crying suddenly. I don't know why. It might have been because I woke up naked in a morgue drawer.

And I couldn't speak!

Mom held me as the horror of what had happened to me in that little house near Hollowell Parkway overwhelmed me.

And I made not one sound.

The Shades moved away. They looked—frightened.

I saw his tongue again in my mind.

More men and woman in scrubs came through the door along with a gurney. One guy pushed in two rolling stands with clear bags hanging from them. I kept banging against the floor, over and over as my body lurched and jerked like some ungodly beached fish. Hands pushed Mom away, then they were on me, steadying me.

Someone pressed something in my mouth and kept my tongue from folding back into my throat.

Fire. Pain. Agony. My blood turned to acid in my veins, and if I'd had a voice, I would have screamed as I felt my arteries and muscles melt and burn away as my blood touched everything.

Everything.

I thought of that tongue snaking down my throat. I remembered Trench-Coat holding up the swirling red hand of death . . . and how he'd put it down as if he'd changed his mind.

"What's wrong with her?" my mother wailed.

I tried to call out to her—but I no longer controlled my body. It was as if it were fighting me. My soul.

Liquid agony!

Hang in there . . . you can do this. It was his voice. Joe's voice. Soothing. In my ear.

Joe!

The men picked me up and put me on the table. The pain cracked my head open like a thunderstorm releasing its rain.

Trench-Coat had done something else to me— something other than taking my soul.

"Get her still!"

Voices, voices, voices . . .

One woman pressed an ice-cold stethoscope onto my chest as another one swabbed my left arm. People held me down. I felt the pinch of a needle, and I tried to tell them to stop. I lurched. I flopped. I had no control.

"You got a handle on the tremors?" one of them said.

The female grabbed a penlight and pried my lids open,

shining the light in my eyes. "Her pupils are dilated. Non-responsive."

"Heartbeat's erratic," the one with the stethoscope said. He told the one with the needle what to put it in my arm.

I didn't want them to do anything. I wanted my mommy. I wanted Joe to tell them to leave me alone! I opened my mouth and screamed at them to stop.

One of them placed a stupid oxygen mask over my face instead. I could hear my mother from somewhere, demanding to know what was happening.

I was looking up into the face of the one with the oxygen. He smiled at me. His face darkened, and Trench-Coat stood over me, naked, warm, and alive.

You are mine now . . .

I saw his lips move, watched them in slow motion as he caressed my lips with his thumb. I knew his voice. Had heard it all of my life.

I knew that voice!

Everything dimmed, faded to black.

Trench-Coat had taken part of me with him.

It was mine!

I closed my eyes as the doctors worked.

He'd stolen my voice.

20

A corridor of hollowed rock stretched out before me. It grew longer and darker the faster I ran. I pushed myself as hard as I could. Disembodied arms, some with flesh, some skeletal, stuck out from the sides of the corridor, and as I ran past them, they tried to grab me. I could hear Rhonda's stereo blaring out Assemblage 23's "Disappoint."

Nails tore at my skin, digging deep rivets into my flesh. Blood oozed over my bare flesh and coated my body, but I continued to run.

Because he was behind me.

He wanted me, small parts at a time. And once he had all of me—there would be nothing left.

His laugh bounced from the walls as I turned a sharp right, and the corridor abruptly stretched out again, elongating as I stood there, panting, watching.

Trench-Coat was there, faint in the distance at first, then drawing closer. Materializing as a movement of shadows at first, and then drawing form as he flew at me.

I gave a silent scream and turned to run back the way I'd come.

But the way was barred. There was no corridor. There was only a wall. I was trapped.

He was there before me. I saw swirling, undulating tattoos covering his bald head where I'd not seen them before. He walked steadily, evenly.

Calmly.

I pressed myself as far back into the wall as I could, willing myself back to my body. Any body!

"There, there," he said.

He spoke.

In my voice!

He reached out and took up a lock of my hair as it fell over my bare left breast. Trench-Coat brought it to his nose. The hair dissolved in his fingers, became a green mist, which he inhaled deeply. He looked at me with white eyes. No pupils. "You're marked now. You are mine. I will devour you piece by piece—and when you are gone—we will become something greater, more powerful than any being that dwelleth upon my master's realm."

I screamed.

He jumped forward and pressed his mouth onto mine.

I felt him pulling me into him. I heard his voice, my voice, in my mind.

Die!

GAH!

Okay—that dream just totally blew chunks.

I expected to wake up in a hospital bed again, with tubes and a beep-beep machine and the call of doctors stat and to which OR over hidden intercoms.

And I wasn't disappointed either.

Wasn't my life just fun? I sure hoped my insurance was paid up.

This time there were tubes in my nose and down my throat. I immediately went to work on those. I can't stand anything in my nose—I even have trouble with shooting sinus medicine up there.

But of course I accidentally jarred something, and that brought several nurses. I was threatened with restraints if I didn't leave things alone.

Mean people.

The edges of the nightmare started to fade.

I sort of remember sleeping again, with no dreams. And then I was awake and watching the nurse change a clear plastic bag over my head.

I tried to talk to her. I tried to move my arm again as I had before, to get her attention.

Abruptly I was out of my body, standing to the side of the bed, *behind* the nurse.

What the fuck?

Going out of body took time and preparation. At least a good five minutes or so of deep breathing, sometimes ten if I couldn't get my head quiet. But . . . I'd just done it in minus seconds flat!

I looked down at my stomach for the cord. Whew . . . and it was there. Still attached at my solar plexus and streaming nonstop to my body on the bed.

That's when I saw myself.

Holy shit.

I looked awful. Gaunt. Pale as a college jock's full moon. The white streak at my temple was back—the artificial color gone. And it was wider. Thicker. And Joe hadn't been kidding about those dark circles beneath my eyes.

It wasn't near as bad an experience as when I'd seen myself after the rape. Not a lot of plastic. Only one beep-beep machine. I sort of looked like I was sleeping. The scene sort of looked calm.

No—it was all different somehow.

In that instant I realized *everything* was different.

From the beginning I'd always been amazed how similar being in my body was to being out of it. You know, that things looked the same, except for me seeing people's colors sometimes. What Mom called their auras or energy fields.

But the sounds, the usual colors, even the textures, had all been the same in both worlds.

Not anymore. Everything had a dingy cast to it now. Like it was all dusted in soot. And the soot moved just slightly, like smoky tendrils of mist, the smoke just after a candle was snuffed.

And there was sound now. Echoing murmurs, like millions of people all mumbling in their sleep. It was above me, below me, around me. Not too loud, but audible. I could pick out a moan here, or a scream there. A snippet of conversation.

And something moved around me, undulated in the air and brushed against the hairs on my body.

The nurse finished with the bag, checked my pupils with a penlight, then left the room, moving *through* me.

Gah . . . she had her lover tied up in the basement?

Sick, sick, sick . . .

I turned and left the room as well, but stopped just outside my door and put my hand to my mouth.

Shadows moved back and forth along the hallway. Sooty black Shades of elderly men and women, and children, in short hospital gowns, sieved through the walls, in and out of rooms, through the nurses and orderlies as they moved metal trays up and down the corridor. I'd seen them in the morgue—but not like this. Not in such numbers!

Joe. Joe had known what had happened. He'd been

there—he'd brought me back. I needed to find him, and he'd said he'd be watching me, right? Or had I dreamed that? But where would I find him? I didn't even know his last name. Would he still be in the morgue? Would someone here know who he was?

I looked to my right, and then my left. I saw the nurses' station as well as the familiar outline of my mom. I started to run toward her, a beacon of light in the midst of all the shadow.

And I stopped in my tracks. Mom really *was* a beacon. Her body seemed to pulse with a golden light that moved up through the top of her head and then back down again. My feet took several hesitant steps closer to the station where I saw her talking to the nurse behind the counter.

I spotted Rhonda nearby in a chair, her laptop pulled open and her many-ringed fingers punching away. She to seemed to pulse with light, only it was darker, more purple than Mom's. I'd never seen these colors before.

Even the nurses pulsed with softer light, like dimmed versions of Mom's thousand-watt-ness.

And through all the light the shadows of people moved back and forth, like a dark wheat moving with the wind.

"Take me," a voice hissed to my left. "Please . . . take me . . ."

A small, wilted little lady in a wheelchair was staring up at me with tiny, black button eyes. The wrinkles in her face came together in a sweet but sad smile. But superimposed on her face was a skull.

A death mask.

Behind her stood a much younger man, maybe her son, dressed in a military uniform. He had short-cropped dark hair and a white smile. He put his hand on her shoulder. She didn't seem to notice.

But of course she wouldn't. He was a shadow. Though he seemed, somehow, more alive than the Shades around him. At least he had some color to him. Kinda like that spot color they used in films these days.

The lady reached out to me, her hand precariously balanced on arms no thicker than matchsticks. "Please—take me to my husband. I'm ready . . . I'm so tired."

I looked at the man standing behind her.

"Please, take her," he said. Ah—this was her husband, not her son. His voice was melodic, and peaceful. "I'm here, and I'm waiting."

I opened my mouth to speak, but of course there was nothing there. I looked pleadingly at the man behind her and touched my throat. I mouthed the words "Take her?"

He seemed to understand. "I know." (He did? Well freak'n fill me in on this plot twist!) "Don't look at it as a loss, but as a gain. The universe balances things out in its own way. For what you lost, you received. And that, my lady, is a gift more rewarding."

And he was gone.

And I had no freak'n idea what it was he meant.

The little lady was watching me. Her hand was still stretched out.

For what you lost, you received.

I took her hand in mine. Light. Incredible blinding light. Orgasmic euphoria filled my body, and I was lifted from my astral feet. I felt myself float in midair and thought I heard the sound of sobbing.

And then it all dimmed to a dull roar of harrowed excitement. I still stood where I'd been, but the woman had collapsed to the floor, and there were nurses and doctors moving over her like a small swarm of ants.

I moved to the side, careful not to let them move through my body. When I looked up I saw Mom staring at me. Rhonda had stood as well. She held her laptop in her right hand, her mouth open, her kohl-rimmed eyes wide.

Guilt pushed me backward, and I turned and ran. I

moved through the wall of my room and I dove as hard as I could back into my body.

It arched on the bed and took in a deep breath . . . and felt better.

Much better.

And I slept. A deep, healthy, dreamless sleep.

IT was Monday afternoon before I woke again. The nurse was back, changing my little IV bag again. The headache was all but a rumor and I felt—better. Of course, no one would listen to me, as I still didn't have my voice back. Three different doctors saw me within an hour before the nurse returned with a message from my mom. She and Rhonda were on their way over.

The door opened, but it wasn't Rhonda. Or Mom. I'd hoped it might be Joe. I really needed to find him and strangle some answers out of him.

Daniel came in. He had a bouquet of flowers in his hand. Again.

He also had a wrapped present. Goody!

The detective leaned forward and kissed my forehead. Yeah, well, I guess the mouth was out of the question, seeing as how the tube up my nose was probably a put-off, as well as my breath.

I really wanted to brush the socks off my teeth.

The package turned out to be a small dry-erase board and pen. I scribbled out WHAT'S THIS?

He smiled. "A means to better communicate. I'm not sure how laryngitis works, but I'm pretty sure you shouldn't try to use your voice."

Now how do I tell the bugger I didn't have laryngitis?

"And I like the new look. Bonnie Raitt?" He nodded at me and reached out to touch my left temple. His hand came back with a very thick mass of white hair.

Oi! I grabbed it away from him and pulled it out where I could see it. White. A thick chunk of soft white strands.

"I'm glad you're okay, Zoë."

ME TOO—THOUGH WAKING UP IN A MORGUE COFFIN IS A BIT UPSETTING.

"Drawer. You were in a drawer."

Erase. Scribble. FUCK YOU.

He smiled and pulled the piece of paper from his back pocket, the one I'd scribbled the message to him on. He held it up for me. "How did you know?"

KNOW WHAT?

"Zoë—no one knows Hirokumi's daughter's been kidnapped. Yet you did—you wrote this for me, right?"

I nodded.

"Remember the phone call I got Friday night? It was about Susan, the daughter. She'd been taken from school that day, her bodyguards shot. I had to get to the station. We kept it quiet—out of the news.

"And then you went missing and no one knew where you were, till some guy called the station reporting a dead body in the trunk of a car, then you show up half-naked in a morgue and I get this note telling me Hirokumi's daughter had been kidnapped by Rollins. How did you know this?"

Okay—truth or dare. I chose truth, 'cause to be honest, I think I'd overmaxed out my dare quota for the month.

I took a deep breath and wrote. I WENT TO SPY ON ROLLINS.

"Oh shit . . . Zoë-ëëëë . . ."

AND I FOLLOWED HIM TO A HOUSE SOMEWHERE ON HOLLOWELL PARKWAY. I DIDN'T KNOW ABOUT THE GIRL—HONEST!

Daniel looked at me like I was a tiny fish. I think he was deciding whether to keep me or throw me back. "And?"

I SAW HER.

"You wrote that in your note—but where is she?"

THEY WERE GOING TO MOVE HER. I WAS GO-
ING TO CALL YOU—THAT'S WHEN I WAS AT-
TACKED AND THROWN IN MY CAR.

Okay—so—a little white lie.

But it sure sounded better and more believable than the
truth.

"They saw you." He took a deep breath. "And they
thought they'd killed you. I'm assuming they're the ones
that vandalized your car, not some joyriders."

Uh. Sure. Why not?

"You saw Rollins?"

YES.

"With Susan?"

I pointed to the board. No need rewriting it. YES.

He frowned. "Did they choke you?"

Uh . . . *point.* YES.

And in a manner Trench-Coat had. Only with lots of
fleshy tentacles.

Ew.

He reached out and took my hand, the one with the
marker in it. "Zoë, we searched the area you scribbled
down, and we didn't find anything."

THEY MOVED HER. CHECK HIS HOUSE.

He rubbed his face with his hand. "See, the problem is
evidence. I can say all day long that Rollins kidnapped
Susan, but I have no proof of this. No one saw him at her
school. There's no reason for a search warrant.

"The only person that saw him was you—and they
think you're dead. I have to get more solid, concrete evidence against Rollins."

I pursed my lips. I CAN TESTIFY.

He smiled but shook his head. "We need more than
that. I need something solid just to get the search warrant—
and I need to do it before Rollins moves her again *if* she's
in his house."

I set the pen on the bed and bent my fingers. They were cramping up. This form of communication sucked.

"You stay here."

I shook my head. HOME.

"Okay. You go home. I'll make sure you stay put this time though."

YOU GONNA HANDCUFF ME?

"Don't tempt me, Zoë. Right now you're my only witness and my only lead in this. I need you safe." He smiled. "I would ask Nona to give me a hand watching over you." His expression darkened for an instant.

I didn't understand his hesitation. IS SOMETHING WRONG W/MOM?

"No, not with her. There was an incident this morning, pretty early, with an elderly patient she'd been talking to."

I instantly knew who he was talking about. The lady in the wheelchair. The one that I touched. WHAT HAPPENED? I wanted to know what it *appeared* happened from the other side, and not through the eyes of a Wraith.

Daniel shrugged, shook his head. "An elderly woman, sitting in a wheelchair just down the hall. Witnesses say she reached out to something—one nurse said she thought maybe she was talking to her dead husband—then she just fell out of the wheelchair. Dead."

Dead.

I remembered the bright light. The incredible feeling of euphoria. How much better I felt—and something else came to me. Deep, overwhelming sadness. A feeling I'd touched something I'd never be allowed to know except in brief glimpses—tiny teasing tastes of peace. I reached up and touched my neck.

Daniel watched me, and his expression brightened. "Wow, even your bruises faded. Looks like the hospital did you some good."

And then he did kiss me. I held my breath, careful not

to breathe on him in case of halitosis. He didn't seem to notice as he pulled back and put a hand to my chin. "You look a hundred percent better now than you did yesterday. Please be careful, Zoë Martininque. You make me laugh, and you confuse the hell out of me. And get better—I want to hear that sexy voice again."

And he left.

I looked down at my board and erased it. He wanted to hear my voice again.

How was I going to tell him some bald guy in a trench coat stole it?

How was I going to tell him that I didn't know if I'd ever get it back?

21

"WHO'S Joe?"

I gave Tim a confused look. Apparently I was going to have to learn to communicate with action and expression. I'd learned the middle finger wasn't exactly making people cooperate with me.

And my expression of frustration—though understood—wasn't appreciated either.

After the doctors released me—after much protesting—but I was technically okay—Mom and Rhonda took me back to the botanica and tea shop. It was just after nine o'clock Monday evening when we arrived, and in the darkness I'd noticed the black-and-white Atlanta cop car parked outside the house along Euclid Avenue. Mom had said they were Officers Mastiff and Harding and would be staying there, compliments of Captain Cooper.

So Cooper believed Daniel, or at least had some bit of faith in his suspicions. Maybe that was good, though I wasn't happy with the watchdogs.

Not that they could really contain me.

Heh—heh—heh.

Other than the distant introduction to the nice police-men when we arrived, Mom hadn't spoken much. She hadn't really looked at me either. Hadn't even asked me what had happened, either at the Park 'n' Ride, or at the hospital with the elderly lady I learned was Delia DeAngelo.

In fact, the only people who'd spoken more than two words to me were Tim and Steve.

I heard the wind banging against the house with the occasional bonk of a pinecone or a sweet-gum burr as it hit the roof or a window. Bundled up in fleece and blankets, I could feel the cold through the foundation of the house itself.

I felt fine. Tired maybe. Insanely cold. But I'd walked the distance to the house from the car on my own, with almost a bounce to my step. Everything seemed to be working—except my voice.

Though the handprint on my arm had turned from a bright red to a dark gray, light tattoo style, it was still there. It no longer ached or burned. And apparently the shock of white hair framing the left side of my face was also going to stick around.

Thanksgiving was less than a week away, and the hardwood trees around the avenue and behind the house were nearly bare.

I also felt as if I'd missed something else. It'd been a long time since Mom had been mad enough to be silent. At least I was too old for a spanking.

Maybe.

I thought again about Susan. I could see the fear in that small, pale face. How her eyes had widened when I'd spoken to her. She'd seen Trench-Coat when he'd appeared behind me.

And seeing such a horrible creature—I was terrified that even if Hirokumi paid the ransom for whatever it was Rollins wanted—Susan Hirokumi wouldn't be returned alive.

I had no proof of this—it was just a feeling.

And my thoughts never strayed too far away from the mysterious Joe. I had no last name, no number, no idea who or even what he was. What he did have was knowledge, and I needed that. Desperately.

Once at Mom's, Rhonda went into the back of the tea shop and started hot water boiling. I moved to one of the cozy couches by the fireplace, which Mom had left burning to come get me.

Steve carried the tea tray and set it on the white wicker coffee table. He was getting better at manipulation. He stepped forward and kissed my forehead, which is something he did very rarely. The flutter of butterfly's wings against my solid skin. "You look like hell, gorgeous."

I smiled at him. Rhonda had my board, marker, and eraser.

He bent forward and, to my surprise, lifted the olive green ceramic teapot and poured a cupful of golden, steaming liquid. "Nona called ahead and had me make this special for you. It'll ease the aches and pains."

I smiled. I needed my board so I could tell him I didn't have any more aches and pains.

Not after I touched that old lady.

Mom had disappeared upstairs.

Rhonda came back in, her iBook in her hands. "Here." She sat beside me and opened the laptop. A blank Word document appeared. "Type out everything that happened. That'll be easier than trying to write it out on that board."

I nodded and shifted my legs around to hold it in my lap. I'm a pretty decent typist when I concentrate, and once I got started on the events, I didn't stop.

When I'd finished, ending it with Mrs. DeAngelo and her dead husband, I hit save. I looked up to see that Mom was sitting in one of the chairs across from me. She was watching the fire, a cup in her hand. Rhonda was stoking the fire.

I set the laptop on the coffee table. Rhonda immediately set the poker aside and grabbed up the iBook before sitting down on the rug with her back to the fireplace and started reading it.

That's when Tim asked his question about Joe. He'd appeared then, hovering over Rhonda's shoulder, reading.

I glared at him and sipped my tea. It really was a good tea. Mellow with a hint of orange. And something I couldn't quite put my finger on.

The small antique clock over the mantel chimed ten o'clock. I waited till everyone was done reading. Mom was last and set the notebook on the floor.

No one spoke. The silence was really getting on my last nerve.

I grabbed up the board where Rhonda had set it beside me and wrote a message. I held it out for Mom to see. She didn't look at it immediately, not until I banged it loudly against the coffee table. The ceramic tea service clanked at the movement.

I felt like some spoiled brat.

I wanted my mother to look at me.

She did. She read the sign and set her mouth in the thinnest line I'd ever seen it in. Nona sat forward then, set her cup on the table, and rested her arms on her thighs. "Am I mad at you? What the hell do you think? Look at you, Zoë! Forty-eight hours ago you were pronounced dead, child. That's the call I got, do you understand that? Then I arrive to see you alive and shaking in a blanket—*in the morgue*! Three hours after they admit you upstairs, they tell me you'd slipped into a diabetic coma and the prognosis looked bad." She stood up, towering over me. "Then I see you in the hallway, and you looked—"

I widened my eyes. Diabetic coma? No one told me that. I didn't remember that. I narrowed my eyes at her when she looked around the room, her hands working into fists. I looked like what?

She sat back down suddenly and put her fists on her knees. Rhonda looked up from her laptop when it looked like Mom wasn't going to finish. "You looked wrong, Zoë. You looked like something from the Abysmal. And then you touched that woman, and she just died."

Mom held up her hand, and Rhonda nodded. "She just dropped dead, right there, Zoë. Then you vanished, and the doctors tell me you're awake and healthy enough to be discharged." She leaned in close to me. "Do *you* think I have a reason to be upset or mad with you?"

I quickly erased my board and rewrote. WOW.

"Oh. Yeah. Wow for you. They tell me you have laryngitis, but we both know that's not true. First that bastard did something to your arm, and you're physical, and now—now you can't speak because you think he shoved his tongue down your throat and stole your voice."

I didn't remember the sensation being that cut-and-dried, and thinking of it raised the temperature in several different parts of my body—parts I didn't want reacting to that thought.

"You have to understand," Rhonda said, and her voice was soft. Which was weird itself—I'd never considered anything about Rhonda as soft. "We were convinced you were going to die. Maddox was sure. Your heart was failing. And then we see"—she sort of waved at me—"what you did in the hall. And you're fine. Near to perfectly healthy. All color and smiles, sans your voice and with an added handprint and white streak."

I wrote, DOES IT LOOK BAD? I realized I hadn't seen

myself since Friday. When I pulled my hair forward I could see the white hairs, mixed in with my darker locks. IS IT A LOT?

"I'd say you've got about this much." Rhonda indicated about an inch with her thumb and index finger. "But you had dyed it, right? Before all this happened?"

But Mom wasn't finished yet. She was on her feet again, pacing this time. "Zoë's hair isn't the issue. That Symbiont or whatever the hell he is did more than just steal her voice and possibly her health. I think he did something else to her."

I didn't have the answers. I DON'T KNOW.

Mom stopped her movements, knelt in front of the coffee table, and slammed her hand down on it. Oooh. Mad. "Where were you from the time he took your voice to the time you came back into your body, Zoë? Can't you remember anything?"

I did remember things, but not things I wanted to share with my mom, even if we were alone. None of us knew or understood what was going on. The only one who seemed to was Joe, and I had no way of getting ahold of him.

I wasn't even sure Joe was real. No one else had seen him.

But there was something he'd said. I grabbed up my board. RHONDA, LOOK UP COPS NAMED JOE IN VICE. He'd said he was going to ask a kid who popped him. Had to be a vice cop, right? Knew about kids and drugs and needed to identify a killer?

I thought about Mrs. DeAngelo. Of me touching her and the sensations that came next. And then I thought of Tanaka and of Trench-Coat standing there beside him. Taking his soul.

Christ. Was that it? Was this what Trench-Coat had done to me? Was that why I felt so much better—because I'd taken her soul?

I looked at Rhonda, who'd stopped typing and stared at me.

I tried to tell her. I even opened my mouth and spoke as if I could. I tried to tell her my fears.

Nothing.

Her eyes widened. "Mother guppy, Zoë. You don't even make a squeak, do you?"

I was ready for a Drama Queen moment right then. I felt like a child who'd lost her favorite toy. And I was terrified. Mommy was mad at me, and she'd made me think of things I didn't want to.

Where had I been for that time? What had I done to that elderly woman?

Arms encircled me then. Mom had stood and joined me on the sofa, and I turned and laid my head down on her shoulder. I could smell Mom's perfume. White Diamonds. And for once, I didn't choke.

Well I did—but I think they mistook it for a sob. A sob takes voice.

I had no voice.

"Why don't we ask the dragon?"

Everyone turned to look at Steve. Even I ceased the waterworks and looked at him, lounging against the fireplace. When had he popped in?

"You mean what's-her-bucket inside?" Rhonda said.

Steve nodded. "Sure. She's the one that first sensed Zoë. She's the one that started us thinking down that road of Wraith. You said this morning the thing could be interrogated."

I looked at Rhonda as she stood, her laptop closed and clutched tightly against her chest. She looked at each of us and took a step back. "I'm not sure if I interpreted that right, though. And it means half-releasing it to do it. What if I goof, and it gets free? It'll try to kill Zoë."

Gee—it's nice to be wanted.

"If it gets free, then I'll kill it myself." Mom released me (go supermom!) and set about pulling stuff off the shelves. Vials, herbs, and a few gitchie-goomies that even I wasn't sure what they were. I watched as she motioned for Tim and Steve to clear the center of the room.

They moved the table, the chairs, the sofas, and the rugs.

This revealed the dark hardwood floor.

It also revealed a honking-great pentagram painted on the wood itself.

I stared at Mom openmouthed. She looked back at me. "Having you silent might actually be a blessing."

22

I wasn't sure how I felt about my own mother having a pentagram plastered on the floor of her place of business. I mean, a girl likes to think her mother reads romances in her spare time, or crochets, not casts spells and summon demons.

This was *so* Buffy.

Unless she was summoning cute demons.

I'd written WTF? on the board, then held the thing up in front of her.

She'd chosen not to answer me as she and Rhonda went around the place gathering up whatnots and suches. So I followed them, trying to shove the board in her face and point at the floor at every opportunity.

Didn't work. She just ignored me.

It really sucked not being able to yell.

It wasn't long before the room smelled like rotten eggs. Sulfur. Mom'd brought out what looked like an old silver chafing dish in need of a polishing. She filled it with sand

and set three cute little round charcoals sparkling and smoking in the center.

It was the nasty powder stuff she tossed on the top that smelled so bad. And smoked. (Cough)

At each of the corners—well—quarters (circles really didn't have corners) Mom and Rhonda placed thick white candles. I took up my board and wrote YOU TWO DO THIS MUCH?

Rhonda smiled. "I'm not as good as your mom."

Oh great. I looked at Mom, then at the circle. Nona Martinique, Atlanta's own Professor Witch.

Faboo.

I wanted to frazzle her with a bazillion mixed questions. When did this start? Were you doing this in our old house when I was sleeping? Is this why I had all those nightmares as a kid? Do you have séance parties and then don't invite me? You talk to Dad like this? Is this why Dad left?

Oh hell. Is *this* why I could go out of body?

But it was just too hard to scribble all that crap down. So I sat in the corner and sulked. At one point I winked an eye and lined Mom's head up in my sights as I crushed her between my thumb and index finger.

I squish your head.

Maybe this sort of behavior was what made puberty a nightmare.

Once they were done, Rhonda set the dragon statue in the middle of the circle. I won't lie and say the thing didn't still give me the heebie-jeebies.

Because it did. And I wanted nooooo part of it. I was still paranoid the thing was going to eat me.

Now—this is where things got weird.

Like my life up to this point wasn't already a case for Ripley's and hunky Dean Cain? You ain't seen nothing yet.

Sitting in my little corner of the room by the fireplace, I

watched as Mom started mumbling something out of a small notebook (one of those black-and-white Composition notebooks), and Rhonda lit the candles from a wooden match. No lighters, for these would be Charmed Ones.

Nothing much happened for a few minutes, except the fraying of my patience. Mom has a nice singing voice, but not a great mumbling one. And it started to really work my last nerve.

The dragon popped, kinda like a kernel of corn on a hot griddle.

I screamed. Not that anybody heard me. I also pulled my blanky up closer. I was still dressed in a pair of sweats and my SpongeBob slippers.

It jumped again.

Shit.

Then it started to jump a *lot* till it was vibrating against the floor. The candles bounced a bit, and I could feel it through my sweats.

Something shot out of the thing's mouth just as an extremely loud scream filled the entire store.

I really hoped Mom had put up the closed sign. This was not the moment some unsuspecting customer should pop in for a late-night visit.

I pressed my hands to my ears, as did Rhonda and Mom. I was also screaming—but that really didn't matter. The thing looped several times, then paused above the dragon, an amorphous ball of green smoke.

The front end formed a ghostly image of Mitsuri's face. Well, not the pretty face, but the oogy one with the hollowed eyes and grimacing mouth. She looked around at everyone, saw me and bared her teeth.

I nearly came off the floor and out of my own body as she lunged at me.

Something crackled in the air between us like lightning, and the smoky Mitsuri-ghost-thing shot backwards as if it hit an invisible wall. I looked at the candles, my hands up to protect me (like these are the hands of steel) as their flames crackled and spit. The whole thing reminded me of a jury-rigged force field of household items.

I looked at Rhonda. *That's my magical MacGyver!*

"Wow," Rhonda said, lowering her own hands. She and Mom had cowered a good two feet away from me (Hello? Victim over *here*!) and now moved forward. "I wasn't really sure that thing was gonna hold."

Excuse me?

"*Wraith . . .*" Mitsuri drew out the name, making it several syllables long.

Rhonda glanced at me. "She's ready to kill you, isn't she?"

Well duh. I gave her a palms-up gesture. If you think about it, she's probably blaming me. There she was, choking me, being a good little minion, and then abruptly she's dragon kibble.

Though she really didn't look much different now than she did when she attacked me.

"*Release me!*"

Right.

I looked over at Rhonda and gave her a gesture that hopefully indicated "It's your show."

But Mom stepped up to the plate. "Who are you?"

Mitsuri hissed.

I stood and looked around for my board. Where did it go?

"I command you to tell me!"

I paused in my looking. *Oooh. Good one Mom.*

"*I am the Bringer . . .*"

And the Bringer was in need of a throat lozenge. Where my stolen voice was a sort of sexy scruffy, this was downright nails on chalkboard. Ah . . . there's my board. I'd been sitting on it.

"Who do you work for?"

"No one . . ."

Rhonda looked over at me. I held up my board. DO YOU WORK FOR REVEREND ROLLINS?

Rhonda asked the question. Mitsuri looked at me to answer. *"I protect the pact . . ."*

Say what?

SAY WHAT?

Rhonda didn't repeat the question, but she did shrug. Mom took over. "What pact?"

"Between the darkness and the false light bearer . . ."

"You mean between Rollins and someone else? There's a pact? Like some sort of agreement? Contract?"

Mitsuri nodded, but she still kept staring at me. I noticed too that her eyes were no longer filled with vengeance, but curiosity.

Mom looked at me. "You think she means maybe the contract as in a hit contract? The one with the Archer and—"

Oh, that name just set little missy here right off. She hissed and started this really weird spin around inside her confined bubble. I didn't know why Mom used the name I'd heard Rollins use instead of my own moniker, Trench-Coat. But it got a reaction. Every time she hit the candle barrier's edge, it sparked, and the candles spit.

I wondered absently what happened if a candle blew out.

I assumed that would be very bad. Kinda like crossing the streams?

Mitsuri finally stopped and got right up against that barrier, looking at me again. *"He has touched you . . . broken the rules . . . you walk between . . ."* She actually smiled! *"He will not suffer such a creature to live. He will fear you."*

I pointed to myself. Me?

Mitsuri smiled. *Ick.* Bad teeth. Or at least so in this form.

I scribbled on my board and handed it to Rhonda. "You mean the Archer. He's stolen my voice."

Mitsuri nodded. *"He had none of his own. The Phantasm does not grant a simple Symbiont such a gift . . . it is not allowed. Even for the Archer . . ."*

Crap. I was right about him taking parts of me. I hate to be right. Sometimes. Trench-Coat was a Symbiont in some sense of the word.

I scribbled another question, and Rhonda asked. WHY IS THE SYMBIONT CALLED THE ARCHER?

The ghostly thing actually looked as if it smelled something bad. *"Because he is branded a rogue. He has defied his master."*

Oh. Right. Made sense to me.

Rhonda nodded. "That makes sense—arch is closely related to rogue." When Mom and I frowned at her, she said, "Sixteenth-century word association." She waved her hand. "Trust me. If he's a rogue, calling him the Archer fits."

I raised an eyebrow at Rhonda. *Riiiiiiight.*

Mitsuri laughed. And it wasn't a good laugh, more of an "I'll get you, my pretty" sort of laugh. *"Wraith . . . the master will not suffer such as you to live."*

WHY?

"You grant absolution, he takes it away. He cannot control you—you must not be allowed to exist. I would take great pleasure in destroying you—but I cannot."

I was not liking the direction this was going. I was also not understanding any of it.

Mom interrupted. "Is there a way to defeat him? Can my daughter get her voice back?"

Mitsuri turned her attention to Mom. *"Release me."*

I looked around the room. Where were Tim and Steve?

Mom shook her head. "You would kill my daughter. You tried once, and you just said you'd try again."

"*I said I cannot!*" I was sure the bookshelves shook at that shout. Mitsuri looked back to me again. "*She is marked. I cannot touch her.*"

"You had no trouble touching her before," Rhonda protested, taking the words right out of my mouth.

"*Different.*" Mitsuri hovered closer to the candle barrier's edge, looking at me as if I were the one trapped inside a pentagram bubble. "*Twisted. No longer living or dead.*"

Yikes.

I waved at Mom and held up my board. DID ROLLINS KILL TANAKA?

"*The Archer killed Tanaka.*"

Well, that much I knew. FOR ROLLINS?

"*Yes.*" Mitsuri narrowed her eyes at me. "*But you were there—you know this.*"

Just check'n the facts, ma'am.

I scribbled again and held up the board. WHAT IS IT THAT HIROKUMI HOLDS OVER ROLLINS?

Mitsuri frowned. "*He holds my master's promise of life eternal.*"

Oh—yeah. That just explained everything. I did my thing again. AND THAT MEANS . . . WHAT?

She shook her head. "*That my master will stop at nothing to get it back.*"

Okay, she was looking at me as if I were the stupidest thing to walk on the planet. What is it with the bad guys and their inability to just spill da beans?

Or was it only on television that the evil dude tells the good guys his plans? Wait—that usually didn't happen till right before the bad dude thinks the good guys are gonna die.

Well, obviously, we were safe since Mitsuri wasn't exactly forthcoming with the information.

She banged against her prison again. "*Release me!*"

"If I release you, you will tell me how to destroy the Archer?" Mom butted in.

Mitsuri looked at her and smiled. "*Yes.*"

I held up my board. NO!!!!! ARE YOU CRAZY?

Mom looked at Rhonda, who was shaking her head with equal fervor. "Nona, don't. You release her, she'll attack us."

"No." Nona shook her head. "She won't." She looked at the imprisoned spirit. "I agree."

"*Release me.*"

Mom shook her head. "Tell me."

The thing screamed. Oh and what a god-awful noise that was. I can only describe it as maybe a billion babies crying at one time. In an echo chamber.

Is that bad enough for you?

"Tell me!" Mom was right against the circle's barrier—too close for my taste.

Mitsuri banged against the field. Sparks. Sputter.

Hrm . . .

"*The full power of the Wraith must be invoked.*"

I blinked. Oh-*kay.*

WHAT THE HELL DOES THAT MEAN?

Mitsuri looked at me. "*You'll find out.*"

I blinked. *Okay—Vague. We're going for vague here.*

Oh for the love of Pete! Whoever Pete was! I wanted to choke her just like she'd choked me.

Let's just go for broke. I erased and wrote hurriedly. WHAT R MY POWERS?

"*Enough!*" Mitsuri banged against the field again. "*You promised to release me!*"

Uh-oh. I looked at Mom. *Pay-up time.* Though I had the feeling that Nona didn't have the first intention of releasing this nasty thing. Or at least I hoped not, and if so, I hoped she knew what she was doing.

I was clueless. My job was to go OOB, gather, and return.

And hopefully with all my parts in place. Evidently Mom's job was a bit more—I looked at the circle on the floor—*complicated*.

At that moment, of all the worst things that could happen, the one particular worst did.

The door to the shop opened. The bell over the opening rang.

And a very cold, very strong November breeze blew out the candles.

All of them.

Poof.

Uh-oh.

Luckily, Mom hadn't turned all the lights off—only the main ones. A light still showed from behind the counter and from inside the tea shop. And that light illuminated a very ecstatic Mitsuri.

Her face took on an almost snakelike appearance for an instant before she turned and lunged through the air toward the poor helpless and unsuspecting patron who'd walked in.

Oh bugger Mom for not putting up the sign and locking the door!

But then I saw the patron.

It was Daniel.

Oh . . . hell!

The next few seconds moved through molasses for me. Mitsuri was heading right for him. Mom screamed for Daniel to move out of the way. Daniel turned and evidently saw Mitsuri barreling for him because his eyes became the size of cue balls through his glasses.

But he was frozen in place.

And in hindsight, I've been scared to one spot loads of times. So I understood.

But this was my possible future husband here (well, a girl's gotta have goals, right?) and Mitsuri wasn't having him for lunch just because she couldn't have me.

I was out and in full Wraith form before I could blink. Later on, Rhonda would tell me how neat it'd been to see my body go plop on the ground. I wouldn't agree, not with the bruises.

Of course I didn't know what I was going to do. I mean, the thing had chased me astrally all around Rollins's office that night, and then back through my cord to my body.

This was also the first time I noticed I wasn't running, but more like flying. Now, I can't fly. It was more like a momentum thing, or an adrenaline thing. Sort of like when a mom lifts a car off of her baby.

I was in front of that bitch in seconds flat, between her and Daniel. She came up short, her smoky form taking on a more human appearance (more like the Lucy Liu we've all grown to know and love), and held her arms out as if backpedaling.

It looked as if she were preparing for something awful. Shaking her head, her mouth wide, her eyes wider. I wasn't sure what the big deal was at the time, other than the fact that I reached out and touched her.

I mean, actually touched *her*.

The world of the physical stopped as if time suspended itself. My hand was thrust through something slippery as oil, yet my fingers had closed around something solid inside. Small. Warm. Tiny.

With a silent grunt I pulled with everything I had and felt something give between me and what I held on to. It shot out of the oily mass I'd known as Mitsuri and clung to me like a small, newborn child.

Only it wasn't a newborn, but it *was* a child. A small, frightened, Asian child. A shadow, lost between the Abysmal and the Ethereal.

I knew this from her—somehow—and as I looked into her face, I saw the skull again, just before she smiled and mouthed the words "Thank you."

She vanished.

She was just—*gone*.

The oily mist disappeared as if cleared away by a fan. The astral world still hung about me in its new hue of sooty shadows. Had I somehow released her spirit? Was that what I'd done to Mrs. DeAngelo? There had been no euphoria this time.

Not even a peep. Was it because Mitsuri had already been dead?

Jesus, I hated working in the dark. I needed an answer book, and there wasn't one around anywhere.

I saw Steve and Tim near the farthest end of the room. Two tiny pinpoints of light, no longer in their physical, human shape. Was I seeing them for what they truly were?

Again Mom and Rhonda shone like twin stars of different colors.

"What the . . . Zoë!" Daniel burst out.

As my hero moved *through* me I saw silken sheets, skin on skin, mouths pressed together in desperate need as fingers interlaced in a passionate, orgasmic—

I gasped as he continued on to my very unmoving body by the fireplace.

I stood by the open doorway, blinking slowly. Man . . . was that what he had on his mind? Right now? Making love? Or had he already made love? And that was simply the remnants of a very nice afternoon? There wasn't any proof that was me I saw. In fact, I'm not even sure that was Daniel, as I'd never seen him naked. But I'd like to think that lean, hard six-pack rubbing against a very flat, tight tummy was his, and mine.

And should I ask him about that? I mean—that image was surely something we could both indulge with—

"What's wrong with her?" Daniel said. He was holding me like a child, cradling my head against his chest. "Nona—she's not responding." He was looking around at the floor and the now very visible pentagram and candles. "What the hell were you people doing?"

Rhonda moved to the door and closed it. She whispered under her breath at me. "Get back in your body now!" she hissed. "Or he'll start giving you mouth-to-mouth."

I really didn't see what the problem was with this.

Nona got up from the floor, glared at me, and moved to Daniel. The boy was distraught.

Wow. He cares!

I nodded and sprinted to the fireplace. There I eased back into my body—which was kinda fun since Daniel was holding it so very snugly, and Mom was telling him to give me room to breathe.

Rejoining was easier—no shock this time—but I'd only gone a few feet away and I'd only been gone a few minutes. I took a deep breath and opened my eyes.

An eyeless skull looked back at me and spoke with the voice of my darling cop.

I screamed.

But no one heard me.

23

DANIEL never saw me in my astral form at the door, nor had he seen Mitsuri at first. It wasn't until she'd been on top of him. He said it looked like a streak of green smoke with a face in it. Then it'd disappeared, and he'd seen me on the floor beside the pentagram.

And I'd seen a skull on his face. A skull. The death mask.

I'd seen one of these before—on that old lady in the hospital. Right before she died.

And on Mitsuri.

"It's part of my séance routine," Nona explained, after she'd made tea, eggs, and some biscuits (mmmmm . . . biscuits) and honey. She set the ceramic green teapot in the center of the table.

I sat beside Daniel in Mom's papasan chair, wrapped up in a blanket and feeling a bit tired. I was hungry too—but just too tired to eat. Of course, that hadn't stopped me from downing three glasses of Sunny Delight.

Oh let's be honest. I was exhausted. I wanted to talk about the whole Mitsuri thing with Mom and Rhonda, but not with Daniel around. I still wasn't sure what it was I'd just done. Either way I was wasted and trying really hard not to fall asleep.

Tim and Steve were present, solid and interacting. Which was something I'd not seen them do in a while. But evidently they also thought Daniel was cute, and being here in their own house, they had the power base or strength or whatever to be visible to him. And quite physical, though I'd noticed none of them had passed any plates around.

And Daniel never seemed to notice that neither of them ate.

My cute cop gave my mom a very harsh look. "You bilk poor believers out of money with séance nonsense?"

"Oh no." Nona was good at this lying thing. "Most of my clients find their answers on their own. I only use the séance as a tool to give them a little push. I never charge for them." Too good. I was beginning to look at her suspiciously and wonder about things during my own childhood.

Like had I really set fire to the living-room rug that day? I never remembered doing it, and now I wondered if it'd been Mom doing some hocus-pocus, and she'd lied about it.

"That's good to know." He looked at me and put a hand on my knee. "It looks like it took a lot out of Zoë. How's your throat?"

I blew him a razzberry.

He smiled. "Well, I came over to let you know Sergeant Danforth is outside, and he'll be there all night. He relieved Mastiff and Harding. You are to stay put and rest."

I really didn't feel much like doing anything else. Mitsuri was gone, the dragon was up on the mantel as a very nice decoration (though I planned on bargaining with

Rhonda about keeping it in my condo—it might come in handy again).

Mental note: *sleeeeeep.*

"What about that little girl?" Mom asked.

Oh. Bugger! I'd forgotten about Susan! That poor frightened kid.

Daniel shook his head. "I see you shared things with your family. Nothing else. If the kidnapper's contacted Hirokumi, he's not talking. In fact, he's not really communicating with us, period. The captain's got people stationed outside his office and his home, but there's been nothing. She's been missing three days now—and that's a long time to keep hoping she's still alive."

I had faith she was, as long as Trench-Coat kept his spinning red hand of death away from her. I only hoped Rollins had enough control over his little minion to stop that from happening.

I took up my board, shoving Rhonda's biscuit off of it, and scribbled. This was going to kill my wrists. WHAT ABOUT FINDING HER AT ROLLINS'S?

Daniel shook his head. "No reason for a search warrant. There's really nothing tying him to her disappearance, and as long as Hirokumi doesn't speak up . . ." He shrugged.

This was stupid. This was his daughter's life he was messing with. I wrote up again. I DON'T THINK PORNO THING ETERNAL LIFE.

I really didn't understand how tired I was till I got blank stares all around. I looked back at my board and shook my head. I erased it. SORRY.

Daniel pushed himself back from the table. "I think I should leave, and you should get some sleep."

I shook my head. I needed to think on this eternal life contract, and what it meant.

I scribbled again. WHERE YOU GO?

"To work."

IS MIDNIGHT.

He stood and leaned over me. "Right, which means you need to be in bed, kiddo."

Too late I realized he was going to pick me up. I pushed at him, protesting that I was perfectly capable of getting up myself. Ah, but of course, there was nothing but silence.

This quiet thing just wasn't me, you know?

He had me in his arms, blanket and all, and Mom was up and leading him up the stairs to the guest bedroom on the right. She'd painted the room a soft blue with white trim. A powder blue comforter adorned the bed, accented by matching sheets and several pillows.

She turned down the sheets and Daniel gently set me down on them. I was becoming more and more impressed with this man. I'm not a small woman, about average height really. And I weigh a good one hundred—

Ah.

Never mind. I get blabby when I get tired.

I'm heavier than you think.

The sheets were cold, and I shivered. Mom's and Daniel's hands collided as each of them tried to place one on my forehead.

Oh please. I'm not sick. Just a bit tired.

Mom started that Mom-tuck thing. You know the one where they go around and shove the sheet and the comforter between the mattress and the box spring. She used to do it when I was a kid, and it worked. I'd been unable to get up for the first ten minutes of the night, and then I'd just go to sleep because the effort of struggle was too much.

Daniel ran his fingers, only slightly calloused and nice, along my forehead. "Rest. Please. And stay put. No more going out. You're my only witness against Hirokumi's assistant. When we find her, I'll need you to ID her."

I looked into his incredibly blue eyes and smiled. No

skull. No death mask. Just pure beautiful. But nothing could quell the niggling of danger I felt when he touched me.

Daniel, please don't go—I'm afraid for your life.

He kissed me (mmmmm . . .) and left the room.

Rhonda was around the corner in an instant, and Tim and Steve appeared out of thin air. The truth is, they could have been there the whole time, invisible, and probably were.

"Okay—what the hell happened down there?" Rhonda sat on the bed with enough force that it popped me up a bit, and luckily freed up some of Mom's tucked covers. "What did you do to it?"

I looked around for my board. Where was my board?

Rhonda had it.

I pushed myself up in the bed and wrote. DIDN'T YOU SEE?

Steve sat down on the wicker chair beside the bed, and I was surprised when it actually creaked. Who knew ghosts had weight? "We didn't see anything. Other than her going at Daniel, then you swooping in all Wraithlike, then you both vanished. What happened?"

I shrugged. Aren't ghosts supposed to have all the answers to these questions? I mean, when you die, aren't you supposed to know all the answers?

Like wasn't there this big stack of spook-lopedias somewhere? Or maybe a spectral library to look this stuff up?

I TOUCH HER SAME AS DEANGELO—SHE GO POOF.

Mom pursed her lips. "You mean you released her spirit."

I looked at Mom. Scribble, scribble. Boy—my handwriting sucks. NO ONE SAW IT?

Rhonda looked at Nona, who looked at Steve, who looked at Tim.

Tim shrugged. "Steve and I lost visibility when the circle went up. It was like watching things through a mist."

Really? Wow. Didn't know that could happen. And from the looks on their faces—they did.

Steve spoke. "Happens when Nona does one of her circles."

I looked back at Mom. YOU DO THIS OFTEN?

And, of course, like all good mothers who don't want to talk about something with their daughters, she ignored me. "We didn't see any more than what Steve's already said. I am noticing you're not as pink and healthy-looking as before. Maybe releasing Mitsuri wasn't the same as releasing the elderly woman."

Scribble. NOT ALIVE. ALREADY DEAD. MAYBE?

I leaned back into the pillows Daniel had fluffed up and thought over things.

Okay—so we have a Symbiont called the Archer hired by the Reverend to intimidate the vice president of a company that now has some sort of document of immortality of said Reverend. Have I lost anyone?

Good. 'Cause I'm toast on this one. None of it made sense. Not if you looked at it from a rational point of view.

And cut the crap—I can be rational.

Sort of. Well, maybe not when I'm sore and wanting sleep.

In the past few decades, rock stars, models, politicians, and even other men of the cloth have withstood sordid nastiness about their pasts. Okay—so we all did things we would avoid the second time through.

Like me—if I had second grade to do over—I'd have never eaten that—

Never mind.

The point is a reverend having a history in the porn industry just seemed so blasé. Capisce? I mean—it was bad drama. Not even TNT would touch this one.

And a reverend hiring a Symbiont—hell—a reverend having the *connections* to hire one—now that seemed a bit serious. If I had access to that kind of connection, then I'd have just sent the thing to steal the document back again.

Why send it to torture and kill a vice president, though memory from that night in Rollins's office surfaced for me then (See? No control), and I remembered Rollins not being happy that Trench-Coat killed Tanaka.

And why have Mitsuri spying? And what the hell did she mean with all that vagueness? And what the hell had Mitsuri been all along? She obviously wasn't a Symbiont, or even an astral Traveler. Maybe she was exactly what I'd assumed at that moment of her release—a lost soul.

I had this really uncomfortable feeling I was missing something. I knew Rollins had Hirokumi's daughter—and yet the businessman hadn't gone to the police.

Why not?

Did he plan on handling things on his own?

And was there something else—something a bit more serious—that Koba Hirokumi had on Theodore Rollins?

I'd originally thought I'd sneak out later and spy on Rollins again and find Susan, the daughter. But I was beginning to suspect my target shouldn't be the good Reverend, but Hirokumi.

I suspected that man knew exactly what was going on.

Barring another one of those dragon things in the house, I thought it was high time I paid the president of Visitar a visit. I made my plans mentally as my eyes drooped closed and I drifted off into pleasant dreams of being fondled and kissed by cute, dark-haired men in red flannel.

24

A bee woke me up.

Or at least that's what I thought it was. I cussed and smacked at the air over my head. But it continued to buzz around in the dark.

My feet were cold where the comforter and sheets had fallen away. Now why is it even when I sleep alone I get the sheets pulled off of me?

The buzzing continued and I suffered my usual irritation when my hair fell in my face, tangled and itching my nose.

I should have braided it before going to bed. Crap.

The bedroom had a small night-light shoved into the outlet to the right of my nightstand. I could see the window (still dark outside), the wicker chair, and my PDA phone. The phone lit up in pinks and blues and vibrated against the stand's wood.

Oh. So that's where the bee was coming from. I'd wondered how a small, annoying bug had gotten into the rhythm of buzz-buzz-buzz-pause so well. Someone was calling me.

And where had my phone come from? I didn't remember having it last night. Unless Mom had gotten my personal effects from the morgue (Gah!) which I'm sure came from my car.

My car!

Moment of silence.

With a snort (the only noise being the air and mucus being driven forcefully from my nose) I sat up fully, turned on the little lamp (Gah! It was my old Mary-had-a-Little-Lamb nursery lamp. Wow . . . and Mary's head was missing . . .) and grabbed up the phone.

The display had a generic picture for the caller ID. Incoming call. No shit.

I paused.

Oh hell. How am I supposed to answer it? I can say hello all day—er, night—and who's going to hear me?

So I held it in my hand, waiting for it to switch over to voice mail.

Whistle while you . . .

Damn—I couldn't even whistle! Lips puckered up (and chapped) and no sound. Just air. When Trench-Coat cleans something out he does it all the way.

Goddamnitsonofabitchpoxonhispeck-

The little unit gave a short jolt and the prerecorded "New Message" came through in its little tin voice through the little tin speakers. I dialed voice mail and put the receiver to my ear.

"You have, one, new message. Message received 3:17 A.M."

It was three in the morning?

There was a pause, then another tinny, automated voice spoke. The words were staccato-like, and very creepy. In fact, it sounded like one of those prerecorded messages available on answering machines now. The kind that usually come on and say "Please. Leave. A. Message."

"Hello. Miss. Martinique. This is. Maharba. At maharba. Dot. Com."

!!!

"I have. Not received. My *full* report from. Tuesday. I am afraid. I am disappointed. With your performance. You have. Until noon today. To submit your true findings. On the meeting. If not. I will be forced. To take advantage. Of my. Knowledge. Of your. Unique. Ability."

The automated T-Mobile response came on then. "If you would like to call back, please press—"

I hit the button for playback and listened to the message again.

What the fuck?

I'd sent in my report after my Fadó experience with Daniel. Of course I had left out a lot of what'd really happened, with Mitsuri and the dragon statue and me and then me becoming corporeal and all.

But how had Maharba gotten my cell number? Rhonda said she'd fixed it up to be impossible to discover my identity. I'd never had a client threaten me before.

And that was a threat if I ever heard one.

How did this asshole know about my *unique* capabilities? What did he mean by he'd have to take advantage of his knowledge? What knowledge? Did he know more about what it is that I did than I do?

Well—anybody knew more about it than I did. Hell— I'm sure the neighbor's cat, Miss Lady, knew. She always hissed at me when I stepped outside my door in astral form.

I hung up the phone and started shaking. What did this guy—or girl for that matter—want? I'd assumed Maharba was Rollins at first—but that proved to be a bust.

I didn't think it was Trench-Coat. But who else would know about my *unique* ability?

Ah! The mysterious Joe! Certainly *he* wasn't Maharba— was he?

"Zoë?"

Okay—if I could have screamed, I'd have popped off a nasty one at that instant.

I looked to my left to see Tim materialize out of the air. He had his hand up in self-defense, and I tried to smack him. Insubstantial. I mouthed "You scared me," but we all know how that came out.

I sighed and looked around for my board. My phone chimed. Two short noises. I had e-mail. I probably had a lot of e-mail.

"It's okay—I got it. Sorry." Tim's voice was quiet, and he looked pale. Well, pretty pale for a ghost. "What happened? Nona told me to stay here and watch out for you. We're not in your protected condo"—he pointed to the roof indicating the whole house—"though she's got some pretty powerful wards up. Sometimes they're hard for Steve and me to pass through. But we're not sure if they're strong enough to keep the Archer from you."

I nodded. Mom had him spying on me. I knew how she thought—and I have to admit—I *had* considered sneaking out and heading back to Rollins's house to find Susan Hirokumi myself. I felt I was better equipped.

I pointed to the phone, then picked it up and dialed up voice mail. Then I hit the speaker so he could hear the message as well. His brown eyes widened, eight balls against a white pool table.

Wow, that was a really bad analogy. Sue me. I was tired.

My phone chimed again.

"Who is this Maharba dot-com person?"

Okay—where was the board? All this shrugging and making faces was giving me another headache. I found it on the floor on my side of the bed. I erased it with my fingers and scribbled. THOUGHT IT WAS ROLLINS—NO DICE. COULD BE MYSTERY JOE.

I then told him Maharba had been a regular client for

about two years, and this was the first time he—she—it—
had ever contacted me on the phone.

Tim pursed his lips. He looked different when he
wasn't scowling. Handsome. He just needed to get over
his death. And oh like I could dispense this advice? I was
terrified of dying. I was too afraid death would be me
wandering around in my astral form with no physical
place to hide.

That would suck. No body to enjoy the physical joys of
living.

Joys like eating.

No more cheesecake. No more ice cream.

*No more sex! Yeah . . . like I've been real lucky in that
department recently. Pout.*

"Zoë—it has to be someone you know, or that's known
you for some time. You did give them a report?"

Isn't it odd how when I thought of food I then thought of
sex? And thinking of sex—I thought of Joe—

No! Daniel.

Dannnnyulll. Not Joe. Don't know Joe.

"Zoë?"

But Joe seemed to know me. Wasn't very comfortable
with that.

"Zoë, hello?"

I blinked at him. Oh . . . question . . . give them a report. I nodded.

"And somehow they know you weren't entirely truth-
ful?"

I nodded again. I had told Maharba the two had met and
been vague about enemies and finding Tanaka's killer. Of
course I'd left out the parts about the faceless secretary
and the huge-ass dragon.

At the time I'd thought those details a bit on the Sci Fi
Channel side of life.

But after the dude's threats—maybe those were the

details he wanted. But why? If he already knew about them, why have me tell him?

Was Maharba a part of this whole freaky mess? Or an entirely new player?

I couldn't exactly go to the police with this either. Especially not to Daniel—as he was the one that I'd been spying on for money.

Chime. Hush phone!

"You might be onto something thinking it's Joe."

It wasn't a far-fetched notion. Joe'd obviously known what I was from the start, and he'd known what to do to jump-start me back into my body from wherever I'd been. Had Rhonda even tried to look for him?

"Are you going to send another report?"

I GUESS SO.

"And Nona? Are you going to tell her about the threat?"

Hrm. I didn't have an answer for that one.

"She's terrified you know. For you." He gave me a slight smile, and I found myself really liking this little ghost more and more. Tim rarely came forward when partnered with Steve, so his personality tended to play in the shadow. "You're her world, even if she doesn't show it. She's proud of you—and of what you can do."

GOOD. THEN ASK HER WHERE MY FATHER IS.

Tim made a face.

Taboo subject. Worth a try.

Chime.

All freak'n right!

I snatched up the phone and scrolled through the menu to the e-mail. As I'd feared, there were a little over seven e-mails—all clients wanting information. All successful eBay transactions.

Great. I had jobs, and wasn't paying attention. That just wasn't like me. But I'd been a little preoccupied with life and death in the past few days.

I checked the dates on each, only vaguely aware that Tim had vanished. I was too late on one of them, the "meeting" having been the day before. I needed to get online and reverse the transaction with apologies.

That left six. Two divorce cases, three of what looked like information-trading snoops—looking over someone's shoulder and taking notes.

And then there was the last one.

It looked like a job. Had the proper header. And there was a transaction.

For one hundred thousand dollars.

One hundred thousand dollars!

Luckily I didn't have a voice or I'd have just woken all of Little Five Points. I looked around the room, not really sure if I should get up and call my bank to see if the money was really there, or wake Mom up and tell her we were headed to Hawaii!

The message was brief.

Must meet IRL (in real life—for those like me that had to ask the first ten times or so). *I need your help, and you'll need mine to save Lieutenant Daniel Frasier. Meet me in Buckhead, the* Storyteller. *Dawn is safest.*

To save Daniel?

Crap! Had something happened to him since he left here?

The message was dated today. Dawn. I checked the clock on my phone. It was now closer to four. So what time was dawn exactly? When did the sun come up? Like I would know these things? I usually did my jobs at night, hung out downtown, then slept way past the time when the sun said morning salutations.

I guessed it to be around sixish. Maybe. *Crap.* And it wasn't like I could call Daniel and find out. It'd be a one-sided conversation with a lot of "Hello? Hello? Hell-oh!" from his end. *Sheesh.*

Well, at least if I heard him answer, I'd know he was okay. So I pulled his number out of my received call list and pressed connect.

"You've reached the voice mail of Lieutenant Daniel Frasier, APD. If you'd like to leave a message—"

I hung up. What was I going to do? Bang pots? He hadn't answered, though. And I didn't know if he had a land line at home. Nor did I know its number.

Crap. He could be in trouble and this person could be either A, the one who'd put him in danger or B, the one who could help me help him out of danger.

My mind skipped several moments ahead and questioned mode of transportation. I was in Little Five Points, and Triangle Park, where the *Storyteller* sat, was northeast, on the other side of downtown. MARTA ceased running at one o'clock and wouldn't start back up till six.

How was I going to get there—either go Wraith or in body?

I could get past the policeman outside if I went Wraith. But then I'd still need a mode of transportation. What if I used my new solid abilities as well? This way, I could leave my body here and then travel where I needed, then travel my cord back home in case this turned out to be a raw deal.

Then I remembered what things looked like when I was in Wraith form. The sooty, smoky things that crawled and spun and flew about. Could I possibly stay in that form to Buckhead? And if I went corporeal, would I still see them all?

And then there was that skull I'd seen on Daniel's face. Twice I'd seen it and twice those people have died. Was it a sign? A signal for me? Something telling me this person was marked?

And was this e-mail meant to cause Daniel's death, or prevent it?

Damn, I hate not knowing anything.

I didn't have a car. But I did know where Mom kept the keys to her beauty.

With no sign of Tim in sight, I rose from the bed and was surprised that I felt just wonderful. In fact, I felt better than I had in several days.

I decided then to go meet this client in my physical form. Lately, every time I'd been OOB, I'd woken up either in a hospital or in the morgue.

And let me tell you, the only thing to top the morgue would be that waking-up-dead thing. Not gonna happen. I found some of my old clothes in the closet and proceeded to get out of Mom's latest clown suit.

Jeans that fit a little too tight (I'd gained weight?). Over-sized sweatshirt with a worn picture of Chewbacca on the front. Thick athletic socks (whose are these?) and—no shoes.

Except for my ugly-duck slippers.

Hrm. Well, they'd have to do.

Careful not to make too much noise, I shuffled to the bathroom and flipped on the light. I jumped back from the face looking back at me.

Now, I'd never considered myself a raving beauty. I was not bad—a little on the unique side. I think it's because of my coloring, being a bit Mediterranean, but having Anglo features as well as a small sprinkling of freckles over my nose.

Never mind the overly pronounced white shock of hair a finger thick on the left side of my face. In the bathroom light it was so white it glowed. There was no time to dye it again—not that it did any good the last time. It kinda looked retro but didn't really detract from the fact that there was something eerie about my face now, something out of place.

I looked a bit gaunt, my cheekbones a bit more pronounced than I remembered them. Dark circles hung beneath my eyes—not attractive, except to a goth lover. The band around my neck where Mitsuri had tried to kill me was little more than a faint red mark.

It was my eyes that bothered me. I'd always called them brown. Plain Jane brown. But they weren't anymore. They were much lighter now, mostly a topaz color. Kinda cool, really. Had that glow-in-the-dark look.

Was this also a side effect of Trench-Coat's meddling?

My hair was in its usual disarray so I combed it down, braided it, and tied it off. It felt a little dry—except for the white streak, which was soft and pliable—and I promised it a nice shampoo at Cortex Salon soon.

Once downstairs, I grabbed my mom's oversized long wool coat, her black scarf, and her knitted hat. The keys were by the back door, and I let myself out. The wind had picked up again, and it was cold.

Damned cold. I should have grabbed her gloves too.

I checked around the house to make sure the patrol car was still there. Bingo. By the curb. I figured I'd put the Volvo in neutral, roll it to the road, and just crank it when I was far enough away. Luckily there was a side breezeway between the house and the woods where the cop wouldn't see me.

I'd just gotten in the old Volvo and put her in neutral when I saw Tim sitting in the front passenger's seat. I gave another silent scream and threw the car back into park.

He looked spooky—real spooky. The only light came from the yard lamp from the backyard of the house that backed up to Mom's fence. Just enough light came through the windshield to show me his face. But the shadows were really shadows, and he was insubstantial. He reminded me of a reflection on glass.

Only there wasn't any glass in the passenger's seat.

Of course I'd not brought my board, much less a scrap

of paper, so I swatted at him. My hand passed through him and connected to the seat.

Tim had his hands up. "Hey, Nona left the rock in here from yesterday. I just decided to use it. You can't just go out by yourself—especially after you promised the nice-looking cop you'd stay put. So I took care of the guard for you." He beamed.

He had a point, though I wasn't sure I wanted to know what he meant by "took care of the guard." I cranked the Volvo and pulled out onto Euclid. The patrol car remained by the road and never followed me.

Tim looked quizzically at me. "Where exactly are you going?"

Luckily the e-mail was still visible on my cell. I pulled it out of my pocket and handed it to him. He became corporeal enough to hold it and read it. Then it sank through him and bounced on the passenger's seat.

"This is a bad idea, Zoë. I think you need to show your mom and Rhonda."

I shook my head and drove. Luckily, there weren't any cars on the road, but there were police. That could always be a problem. Especially since I didn't have my license or insurance with me. I realized this about halfway up Monroe Drive, past my condo. They were with my purse, which I was sure my mom had hidden somewhere.

Tim faded in and out (which was a bit distracting) but kept very quiet. I didn't know if he was saving his strength or testing his abilities this far away from his home.

I turned down Peachtree Road and cruised past Lenox Square Mall, Hotel Nikko, and Dante's Down the Hatch (a killer fondu place that once had real alligators—don't know if they do anymore).

Triangle Park came into view (*Yay!*), and I turned right into the bank parking lot just before it. I cut the engine and sat still, the windshield facing the statue.

The *Storyteller* was an imposing bronze statue of a man with deer's hooves and a buck's head. He held a two-pronged staff in his hands that reminded me a bit of Neptune. The statue had been created by Frank Fleming and sat in the center of Triangle Park, which was little more than a triangle of land where Roswell Road and Peachtree Road intersected.

Supposedly this is where the infamous Buckhead tavern once stood, and the Buckhead is telling the story to the woodland friends (a bronze assortment of forest creatures) of how the tavern got its name.

Or so I'd heard. I just thought it was a cool landmark. Looked more like Herne the Hunter of the wood who tells tales to Snow White's menagerie.

Tim reappeared, looking a bit more solid. "What now?"

I reached through him and grabbed my phone. It was 5:32. I looked at Tim and mouthed the words "We wait."

We were behind the *Storyteller*, a couple of yards from the circular brick area where he sat on his bronze log. His twin lamps were lit, illuminating the little woodland friends, though I really couldn't see any detail from this distance, or through the few trees.

It started getting cold in the car and I wished I'd brought some sort of blanket. I cranked the car and put the heat on. I certainly hoped the mystery e-mailer wasn't expecting me to sit out there in the cold next to the old buckhead.

That wasn't happening.

About twenty minutes after we parked a huge-ass black limousine pulled in on my side of the car. I squinted at the black window, wishing I had x-ray vision to look inside. It sat quietly, and I glanced to my right. Tim was gone.

I snatched up the rock Mom kept in there for him and shoved it into the pocket of my sweats. No matter what happened, I wanted him with me.

I'd just grabbed up my phone when the passenger-side

door opened, and a large sumo wrestler stepped out, dressed in a well-cut black suit. I recognized his face.

Tiny.

Shit! These were Rollins's men!

I realized then I'd been keeping hope up that the e-mailer had been Joe, and this had been his way of contacting me. And he was very rich with a payoff of a hundred thousand dollars.

Beckett emerged from the other side. *Damn!*

The car was still cranked and I threw it into reverse, intent on backing the hell out of there, even if I backed over Tiny (though I think that would put a significant dent in Mom's car).

Something tapped the driver's window, and I turned to my left. A very large gun was pressed against the glass. Beckett had moved behind my car, and I looked in my rearview mirror to see him aiming his own gun at me, through the rear window.

Shit! Damn! I'm toast!

Tiny motioned me out of the car with the gun. I shut off the engine and unlocked the door. He opened it.

I slid out of my body. It wasn't a conscious thought, just instinctive. My Wraith self sieved through the car's glass and I found myself standing next to Tiny. He looked inside the car at my body, now slumped to the right into the passenger's seat.

I thought of Daniel, of the thoughts I'd picked up when he'd passed through me last evening. My body tingled, and I knew I was corporeal.

And pissed.

Tiny sensed something as well as he turned to his right, closing the car door on my untouched body. His eyes widened as he saw me. I smiled, waved, blew him a kiss, then took a deep breath of astral chi, and rammed the very physical heel of my palm upward into his nose. I heard as well as felt the cartilage break.

Blood splattered both cars along the doors and glass. He screamed really good as he grabbed his nose and fell backward, landing on the curb and grass beyond.

Wow—I did it! I'd never done that before!

Heh—don't mess with a woman's astral anger, baby.

One down, one to go, and I'm out of here.

Dizziness washed over my vision. Sooty little creatures like black thread scurried over Tiny's writhing body as I turned. I nearly fell and put my hand out on Mom's car—but it sieved through.

That's when I saw Beckett, the smart one. He'd used mine and Tiny's little fight to open the passenger door to Mom's car. He had Mom's coat half off my right arm, and was pulling a very long, very sharp-looking needle out of my flesh.

Sonofabitch.

What had he shot me with? Why was I dizzy in Wraith form? I lost momentum. I lost control.

I felt myself slip back into my body, pulled there by my cord. I had no control over my muscles, and my head lolled a bit as Beckett lifted me out of Mom's car and then fireman carried me over his shoulder. I watched the pavement, only faintly aware I wasn't wearing the coat anymore. I shivered from a distance before I felt myself lowered into what I recognized was the limo's trunk. It was getting hard to focus, and a very scary warmth spread throughout my body to block out the November chill.

I blinked slowly up at Beckett. He gave me a catlike smile. Tiny appeared, his face a bloody mess. He'd used his handkerchief to staunch the flow, but he watched me with intense, wide-eyed fear.

"Did you see that, Beck? I mean, was that her? That . . . that thing?" His voice sounded nasal.

"Yeah, that was her."

I blinked at him again. I was losing consciousness. This just wasn't acceptable. I needed to stay awake. I needed to know where we were going.

"Don't touch her, Tiny," Beckett said from the front. "Boss said as long as she stays doped up on his special sauce, she can't do that again."

"But what the fuck was that she did?" His voice was several inches above normal. I thought he was bordering on hysteria. "That ain't natural, Beck. She ain't natural."

"Neither was Mitsuri before she went missing. And that dame right there scared *her*. She's more than what she looks like. And if I were you, I'd keep my hands to myself."

My last thought was that I should have grabbed the antique key, the one Steve was attached to. Steve was a lot bigger man than Tim, and given the proper incentive, I had faith he could kick some serious butt.

25

I wanted to throw up.

I was cold and covered in sweat at the same time. A cold towel was placed against my cheeks, then my forehead.

"I do apologize for my men's lack of . . . restraint with the drug. You weren't meant to receive so much. But I'm afraid you frightened them."

I processed the voice. The information.

Drug? What drug? Was I still in the hospital? They OD'd me in the hospital?

Sue!

The voice sort of sounded like a doctor. It was smooth—someone accustomed to talking to people. But since when did the doctor call the nurses his "men"?

I rested back on something very cold and smooth. It felt like leather. I needed to open my eyes, but I was afraid to. My stomach still roiled with displeasure. I was just happy I hadn't overloaded on Mom's biscuits.

"Feeling better?"

I nodded. That voice. I finally forced my eyes open—felt they'd been glued together with Elmer's.

What I hadn't expected was to look up in the face of Reverend Theodore Rollins.

I'm sure my mad scramble to get away from him was opposite the usual reaction he had from his followers. And I just wasn't one of them. I was in some sense terrified of this man.

He reached out and put a hand to the side of my face. I remembered at that moment what had happened—at Triangle Park. Tiny and Beckett. I took a quick assessment of my body—wrists bound with plastic, as were my ankles. But everything seemed to be in working order.

I tried to go all Wraithy on him at that moment—but nothing happened. It felt as if the Elmer's in my eyes was sticking my astral to my physical.

A quick look around proved I was back in Rollins's office, sprawled out on one of his couches near the floor-to-ceiling windows.

Using that self-assessment gesturing, I felt in my pocket for the rock—it was still there. Which meant Tim was nearby. Though I wasn't really sure what good that was going to do me if I ended up with cement shoes.

Interesting how I'd absently equated organized religion with the mob.

Go me.

"Shhh . . ." Rollins's voice, as well as his mannerisms, were gentle. Fatherlike. Yeah, and most fathers kept their little girls tied up on the couch and drugged. "Miss Martinique, I presume?"

I stared at him. I nodded. Was there really a point in lying? I was the one who showed up at the park. Unprotected. No backup.

Stupid, stupid, stupid.

I'd make a lousy cop.

"I am the Reverend Theo Rollins. I apologize for the way in which we have to meet—but with your rather *unique* abilities, I'm afraid it was necessary."

He used the word *unique* the same way the message had. Maybe he *was* Maharba. I stared at him.

He just smiled that perfectly white Betty White smile. Dentures?

I was very uncomfortable this close to him. And it's not because I thought he was a slimeball as much as there was something . . . well . . . oogy.

Close to the same oogy I'd felt that first night I'd stupidly stepped into the Bank of America building, so gung ho to check out the oogy there.

But whereas Trench-Coat had been überoogy, Rollins seemed like a minor oogy.

Mental note: *Oogy bad. Bed better.*

I really should have just stayed at my mom's house.

Rollins frowned at me. He sat on the coffee table in front of the couch, dressed casually in a pair of khakis and white shirt. The sun shone through the windows, over the buildings in the distance.

Daylight. Full-on daylight. What time was it?

"You seem very quiet for someone who's just been—for lack of a better word—kidnapped."

Kidnapped? Hey, no one said anything about being kidnapped. And I hoped the look I shot him said that. I motioned with my hands, making a flat palm with my left and indicating a pen and writing on it with my right.

"You need something to write on?"

Duh.

Rollins moved to his desk and looked around. He came back with a blank legal pad and a pen. I scribbled down a few things and held them up to him. YOUR BOY STOLE MY VOICE. I WANT IT BACK. I ALSO KNOW YOU HAVE SUSAN HIROKUMI.

Rollins's eyes widened, and then he smiled.

And that's when I realized I'd probably just blown my wad. I suspected up until that point, this guy had no idea how I was involved. Now he did. Even with no voice I've got a big mouth.

"First, let me assure you, I don't have anyone here but you and my men. As for what you mean by 'my boy' stole your voice, how can someone steal your voice?"

I smirked. Okay, we'll skip Susan for the moment. Scribble, scribble. You know, if I didn't get my voice back, my handwriting was either going to get better or absolutely unintelligible. Much worse and I'd fulfill the first qualification for doctorhood.

YOU TELL ME. YOU HIRED HIM TO KILL TANAKA.

Rollins's expression wavered only slightly. But I saw it! I'd hit a button. I only hoped it wasn't a self-destruct button, and checked to make sure I'd not worn a red shirt.

"I never hired anyone to kill William Tanaka. And I suppose you'll accuse me next of being a gay porn star and wanting tapes back from Visitar. I'm afraid you're as delusional as the cop you've been sleeping with."

Ah! I have not! And I resent you accusing me of something I haven't done . . . yet.

He narrowed his eyes at me. "You have *no* voice? None?"

I shook my head.

"And you say someone who works for me stole it?"

I nodded again. Oooh, the Reverend was a bright boy!

BUD, I SAW THE ARCHER AT THE HOUSE YOU KEPT SUSAN AT. THAT'S WHERE HE TOOK MY VOICE.

Rollins sat up straight as I watched the color drain from his face. He stared at the legal pad, then snatched it away from me.

"You saw the Archer? Where?"

Okay—I knew faces. Or rather, I understood expressions. And this was a man abruptly on the edge of sanity. He screamed panic at me with his wide eyes and sallow skin. If I hadn't known better, I'd have said this man was terrified.

I shoved my finger at the legal pad he had in a death grip. I'd written right there where—at that stupid project house.

Rollins stared at me. "The Archer was there?" He looked down but wasn't really looking at anything. "He was there with us—and never made a move. He could have extracted me then, but didn't." Rollins focused his gaze back on me. "He took your voice? He attacked you—and took your voice? Tell me." The good Reverend grabbed my shirt and pulled me closer to him. "Were you out of body?"

I nodded and felt creeping tendrils of fear—this man's terror became contagious. He released my shirt and stood, tossing the legal pad back at me. I pulled myself up straighter and into a sitting position.

"*He* knows. *He knows* I'm here—which means he knows I don't have it anymore. Otherwise, he'd never have sent the Archer here—to the physical world."

What—the hell—is he on about?

Was this man losing it? From the speed of his pacing, I'd say yes. I grabbed up the pad and turned to a new page. I scribbled some more but had to slam the pad on the coffee table to get the asshole's attention.

WHAT THE HELL'S WRONG WITH YOU? YOU HIRED HIM, DIDN'T YOU?

Rollins looked down at me after reading the pad. He actually sneered. "I never hired the Archer—no one but the highest of the Phantasms can call upon a Symbiont like it to do their bidding. I had Mitsuri conjure a simple Symbi-

ont to attack Tanaka and frighten him so he'd get my property back for me." He put his hands to his face. "All this
time I thought *that* Symbiont had killed Tanaka. But no . . .
it was the Archer. It could have had me at any time—but
now it's focused its attention on *you*. Tell me"—he fixed
his crazy eyes on me—"is that when you first saw him?
With Tanaka? Did he touch you then?"

I nodded, then tried to press myself back into the couch
when he came at me and yanked up the sleeve of my
sweatshirt. "This? This is his touch? You were still connected to a body?"

I nodded dumbly. Why did he look so excited?

And that smile! I felt like the cornered little rabbit in
front of a very hungry mountain lion. "It's perfect, then,"
Rollins said. "You've taken his and the Phantasm's attention away from me. A Wraith! A real Wraith! Neither of
them can let you live. They're not looking for me!"

Now I was shaking. *Phantasm? What. The. Fuck?*

But Rollins wasn't looking at me anymore. He was pacing again and thinking out loud. Lucky for me.

"Mitsuri warned me there was something more powerful at work here. She sensed you." He looked at me. "I'd
brought you here to help me get back what's rightfully
mine—maybe threaten the life of your little cop lover so
you could steal it for me." He stopped and pinned me to the
couch with his gaze. "As a Wraith, you can become corporeal, correct? Yes?"

I nodded. Shouldna done that. Dizzy. *Ouch.*

He looked happy. Just as long as he didn't look crazy, I
figured I was fine. "Good. Good. But this is better . . ."

Oh hell. I tried to pull the hard, plastic closure open.
But it only cut into my bare wrists and bare ankles. If I
could go Wraith, then go solid enough, I could find some
scissors? Or a knife? But it was hard to concentrate on
much for very long. I just wanted to go back to sleep.

"I can use *her* against Hirokumi to get my things back, and you—" He stopped then and focused on me. I sat up and smiled. "You—I can use you as leverage! I can trade you to him!"

I did not like the sound of this. Especially the part about me being traded to him. *Who's him?*

Oh I think I'm in deep doody.

Rollins was on me—so to speak—in seconds. He sat on the couch beside me, his hands taking up my wrists and holding them tightly. I tried twisting away from him, but he was strong.

Strength of the insane.

And he was close—way too close. And his breath smelled foul. Like something had died in there. *Ew.*

And that oogy feeling? Well, it was washing over me like ocean waves. There was something really not right about this man. I felt nauseous.

"It's a perfect plan. I can keep this life, and they'll never know what I've done. They'll never suspect. The Archer will know—but with you as a trade—I can lure him into the game with me." He smiled, and I saw it again.

The same image I'd seen on Daniel's face.

The skull. Death.

"When Mitsuri swore she'd sensed a real Wraith I'd been afraid then. Do you know how many Wraiths there are in my world? None, Miss Martinique. And do you know why? Because once a soul transmutates into one, the Symbionts hunt it down and eat it. And do you know why?"

I shook my head. I was still getting over the "eat it" part.

"Because Phantasms fear them. Wraiths are the harbingers, Miss Martinique. The bringers of life and of death. I had to find you, and it was so easy. And then I learned you were the same woman my men had seen with the cop."

You know, instead of concentrating on my own abilities at the spy game, I've really got to be more careful about other people spying on *me*!

I struggled against him again. Geez . . . me as helpless female was getting old. I wanted to slap him. I wanted to scream. I wanted to go Wraith on him and club him from behind.

I tried harder this time, focusing my concentration. Oh, I felt the usual slip, and the physical and astral worlds did a weird slipstream on me, but I couldn't move any farther. I was half-in and half-out.

It was as if my feet were cemented to my body.

"Please, don't wear yourself out, Miss Martinique. The plastic ties are spelled with binding mist. You can't become a Wraith as long as you wear them. You are mine, for now." He smiled and squeezed my wrists tighter. "Mitsuri saw you here—that night. It was you, watching me. Listening in. She went after you, and disappeared. Did you kill her, Wraith? Is that why she never returned, and you still live?"

I'd let her go. I knew that now. I'd released her from a life of servitude. Now how did I *know* that?

"You really can't make a sound, can you? If it's really the Archer you've seen"—Rollins narrowed his eyes at me again and leaned in closer—"then it's not so strange he would take your voice. His master removed his long ago when he dared to speak against him."

Now by this time the asshole was less than two inches from my face.

And being that close, it was hard for me to relax. I couldn't slip out of my body. I couldn't kick him because my feet were bound. He had one hell of a grip on my wrists.

So I did the next best thing.

I bit his nose.

And I bit down hard and wasn't about to let go.

He cried out and let go of my hands. Okay—so biting was a form of girl fighting—but it got the asshole off of me.

He also pulled me up by sheer force, trying to tear his nose away from me. But I have good jaws (*ah! I know what you were thinking! Don't go there!*). But when I clamp down I really clamp down.

I had a boyfriend once, made the mistake of calling me the wrong name during a very heated and intense session in his car. And let's just say, I doubt he ever again asked a girl to—

You get the picture.

But this time I tasted blood. I felt something tearing.

Rollins howled and grabbed me around my neck.

That did it—I was choking again. I let go of his nose. I thought he'd let go of my neck, you know a courtesy thing—but he didn't.

Shit, shit, shit—not again! I'd just got past the last bruising. Was Daniel ever going to see me non-beat-up? Rollins had me on my feet, with me unable to kick. I tried to pull his hands away, but my own bound wrists were useless.

Abruptly, his hold disappeared, and we both fell to the floor. Rollins flopped to my right, hitting the coffee table and crashing through it. He lay still, his nose a bloody mess. I hadn't ripped the end off, but he was going to have my dental impression in it for a while.

I'd fallen backward, unable to balance with my ankles locked together. But I didn't hit the ground. Someone caught me and lowered me to the couch.

I turned and looked up at Tim's face. He was smiling, his eyes wide, and his physical skin bone white.

"I did it." His voice was breathless. And I think that was a turning point in the ghost's life, helping me like that. "I'm sorry it took me so long, but I had to gather enough strength to pick up that paperweight and hit him with it."

I looked on the floor and saw the lead cross Tim had used to kayo the good Reverend. I remember seeing it on my first visit. A paperweight.

I pointed to the binder on my ankles and wrists. He nodded and went back to the desk. He found a pocketknife and tossed it to me before abruptly disappearing. I was able to cut the plastic, coughing the whole time, and sputtering.

My throat hurt again. And I figured—if Trench-Coat hadn't of absconded with my voice, then I'd probably have lost it anyway from being choked all the time.

And what's with that? I'm a nice person. Why are people trying to kill me?

I absently shoved the plastic as well as the knife into the pocket of my sweats (better to have Rhonda take a look at the mechanics of something that could prevent me from going OOB) and stood—and sat back down. Oh man . . . I was woozy. *Drugs. I hate drugs. How can people function on drugs?* And I didn't even know what it was those assholes had shot me up with.

Speaking of Tiny and Beckett, where were they? Evidently Rollins had deemed me meek enough to be in a room with him alone, but that didn't mean they weren't just outside the door.

Or worse, watching on some monitor screen somewhere.

I quickly dismissed that second thought—if there had been someone watching and seen Tim bludgeon ole Teddy here—they'd have already been through that door. I was guessing he'd ordered our little meeting to be a closed one.

But why?

And come to think of it, what the hell had the man been talking about?

"Zoë—you okay?"

It was Tim's voice, near my cheek, but I couldn't see him. I figured he'd pretty much used all the tangible energy he had to become solid for that brief instant and was now little more than a wisp.

I nodded and stood again—a little slower this time. I continued to cough, now and then. Soundless. Very creepy.

I looked at the door, then I looked back at the desk.

You know, since I was here . . .

Shuffling to the desk in my ugly-duck slippers was arduous—especially since the room kept moving sideways. Long-lingering whatever-it-was drug. But then again, in the past week, I'd had a concussion, been pronounced dead, had some ethereal, undead thing shove his snake's tongue down my throat and rip out my voice, been kidnapped by the bad guy (I should add voluntarily—'cause if I get down to it, nobody made me drive Mom's car to that damned park, stupid), and summarily drugged.

Wow, with a week like this, is it a wonder I'm still single?

Luckily, Mr. Crazy-Reverend had unlocked his desk, and I was able to open all the drawers.

Unluckily—I didn't find Jack Shit (ever wondered who Jack was—and why on earth his mother married a guy named Shit?). Not even a document. I did find a few books on the occult—one of them even looked like a pocket-pal kinda thing—like one of those five-inch-by-eight-inch books to use when visiting a foreign country.

And when I thumbed through it—it read like one. Only this wasn't to visit France or Germany or even England (hey, they may speak English, but they drive on the wrong side of the road over there)—it was a how-to on visiting . . .

. . . uh, the physical plane.

I opened up the front to see the publisher. And—there wasn't one.

I ignored the *Twilight Zone* theme in my head and shoved the thing into the pocket of my sweats and kept looking.

I'd hoped I'd find something telling me where the little girl was, and if she was okay. The way old Teddy was talking, it sounded like she was still alive. And maybe if I'd just played it cool, he'd have taken me to her.

Yeah, bound and drugged. And exactly what good could I have done like that?

Well you sure as hell weren't doing any good in your body wearing ugly-duck slippers.

"Zoë, I know you've got the curiosity of a cat," Tim said on the wind beside me. "But there's someone coming."

Shit. I closed the desk drawers. I didn't immediately see a place to hide. *Great—now what?*

I saw the phone and picked it up, my fingers poised just above the numbers, ready to dial.

Yeah, and say what? Damn. The reality hit me at that moment—I couldn't even use the phone to *call* someone much less answer.

Moving more like a Weeble—wobbling but not entirely falling down—I made it to where Teddy was. I grabbed up the paperweight—heavy!—and shuffled to the door. I didn't have much of a plan, figured once they came through the opening, I could hit one of them with the weight and hope there was only one.

Someone tried the handle. It was locked.

Knock, knock. "Boss? You okay? Silent alarm's picked up an intruder on the grounds."

An intruder? Were they detecting Tim's presence?

"Boss?"

I turned to look at Teddy—who wasn't sprawled on the floor anymore.

"Zoë!"

I didn't duck as much as fall out of the way of Rollins's

grip. He'd moved behind me and fallen into the doorframe as I turned too fast and lost my balance.

The goons outside, Tiny and Beckett, pounded a little harder on the doors. It wouldn't be long before they broke through, and I was no match for the two of them. Even if I wasn't in bad shape, my defense training would protect me from maybe one, but not all of them.

Hey, Jackie Chan I am not. But the more I thought about the past few days, maybe I should look into it.

I stumbled and regained my balance. The drug's effects lingered still, though not as bad—just enough to make me clumsier than normal. Rollins was also moving a bit like a sailor with no sea legs. But I was thinking Tim hit him a little too hard with that cross.

The pounding got louder, and I heard wood crack. Rollins moved toward the door—if he let them in I was doomed. Especially with their guns.

I have a more-than-healthy fear of guns.

What I needed was a back door. Surely a guy as crooked as Rollins had a secondary way out of his office—just in case of a police raid or—or if a stampede of loyal Jesus freaks broke down the door.

Of course my first instinct was to call out to Tim and say "Look for a secret door!"

It really bites not having a voice.

I heard the door give.

"Boss—you're bleeding!"

Awwww . . . how sweet. Not.

Rollins growled, "Get her," loud and clear. Going down on hands and knees, I shuffle-crawled to the other side of the couch as Tiny and Beckett moved in the opposite direction.

See—I'd watched them long enough to know the two wouldn't think of dividing and conquering.

Now at the end of the couch closest to the door, I peeked

around the side to see Rollins stalk back to his desk. Drug
or no drug—I had to get out of there.

With a silent scream (so it was a good thing this time), I
stood and bolted for the door. Once through, I ran-
stumbled as fast as I could down the hall of Theodore (all
those pictures, remember?). It wasn't as fast as I'd have
liked—the ugly-duck slippers didn't have the kung fu
grip I wanted.

"There she is!"

Yipes!

"Just wound her—boss wants her alive."

Wound? Gosh . . . didn't these guys have like a tran-
quilizer gun or something? Some means of subduing a
prisoner without resorting to slugs?

What the hell am I thinking? I didn't *want* to be tranqued
any more than I wanted to be—

Gunshots! *Pow! Pow!*

Something zinged past my ear and exploded onto the
doorframe leading into the main foyer. I burst forward,
stumbling and sprawling into the main room behind the
staircase.

My sweats also caused me to slide a good bit too—my
momentum pushing me forward so that I was totally
missed by the two WWE suits running by the staircase
and into the hallway of Rollins's office.

I scrambled back up and ducked behind the back of the
stairs. Three guards stood outside the door, each with assault rifles.

Uh-uh.

*Now what? The bad guys are going to come out of that
hallway any second.*

So I went up the stairs. On hindsight, it probably wasn't
the best move I could have made, but I was running on
pure adrenaline now.

The thing split into two paths—right or left.

I took left—it was less lit. And I had a faint memory of heading down this way before.

The corridor dumped out into another one of those long hallways. I stopped at the entrance and listened for the goons.

What I heard was . . . Fosters Home for Imaginary Friends.

Hey, I watch Cartoon Network *too, you know.*

Susan!

Using a bit more caution, I moved to each door until I heard the television the loudest. The door was locked. *Oh duh. And shouldn't there be guards?*

Now, that thought didn't register as strongly as it should have.

Susan? I hissed with absolutely no voice and rapped a knuckle loudly on the door.

I heard something inside and the television stopped.

I knocked again even softer.

"Hello?" It was a child's voice. Frightened. Scared. But alive. "Who's there?"

Oh, it's me. That lady you saw get French-kissed by the bald guy in the trench coat. Man, come to think of it, I was sure that whole scene was probably going to scar her for life—thinking if she kissed a guy he'd hurt her.

Hrm. Maybe at her age that wasn't a bad thing. Might keep the bogeymen away.

Damn, damn, damn. How was I going to get in there and reassure this kid I was a friend when I couldn't speak? I was contemplating this when a hand came from behind me and clamped over my mouth.

Another one encircled my arms, pinning them to my sides. Instinct went into action (not to mention all that adrenaline). I leaned into him, stomped his right foot (not very successful with ugly-duck slippers on). But he hissed and released his hold on my arms. I spun right, pushed with my left, and power-drove my right elbow backward into his fleshy middle.

After hearing a satisfied "oof," I spun the rest of the way. Recognizing Tiny, I gave a silent yell and kicked up with my left foot into his already-swollen nose.

It was a beautiful move—too bad I wasn't paying more attention.

A bigger goon with cheap aftershave moved behind me as I kicked. When I turned to make my way to the stairs, he nailed me with a two-by-four against my left cheek. Stars momentarily filled my vision, and I staggered. That second of lost footing gave my attacker the window he needed to grab me around the neck and press a gun to my head.

"I got her!" this guy yelled out. *Ow . . . not so loud!*

I could just see Rollins and six more WWE hustling up the steps through the stars in front of my eyes. Beckett flanked his boss. I could hear poor Tiny moaning nearby. Two hits to the same face. *Yow.*

The stars cleared as Rollins's bloody face loomed closer, though he didn't look at me. "Where was the intruder detected?"

"Near the east wing, lower level."

"Which signal was it?"

The man holding me said, "Blue."

Rollins nodded. "Physical. Could be the cop, come to save his little girlfriend." Then he looked at me. "Stash her in the trunk of the limo. I want her bound and drugged, but unharmed." He reached out and touched my forehead. The sense of oogy radiated off of this man, about like it had with Trench-Coat, and I tried jerking away from him.

"She's my insurance policy with the Symbiont. Move the girl as well. We leave now." Rollins and four of the goons marched back down the stairs.

Oh hell! Not the trunk again. I had a permanent phobia

of trunks—not that I really remember my joyride in my Mustang's trunk—but I do remember the aftermath.

When held from behind by an assailant, the proper thing to do is stomp down on his foot, turn, and knee him in the groin. And normally that works for me. Except I missed his foot, and when I tried to move, he clocked me with the gun.

Sonofabitch! That hurts*!*

Stars again, followed by a wee bit of nausea. Wraith . . . I needed to go Wraith. I also needed to get that ringing between my ears to stop.

I thought about Tim. If he had any tricks up his sleeve, now was the time to play them.

"Zoë."

Speak o' the devil.

"I can't manifest, Zoë. That took too much out of me. If you could jump, maybe you could go corporeal and stop them. But if they hit you with that needle again . . ."

If I went unconscious, I would be immediately pulled back into my body and trapped inside. Same as before. Wash. Rinse. Repeat.

Time to go Wraith and get the hell out of here.

I relaxed as the big guy half dragged, half carried me.

I was amazed at how easy this was becoming, to just slip in and out of my body. And I wondered for a second if all the popping in and out wasn't somehow like wearing down the silver cord connection.

Was it possible to break the cord? Could I sew it back on if I did?

"Hey, I think the broad fainted."

I stood to the side of them as the guy holding me paused near the stairway. Tiny had moved from the floor, another bloodied handkerchief over his face. Beckett turned and peered down at me.

Wait—broad? Who uses broad *to refer to a woman nowadays? How quaint.*

Jerk.

I wasn't as wobbly in my astral form—evidently not experiencing the same physical effects as my body did. I watched my head roll to one side. *Ew.* My eyes were open. Staring. Hadn't noticed *that* before.

He knelt and set me down on the floor. He was really kinda gentle too. "She's purdy."

Awww . . .

"She's dangerous," Beckett said, and I noticed he was looking about the hallway. "Shit, she's out again. I say we tie her up right here and drug her." He handed his gun off to Tiny and knelt beside me. I watched him pull out another set of those plastic things. Were these spelled too?

Tiny started going through my pockets. He took out my phone as well as the rock. He pocketed the phone but tossed the rock to the side. It knocked against a nearby wall and rolled still.

Uh-oh.

Tim appeared beside me. "You've got to get that rock back."

I did. I became corporeal more easily this time and snatched up the rock. I was on Tiny before he could turn and smashed the rock into the side of his face. His gun went off, the bullet lodging in the throat of the one who'd hit me in the head.

Two down, one to go.

But I hadn't been watching Beckett for a second time. With wide eyes he grabbed up the syringe and jabbed the needle into my neck.

Damn. I had only a few minutes before I'd get sucked back in again.

The lights dimmed.

"Zoë!" Tim hissed. "They've got company!"

Shadows moved to our right and left. People in black pajamas.

I looked at Tim. *What the hey? Ninjas?*

I counted six in all, three from the right and three from the left. It was at that moment I realized I could see them because I was Wraith—there was that heightened sense of the dark. It wasn't that the lights dimmed—the lights had gone out!

Rollins's men were blind!

They didn't see the guys in pajamas. So they didn't see what hit them as each was clubbed from behind or the side by a black-clad intruder. The men whose faces were as well hidden as their bodies bent over Rollins's goons and disarmed them.

One of them grabbed my phone back out of Tiny's pocket and shoved it into a black bag over his shoulder.

Popular phone.

To my surprise one of the larger shapes leaned over me—er, my body—and put two fingers to my neck. He looked at the others and nodded. And in one graceful move, he lifted me up over his shoulder and carried my body fireman-style down the stairs.

What gives? I was convinced now that he wasn't Daniel—unless Daniel was some clandestine member of a Black Dragon Yakuza cult or something.

"I think you're being kidnapped—again."

What the fuck? I looked at Tim. *By who now?*

The men were as quiet leaving the building as they had been entering. I heard the sound of several silencers, followed by the thuds of bodies hitting the floor. Tim and I peered over the side railing to see the six men leave out the front door.

I turned to Tim and noticed the rock on the ground.

The rock! Without it, Tim couldn't travel with me—wherever that might be.

Tim was on the same page. I managed to become corporeal enough to pick the rock up, but when the same dizziness and nausea I'd had before returned, I tossed it inside one of the urns of a potted palm tree.

Tim spoke. "There's nothing you can do, Zoë. You're already fading."

He was right. I could feel the pull of my body even at this distance. Oh this sucked. I couldn't just leave Tim here! How was he going to get back to the house in Little Five Points?

This was just a really odd turn of events. First I'm kidnapped by Rollins's boys, and now my body was out the door with a whole other group of kidnappers.

What gives? What is so all foul important about me?

I was lifted through the air as my cord pulled me back. Rollins's men were scattered about the little drive area beneath an extinguished chandelier. A black limo, the trunk open, sat idling in front of me.

I had no idea which way the boys in pjs had gone. Until I heard a car start to my right. I looked down to get a good view of the cord at my belly button (you think there's a connection between the fact that the silver cord holding the spirit to the body is located where the body was once connected to Mom?).

I blinked.

This probably wasn't a good time for philosophical speculation.

But my cord did trail off in that direction. Which was the direction I was now traveling. Very quickly.

I came upon a black kidnap van (the kind with no windows on the sides or back) parked just outside the gate entrance. I arrived just as the little group of six did with my body.

That's when I realized none of them were speaking English.

The one carrying my body was helped inside by an Asian man in a black suit. He wore a headset with a mic in front of his nose. The interior of the van was a mixture of ambulance and surveillance utility.

The pull on my cord strengthened, and the entire scene faded away as I slid back inside my body. There wasn't any pain as I slid into unconsciousness, only the stray thought of what would happen to Tim.

Mom's gonna kill me.

26

ONE day I'm going to take a tape recorder and walk along the streets of downtown Atlanta, and ask passersby what they did a week before Thanksgiving (this was all contingent on me kicking Trench-Coat's ass and getting my voice back).

I'm sure most of them were busy buying groceries, baking cookies, calling friends and family, or even flying out to their destinations. You know, normal holiday stuff.

NONE of them were bouncing around from one kidnapper to the next, waking up from drug-induced sleeps (much less inside of morgue drawers . . . shit!) or being choked by wacky, strung-out televangelists.

No—that would be *my* life.

Waking up this time wasn't as bad. I was in a real bed, not on a couch, and I wasn't tied up in any fashion. Still had a headache though. Might be a lack of caffeine for the day.

Wait . . . what day *was* it anyway?

I smelled food—and my stomach let out a very embarrassing growl. When was the last time I'd eaten? Mom's? She fixed biscuits, right? What time was it?

I felt soft sheets against my thigh and rump.

That opened my eyes. I pulled up the sheets and looked under them.

And where were my clothes?

I realized then I was on a very soft pallet on the floor. Several dim lamps sat around the room, giving things an eerie, brownish glow. I couldn't see any other furniture, other than a low-legged black lacquered table to my left beside the bed. On top rested a small ceramic cup and a matching ceramic carafe. Condensation beaded on the outside.

Water?

Thirst overwhelmed all sensation, and I sat up, exposing breasts and all as I bypassed the tiny cup, took the carafe in both hands, and guzzled the cold water inside.

Ouch. I winced from the cold. Brain freeze. But I didn't stop. I was too thirsty.

I heard something and moved the carafe from my mouth, vaguely aware some of the water had spilled over my mouth and now dripped onto the blankets in my lap. The wall to my left and near my feet slid away.

"Ah, you are awake."

An older Asian woman, maybe just the other side of a hundred, bowed. She wore a light-colored kimono that shimmered in the dim illumination. Her snow-colored hair was pulled back from a face devoid of any blemishes. Oh, she had wrinkles, but her skin was incredibly smooth to look at.

You know, that whole baby's bottom kinda thing.

She knelt on the floor with a grace I'd never have. I felt my cheeks go bright red with the heat of embarrassment and wiped at my water mustache.

With a nod and bow, she took the now empty carafe

from my hands and smiled. "I will have Dojima bring in clothing, food, and more water."

This woman stood—a single fluid movement—and glided along the floor to the door. Just as she turned the corner another woman appeared. This time I yanked the cover up over my breasts. This kimono was much younger, with black hair that hung over her shoulders.

She brought in a small stack of clothes, set them inside the door, then came back with a tray of small plates and a larger carafe. To my surprise she winked at me before sliding the door closed.

Where the hell was I? Japan?

I stood, naked, and grabbed up the clothes. They were smooth, made from silk and cotton. It was a kimono of dark green. Simple. Luckily I'd worn one once, so I kind of knew how to put it on.

Afterward, I found a brush and comb on the table beside my bed and attacked my hair. It'd been washed—I knew this because it had a shitload of static in it. Which then made me freak out that I'd been bathed while unconscious.

Yow!

And tangles. I finally managed to separate it into three pieces and braid it. But with no rubber band—ah, there was one on the floor. Probably tucked in the kimono.

The food was incredible. Small dishes of things that smelled great, tasted better, and I couldn't identify. That was okay. I used my chopsticks with gusto and almost gave myself a stomachache.

I'd finished up the entire carafe and was on my third cup of tea when the door slid open again. It was the nice older kimono. She bowed and beckoned me to come with her.

I hesitated. Call me suspicious—but my life in the past week had been no less than a roller-coaster ride of just way

too much fun. I didn't want to be led somewhere else I
might be vulnerable. And in my physical body—I was just
as susceptible to any physical danger as the next person.

I was positive I was going to see Hirokumi—who apparently knew more than he'd told Daniel in their meeting.
If I could fool him—I believed I could fool anyone.

But where to put my body?

I looked at the old kimono in the doorway and held up a
finger. She seemed to understand the "wait a minute" gesture and slid the door shut.

A bit more exploring and I found a narrow closet near my
sleeping pallet. The door slid to the side, and there was just
enough room in there for me to sit against the wall.

With a glance at the other door, I scooted in and shut
the closet. It was dark—darker than I'd thought it would
be—and I settled myself. I got as comfortable as a five-
foot-nine body could get in a three-foot-five space. At least
this wasn't a trunk, and no one was gonna joyride a closet.

Once again I slid out of my body and opened my eyes to
a world of sooty shadows and washed-out colors.

Whoohoo.

I held up my hands—transparent. I thought of Daniel. I
thought of taking Daniel on my bed, of him beneath me, of
him writhing in extreme pleasure.

Pop! I was solid. *And what's up with that? Thinking of
sex makes me corporeal?*

The world wasn't as dim in this form, though I was still
aware of a few things that scooted here and there. Things
that—if I really analyzed their shapes—resembled wee little
shadowy dragons. The colors of the room still looked muted.
I didn't know how long I could stay this way—as I believed
Rhonda's battery theory—but I'd rested (more than I'd
wanted to) and I'd eaten. I could probably stay traveling for
several hours, as long as I didn't stay solid all the time.

I also didn't have my watch. Come to think of it—where *was* my watch?

With a deep breath, I slid the door over myself and, after a well-subdued burp, followed her. I found myself trying to simulate her gliding walk—ain't gonna happen.

I was too clumsy, even astral. And too tall.

We went through a maze of paper-covered hallways before turning a corner and confronting a large, double, sliding door. The old kimono knelt in front of the door and looked up at me.

Oh. Me too?

I knelt (oh man, my knee actually creaked—I wondered if the knee on my physical body had done it too—the noise echoing in my room), but I didn't lower my head. I was too fascinated with the picture painted on the smooth paper doors.

At first it looked like two dragons fighting. But then it changed and I saw two people, on either side, apparently controlling the dragons. And as I looked at the door's carvings, I noticed things *in* them. Painted ever so subtly were faces, bodies, animals, all worked together to create the image of the dragons.

It was really impressive.

The doors parted.

"Please, come in, Miss Martinique."

I glanced at the old kimono. She was bowed completely over, her forehead touching the floor.

Standing, I moved through the doorway and into the room beyond.

It was like stepping through a time portal, from old Japan to present day.

The floors were polished hardwood, covered in deep green oriental rugs. The walls were made of dark wood as well, decorated with evenly spaced portraits. It reminded me just a bit of the hallway leading to Rollins's office, only I couldn't see who was in these pictures.

A large, ornately carved desk sat as the centerpiece of the room. Behind was a gold paneled screen painted with a similar scene as the one on the front doors. Two potted palms flanked the desk, giving the room an organic feel, and I heard the running water before I saw the fountain tucked into the right corner.

Very feng shui, you know.

Hirokumi sat behind his desk. He stood as I approached and moved around the desk. He wore what I guess was the equivalent of a man's kimono. Black, wide sleeves. Looked comfy.

I was thinking that Daniel would look nice in one of these, with nothing on underneath.

Heh.

Hirokumi stepped toward me, his arms extended. "I hope you will accept my apologies, Miss Martinique. My name is Koba Hirokumi. I am a friend of Detective Frasier. I had no idea the Reverend's men would intercept my message to you."

His hands were warm as he took mine in his. I was afraid I'd go all transparent-like when he touched me, but I was apparently solid to him. His hands were strong too—solid. And I sensed something.

Power. This was a man to be feared.

Then what he said clicked in. *Hirokumi* had sent me the message to meet him, not Rollins. And he'd paid me. Which meant he knew my profession.

Ouch—people with money. Think they can just do what they want.

Sigh. Wish I was one.

When I didn't speak, he gestured for me to take one of the chairs in front of the desk. I did, and instead of taking his position of power behind the ornate masterpiece, he sat in the chair beside me.

"I was very troubled when my men found your car abandoned and you missing. I knew then he'd either intercepted my e-mail to you, or had someone watching your mother's house and followed you. But, in his rusting life, my foe has grown easy to read. I knew where he would take you and where he would keep you.

"You also left your phone on, which made it easier to track you."

I know my eyes probably widened to the size of silver dollars. I was impressed, but also made a mental note to turn the damned thing off in the future. I'm not sure how comfortable I was with being tracked. I also didn't think that was legal.

He narrowed his eyes at me. "Your detective friend is very worried about you. Apparently your mother found your room empty yesterday morning, and they identified the car left at Triangle Park as belonging to her."

Yesterday morning? I frowned at him, trying to convey my own confusion.

"It's Wednesday evening."

Wednesday? What the hell happened to Tuesday?

Hirokumi gave me a very fatherly smile. "I'm afraid Rollins kept you sedated longer than you realized. And with good reason—with what you can do—he is afraid of you. More so now, if I suspect what has happened to you, has."

I blinked at him. I really didn't know this man—wasn't sure I could trust him. I didn't know how he knew about me. Or how he was really involved in Rollins's weirdness.

I used my right hand and mimicked writing on my left palm. When Hirokumi frowned, I put a hand to my throat and shook my head.

His eyes widened. "Then it's true . . . the Symbiont Archer has stolen your voice."

Wait—is this like broadcast news? Is there a paranormal podcast out there just letting everyone know what happened to me?

I made the gesture again, and the businessman went to his desk and pulled out a pen and paper. The paper was a notepad with the logo of Visitar Incorporated on it.

HOW DO YOU KNOW ABOUT ME? AND YEAH, HE TOOK MY VOICE.

I'd hoped my writing hurriedly would convey to him how upset at this whole thing I was. But it just wasn't the same—not having a voice to get really mean with.

Hirokumi read quickly and gave me another one of those fatherly looks. Only there was something else in his expression. Wariness?

He also looked dejected—kind of like a father who suspected his kid used drugs, then discovered his suspicion was right. And didn't want it to be.

"The moment Mitsuri said a Wraith was present, we had a problem. If any unseen spirits were to be in that office, it would be the Symbiont we all know as the Archer."

Ah-HA!

No wait. What?

I grabbed up the pad. YOU KNEW HE KILLED TANAKA.

Hirokumi nodded. "I tried to warn Daniel away from it all—to tell him things weren't as they seemed." He turned and pulled the small book I'd swiped from Rollins's desk from beneath a stack of papers. "You got this from the Reverend's office?"

I nodded. I'd forgotten about it.

"While you were there, did you see Susan?"

I shook my head, but I also scribbled. I THINK I HEARD HER BEHIND LOCKED DOOR.

"Then she was there and she was still alive," Hirokumi said in a low voice. "What did Rollins say to you? Do you realize what this is?"

1ST: HE SAID THINGS NO SENSE. 2ND: NOPE.

I rechecked my writing and realized I was starting to abbreviate things. And not in a good way. I was feeling a bit tired already.

Uh-oh. So soon? How much energy do I burn up when I stay physical like this?

"Did he tell you the reason for all this madness? What it was I possess and he would kill to have returned?"

I shook my head on that. I was pleading dumb on this one.

Hirokumi stood and tossed the book on the desk. He went to the other side and unlocked either a drawer or safe out of my line of sight. After a few seconds he pulled out a manila folder with a blue tab on it. I'd seen folders like this in the doctor's office. Sort of like a patient file.

He slid it across the desk at me. I picked it up. The side tab read Theodore Rollins. Uh-oh. I opened it. Lots of typed paper. There were a few of those red, pointy stickers—kinda like the ones used on documents nowadays to let you know where to sign—stuck in several places.

I read those places first—and then read them again.

I looked up at Hirokumi. He was sitting in his chair, his elbows on the desk, his hands clasped in front of him. He'd read my expression perfectly. "Yes—Rollins had cancer."

Had cancer. I looked back down at the dates. This was impossible. These papers said he was diagnosed—twice with a second opinion—over twenty years ago.

Could someone survive with cancer for twenty years? And come to think of it, that would have made him in his early thirties at the time of diagnosis. The man that had had me by the throat didn't appear to be suffering from anything—except maybe overexcitability.

"Those are the documents of a man who should be dead."

I looked at the papers in my hand again. I thumbed through them, scanned the doctor's scribbled notes—okay—I deciphered what I thought they said. All of them gave a diagnosis of death within a year.

"His body was riddled with it—two surgeries exposed the cursed poison to oxygen. There was nothing anyone could do. He would have died before he was thirty-one."

I looked at Hirokumi. "How?" I mouthed this to him.

The businessman reached for a small, ornate wood box on the top of the desk. It was set askew to the side, and I thought maybe it had cigars in it.

Hirokumi brought out a dragon statue, which I assumed was the one Mitsuri had had in his office, and lit the tongue. I forced myself to remain calm. If I got sucked into the thing, then well—cover was blown, and I was so toast.

But the smoke didn't rise into a dragon, nor did it seem to be paying attention to me at all.

The man clapped his hands and spoke some weird words. I swear I saw something move in the air between it and me as the lid popped open. Hirokumi opened up the box, and all hell broke loose.

At least for me.

They were shadows at first, little glimpses of black wisps of smoke that dove about in the air. I thought for a minute that they were little gnats wearing bits of gauze—but that was silly.

Then several of them flew at me and hovered in front of my eyes.

They had faces—human-like faces—with big teeth and bug eyes.

If I'd had my voice, I'd have been screaming like a girl

as I swatted at them, though not one of the gnats actually bit me.

Then abruptly the smoking dragon came to life—or the smoke did—and I swear I heard those little creatures squeal as they were sucked into the dragon.

"You can *see* the guardians?"

If you mean the gnats from hell—fuck yeah. I nodded but kept looking around for them.

"Interesting." He reached in his desk and pulled on latex gloves before reaching in the box and removing a single, folded piece of parchment.

Okay—that definitely wasn't a porno tape.

He unfolded it carefully, placed it on the table, turned so I could see it. It looked like it'd been written with a quill pen, all blobby and sketchy. And like anything set in front of me, I started to read it.

It was a contract, set forth between one Theodore Rollins and something that just wasn't pronounceable. At least not for me anyway.

But that wasn't the weird part. No . . . that was several lines down in the archaic script.

According to this, Rollins had sold his soul for long life and good health.

Oh . . . was that *all*? Where was the tag line asking for wealth and fame? If I sound sarcastic, it's because I was. This was soooo cliché. I mean . . . a contract between Rollins and what I assumed was the devil over his soul.

Oh how ultimately formulaic can we get here people?

I grabbed up the paper and shook it at Hirokumi. That's when I saw the man's horrified expression.

"What?" I mouthed at him. Oh I REALLY wished I had my voice back.

He stood slowly, and shakily I might add, before pointing at the paper. "Your hand . . . it does not burn?"

Burn? I set the paper down on the desk and looked at my hands. No—no burns. I turned them to face him. See?

Hirokumi took the paper and refolded it before setting it back inside the box. After closing the box and relocking it, he removed his gloves. I waited impatiently for some sort of explanation.

Instead, he turned to a compact cell phone and flipped it open. Speed dial, and he was speaking Japanese into it.

As he hung up, I heard the sound of a door sliding open. I turned to see a wee little man in a black suit enter the same door I'd come through. White, stringy, thin hair hung in a semicircle from a bony head and pooled against his black lapels. A Fu Manchu mustache hung over his upper lip, and the light from the room's lamps shone off of the top of his bald head.

Hirokumi returned the bow.

"This is my seer, Rai Keitaro."

Sure it was. I stood from my chair and faced the man. Standing at full height, he barely came to my navel.

Rai bowed and peered up at me through heavy, folded eyes. He nodded as he started walking around me. Hirokumi moved to drag my chair out of the way. I felt like the center of a merry-go-round.

The little fucker was making me dizzy.

Hirokumi said something in Japanese and nodded to the box. Rai nodded but held up his hand as if to indicate silence.

I noticed something then. It was soft at first. Whispers in my ears. Vague, wispy images moved in the air around Rai, yet somehow I knew that he knew they were there.

"Yes, yes," Rai said as he mumbled to himself and stopped in front of me. He glanced at Hirokumi. "Kado."

Kado?

Like in OJ's houseboy?

Rai shook his head. "No—Kay-doe. Not like 't' sound."

I blinked at him. Did he hear my thoughts?

Rai shrugged. "Some of them. Very untrained. American woman. Brash. Unpolished. You look Greek."

Irish-Latino, bud.

The little man shrugged again and clasped his hands together. "Same difference. You all look alike. Very beautiful."

I laughed. Well, in theory I did. Looked kinda funny with no sound. I liked this old guy.

Hirokumi stepped forward. "Is she a Wraith? Was Mitsuri correct?"

Like we needed clarification from the little toad?

"Yes and no—not quite. Unique." Rai touched his own throat. I noticed the wispy things again, just briefly. What the hell were they? "Not like me anymore."

Not like him . . . was he a Wraith too?

Rai looked at me. "No."

"You can hear her?" Hirokumi said.

Rai nodded. "I told you already—some things. Some thoughts are loud, others muddled. Very chaotic up here." He reached up to his own temple and tapped. Then with a frown, he reached out and poked my middle with a crooked finger.

Ow.

Okay buddy, if you can hear me, I'd like some answers, like did Trench-Coat turn me into a Wraith, and what does all this have to do with Rollins?

Rai gestured for me to sit. I grabbed up the chair Hirokumi had moved away and turned it to face the little man. I wasn't missing this—I somehow knew I was about to get the first real answers since my first encounter with Trench-Coat in that building.

"Trench-Coat—very amusing. American moniker. Many worlds center around this one—this world is the physical plane." Rai held his right hand out in front of him, palm down as if indicating a flat surface. "Middle of things. There are worlds above, and worlds below."

Okay. Physical plane is the middle, yadda, yadda, yadda. Above and below, like Heaven and Hell?

The man shook his head. "No. More complicated than that. No good. No evil. Simply is."

Ah . . . like the mental, the astral, then the Ethereal and the Abysmal?

He smiled. Little gnome was missing quite a few teeth. "Yes. Exactly. You saw guardians." Rai nodded toward the smoking dragon.

I nodded. Then I frowned. *Now, how come the smoky dragon inside didn't come out and try to eat me this time? Is it because I'm corporeal?*

Rai smiled at me and winked. "Yes to that. But they are on one plane of existence. Several levels above and below, existing within the Abysmal." He gestured to a space below his hand. "The closer to the physical plane, the stronger the being. Mortal existence, the soul"—he pointed to Hirokumi— "come from one plane, experience this world, and then move on to the next. Sometimes return for new lessons."

I glanced at Hirokumi. How come Rai didn't point to me or to himself?

"Mortal souls are different because they can transcend planes. They can move beyond levels of existence to become all things."

I nodded. *Okay, so a soul can reach enlightenment. Basic Religion 101.*

He nodded. This kind of communication was better than the notepad.

"They—other beings—they want physical existence. They want carnal pleasure. They crave this plane, but forbidden to be born. They have no soul, no transcendence."

That would suck. So they just float around watching us?

"Some can, some can't. Different levels of being have

different abilities. They have their own world, one a mortal cannot see." He smiled at me. "As what you call a Traveler, I live in two worlds, the physical and the astral. But as a Wraith, you . . ." He smiled when he paused. It was very creepy. "You live in all worlds. One foot in, one foot out. You bring death, and you bring life. You live in all"—he leaned toward me, his expression abruptly sad—"but you can never reach peace in any of them."

I blinked. *Never reach peace? No shit.* Ever since I'd met Trench-Coat, I hadn't known a moment's peace. Things had changed since he first touched me. I thought of the way things looked now when I went out of body, and wondered if instead of viewing life through the astral, I hadn't been viewing it through the Ethereal instead?

Rai nodded. "That is precisely correct. The Symbiont Archer—his touch changed you. Broke rules—probation and doing well—until you came along."

Say what?

"He in big trouble." Rai shook his head. "The Archer was making amends with his creator—asking for pardons—no longer Archer. Then you show up. But you were different when he touched you. You are Kadobashi. The gateway's bridge. Through you he can attain the physical, but only if he can possess you. He must take and master you piece by piece, before you master him."

You mean like my voice?

"Honorable sir," Hirokumi said, interrupting us. How rude. He bowed. "I do not wish to hurry you, but my daughter. I must know what to do. Does she possess the power of a true Wraith?"

Rai nodded to Hirokumi but looked immediately back to me and our two-sided conversation. "Yes, your voice. But know that a balance must always be maintained between the worlds."

I was getting a bit frustrated, basically because I felt

like I was missing something. I didn't understand what any of this had to do with Trench-Coat and my voice, and what Rollins was so upset about.

The little man pointed to the box. "By the terms of this contact, the Reverend was given a Symbiont that lived alongside the soul. It protected the Phantasm's prize while it healed his physical ills. Destroy all cancer. It gave him long life and it gave him power. But the Symbiont grew more powerful the longer it remained in the physical world. The Reverend was a weak man." Rai shook his head. "He succumbed to the Symbiont and now lives in the mental plane, within his body. He may see the world, but he has no control."

Hirokumi jumped in, evidently thinking his own seer wasn't fast enough for him. "As long as Rollins possesses this contract, the Symbiont's home inside of his body is safe. But if he loses this contract, then he forfeits his rights and Rollins's soul belongs to the Phantasm and the body dies. The Symbiont ceases to be if the Phantasm dismisses it."

Oh ew. That creepy man isn't really a man? And he'd been in my face?

"Yes." Rai said, taking over the info-dump again. "The Archer was sent to retrieve the soul of the Reverend since the contract was no longer in his hands."

Ah! So if he still had the contract, Trench-Coat wouldn't be here.

"Yes." Rai glanced at Hirokumi. "Koba has the contract and somehow a stray spirit or creature discovered the original owner no longer possessed it."

I was thinking one of those little nasties I'd seen come out of that box was probably the narc. Then again, all bets were on the Symbiont Rollins said he conjured to taunt Tanaka. What you wanna bet that thing ran home and told the Phantasm?

And in comes Trench-Coat.

"Tanaka had tried to barter with Rollins, claiming he could get him the contract. He wanted money. Power. Things I would never give him."

Talk about greedy—Tanaka had been the vice president of a multimillion-dollar company. And he wanted more?

Sheesh.

Hirokumi looked sad, which explained to me the look he'd had on his face in his office when he'd spoken with Daniel. "William tried to take the contract, and it burned his bare hands. The document marked him so the Archer could track him like a bloodhound. When it did not find the contract, it became angry and took Tanaka."

Okay. In laymen's terms, Tanaka's death had been his own fault. And Trench-Coat was an otherworldly bounty hunter.

Greeeeat.

I looked at my own hands. They weren't burned and I'd touched the damned thing.

"I believe you were unaffected because you are already a part of the Abysmal world." Hirokumi took a step forward. "As a Wraith."

That freaked me out. I was a part of this dark, invisible world? I started rubbing my hand on my thighs, the rough areas on my palms snagging on the silk.

"The Archer's goal is to retrieve the soul, destroy the body and the Symbiont housed inside." Rai clasped his hands again before him. "And I believe it would have, and things would have righted themselves." He narrowed his eyes at me. "Until it encountered you. You drew it away from its purpose, enticed it. It broke rules when it took your voice and if the Phantasm that sent it discovers the betrayal, it will send more Symbionts, more chimeras and nightmares to destroy it as well as Rollins. Because if the Archer possesses you, then it could become more powerful than the Phantasm that created it."

Hirokumi shook his head. "We can't allow that."

This did not sound good at all—especially because it sounded like it was my fault. And that wasn't sitting right with me.

But it made Rollins's—uh the thing's—well Rollins's words make sense. When he said he'd barter the girl he meant Susan Hirokumi for the contract, and when he said he'd barter me, it meant to appease the Archer. Trench-Coat.

I was supposed to be Ethereal fodder.

And to be honest, I wasn't liking the way these two men were looking at me.

"We will agree to Rollins's offer to trade the contract for my daughter." Hirokumi moved around to the back of his desk.

Rai looked sad as he reached out and touched my arm. "I am sorry, my daughter. But the balance must be maintained. Pity—Wraiths are so rare these days. Most have been exorcised by the living to near extinction. Or hunted by rogue Symbionts for their souls."

What the hell? I turned to look at Hirokumi. He looked upset. More so than when Tanaka died.

So now they meant to offer me to Trench-Coat just as Rollins had?

"No," Rai said. "Once Rollins possesses his contract again, the Archer cannot take the soul and will not be allowed to destroy the body or the Symbiont. It is the Symbiont within Rollins that wishes the contract. But because he has your voice, the Archer cannot return either. So there is only one way to rid ourselves of such a powerful Symbiont."

I swallowed as I stood and backed away. I looked from Rai to Hirokumi.

Hirokumi held a Glock in his hand, aimed at me. "Your death."

27

I don't know how many times in my life I'm going to wish I could go back to one particular Tuesday night and strangle the curiosity right out of myself. I might not really strangle myself, but I sure as hell would stop me from going into that freak'n building with a really good bitch-slap.

Then I'd never have seen Trench-Coat kill Tanaka.

I'd never have been attacked by some harpy spy spirit.

And I'd still have my voice!

But—I might never have met Lieutenant Frasier (not that much had been happening on the romantic front with the cute cop).

I know I wouldn't have found myself facing the wrong end of a Glock 9mm.

Oh nooooooo.

I'd be shopping. Buying shoes. Trying on jeans. Drinking a mocha at Starbucks.

Or even better—eating greasy, fake-butter-covered

popcorn while I watched a movie in the dark, my only worry being which hip the butter was going to sit on.

Now—as I faced my imminent death, I thought some serious thoughts.

Of survival.

I stared at the gun. If he shot me while I was Wraith/ solid, what would happen to my body in the closet? Would the bullet pass through me if I became invisible in time? But then they'd know I wasn't really here. If I became incorporeal right now, I might be able to move past Hirokumi, invisible, go corporeal again, and grab the gun.

And then what? Shoot Hirokumi? Shoot wee Rai? And what about that smoking dragon?

To my surprise the little gnome sidestepped to stand in front of me. If he hoped to protect me or deflect any bullets, I hated to tell the fucker I was still vulnerable from the boobs up.

"No, Hirokumi. Her death will not release the Archer from this plane."

The businessman looked really upset, and the gun wavered. I ducked behind the gnome. Okay—call me chicken shit. But the guy was obviously unstable, what with the kidnapping of his daughter, and was willing to do anything to get her back. "Without her, he would have no reason to remain."

"He has tasted physical gifts. By taking the Wraith's voice, he may now use it to influence the living. True, he will continue to pursue her until he possesses all of her. But if she dies, he will intercept her soul."

Wait—what? You mean that asshole would prevent me from going to Heaven?

Or at least I was hoping I'd go to Heaven. After that incident with the little old lady and then with Mitsuri, I really wasn't sure of anything at the moment.

"Koba," Rai said, and his voice was gentle. Soothing.

"Susan will be all right—we will trade with the Reverend's Symbiont, and she will be home. It will receive its own punishment for what it has done. What is more important is the destruction of the Phantasm's charge."

I think it was at that moment, standing behind a little old Japanese man, that the epiphany of being in over my head finally came crashing down on top of my shoulders. There were things out there on the astral plane I'd never encountered before—not in my little realm of it.

And somehow that had changed—my realm. It had gotten bigger, and I didn't want it to. I was of the belief that if I could see it, it could see me.

And I didn't want to be seen. Not by things that I didn't understand.

At least not yet.

I got the feeling I was no longer a wee guppy in a vast sea. I was now a wee guppy with a honking-big neon sign in a vast sea. The message "Eat Me" could be seen for miles.

Was it possible not to astral travel anymore? To not be a Wraith anymore?

I somehow doubted it.

It was like ice cream. One bite, and you were abruptly looking down at the end of the cone—or cup in my world. Not a big eater of crunchy sugar.

Even when you get a taste of something you don't really like—like pistachio or black walnut—you keep sneaking more bites until the whole pint (who're we kidding— gallon) is gone.

Hirokumi lowered the gun as well as his shoulders. He looked defeated, and I felt sorry for him.

Well, only a little sorry. The asshole had pulled a gun on me.

"What do you propose?"

Rai nodded, and I was surprised to see the gnome's

shoulders relax as well. Ah—nice to know the omnipotent also panic. "We must arrange a meeting between Rollins and you to exchange Susan and the documents. The Archer will be nearby, watching. It is my guess Rollins had planned on trading Miss Martinique for his safety. Offering a starving man water."

I recalled Trench-Coat to mind. Starving? Hardly. But Rai was right—that was what old Teddy had had in mind. Not that I'd understood any of it at the time I'd been in his office.

Rai spoke. "I propose we do the same—use Miss Martinique as bait to lure the Archer to us."

I looked down at the little troll's shiny head. *Excuse me?*

"But, Seer—that would be giving it the power to fully enter this physical world."

"Not if we trap it inside the mouth of the dragon." He nodded to the statue still smoking on the desk. "The Symbiont is still largely a part of the spirit realm. He is as susceptible to capture as any other Abysmal or Ethereal creature."

I looked at the dragon statue and dismissed the idea of becoming invisible to escape. It sought out spiritlike beings. So I sort of suspected that if I went invisible, the thing would take a look at me and think, "Oohh, munchies and crunchies."

Either way—I figured I needed to get out of there before Hirokumi changed his mind.

The big deal was how. If I just vanished out of sight, I'd blow my wad, and there was no way I'd get out of here in one piece with my body. I checked the little clock on Hirokumi's desk. I'd been out of body for nearly an hour, but I'd been corporeal the whole time. So, what did that translate to time out? Two hours equal to not being visible?

And there was the dragon. Argh. Why couldn't this

business be easier? Even better, why didn't I just stay in Mom's bed?

I needed a diversion.

Shouts from outside the doors.

Ooh. Good diversion.

But I wasn't quick enough. Who knew there were guards *in* the room with us? I didn't. But obviously there were hidden panels in the wood walls because before I could say "what the f—" there was a big man behind me. He grabbed me around my chest, pinning my arms to my sides, and clamped a hand over my mouth, smashing my lips into my teeth.

Ow. What? He not get the memo either? Hell-o. No voice!

The big guy—who smelled of Aqua Velva I might add—dragged me backward behind one of those real pretty screens.

He released my mouth and I started to bite him, stomp his foot, you know—be that action heroine I loved in the movies—till something metal, solid and very much like the barrel of a gun, banged painfully against my lips and teeth.

Ow. He had the gun . . . in my mouth.

Now—here we go again with the fill-in-the-blank. If he shot me, while I was physical, would it hurt? And if it hurt, would it affect my physical body? I mean—would it suddenly go into death throes (bullet to the brain—I was assuming it'd be a death shot) and a bullet hole appear in my head? Would I abruptly snap back into my body?

That would be bad.

I think it was a great theory—but not one I wanted to test. So I stayed still in his burly arm, my head pinned to his chest with the gun.

The doors slid open, and the yelling became clear—it

sounded like what I imagined a harpy would sound like—
if she were Japanese. Since I couldn't see anything through
the screen, I listened.

I imagined it was the old kimono. Very unhappy.

"Ahhh . . . Detective. What an alarming surprise."

Detective? Daniel? I started to struggle and big guy
shoved the gun farther between my teeth. I quietly gagged.

I promised myself I would get even with him.

"Really? Not as alarming as the one I got when I saw
your men carry a young woman out of that house. Where
is she?" It was Daniel all right. It felt like ages since I'd
heard his voice.

"I'm sorry, Detective, but I have no idea of whom you
speak. I'm afraid I must protest your intrusion into my
private home. I'm sure Captain Cooper would be very unhappy to learn of your actions."

Uh-oh.

"Koba—I was pulling surveillance outside of Rollins's
residence. I saw your men bring someone out of that
house. Either it was your daughter, or it was Zoë. Where.
Is. She?"

My hero.

But Daniel, for all his cute bravado, really had no idea
what he was dealing with here. I know he believed I was
here, and not Susan. And I was afraid he was going to get
hurt if we didn't get out of here. He wasn't going to just
leave, and he was the only way out for my body that I
knew of.

Need another diversion.

I knew what I had to do, but wasn't sure how quick I
was going to be against smoky dragon. I had to try, right?

Sometimes I'm not the brightest bulb in the sign.

With a deep breath, and no clear idea of what I was doing, I closed my eyes and thought about being astral, like
smoke.

I slipped from my bully's grip and moved away. Big guy gasped and lowered his arms, his gaze looking all over the place. I immediately turned and passed through the screen.

Daniel was there, dressed in his usual suit and round glasses. He looked damned good—enough for me to jump right there.

Wrong thoughts, wrong thoughts (notice I didn't say bad). *That roar you're hearing isn't your libido, child.*

It was the dragon awakening.

Any second now that thing's smoke was gonna take on the look of a *Yu-Gi-Oh!* monster and try to eat me.

I moved to the other side of the desk—to the other screen—and hid behind it. I felt dizzy for a second as I thought of myself as physical, just like before.

In fact, the dizzy feeling got worse before it got better. I was stunned and fell back against the wall behind the screen just as the dragon plunged through the screen at me—

—and stopped, jaws wide. It snapped its jaws shut and blinked.

The thing actually looked disappointed.

Ha! Missed me. Neener-nee.

Oh . . . but I felt awful. And I immediately thought maybe I'd overused my body battery. I needed to get back to it. I needed a watch. I needed—

"Zoë?"

I turned to see Daniel peering behind the screen, his gun drawn and held in both hands. I gave him a smile and nodded.

"You look nice in that." He reached out to me, and I took his hand. "You ready to go home?"

Daniel pulled me from behind the screen with one hand on my shoulder and one still clutched around his gun. "Kidnapping, Hirokumi? But why Zoë? What is Zoë worth to Rollins? Why did he, and now you, kidnap her?"

I could only imagine Daniel's surprise to be spying on

Rollins and see men in black pajamas sneaking me out of the house. I was surprised at Hirokumi's apparent calm as he sat at his desk, his hands clasped on its surface. He'd just been caught with his hand in the cookie jar, and he looked pretty okay about it.

Smug.

I didn't see Rai anywhere though. Maybe he was under the desk?

Oh. Ew. Bad image. Nasty.

Mental note: *wash mind out with soap.*

"I've warned you before, Lieutenant, things are not as they seem. You are meddling in a world far beyond your everyday good guy and bad guy." Hirokumi smiled, but didn't show any teeth. I was glad of that. I was beginning to think those teeth might be pointy and razor-sharp. "Those areas are now blurred gray."

Didn't like the sound of that either.

"Is that a threat, Koba?" Daniel sounded frazzled. Sort of like I used to when my day had just started at worse and got increasingly . . . uh, worse. "Your daughter is missing—and you kidnap a grown woman as a trade? What does Rollins have going that he'd want or need Miss Martinique? Is it because your former secretary tried to kill her?"

I hated to tell Daniel that Hirokumi already knew Mitsuri was rotten, but we didn't really have time to stand here and chitchat.

Rather, *I* didn't have time to stand here and chitchat. Not that I could really even chat about any chits. I wasn't feeling oh-so-spiffy and needed to get back to my body.

I already knew I was going to be hungry and thirsty. Really thirsty. That seemed to be the new side effect. I glanced at the nicely glowing white hair on my left shoulder. Besides that.

Oh, and the tat.

So, if I was any good at guessing symptoms with time

spent OOB, I gave myself half an hour more in solid form and blammo. Back in the body I went whether I liked it or not.

I could probably travel my silver cord right now and join Daniel in my real physical body, but my sudden disappearance would A, probably freak poor Danny-boy here out enough so that Koba's men could capture him, and B, alert the disappointed dragon that I was back in munching form.

No, we needed to get to my body or close enough so I could zip back in.

Wow . . . a week ago I'd never considered just zipping back into my body. It was getting too easy. And I'd hate to be out in public and sneeze and poof! Out of body.

Not good on dates to go all dead-like, then poof! Back in again. It'd give a whole new meaning to the old belief that Southern women swoon.

Koba looked as disappointed as the dragon had. "I'm afraid things aren't that simple, Lieutenant. Nor can I allow you to simply take such a prize from me."

Prize? Little old me? Wow—I felt so loved.

"Prize? Zoë?" The incredulity in Daniel's voice was palpable.

And offensive. *Hey buster, I'm one damn great prize.*

Daniel held his gun up higher, aimed at the businessman's chest. "I'm not here alone. Cooper didn't officially approve this little venture of mine, but he's here nonetheless. And he can hear everything you're saying."

I turned and looked at my hero. Cute, and wired! Loved it.

I'm not sure Hirokumi believed him, but I do think that, as a businessman, he knew when not to gamble. "You may go, Daniel Frasier. And you may take . . ." The man smiled and looked directly at me. Oogy. "Whatever it is you have with you."

I don't think the lieutenant got it—but I did. Hirokumi *knew* the only way I'd been able to get away from my captor behind the screen and arouse the dragon was to become a Wraith.

He knew I was out of body. And what about Rai? Where *was* he?

Daniel pulled at me then, and I gave Hirokumi a narrowed look. He merely bowed from his neck with a smug smile.

I really hated smug. Did I mention that before?

Cutie-cop wanted to go right, but I pulled him left. "Zoë, we have to get out of here this way. My car's parked by the road."

I shook my head and was insistent. I needed to get my body, and it was three turns and a hallway back this way.

He wouldn't let go of my wrist, so on a whim, and really not sure if it would work, I concentrated on just my wrist being invisible.

It worked all right. I snapped to the left, and he nearly stumbled to the right. Righting myself, I motioned him to follow me.

With a few choice words (my, my what language! Must take notes!) he did, and I moved a bit shakily back down the maze to the room where my body was stuffed in a closet.

"Zoë . . . what did you leave in here?" Daniel said, as I slid the door to the room open.

It was the same. The food tray had been removed and the bed straightened. Hopefully the help hadn't opened the door and gotten a shock. I doubted they would—I mean—I didn't have any clothes other than what was already on my back.

I gave him the index finger of my right hand, indicating to wait one second as I moved to the closet and slid the door open.

If I could have screamed, man, I would have. And probably pierced a few eardrums.

Either way Daniel read my body's reaction and came to my side. He definitely helped prop me up because I was about to give an old-fashioned swoon.

He looked into the closet. "Was it that envelope you needed?"

No! I wanted to shout. *I had a body here! I left it here for safekeeping! Where the fuck was it?*

Daniel moved forward and bent down to grab the envelope that was there. It was addressed to me. "Let's go before Hirokumi changes his mind, and we're trapped here." He grabbed my wrist again and dragged/pulled me from the room and back down the hall.

I was looking down at my bellybutton area and trying really hard to find my cord.

My first thoughts of course were centered on where my body was. Until I looked down at my bellybutton area to find my cord.

That's when I lost control and vanished, completely.

28

THE ABYSMAL

IF my body was my battery, then I had to believe it was still alive, and I was still attached. Somehow.

The little adventure with Trench-Coat that subsequently zapped my voice had proven I could stay out longer. But Joe had said he'd used a cocktail on me, his own recipe, to pull me back in my body. And then there had been that recovery period—with me in the hospital. Again.

So—did that mean I could stay out of body for a longer period of time as long as I had Joe's cocktail? And exactly what had that been? I had no way of getting hold of him. Maybe I could go back to the hospital and ask around. Find out his last name.

That is, if I survived my present nervous breakdown.

During the drive from Hirokumi's estate north of the city, up Interstate 75, I thought about what'd happened in Hirokumi's home, in that room as I realized my body was gone.

Daniel had lost his grip on my hand and turned, and

could no longer see me. He brandished his gun and called out for me, but of course he couldn't hear me.

We both heard footsteps in the hallway.

Then I was somewhere else.

I was *someone* else.

I stood behind Hirokumi—and I was talking. Actually speaking. But not in control of what I wanted to say. I knew on some level I was back in my body, but not in *ownership* of it. I was more of a bystander—sort of watching things unfold from the wings.

And then blam! I'd been kicked out and found myself back in my room. Daniel was gone and I'd half stumbled, half run out of there looking for him. I heard shouts down the hallway and went in that direction. Three, maybe four turns later and I was at the front door.

I'd heard the dragon roar.

Daniel had been getting in his car as three of Hirokumi's men pointed really big automatic guns at him. With a glance at the men, I decided going with Daniel was preferable to sticking around here.

He'd looked upset. Really upset as he backed the car out of there, unaware I'd been sitting right there beside him in the passenger's seat.

And even now, as I watched him punch numbers into his cell as he drove, it happened again. I wasn't in the car anymore—but back in my body.

And I was *speaking*, not writing. I was actually speaking out loud.

And I sounded an awful lot like Rai.

Ew.

And then I heard my own voice.

My voice!

I looked up.

Trench-Coat, in all his hulking, black leather forbode-i-ness, stood on the other side of a desk. Hirokumi's desk.

The desk I'd just left. The dragon still expelled smoke. But why wasn't it going after the Archer?

Wait . . . everything sort of fell into place at that moment. Someone—Rai?—was in my body, talking to Trench-Coat, who then answered in *my* voice!

What. The. Fuck?

And then Rai, in my body, abruptly held my body still. "She is here . . ." was all I heard myself—himself—us—say before I was abruptly back in the front seat of Daniel's Crown Victoria.

What was going on? And was it going to keep happening?

I needed more than to lie down.

I needed my mommy!

I doubt Daniel actually heard my unspoken plea, but he did increase speed.

I was surprised when he drove straight to Mom's. Which was good, because that's where I'd wanted to go. And because by the time I hit the door to the botanica and tea shop, I'd guessed I'd been out of my body for nearly four hours.

Ding, ding, ding.

Time's up?

Mom knew I wasn't in my body the moment we stepped through the shop door. In fact, she immediately closed up the store after we stepped in.

Daniel went to her and took her hands in his. "I saw her, Nona . . . She was there, and then she just . . . vanished." He busied himself telling her what he'd seen at Rollins's, and later at Hirokumi's, then he moved away into the botanica to call Cooper on his cell.

Mom and I stood in the middle of Mom's shop, in front of the counter. She still wore one of her numerous knit pantsuits. A dark, emerald green one this time, with a white turtleneck and her old standby necklace—a green stone set in a gold filigree that hung just above her breasts—only now it hung above an embroidered Christmas wreath.

Christmas. Was it Thanksgiving yet?

Had we had Thanksgiving yet?

"Where's Tim?" was all Mom said in a low voice.

Then Steve appeared, looking more washed-out than I'd ever seen him. I wanted to tell them about Tim and what he'd done to help me, and that he was still trapped inside of Rollins's estate.

At least I'd hoped the rock was still in the potted plant.

No one really bothered taking rocks out of plants.

Did they?

But I didn't have a pen, or a pad. And I'd lost the juice to go corporeal.

"I need to know"—Mom's voice was stern, even, low. Scary—"exactly what happened. After Daniel leaves."

And I needed to process and understand everything I'd heard and seen. There was so much knowledge. And there was knowledge I needed to research somehow, either on the Web, or in a library.

Rhonda came through the front door, the bell overhead banging loudly against the motion.

And sometimes knowledge arrives in a noisy, gothic package.

Her hair was down, which was odd. Matt black, it splayed over her shoulder like the broken strands of a spider's web. Her eyes were shadowed as usual, but not with the precise care she usually took with them—this looked more like eye shadow gone wrong after sleeping in it.

The little geek was dressed in plain jeans and a gray Celldweller sweatshirt. She had on her black leather jacket and matching black combat boots.

It was sooooo good to see Rhonda again.

On her shoulder was her leather book bag, and she

dropped it to the floor when she saw me standing in the archway between the herb and the tea shops. "Zoë!" Her eyes widened. "He found you!"

I shook my head.

Mom put her finger to her lips and nodded to the botanica, where Daniel spoke on his cell. "Daniel doesn't know she's here—he didn't find her body."

With arched eyebrows, Rhonda stepped toward me, her index finger making zigzagging motions in the air. "Love, the kimono." Then she paused, her eyes wide with dawning horror. "Where *is* your body? How long have you been out of it?"

And therein lies the rub.

Daniel stepped out of the botanica as he tucked his cell back into the inside pocket of his suit jacket. He smiled at Rhonda, but not even that managed to brighten his beautiful face. "I'm sorry. I'm so sorry. She'd been right there. I can only guess one of Hirokumi's goons snatched her again. But what I can't understand is why." He absently scratched his head.

Mom stepped forward and put a hand on his shoulder. "It's okay, Daniel. You tried. And your hunches paid off. We know Hirokumi has her, for whatever purpose." She glared at me, which meant "and you're gonna tell me."

"But why, Nona? The only connection Zoë has in this is her snooping, and that Mitsuri saw her while she'd been leaving Rollins's place. That's where it made sense that Rollins's men would have her, but why Hirokumi?"

But the shop owner was fast on her feet. I also knew she wanted to get Daniel out of her house for now. "I don't know yet, Daniel. But we'll find out."

"He called her a prize, Nona. What the hell did that mean?"

Well that comment got me looks all around the room.

"Daniel, perhaps you should get some sleep, and regroup. You know she's alive, and now I do too, and that's okay for now. You should be able to get Captain Cooper to back you up on this. And if Cooper won't listen to you, he sure as hell will listen to me."

Daniel left with promises to call back if he heard any word. Mom stood by the door until the Crown Victoria was out of the driveway.

I lost myself when the door closed, as if I'd been holding my astral pieces together while Daniel was there. Why? I don't know—maybe I thought in some weird way he'd see me or something.

I must have vanished for a moment. When I saw Mom and Rhonda again, they were above me. I lay on the floor— or rather lay as easily as any astral form could. I felt weak, shaky, drained of energy.

A hand touched mine—soft—the delicate tickle of a spider's web against my astral skin. Steve knelt on the opposite side of Mom and Rhonda, and he was touching the back of my hand.

"Nona—I'd say that's a bad thing." Rhonda pointed to the contact. I could only imagine what it looked like from the living's point of view.

"Zoë"—Mom's own skin looked as pale and ill as a full moon—"get back to your body! Now!"

"I can't," I mouthed to her. I needed to tell them what happened. But how? I didn't have the strength to become solid enough to hold a pen.

"Grab my hand, Zoë."

I looked back to Steve. I saw pain in his eyes. He needed to know where Tim was. How awful it had to be for him to be alone in this house after all these years. And I'd left Tim in a potted plant.

I didn't understand the request to hold his hand—wasn't even sure I could. I'd never touched the boys, as Mom called them. No one ever had.

Turning my palm over, he slid his hand into mine, and I realized too late what would happen. I should have known.

There was no euphoria as I watched the color drain from Steve's face. I felt strength, a surge of energy, as my new Wraith condition pulled Steve's ethereal juice from him.

"Stop it!" My mom's voice was a shriek.

It was also enough to jar me back into myself in a sense. I wrenched my hand free of his—knowing it was what I'd *intended* to do when I'd seen what was happening to him. Intended, but hadn't.

My newly stolen strength sustained me, but Steve faded to little more than a hint of his physical appearance.

"What did you do to him?" Mom was on the floor beside him, next to me, but unable—or in my case unwilling—to touch us.

"Quick," Rhonda said, as I pulled myself into a sitting position. I thought of Daniel again, saw his face in my mind, and within seconds I felt the dusty hardwood beneath me, felt the chill in the air from the windows. She knelt beside me and handed me a pen and legal pad.

"Tell us," Steve said softly. His voice was a projection. A memory on the wind.

I hesitated—he'd known this would happen. He'd given me his strength, his ethereal essence, so I could tell them what happened. I sat wide-eyed as I watched him sustain a shadowy physical form, the pen and paper in my hand.

"Write, Zoë." Mom continued looking at Steve. She wouldn't look at me. She was still mad at me. "Don't let Steve's sacrifice go to waste."

So I wrote. I told them everything that had happened, from the time I received the message on the phone (though I left out the threat from Maharba) to when Daniel and I arrived here.

And after I'd finished, and Rhonda read as fast as she could, I watched Mom. Willed her to look at me, her daughter. Please. Steve gave me a smile and a wink, and I pulled my knees up to my chin and wrapped my arms around them.

"I'll be fine, Zoë," Steve said.

But somehow, I knew that wasn't true. I'd taken something from him. Something vital. I'd crippled him. And for what? For a brief moment of strength? How long would it last? Would I spend through it as I had my own strength? Would I devour it as a drunk devours whiskey? Already I'd felt the disappointment inside of me when the euphoria I'd known with Mrs. DeAngelo hadn't returned. How long before I too became addicted to this method of thievery?

Whoa—that was deep. Was that me thinking such melancholy thoughts?

And it got worse. If we got Tim back—would Steve ever be the same?

Rhonda spoke. "So you think this Rai character is in your body, and that's why you can't get back in?"

I guess I'd sort of thought of that, but I hadn't given voice to it. Sounded weird even to me, but I nodded.

Rhonda seemed to agree. "Me too—but what is he? Is he an astral Traveler?" She stood and pulled a massive book from her bag and returned to our little floor party. The thing looked like a Merriam-Webster dictionary.

It wasn't the usual book of everything, the one in Mom's shop. This was something I'd not seen before. The cover looked more like the old tattered weave of a hard cover, without the dust jacket. It was black, with the faded gold embossing of the words "PASSAGE OF THE DEAD."

Needless to say, I don't think this one had ever made the top ten in *Publishers Weekly*.

Rhonda flipped to several pages marked with ripped pieces of lined white paper, and I noticed Mom taking up the legal pad. When she started to read, I moved next to

Rhonda and peered over her shoulder to look at the illustrations and really wished I hadn't.

Whatever artist had been commissioned on this one had definitely taken his cues from H. R. Giger. *Eewwwwwwwwww.*

The left page was covered in bulky, eye-blurring text. The right page showed a black-and-white picture of what I would call a cat on steroids. Or maybe a really pissed-off cat. The size of its maw had to have been the diameter of a bowling ball.

Garfield meets Darth Sidious.

And the artist had warped the thing to where its tail had looped back around and snaked down into its throat, which might be why it looked so mean.

I noticed an interesting smell. It was nice. Spicy. And my stomach growled. Was there something on the stove?

"This," Rhonda was saying, "is a Symbiont. Or rather, a sort of idea of what they look like when not in symbiosis. And as I figured, they're created by Phantasms from the mist of the spiritual plane, both Ethereal and Abysmal. Most of the time they're benign, or even at times used as pets."

"Pets?" Mom and I said at the same time (only my voice wasn't heard by anyone).

Steve nodded. He looked a little better—or as better as a ghost could look. "I've seen one or two of them here and there."

Mom pinned him with a wide-eyed stare. "In *my* house?"

"Harmless, Nona, really," Rhonda said. "Sometimes they're just simple, old afterthoughts of the Phantasms. Sort of like cats and dogs. There are some schools of thought that small creatures like them—pets, or familiars—are like extensions of our souls. Actually, some witch's familiars are Symbionts possessing animal bodies."

"That would sure explain my old bird Hermes. Little fucker was smarter than he should have been." Mom scowled.

Hermes had been a kestrel, the smallest of the falcon family, and indeed the smartest. It'd had a love of boiled peanuts and ginger ale, and made a break for it one afternoon while Mom got groceries out of the car.

I don't think Mom ever forgave the little creep for running off on her. Kinda like my dad.

Wow . . . what is that smell?

Rhonda nodded. "It rings true from what I read here on Symbionts. They can become physical—which means they can enjoy the pleasures of the flesh in two ways. They can A, take over a body." She looked at me. "Or B, they can take in enough souls to transmutate its own body into becoming physical. The key ingredient for that little spell is an astral Traveler."

I gulped. I looked around for a scrap of paper. The pen was on the floor and easily retrieved. Mom irritably ripped a sheet out (she was still reading) and thrust it at me. YOU THIK RAI WAS A SYMBOTE?

Gah. My spelling. Awful.

"I'm not sure. He could be either astral or ethereal. From this book I found that either could possess a body. The difference is an astral entity can only possess for a short time. They can maybe ride along, but it takes a buttload of willpower to manipulate a body."

Really? I pursed my lips. I didn't know I could have possessed someone. I'd always been told I had a lot of will. I leaned in close to Rhonda . . . was it her that smelled so good?

"On the other hand," Rhonda said. "For a Symbiont, it's easier to take hold of a body, especially if the original owner is weak-willed."

I scribbled. OR THE BODY EMPTY?

She nodded. Crap. So the wee man with the Fu Manchu mustache was actually a Symbiont. Maybe. *Damnit. I just want my body back!*

"Now with Trench-Coat, we've established that he probably intended on eating you the way he did Tanaka, only you weren't really dead, which caused a weird glitch, and there was a transferrence. He took your health, and your voice."

Honestly, I'd have preferred Trench-Coat take something else, like the cellulite on my left thigh.

I leaned in close to Rhonda again. The smell was coming from her. It was like stepping into Macaroni Grill at lunch, all garlicky and spicy. I could just eat her alive.

Rhonda was still talking. *Whups. Was it important?* ". . . dealing with Phantasms."

"What the hell *is* that?" Mom abruptly spoke up.

"What? A Wraith?"

"Phantasm. You keep saying that. What is it? Is it the devil?"

Good question. I got the idea it was a big bad and something the Symbiont in Rollins was deathly afraid of. That was about as far as I really wanted to go.

"We can't look at this situation in the contemporary religious context of god and devil, Nona," Steve said.

Everyone turned and looked at him.

He looked so pale. Gaunt. Shadows crept into his handsome face, and I felt a twang of guilt. *I did that to him.* "When we realized we were dead, disappointment in the lack of manifestations of our shared belief kept us little more than Shades here in this house."

I stared blankly at Steve. English?

Mom shook her head. "*English?*"

Ahhh . . . like daughter like Mom.

"He means when neither of them ascended to Heaven or descended to Hell, the realization that there may not be such places caused them to go into a really hard depression." Rhonda the psychologist.

Mom shook her head. "There is a God, and there is a Devil."

"Maybe, maybe not," Steve said. "I've never seen either as a personification. I've seen beings of light at times, and felt an overwhelming sense of peace. I would categorize those instances as coming close to angels. And if there is a Devil"—he looked at me—"then the beings would be the Phantasms."

"Plural," Rhonda said. "More than one?"

"A hierarchy. I've only seen one. And it terrified me. They have no real shape, save the one you give them. And it will use that image, that nightmare you have, to destroy you. Phantasms hate the living."

I felt a chill and shivered.

"They rule the realm of the Abysmal," Steve said, and held his hands at his sides. "The world between the spiritual and the physical. They can *see* the physical side of life, yet never touch it. And they can see the ultimate ascendance, and never achieve it."

I got the feeling at that point that Steve knew a lot more than what he was telling us. But at that moment I wasn't paying attention to anything except that wonderful smell.

"Zoë?" Mom said. "What are you doing?"

Doing? Nothing. I'm just pushing my face into Rhonda's hair. So niiiice . . .

"Zoë! Stop!"

I stopped at the sound of Rhonda's voice. I realized too late what I'd been doing.

I was on my knees, my hands gripping Rhonda's exposed wrist. And she was fighting me.

And losing.

Euphoria . . . orgasm!

I let it fill me, surround me, strengthen me—the taste of the living!

Until something very sharp struck the side of my face. I let go of my prize—

I felt myself fall at that moment. And again I was back in my body. I was looking at Susan. She was dressed in a blue corduroy dress over a white turtleneck.

She was watching television, and her eyes were glazed.

Drugged. I knew she'd been drugged. And on her face . . .

The death mask.

But I couldn't quite make out the room—where she was—but I also knew there was someone else in the room with us.

Rai's gnomish face blocked out my vision, and I cried out in surprise.

Suddenly I was looking up into Mom's face, and Rhonda's, and they looked scared as shit. Well, Mom looked pissed.

"Keep away from her. Just do it," Mom said.

Do what?

I was on the floor again and pulled myself onto my hands and knees. Yow . . . I felt good. And there was that smell again.

"She's changing . . ."

"Rhonda, light it!"

Light what? I pushed myself onto just my knees. Mom stood in front of me, smelling all sweet and good, but looking like Darth Vader himself. She had a white candle in her hands and lit it with—

Her finger? Wow . . . when did Mom start doing that?

"I bind thee! I bind thee! I bind thee!"

I was abruptly on the floor, unable to move, pinned to the hardwood by an invisible pressure. Panic came and went as I wondered if I would eventually disappear or sieve through the floorboards.

I think the latter bothered me more, as I was sure there were all manner of creepy crawly things under the floor. *Ew.*

I wasn't sure how long it took before I heard a terrible, familiar rumble.

"Are you sure she'll be safe in there?" Mom screeched.

"Calm down, Nona," Steve said.

What? Put me in what? I turned my head to see what the fuss was about—and nearly came unglued. Facing me was the dragon statue, smoke curling from inside its open mouth.

I screamed. A silent cry for help.

No dragon came at me. No beast intent on chewing me up like that morning's Cheerios.

No . . . only smoke. It moved like the sooty mist of the Wraith's world and enveloped me in soft, feathery caresses. I closed my eyes as the mist became flesh and folded me into the arms of the dragon.

29

I went in screaming—

—and I came out screaming.

With absolutely no memory of the time between.

Yet Mom said it was Thursday afternoon. Thanksgiving.

And I instantly craved buttery mashed potatoes and pressure-cooked green beans.

Light came through the shop's windows with a subdued intensity—it was still overcast outside. I hadn't noticed that nearly all the leaves had fallen to the ground from the hardwoods. Everything had a monochromatic look to it, one of the first signs of winter, even though the pine trees in the backyard would stay green.

I stood at the window, a ghost of my former self. Literally. Odd how I'd spent the past few days avoiding the dragon, only to be welcomed by it and obviously nurtured.

Weird.

I put my hand to the window. The glass was cold, smooth. No, not a ghost. A solid ghost.

But all in all I felt—wrong.

I turned and saw the exposed pentagram on the floor with the dragon at the center. The candles smoked, and I smelled the obnoxious odor of sulfur.

"Zoë, you back now?"

I turned to my right, where Rhonda stood. She still wore the same smudged makeup and clothing she had when I'd arrived here with Daniel. I nodded. I motioned for a pen and pencil.

She brought me her laptop with a blank file up. I took the machine and sat on the floor. I was only mildly surprised I didn't zap the electronics of the machine itself. Unless that didn't happen when I was corporeal.

I'M SORRY I TRIED TO EAT YOU.

Rhonda knelt on the floor beside me but kept a discreet distance. "It's okay—Nona and I figured it was simply your self-preservation kicking in. You need strength, and normally you get that through food and water. But since your body's still MIA—"

Then I turned to a new food source.

Souls.

"It's really my fault." Steve appeared by the fireplace. He looked better, though not as bright as usual. Dark circles hung beneath his eyes, and I wasn't sure if that was from me or from worry over Tim. "I shouldn't have shown you what you could do."

I typed. I SORT OF ALREADY KNEW HOW.

Mom came down the stairs then. She saw me and smiled. "I see Rhonda's idea to stick you in the dragon statue worked. We charged up the pentagram last night and fed it juice with the statue in the center as a conduit. You feel better? You look much better."

I shrugged. So that was what'd happened. And I had no memory of it at all. To me, it was as if I'd just gone to sleep.

Mom nodded. "Good. That way Rhonda and I don't look like food."

Astral kibble.

"You're sort of like an ethereal vampire." The goth chick beamed.

I frowned and mouthed the word "ethereal?"

Nods all around, even from Mom, who stood in the center of the room, holding the laptop and reading. "You're no longer limited to the astral, Zoë, that's just it. You're part of the greater picture now, which makes you powerful, and it makes you vulnerable. Before you were seen by the Ethereal/Abysmal but you couldn't really be touched. Now you can be."

Did not like the vulnerable part of that statement, but given my present situation, I believed it. Didn't like the touched part either. I pointed to myself and gave them both a palms-up. I was curious about my physical condition.

When the impromptu sign language failed, I grabbed back the laptop and typed in my question.

Rhonda answered. "You should be okay. This Rai dude is in your body, or was. And as long as it gets juice from some sort of soul and presence, you should physically be all right. Now, I can't say whether that's healthy for your body on other levels—let's say Rai taints your body somehow."

Taints? Great, so now my body is going to be all oogy.

Mental note: *Lysol for the Wraith, kills possession germs dead.*

Mom sat on the couch. She looked at me and her lips formed a firm, thin slit beneath her nose. She wasn't happy. "You should have stayed home, Zoë. You should never have left this house."

I know, I know. Blah, blah, blah. Too late for stating the obvious.

Heh . . . maybe it was good that I didn't have a voice, 'cause that would've just rolled off my tongue.

THEN I WOULDN'T HAVE ANSWERS TO QUES-
TIONS.

Rhonda nodded. But then again, she wasn't blinded by
motherly anxiety either. "Look, this is all quaint, but we
have two larger problems here. One, we need to get Tim
back, and two, there's a little girl out there being used as a
pawn between two major assholes. Anyone got any idea as
to what we can do?"

Type, type. YOU FORGOT GETTING MY BODY
BACK.

She narrowed her smudged eyes. "You tried getting
back in since you came out of the dragon?"

I drew in on myself. Truth told, no I hadn't. Didn't want
to try either. Not without actually seeing myself first. The
three times I'd slammed into Rai *in* my body hadn't been
bad, but I'd felt dirty. Used. And a bit upset at being re-
jected by my own flesh and blood.

It was hard to describe. Especially when one was limited to paper and pen. A writer I'm not.

"No." My mother moved forward. "Don't even think it.
If you get back in that body, you'll be even more vulnerable. And they'll have you, not just your shell."

I realized at that moment that a lot of Mom's stern behavior came from worry. In a clearer situation, her baby
had been kidnapped and was being held who-knows-where
and having who-knows-what done to her.

But my world wasn't so clear, or cut-and-dried. No, my
world was as choppy and fucked up as they come.

I pulled up the laptop again. WHERE IS DANIEL?

Rhonda and Mom looked at one another, but didn't
speak. Okay, that bothered me. I looked at each of them
and glared for emphasis. Not as effective as . . . oh . . . a
scream. *It was real simple guys—you tell me now or I'm
out that door looking for him.*

Well, that's what I'd have said if I could.

Rhonda broke first. "He called about a half hour ago. He said there had been a lead in the case."

I glared at her. Tell me or I'll give you the Wraith evil eye. Absently, I wondered if there was such a thing. After all, I was the harbinger of death and life.

Wow. I had a cool title like a superhero.

Type, type. LEAD?

"Apparently Rollins uses a few of the buildings down off of Tenth, near Georgia Tech. It's where he does a bit of his prerecording for his shows on Sunday morning. A studio setup, really. The building and studio are owned by a company called First Sons, Inc. They own a lot of real estate in the city and lease these buildings to Rollins's televangelist empire."

I moved my index finger in a circle, indicating to keep talking.

"Captain Cooper had surveillance set up on all properties used by Rollins, just in case. Daniel said there'd been activity at this one pretty early this morning."

DID HE GO THERE?

Mom spoke up. "We don't know, dear. But you're not."

I looked at her. Like hell. I was going wherever Daniel was and Susan Hirokumi could be. I knew they planned on trading her back to her father; but in kidnap cases, I was sure the statistics were bad that the child survived.

Or so I'd seen on television.

I don't know why, but at that moment I thought of the skulls I'd been seeing on people's faces. DeAngelo, Mitsuri, and even Daniel.

And on Susan Hirokumi.

I couldn't let that little girl die. I asked about the image and what it meant.

Rhonda gave me a grave look. "You're a Wraith, Zoë. And Wraiths appear to people who are dying or will die soon. If a Traveler sees herself, or a Wraith along the way, it means their death is near. As for being a Wraith in the Abysmal sense—it's like you've heard several times now—you're a harbinger."

SO IF I SEE A SKULL ON SOMEONE'S FACE, IT MEANS THEY'RE GOING TO DIE?

Mom and Rhonda nodded.

Rhonda backed up. "You didn't see one on us did you?"

I shook my head and grabbed up the pencil and legal pad by the couch. The laptop was too taxing. DANIEL.

I scribbled again. SUSAN.

I stood and let the pencil and paper fall to the floor. I had to go to him—but how? And where?

"Stop, Zoë," Mom was saying. "You can't go."

I glared at her. There wasn't any point in threatening Mom. Besides the fact that a good Southern-born woman never threatened her mother, I was just damned scared of her sometimes. Like now, when she looked all mean-like.

But I couldn't stay here. I needed to check and see if my body was vacant. I needed to find Daniel. I couldn't let my cute cop die, now could I? We hadn't even boinked yet.

Mom turned and grabbed up the dragon statue. What the hell? "Zoë, I'm sorry. But I can't let you do this. It's too dangerous."

Rhonda stood and backed away from Mom. "Nona—what are you doing? You can't hold Zoë here that much longer. She needs to get back in her body."

But Nona wasn't listening. "I can hold you in here, where you're safe. I won't lose you, Zoë. I can't lose you—not like I lost your—"

My what? I took a step closer to her. *My father? Christ this is no time to go all mysterious!*

But Mom had turned and grabbed up a book of matches on the counter. She set the statue down before fumbling with the book in her haste to light one of them.

Rhonda turned to look at me. "Get back in your body!"

Aye, aye! I looked down for my cord. And it was visible! At last! Was this a sign that my body was no longer occupied? Who the hell cared right now?

Mom had a match lit.

I concentrated and closed my eyes just as she touched the match to the dragon's tongue.

I felt myself melt away—but to my body or to the statue—I'd know when I got there.

30

AFTER being a free spirit, so to speak, for a while, having a body back was sort of like putting on a comfortable, well-worn winter coat.

In July.

It was comforting on the one hand because I felt protected again and not so exposed to the elements. But then again, it was just damned scratchy.

The room I found myself in was another office. The lights were out, but afternoon sun filtered through blinds in the windows. It was almost as opulent as the one Rollins had in his house. The back and right walls were made of the same floor-to-ceiling windows. Rollins's desk, a replica of the one in his home office, sat sideways in the right back corner.

Same cross and world logo in front as the desk in his home.

Along the wall was a black leather couch.

This is where I was. And I was on my back. I blinked

several times, moved my arms up to where I could see them. I still wore the green kimono, though it was bit dirty along the sleeve edges. There didn't appear to be any of the normal pain I was accustomed to when I came in through the cord, so to speak.

Was this a side effect of my new Wraithy status as well?

I moved slowly and propped myself up on my elbows. I wasn't bound as before. There weren't any kind of tethering spells on my ankles. So—why leave my body unattended?

"Because I'm supposed to be watching it."

Marymotherofgod!

If I could talk, I'd have squeaked out a noise to set off any alarms in the building. I turned to my left, where a matching leather chair sat beside the couch.

In it slouched a very pale, ghostly image of Rai.

Uh-oh.

I sat up and stood, one fluid motion. Oh, there was an instant of dizziness, but only because I got up too fast. He held up gnarled hands. He also looked like he was breathing really hard. I knew I sort of simulated breathing in astral form, but didn't really. I'd often wondered if I could like, move OOB underwater for a while and watch the fish.

Hadn't tried it, as I'm deathly afraid of water.

That whole drowning thing.

"I can't hurt you. I can't even maintain control of your body. It took all of my energy just to keep it ready and healthy."

Well waaah. I was really upset for him.

I also wished like hell I had my voice so I could *chew him out.*

"I can hear you, Zoë Martinique. Quite clearly."

Uhm . . . that's right. I forgot you could.

"Yes."

I pursed my lips. *As a bad guy, are you here still so you can tell the good guy—that would be me—what your insidious plan is?*

He smiled at me. It was absolutely the most hideous thing I'd ever seen. All teethy and cheeky. Yuck. "Wraith—there is more working around you than you could imagine." He shrugged. "But, as for now, this much yes, I can tell. It is why I'm still here, and expended most of my energy to maintain your physical health."

Okay, that was like . . . vague

Maintain? Why? What the hell are you?

"Ah." He nodded and looked like a teacher pleased with a student. I had to remind myself this was the man who had been in Hirokumi's office and *so rudely absconded with my body!* "I was once like you, not a Wraith, but an astral Traveler. I called myself a spirit walker. There aren't many in this world."

I nodded. *Yeah, got that.*

Rai seemed really talkative though. "I abused my power on many levels during my life, until one day I lost time. I lost my body. My cord was severed, and I remained between worlds. Not living, nor dead."

Oh ooogy.

"I have no real standing on the Abysmal plane. I am nothing. A servant to Phantasms and their Symbionts. I've worked for bogeymen and chimeras. I am an aberration. Phantasms would as soon destroy us as suffer us to live."

Phantasms. That word just kept popping up.

"Hirokumi called upon my help long ago, and I have remained in his service because it gave me hope, and a purpose."

Hope?

"Hope that one day, with Hirokumi's help, I could transcend, and know eternal life."

Wait. I held up my hand. *You're basically a bodiless*

*astral Traveler. And you possess bodies and do Hirokumi's
bidding so that one day you can, like, disappear, like go to
Heaven or something?*

He nodded.

*Okay, just making sure I was still on the same avenue
here. Please, go on.*

"But because I'm not a Symbiont I can't possess bodies
for very long. A Symbiont would use the body's energy to
survive. When I am inside a body, my energy is taken by
the host."

Damn skippy.

So you're pooped because my body sucked your energy?

He nodded.

*And I feel okay—except for this slight headache—
because it's sort of like what happens when I release a
soul.*

"You've learned much."

*Yay. Go me. What I'm not understanding is—Hirokumi's
plan was to kill me. So, you kept my body. Why didn't he
kill me? Just you know, shoot me?*

"Because he's more afraid of you than you realize." He
coughed. A nasty, phlegmy sound. "The truth is you're
more valuable to me as a Wraith, not as a Shade, which is
what you'd become if your body died while you were out
of it."

Hrm. School time. Care to explain that to me?

Rai checked his wrist. I didn't see a watch, so I was assuming it was an old habit he'd gotten from when he was
alive. "We don't have time. Your police friend has arrived
and will be engaging the Archer in just a few minutes." He
looked at me as I stood really fast. "Though Detective
Frasier is in good shape, I'm afraid he's no match for a
Symbiont."

Daniel's here? Where at? Why? Where's Susan?

With another shuddering cough, the gnome pushed himself up from the chair. His shoulders rolled forward. You'd think he'd aged twenty years in a few seconds. "The detective had become an irritant, and my master believed by leaving you here, unguarded, the Archer would emerge. By making an anonymous phone call to the police with a mention of seeing an unconscious female being trundled into this building, he also believed the good detective would join the party as well."

Damnit. And I figured the expected outcome was that Trench-Coat would take me as well as kill Daniel. All in one fell swoop. I glared at Rai. *They're still making the exchange, the documents for the girl, somewhere else. That's where Susan is.*

Rai nodded. "She will not survive. She's the prize, the vessel in which the Symbiont will hide."

I blinked. *Come again?*

He shook his head. "No time. You must go."

But what do you want in all of this? Why be nice to me?

"I'll be there when you need me, and when you find the power, when you ignite the full potential of the Wraith against the Archer, then I'll give you the secret to defeating him, though you might find it's not truly what you want. And then." There was that smile again. Yuck—yuck. "You will destroy me."

And he was gone. Not even a puff of smoke. Just pop.

Riddles and innuendo. Fuck 'em all. I was getting just damned tired of no one giving me a straight answer. Ignite the Wraith? What. The. Hell? But no matter—he said Daniel was here, and I needed to stop him before he tried to take on Trench-Coat. It was me the Symbiont was after.

Or rather, pieces of me.

Why was it at that moment I felt more like Captain Hook and Trenchy was the Crocodile after the rest of me?

Gunshots again, then a shout.

Fuck! That was Daniel.

And I knew—I just knew—Trench-Coat and my cop had met.

And the two weren't dancing.

31

THE office let out into a boardroom. Floor-to-ceiling windows gave me a spectacular view of the Atlanta skyline. The sunset over the IBM Tower splashed the scene with brilliant yellows, indigos, blues, azures, and subdued reds. Happy Thanksgiving!

A long, oval table with about a dozen high-backed chairs took up most of the room's center. The room smelled of artificial air freshener, Hawaiian scent if I wasn't mistaken. And it was cold, as if the building's heater was turned off. I padded around it on top of soft, sink-into-it carpet with the realization I was barefoot, in a green kimono, with my hair billowing out around me.

I'm sure I looked scary as hell.

I found an elevator at the other end of the room but wasn't sure which way to go. Up? Down? What floor were they on?

Would Trench-Coat sense me and come hither?

Gunshots again.

Up—definitely up.

I avoided the elevator and decided on the stairs to the right. Figured I'd make better progress on my own power and not the building's. The drawback was the stairs were ice-cold on my bare feet.

Yow!

Luckily there were only two flights, which meant up was the roof. They were on the roof?

The door wouldn't open at first even though the knob turned several times. I threw my weight against it twice before it gave.

Icy air greeted me as I exploded outward onto the asphalt and rocks of the building's roof. The momentum I'd used to get through the door carried me onto my knees. Fire burned through both of them as my unprotected skin scraped against the asphalt.

The sounds of fighting caught my attention. I looked to my right to see Daniel and Trench-Coat exchanging blows. Real, *physical* blows.

And from where I half sat, Trench-Coat looked about as whacked as Daniel did. They both bled from various cuts on their faces. Even as I stood I watched my cute cop deliver a well-aimed roundhouse kick to Trench-Coat's side.

But Trench-Coat grabbed Daniel's leg and, with a grunt, twisted the detective to the right. Daniel sort of spun a bit and went down on his side.

Daniel!

"Well, well, well." Trench-Coat spoke in an all-too-familiar gravelly voice as he wiped the blood from his lip with the back of his wrist. "It's so nice for them to leave me dinner." He looked at me. "And dessert. Hello, Zoë."

The way he said my name, in *my* voice, plucked at the strings of my spinal cord. The way he drawled out the *e* sound had an odd effect on me, much the way a light touch along my naked thigh would.

Ack. Yuck. Stop it.

I took a step forward. *Don't you dare hurt him.* I didn't know if he could hear me the way Rai had. Either way, with no voice, I was sort of stuck *thinking* my threats.

He grinned beneath his black shades. "Oh, I wouldn't dream of it. As long as you do as I say. I've been waiting on you. Playing with my toy." He glanced at Daniel, who was grunting in a moany sort of way as he got to his knees. Trench-Coat held his right hand, his index finger wiggling at me. "Come to me, and I let the little man live. Relatively."

I didn't believe him, not for a minute. But I wasn't sure what sort of choices I had. Oh, I knew *some* martial arts. I wasn't a black belt. But somehow I wasn't sure if any of my training would be effective.

But other than that, I really didn't have any superpowers to speak of. I didn't own a gun, and I'm sure Daniel'd already fired on the spook with no luck. I didn't have pepper spray, or even Mace. *Ooh. Go me. Fearless Wraith.*

I saw Trench-Coat hesitate.

Wraith.

There it was again, only not as physical. He could obviously hear my thoughts, just as Rai could. So—why did my thinking of myself as a Wraith bother him?

Unless he was afraid of me. Just as Rai had said Hirokumi was.

Trench-Coat laughed. Daniel was almost on his feet. And the two were pretty close to the roof's edge. The brittle wind whipped my hair about my head, and I shivered violently. My toes were little ice cubes on the sticks of my feet, and it felt as if my kneecaps had slid down my shins.

Hrm. Maybe being a Wraith would feel better?

But then, where would I put my body?

Trench-Coat made a tsk-tsk noise. "So hard, having flesh, isn't it?" He turned just as Daniel stood and hammered a fist into the detective's midsection. Daniel bent over with a loud noise, and I watched his glasses fall away to the asphalt.

"Don't become the Wraith, Zoë."

Or what?

"Or this." And he turned and lunged at Daniel, planting both of his hands against the detective's middle. Daniel teetered over the edge.

I screamed silently and ran at the edge, my arms out to catch Daniel as he fell. But I missed him as he went over the side.

And Trench-Coat grabbed at my right, outstretched hand and yanked me to him. I used the momentum from his motion and brought my left knee up into his side, using my powerhouse (that's the torso, solar plexus, and hips) as the nexus of my body twisted.

Hell, if he was physical enough to hit Daniel and grab me, then he was solid enough for me to have done a little damage too.

Daniel!

Trench-Coat actually gave an "ooof," and I didn't waste a breath as I pulled my wrist free, spun to my right and came down with a full fist on the back of his neck.

When he went to his knees, I took a chance to look over the edge—not that I really wanted to see Daniel's body splattered all over the parking lot below—but I had to know whether to get mad.

Or to get even.

Since I hadn't arrived in the building by walking up to it, or in through the front door, I didn't really know where I was or how high I was. Daniel could have fallen sixty feet—or sixty inches.

No luck. We appeared to be up several floors—five at the most. But Daniel had landed on a fire escape just below where I stood. It didn't look like a very comfortable position. I was sure his leg was broken, or even more than that. He lay at an odd angle.

And he wasn't moving.

A hand yanked me backward by my hair. I lost my footing and stumbled just as Trench-Coat's arm snaked around my neck. The enemy was back up and in the game as he bent me forward and pulled me into his side. He had me in a nuggy position.

Yippee.

Mental note: *Do not turn one's back on a Symbiont. Especially one wearing Vin Diesel's face.*

I stared at his boot and noticed I could see the asphalt through it. What's this? Was Trench-Coat not fully in control of his corporeal ability? I was able to reach down and run my fingers through the boot and touch the roughness of the roof before he yanked me up into a standing position.

He wasn't fully manifested. So—how did I use this to my advantage before he literally sucked up something else out of me?

I could go Wraith, then go solid and mess with him from behind. But then he'd probably just toss my body over the edge, and I wouldn't be as lucky as Daniel and land on the fire escape.

In martial arts we're taught to use the attacker's offenses against them. Look at their strengths and turn them backward. Well, old TC here had me around the neck with his left hand—so where was his right?

Too soon I found out as it came around and he cupped my chin in his palm. I grabbed at his hands and tried prying them away as he pulled me to his front and leaned in to kiss me.

Over my dead body!

Ooh. Bad idea.

I have an uncle, on my mother's side, Uncle Chester, who loves to press his tongue into my mouth when he kisses me.

Guy's got to be nearing a hundred years old. I used to complain to Mom about it, and she finally just shrugged, and said, "Tell him you don't like it."

Well, that'd never worked.

So, next time he did it, I took matters into my own hands. I figured if he didn't hear me when I expressed my discomfort, perhaps he'd listen when I showed him.

So I bit him. Hard enough to draw blood.

I thought of Uncle Chester at that moment as I felt the tips of Trench-Coat's tentacled tongue press at my lips.

I thought of Rollins so close in my face.

So I bit it.

In fact, I bit it so hard, I bit the tip of it off.

I knew I'd done it the moment he let go of me and screamed. My voice screaming—not a pleasant sound even when it was from me, the rightful owner. I stumbled away and spit hard. *Foul! Yeck!* I spit again and nearly gagged at the thought of any of Trench-Coat's tongue in my mouth.

I managed to move to the ledge and watched as Trenchy started doing the pee-pee dance. What? Had it been his penis I'd bitten instead? Was I so out of it not to realize I'd been at his crotch and not his mouth.

No, that'd been his tongue. Ew. Were the two related?

I was happy to realize I felt none of the erotic quality I had earlier when I thought of the bastard. No—I just wanted him dead and gone so I could rescue a little girl and get my cop to the hospital.

Trench-Coat reared his head back and screamed. The sound carried up and out in waves. It vibrated the building. Even the wind in the evening air gusted in response. Damned eerie.

Well, while he was having a hissy fit, I climbed down the reverse-U-shaped fire escape ladder to check on Daniel. Clouds billowed out from all sides of the city. I glanced at it briefly, but was more concerned for Daniel.

He lay on his side, his head turned away from me. He bled from his mouth, his head, and a few other places. I checked his pulse. Alive. Faint. He needed medical attention. What if there were internal injuries?

Just then the metal of the fire escape groaned, and the whole landing lurched to the right. I grabbed the sides as it moved again, and leaned to the right.

Daniel's prone body rolled away, and I reached out with a hand and caught his suit jacket, preventing him from rolling farther. What was happening? Was our combined weight too much for the damned thing that it chose now to pull away from the wall?

I heard a laugh and looked up. Trench-Coat sat on the roof's edge, his large, booted feet dangling over. He waved at me and smiled. White teeth. Blood dribbled over his lips, and I assumed it was from his damaged tongue. He widened his eyes and the fire escape lurched again.

The angle we tilted at took away the leverage I had in keeping Daniel's body still. His legs moved and dangled off the fire escape's edge as it teetered forward and threatened to dump us both onto the parking lot below.

I'd become the pin between the two beams, what kept it together. I had Daniel in one hand, and the fire escape's main support in the other. The prone man's body was heavier than what I was accustomed to holding.

My own grip on the metal was weak, precarious. And Daniel was slipping out of my grasp. If he fell, if I let go, he'd die for sure when he hit that pavement.

And me? What would happen to me?

"I would save you," Trench-Coat said from above. "I have plans for you, *Wraith*."

How was he still talking with a damaged tongue?

Plans. I still had the taste of his tongue in my mouth as I took in a deep breath. What do I do? If I stepped out of my body, both Daniel and I would fall. And what then? What could I do against Trench-Coat?

"You can destroy him," Rai's voice whispered in my ear. I nearly jumped out of my skin but I kept my hold, gritting my teeth as the cold wind whipped my hair all over my face.

How? I grunted.

"Let your lover die."

What? I frowned, glanced around. I didn't see Rai anywhere, but I heard him. *I'm not going to let Daniel die.*

"You have to. Your lover's release will give you, as a Wraith, enough rage and power to destroy him."

But how? I didn't see it. If I let him die, then the skull was indeed the signal I feared it would be. I—I didn't know what my feelings were—but I cared. Deeply. And wanted him with me.

"Wraith—if you release your lover, you gain a part of him. Use it. Channel it. The anger. Look what the creature has done to you. To your life. To your lover."

I didn't need prodding to be angry—I was so pissed off I felt the tears run down my cheek. Let him go? It would be easy. And he'd strike the pavement.

Just let him go. Destroy the evil behind me.

Free him.

I looked at Daniel's calm face, his closed eyes. I looked at the blood on his forehead, on his lips. It was my fault—a trap for me that lured him here, where he would die.

"Release him!" Rai's voice was insistent in my ear as I also heard Trench-Coat laugh above me. Mocking me.

Release him.

And I did.

If only he hadn't have opened his eyes and looked at me as I let go.

I watched him watch me as he fell away and I screamed, and screamed and screamed.

Blood.

Laughter from above.

I scrambled, shaking, down the steps of the leaning fire escape. I moved slowly, as carefully as I could, until I could jump the rest of the way. Daniel lay on his stomach, his head turned away from me. His eyes were closed.

I felt a presence beside me, begging me to release him. I thought of the euphoria I'd experienced before—of the surge of power. Sobs racked my body, and I collapsed on the ground beside him.

I stepped out of my body and faced what I believed was the Shade of my lover. I'd expected him to look so much like himself, just as I looked like me when I went OOB. He was shadowy instead, not even as coherent as a Shade, and maybe that was because of the nature of his death.

His body lay broken, but he was still anchored. Somehow.

I had to release him, to gain the power, to destroy his murderer.

I reached out in my incorporeal state and touched him.

"No! That's not—"

I heard the voice just as the power exploded inside of me. A whirlwind of joy! Of happiness!

Was it mine? Or was it Daniel's?

And there was a whisper as the lights of forgiveness enveloped me. So close to my cheek. A caress, a kiss. "Thank you."

And that was it. No more words. Nothing except the overwhelming madness of sorrow. I felt I had wings as I looked up at the roof's edge and saw Trench-Coat, a burning, red light like a pulsing, raging fire.

And I was there to quench it.

"You're mine!" I heard him shout from above.

And I shouted back. I screamed at him for what he'd done to Daniel, to me, to Tanaka. I felt myself lifted into the air to the level of the roof. Into the wind I screamed. The air before me shook and vibrated as if it were a summer heat rising from steaming pavement.

I watched as it moved like waves out and up and bowled into Trench-Coat. He fell back onto the roof and writhed, his corporeal skin turning a bright pink and then red. He screamed and screamed, until there was a brief instance of silence.

And he imploded.

No great shower of ethereal goo. No ectoplasm. Just a simple pop, and nothing.

I stared at the empty roof for several heartbeats before I realized I really *was* in the air. I didn't have wings, but I wasn't on the ground. I wasn't really myself either. I looked down at myself and saw . . .

Something else.

Something not entirely human.

Oh dear. Was this what Mom and Rhonda saw that day in the hospital?

I eased back to the ground as the sound of sirens filled the void left by Trench-Coat's screams. My body lay to the right of Daniel. We were face-to-face, like some tribute to the death scene of Romeo and Juliet.

Yet it was *Hamlet* that came to mind at that moment (I really didn't know *Romeo and Juliet*—too sappy). I knelt beside Daniel, corporeal, spent, alone, in shock at what had just happened.

"Good night, sweet prince, and flights of angels sing thee to thy rest."

It was nearly an hour later before I realized I'd spoken those words out loud.

32

WHEN the paramedics said they had a pulse, I lost it. Full-blown female PMS drama moment. Oh I even weirded out myself on this one.

I had my voice back, and I was putting it to good use.

Alive! He was alive! Never stopped to wonder how, or why. Or even if I was sure it was really Daniel fighting for his life inside that body, and not something else. I just *knew* it was him.

So like any good EMT team would do, they threatened to sedate the crazed, wild-haired chick in the ragged green kimono. I agreed to succumb to tests to make sure I was okay as long as they kept me informed on Daniel's condition. The nicer of the two ambulance men said Daniel had a concussion, possible broken neck, fractured leg and wrist, as well as internal injuries.

He was in bad shape. But the doctors had him, and Captain Cooper was there. I avoided him, not wanting to risk his anger and have him sic officers on me. In his version of things, I was a witness. I had to go.

I had to finish the job Daniel and I started. There were bad men, and some bad things out there, and I had to rescue Tim, and Susan, and set things right.

Daniel would want it that way.

It was close to one in the morning, the day after Thanksgiving, when Mom and I arrived at Rollins's house. It looked cold outside. I could just see sleet against the Volvo's headlights, and the automated computer guidance system reported the temperature at 1.67 Celsius.

I figured that was really cold in Fahrenheit.

It wasn't unheard of to be that cold in November in Atlanta, it just wasn't normal. But then, nothing about the past two weeks had been normal.

I'd assumed that the Reverend had vacated the estate after Hirokumi's little raid that night and hidden himself away in some secret location. So of course there wasn't supposed to be anyone home, right?

So it should be deserted?

Sure it looked deserted, except for the three white limousines in the front drive, the copious lights on from inside, and well—a yammering alarm system.

"Somebody's home . . ." Mom said as we parked the car across the street in an opposing driveway. "You think that alarm's on because of Rhonda?"

"Rhonda?" I turned and gave her a piercing gaze. "Rhonda's in *there*?"

Mom nodded. "She wanted to go in all Rambo-style and rescue Tim. So I wanted to make sure you were here when she came out."

I wanted to punch her. No wonder she'd been all agreeable to help me sneak out of the hospital.

Mental note: *never trust agreeable mommies.*

"Don't you think you should have told me this before now?"

"What, and have you all worried and not listening to my advice? Trust me on this one, Rhonda's fine. But you do need to get in there and help her out."

Second mental note of the moment: *snarl*.

I moved into the backseat and slipped out of my body. Then I moved as fast as possible through the gate and across the yard. The dogs weren't out, which was good, since they'd all sense me and want to play fetch.

My thoughts returned to Mom's theory on Daniel's survival, the one she'd expressed to me in the car ride over here. I'd indeed taken someone's soul. And if it wasn't Daniel's, then whose?

My first assumption was Rai's. He'd been an astral walker, like I was now that Trench-Coat was gone, and he'd been able to possess my body. He'd also been damn insistent on me somehow killing him. It would explain why Daniel's astral self looked all wonky right before I took it—Rai had figured I wouldn't do it if it wasn't Daniel's—maybe that my anger wouldn't be great enough. But he couldn't actually take on Daniel's form.

I also remembered someone screaming out in panic right before I took him, and I had to wonder what it'd done to me, being a Wraith at that moment, that someone would object. Had it been Trench-Coat?

Gah. Theory. Speculation. But Rai could apparently possess bodies as an astral Traveler. He'd obviously been inside of Daniel's. He'd said he couldn't do it as long as a Symbiont could. Well—I was an astral Traveler again. I wondered if I could slip inside a dog—that would get me inside the house pretty easy. No one was going to shoot a guard dog.

And then I thought about my old German shepherd drinking out of the toilet.

No thanks. I'll pass.

With that unpleasant consideration behind me, I slipped past the black-suited hoodlums in front (several of whom I recognized from my previous stay at Chez Rollins) and stopped just inside the foyer.

Okay . . . Susan had been housed in the room upstairs left. I had tossed Tim's rock upstairs right. So I scrambled upstairs right with the intention of making sure the rock was still in the planter . . .

. . . only to find that the planter with the tree wasn't there.

Uhm.

Uh-oh.

I ran in the other direction down the left hall to the door where I'd heard Susan before. I sieved through and stopped just inside the door.

Plushy hell.

The room was covered in floor-to-ceiling stuffed animals. Bears, foxes, wolves, seals (did seals have fur?), camels—you name it—it was stuffed into the room. The carpet was pretty tame, a sort of long-pile beige.

To the right was a princess bed complete with canopy and soft, pastel pink curtains. Would have been even nicer if it hadn't had hospital straps attached to the mattress.

I heard footsteps outside, and the door shot open. Two men with machine guns stormed in and then stopped right in front of me.

"Where's the kid?" the one on the left said. I narrowed my eyes. Was that Tiny? His face was black-and-blue—my handiwork.

"Already in the limo. Boss says to check all the rooms. The intruder's gotta be on this end."

I watched them turn and leave.

Well—so if Rhonda set off the alarm, at least she hadn't been caught yet. So where was she?

And which of those three limousines was Susan in? I followed them out of the room, but when they turned right, I went left and back down the stairs to the three large luxury automobiles.

Without any sort of guide I just started on the left and sieved inside the back, then the trunk. Nothing.

I repeated the same with the second. Nothing.

But on the third?

Nothing.

I stood in the center of the front, the alarm still blaring out around me, suited men with guns running here and there, and scratched my head.

What the fuck? Where is Rhonda? Or Susan for that matter?

Okay, I didn't see any more limousines, unless there had been one I'd missed before we got here. So, my next plan of attack was to find Rhonda.

I went back inside and hurried into Rollins's office.

And walked right through Rhonda, who'd been leaning against the door, listening out. I of course knew it was her before I turned back because when I passed through her I caught the constant play of Celldweller music in her head.

Sheesh.

She of course knew it was me because Rhonda could see me.

"Zoë?" she hissed.

I turned and did a palms-up. I also dropped my jaw when I looked at her. She was wearing my outfit!

Complete with black bunny slippers!

I cocked an eyebrow and pointed at her, moving my index finger up and down from head to toe. "Excuse you?"

She actually blushed. "Sorry—but I always thought you looked really cool dressed like this." She blinked and her eyes widened. "You *can* talk again. I thought Nona was a bit off when she told me that. So . . . you're not all Wraith anymore?"

"No, just ordinary old me again." That is, if slipping in and out of my body to snoop on people was normal, then go me.

I just couldn't take my eyes off of Rhonda. She'd even donned a hair extension to give her a long braided ponytail in the back. I wanted to sniff and feel pride. I had a five-foot-three goth live-action figure.

A mother couldn't be more proud.

Not.

"Zoë!"

I turned to see Tim standing there. I ran to him and gave him a hug—luckily astral can touch ethereal. At least in this situation. Steve materialized nearby.

Steve is here too?

Wow, a real ghost reunion. That's when I noticed the potted plant I'd tossed Tim's rock into was now in Rollins's office.

I turned back to Rhonda—and that's when I noticed the gun—a .38 Special.

Oh my. I glared at her and pointed to it. Man, I was so accustomed to gesturing and pointing it never occurred to me to simply say "What the fuck?"

She shrugged. "Sorry, Zoë. I don't have any cool powers like you—so I had to think Lara Croft."

Well, not really. "Lara would have brought a bigger gun. And I don't have any cool powers anymore. Was Rollins here? Did you see where they took the kid?"

"Rollins left out that door over there"—she pointed to a shadowed area to my right behind the planter—"when I set off the alarm. I was stuck in here when they came in."

"They?"

With a nod, Rhonda said. "Rollins, two of his wrestler types, and the little girl."

Susan.

"Mom's outside the gate in a Volvo. She's waiting on—
something to come out of the house for a rescue. I need
you all to get in her car and haul ass."

"Where are you going?" Steve asked.

"I'm going to follow Rollins. I've got to make sure Susan's okay. And I have to know what happens with Rollins's Symbiont. With no more Trench-Coat around, he's
probably feeling a bit superior right now. Now go!"

I ran through the wall and stopped. I heard voices to my
left. There was a black limo parked a few feet away. I saw
Tiny, and Beckett, and had a brief glimpse of Rollins in the
backseat.

Beckett closed the trunk of the hulking machine.

I saw the exhaust start as Tiny cranked the car.

The trunk! She had to be either in the trunk or in the
back with Rollins. The Symbiont inside of Rollins could
see me, so I had to be careful.

I ducked and went around the driver's side to keep out
of Rollins's sight and sort of sieved/fell into the trunk.

And landed right beside Hirokumi's daughter.

She was alive, but unmoving. I assumed she was still
drugged, easier to handle. She wasn't bound, which would
help a bit. When the limo started moving, I remained still
and waited.

When the limo stopped, I took in a deep, astral breath
and sieved out of the trunk.

I'm not sure what I'd expected—maybe some really
cool place with a new neat building. But no—I knew this
location.

We were parked outside the newly uncovered three-
story spooky building on Perimeter Center Road, just across
from Perimeter Square. I could see the signs of all my favorite stores: Comp USA, Bed Bath and Beyond, and even
PetSmart! Though I don't have a pet. Next road up was The

Container Store and Borg and Chernoble (Barnes & Noble to you laypeople).

For years I'd always half tagged the area as wooded, one of those nice features of the South and all her greenery. Then driving out of Bed Bath and Beyond, Rhonda and I saw the trees had been razed, exposing this lurking behemoth of cracked concrete and shattered, half-boarded windows. Who knew there were twentieth-century ancient ruins behind all those pines and oaks?

In the daylight this place looked unfriendly. At night— we were talking überunfriendly. Illuminated from the streetlights and the buildings to either side, the thing looked alive, as if it would suck your soul. If you went in, you'd come out a changed being.

I'd heard it was gonna be a Super Target—same thing.

They'd parked to the right side, well out of the view of any nutsies awake at one in the morning after Thanksgiving. The moon was full, and it was easy to see, though two of Rollins's WWE pulled camping lanterns from their limos and set them up on the luxury car roofs.

I stood just outside the limo I'd hitched a ride in and looked around. Something was different. I could still see the sooty, spooky images I'd begun to see after Trench-Coat's touch. But I wasn't Wraith, was I? The hairs on my astral arm rose and I felt like being in the middle of bloodied waters with no shark cage around me.

Yeah, I think that was a good analogy.

And they were all there, on the edge of the field's trees, watching. And we were pretty much cut off here, with only a single dirt road back to Perimeter Center Road.

Mental note: *I will not scream like a girl, I will not scream like a girl.*

A voice on the wind spoke to me. "The wicked comes."

I heard the crunch of cement stones on cracked asphalt as a white limo pulled up slowly. It moved lazily around the building and parked several yards away. Two of Koba Hirokumi's men got out just as Tiny and Beckett got out of Rollins's limo.

The four gunmen of the apocalypse took up positions with guns drawn, flanking their respective bosses. I stood to the side and watched.

Rollins got out first, dressed in a black suit and trench coat. Koba then stepped out, dressed in a white suit and black trench. Polar opposites, yin and yang.

As far as I figured, Koba Hirokumi was a semi-innocent bystander in all of this. Albeit a very informed one, but still—he'd found the contract and the information on Rollins's health, then Rollins kidnapped his daughter. I mean, threatening to use me as bait and killing me, that had all been show, right?

"The Archer is dead."

Rollins nodded. "I must say—I had not thought it possible. Your plan worked. You tricked the Wraith into this?"

Hirokumi gave a short nod. "*Hai.* And in doing so, she has destroyed her own powers. She can trouble us no more."

!!!

Wait a damned minute. Tricked me into destroying Trench-Coat? I thought the outcome was supposed to be me and Daniel dead.

Rollins nodded. "And what of the detective?"

Ah-ha!

Hirokumi clasped his hands in front of him. "The detective miraculously survived his encounter with the Archer. But if he becomes a problem later, he can be easily dispatched. We can use him to control her."

"What about Him? Is He appeased?"

Hirokumi looked really smug. "The Suzerain is always appeased."

Susi—what? What the hell was that? Was that French? Was he talking about the Phantasm thing?

Did I mention that I hated smug?

Rollins stepped forward, and his gunmen held out their weapons. Hirokumi's moved as well. "Is *He* here?"

"We have not seen Him." Hirokumi cracked a smile. And let me tell you—it looked ghastly in this light. Ever seen a scarecrow smile? Shiver.

Rollins held out his hand. "Give me my contract, and I'll have your daughter given to you."

Here we go, I thought.

Boy was I wrong.

Hirokumi shook his head. "I give her to you, with no regrets. She can be your way station." He smiled again. Ugh. "When you accept my offer."

Way station. Rai's words came back: "*She is to be the vessel.*"

Now I was really confused. And so was Rollins. He looked from Hirokumi to his own men and narrowed his eyes before continuing. "What trickery is this?"

Hirokumi took several steps forward. Rollins's men held their guns up and aimed, as did Hirokumi's men, but Koba motioned them to lower their weapons before he spoke. "The body you now possess, it still grows old, and feeble. It will die, and the contract will evaporate as ash in your hands. You know as well as I there is no protection from the Suzerain's claim. He will have Rollins's soul and you will be destroyed."

I felt just as dumbfounded as Rollins looked, though I was pretty sure this Suzy-rain guy was the Phantasm that created Trench-Coat, and wanted Rollins's Symbiont. I still think it's a French word.

"I offer you my daughter as a place to hide away from His attention. Inside of her, in the place made for you by my seer, the damned, you will know peace and rest. There, you may feed from her soul and grow powerful, before I offer you my own body." He put his hands to his chest. "In here you will have more money, power, women, and wine."

What the fuck?

Rollins cocked his head to the side. "You—would give me—so wonderful a gift as your daughter's soul?"

No . . . no, no, no. Hell no.

Hirokumi nodded. He actually beamed with delight as he gave a short bow in agreement. "*Hai.*"

"What's *wrong* with your body?" Rollins said, and shoved his hands into his coat pockets. "Why offer me this, and suffer His anger and vengeance?"

My question precisely.

"I was diagnosed with Parkinson's a year ago," Koba Hirokumi said quietly. "The disease's effects have started over the course of this year. It is a death I do not wish to succumb to. I wish a longer life—there are things I must accomplish, an empire I must finish building."

"So why not allow me to enter you now?"

"Because I still have safety precautions to set in place, so that if you overcome me, you will not win, as you did with Theodore. I will still have control."

Pissed. Oh I was pissed. This motherfucker had Parkinson's, and was offering his daughter's life up to get an oogy in him?

But Koba was still talking. "But please, do not think of me as an enemy, but as your only hope. The Phantasm comes. The contract will not save the soul you hoard within that body. I have removed your adversary. The only thing on the physical plane that could harm you."

Rollins spoke. "But when I didn't respond to you, you sent out a signal to the Phantasm that conjured me. Because you knew he would find me, and I was forced to show my hand."

I put my hands to my ears. This was all becoming very upsetting. We'd all been played. All of us. By Hirokumi.

"So the girl . . ." And I thought I saw real hunger in Rollins's eyes. "She is here to wet my whistle?"

"I instructed your men to take her, so that you would be tempted by her sweetness, her innocence."

"She is your daughter."

But Hirokumi shook his head. "I have no use for her. If I had had a son, then my line could have carried on the name of Hirokumi through my holdings in Japan as well as here in the States. The girl is expendable."

Boo! Hirokumi sucks.

Rollins narrowed his eyes. "I discovered your little spy inside your daughter, Hirokumi. Perhaps too late, as I do not possess the magic to see housed spirits. But my seer would have known of the soul-damned Traveler inside your daughter. Is that why Mitsuri disappeared? So that you could spy on me even as I took the child into my home?"

"It was how I knew of the Wraith you kidnapped. It was how I knew your moves, and what touched the Wraith's heart, before you did."

Played. We'd all been played. And Rollins looked as pissed as me about it.

"What makes you think I won't kill you now, Koba?" Rollins said. "As a Symbiont, I can take another form."

"No." Koba smiled. God I hated that smile. "As Symbiont you are bound by rules—the ones in this contract signed with Theodore Rollins's blood. Since I hold the contract, only I can free you. Yes, you could run then, and be free. But you could never possess a body again—you can hide in them, but you can't own them. You would never be able to feel, or taste, or smell again unless you are bound."

I knew from the expression on Rollins's face Hirokumi was right. Educations galore!

"I like my life," Rollins said finally. "I like doing what

I'm doing. I may not believe in it—in God and the Devil—the way most folks do. But I give people hope. I don't kill, Hirokumi. Not like you."

Koba lowered his head. "I had believed you would say such. There is another way for you to leave this body, Symbiont, if you won't do it willingly."

That's when I realized the eyes watching us weren't all from the oogy realm. They were living. And they were dressed in black pajamas.

And they were carrying Uzis.

I ducked toward Rollins's limo first and went through the trunk as the bullets started flying and pinging. I held on to Susan in that limo trunk, as hard as I could. Luckily, the limo was bulletproof, but the noise was deafening.

When the noise stopped I listened for a brief second before I sieved my head out.

The cleared area was riddled with bodies, both in black suits as well as black pajamas. Rollins had had his own men in position as well.

I saw Rollins sprawled on the ground against the passenger, right-side tire. His eyes were open, and he wasn't moving. Tiny and Beckett lay in heaps beside him. I knew Tiny was dead.

Rollins—there was still life.

To my utter surprise, Koba Hirokumi was still alive. He was struggling to stand up, having taken a hit to his left knee and arm. I assumed he had Kevlar on everywhere else. He'd banked on this happening.

Something wispy materialized around Rollins—almost gossamer. And I knew it was the Symbiont. I'd sort of figured it would be like that Garfield cat thing, remembering the picture Rhonda had shown me.

But it was beautiful. Sparkly.

And Koba had his arm out to it. "I offer you my daughter. If you refuse"—he again smiled—"you will be hunted down and destroyed." I noticed in his hand he held a folded piece of parchment.

A new contract? Or the old?

Oh no you don't.

Son of a bitch just had a reverend shot and all his men in pajamas as well—and he was still bargaining for the Symbiont's long life.

Wrong. So wrong.

I wanted to shatter the Symbiont then—I wanted to destroy Koba's hope of longevity. I wanted to hurt him for hurting everyone else he'd touched.

Especially me.

And Daniel.

I knew if I still possessed the strength and ability Trench-Coat had given me as a Wraith, however ill planned, I could wipe the Symbiont from existence. I could destroy it. I *knew* this.

But Trench-Coat was gone. Destroyed. And I was nothing but an astral image of myself.

I fell to my knees and watched as the Symbiont moved toward the trunk, to me, and to the waiting girl inside. She would die from this—I'd seen it. The death mask.

"There is another way," the wind whispered again.

The voice was Dark. Spooky. Sexy.

Familiar.

It was my own.

Something brushed against me, to my right side. I turned my head to my left, and saw the faint, washed-away image of Trench-Coat.

He was facing the oncoming Symbiont same as I, and kneeling. He wore his coat, and his boots, his dark shades, and his smirk. I frowned at him. Oh—I was shocked. Scared to death. And smitten. "You—you can't be here."

"I'm not. I'm simply a figment of your imagination, Zoë." Smooth words, rich as chocolate melting in my mouth.

I felt heat rise in the right places at the wrong time. No . . . I would not get all turned on from a memory.

"More than memory, Zoë." He turned and faced me. I could even see my own ghostly reflection in his shades. "You destroyed me with a Banshee's curse, a little something I picked up in my long life and somehow gave to you. But I'm more than Symbiont—I am Archer—and I claim you."

I looked back at the approaching Symbiont. *Man that thing is moving slow. Is this normal?* I looked around at Hirokumi, then to Rollins. Actually—*no one* was moving.

What the—

"The Suzerain comes, Zoë. He doesn't want you to become a Wraith."

"To become a—but I can't. When I killed you, I lost it all."

"Not entirely. It's still there, Zoë. Just under your skin, lodged deep inside your twisted soul." He grinned. Straight white teeth. "With me."

"You're in my soul?" *Oh no—we ain't having none of that.*

"When you destroyed Rai, you took a damned soul, Zoë. That's a mark that cannot be erased in the Good Book."

"But he tricked me." I glanced around at the scene again. Things were unnaturally still. Quiet. No traffic noises. Not even a cricket (though it was a bit chilly for bugs this time of year).

"So I simply moved inside of you, my love." He stood and took a step closer to me. I scrambled to my feet and backed away, careful not to sieve back into the limo behind me.

I put up my hand. "Wait. Whoa—you're inside of me? In my soul?"

He stopped, but he was still grinning at me. And it was a smug grin.

I really hate smug.

"We're two of a kind, Zoë. Different. Aberrant. We belong together."

No, no, no, no . . . I belonged with Daniel. Or at least some facsimile of a normal, breathing, non-Abysmal-planed thing. "You get out of me right now!"

"Only you can release me, Zoë."

Uh-oh. I heard strings. There were always strings. "What happens to me if I do release you?"

"*You will not!*"

Yow!

I spun to my right and was aware of Trench-Coat's own quick movement.

From the shadows came the image of a young man, walking with determination, toward us. He wore a jacket and hood like a rapper, his face shadowed beneath it. His hands were clasped behind his back as he glided closer.

I watched with mounting, fascinated horror. He wasn't completely there, having no form from the waist down. And he was made of shadows and soot, as if he were a part of them.

He stopped inches from me and lifted his head to look at me as he pulled a masquerade mask from behind his back and held it up in front of the dark maw of his hood.

The mask of a harlequin. The same doll my mom had bought me when I was eight, thinking it would be something I'd like. White face, black diamonds around its eyes, a single bloodred tear and black lips. I'd buried it in the backyard because it frightened me. And I never talked about it again.

No one knew about that damned doll except my mother, and me. I took in a quick breath of astral air and stepped back, closer to the image of Trench-Coat.

The black-painted lips on the molded mask turned up in the corners as the black, eyeless sockets seemed to stare right through me. *"They take on the image of what scares you the most,"* came Steve's words from a morning breakfast, so long ago.

Power radiated from this thing in waves of überoogy.

Phantasm.

"You cannot touch her." Trench-Coat was quick on the defense there.

The Phantasm's mask seemed to nod on its own. I leaned to the right, trying to see what was behind the wretched mask. I saw nothing. The molded black lips moved when it spoke, but not quite in sync with the words. "Not yet—but if you continue confusing her, slave, she will become my enemy." The mask turned on its wooden dowel. That's when I noticed the hand clutching it was little more than a shadow, and it still held the other hand behind its back. "And I hers."

Trench-Coat turned to me. "He is afraid of what you'll become, Zoë Martinique. Of what I'll become." He looked back at the Phantasm. "Something he cannot control on any plane of existence."

"Do not task me, Archer." The last name he spit out as if tasting something bad. Well, I did remember hearing about these two fighting before, and the Phantasm here had taken Trenchy's voice. "You have disappointed me since the day you were created."

"I'm flattered."

Oh geez. "Look." I glanced over at the frozen Symbiont, trying to silence my rising gorge at the nearness of the harlequin's mask. For years I'd trained myself to ignore clowns and masks—but the harlequin face—it haunted my dreams. "I'm really sorry you two can't get counseling, but there's a little girl in this limo who is going to die if your Symbiont takes her body. Now, aren't you upset that that guy over there"—I pointed at Hirokumi—"has the contract you established with him"—I pointed at Rollins's still-inert form—"and is going to destroy it as long as he"—I pointed back to Hirokumi—"gets the Symbiont for himself? I mean, you need to destroy the Symbiont so you get your soul, right?"

I couldn't believe I'd just told a bad guy to take a reverend's soul. Oh I'm so going to a special kind of hereafter.

And I was surprised when the Phantasm only chuckled. "What is an old, worthless soul to me when I can feed on that of a child through my Symbiont? Let him take her, then let him take the fat man." Again a laugh. "I can have them all."

I heard something faint, soft. The voice of a child. It came from the trunk of the limo.

Oh God. Susan was awake and beating on the hood.

The Phantasm had started the world moving again. The Symbiont was closer to the trunk now, and in seconds he'd have Susan Hirokumi.

"Zoë." Trench-Coat turned to me. "Join with me—be the Wraith—be one with me as we did that night in endless lovemaking."

Abruptly I relived images, sensations, of soft sheets and warm bodies, sensual caresses and ethereal whispers. My God . . . it hadn't been a dream. I'd made love to him.

I'd made love to him!

In those missing hours before the morgue, I'd known Trench-Coat in ways I'd only read in Mom's thick romance novels.

EWWWWWWW.

But I'd enjoyed it.

"*Doe-da*?" came Susan's voice.

I felt the wind beside me chitter. "Choose. Save the girl"—the trees moved overhead in the starless night—"or let her die. Be the Wraith and destroy the Symbiont."

"No . . ." I shook my head. "I thought I'd destroyed you,

but now you tell me you're inside of me. I don't want that Symbiont inside of me too!"

"It will not!" Trench-Coat said. "You and I were linked the moment I touched your arm."

I glanced down at my arm. The imprint of his hand was gone. I hadn't noticed. Was the color of my hair back to normal as well?

"Let me touch you again. Free me, and yourself."

"No!" The Phantasm stepped forward. I stared at the mask in horror. The eyebrows moved into sharp, angry arches, and the black lips turned downward. "You will *not*. I command you."

Oh ho ho? I felt my own anger rise again. It never replaced my fear of this thing standing before me with its mask of harlequin rage. If I gave in to my fears at that moment, I'm sure I would have melted on the ground and screamed in terror of the harlequin mask. I'm sure in hindsight, I should have just let them all go at each other and gone straight to my parish priest and gotten Trenchy exorcised out of me.

But I was pissed. And I wasn't going to let an innocent child die. On the other hand, if I let him touch me again, then I was in a sense letting Tanaka's killer free.

Which was the right choice?

In the end, I figured there wasn't one. But I sure as hell wasn't going to let some mask-wearing blank-faced Phantasm feed off of a little girl.

I made my decision and reached out to Trench-Coat. I looked at the Phantasm's mask and felt the cold rage as it focused on me through the narrowed eyes of the mask. "Eat me."

In hindsight—probably it wasn't the brightest move.

But then Trench-Coat touched me. Ice ran through my veins, followed closely by warmth. I could almost hear

Mom's voice, and Rhonda's, from wherever they were with my body. Could they tell I'd changed again?

I could. I was stronger. I felt light, my soul woven into the very night air, a part of all things, then somehow not at all.

Celldweller's "Symbiont" played in my head, and I felt myself spiraling into the air. And he was with me.

Trench-Coat.

TC.

Abruptly the tidal wave of power lessened, and I opened my eyes.

The Phantasm was gone. TC stood to the right, and the Symbiont was beside the car.

Oh no you don't. I reached out with my hand and grabbed the Symbiont's core. The sparkling lights abruptly vanished, exposing the hellish cat Rhonda had shown me in the book. And it scratched!

Ow!

Littlesonofabitchyoumother—

Only I yelled at it. With that special kind of yell. The one with no real sound to it. The thing started to mutate and stretch, as if being pulled into a million directions. I flung it off of me like a bad bugger.

It exploded on impact against Rollins's car.

Ew. Ew. Ew.

That's when I heard Hirokumi scream.

I turned to see TC take the corporate president's soul into the whirling red circle of his palm.

No!

But he didn't stop. He did turn and look at me. "I have to have a prize too," my own voice said back to me.

And I knew I could no longer speak. Not unless I destroyed him again.

He held up a hand. "Uh-uh-uh. You asked for my touch this time, Miss Martinique. You invited me in. We now have a binding contract."

Our deal. And I knew I'd made a deal with the Devil. Oh wouldn't Faust be proud!

"It's worse than that, Zoë." He smiled at me as he straightened his coat. I glanced at Hirokumi's soulless, staring body on the dark ground by his limo. "You've made a deal with what the Devil fears."

And he was gone. Only a whisper on the wind. And a voice in my mind. "I'll be around, my love."

Bleck.

I learned at that moment as ethereal tears streamed down my face and I opened the trunk to comfort a frightened little girl. There are worse things than losing.

There was always winning.

EPILOGUE

Two Weeks Later

I listened to the soft beeping of the heart monitor in the ICU unit at Northside Hospital as it played an accompaniment to the CD *The Piano*. I'd learned it was Daniel's favorite sound track, and so I played it as much as I could. It was very nice. Soothing.

They expected Daniel to wake up any day now. His leg was mending. His ribs. His patched spleen and even his fractured left pinkie.

But his head? No one knew yet. He'd taken a hard crack to his skull, which had put him in a coma. So—I'd spent a lot of time here.

And Mom and Rhonda came at noon each day with biscuits, ham, tea, and jelly. I was hoping he'd smell Mom's buttery cooking and wake up.

Nothing yet.

And so I sat in the spare chair, listening to the nurses and doctors, sort of guessing which doctor they'd page to the ER next. I wanted to think of anything except what I'd done. What I'd become. Of what I'd done to my soul.

I thought of the aftermath instead.

The doctors attributed my muteness to the brain damage. Of course, when was it I received this "brain damage"? Maddox said it was my time without oxygen in the morgue. Those seizures, remember?

And, I had been officially declared a Type II diabetic, which of course Mom said was ridiculous. But, to make her happy, I tested my blood after every meal. I reeeeeeeally hated doing that. Luckily I got one of those little blue things that will test a really small amount of blood.

Go me.

Luckily, Reverend Rollins survived his ordeal. Though the damage done by the bullets in his chest severely limited his appearances around the world, he still delivered the message of God, in a much more subdued fashion.

I still wondered days afterward why TC took Koba's soul and not Rollins's. Rollins's fulfilled the contract. But maybe the old Symbiont had his own sense of justice.

Weird.

Koba Hirokumi's death was listed as unsolved. Cooper pretty much glossed over the finding of Susan Hirokumi in Rollins's trunk, and since the girl didn't remember anything and was now with her mother in Japan, everyone kept quiet.

Tanaka's murder? Cold-case file for all I know. Captain Cooper, on his frequent visits, really didn't want to talk to me. He blamed me for Daniel's condition.

And he was right.

I'd tried that first night with Daniel in the hospital, after the incident across from Perimeter Circle, to revive him, to mend him in some way—but instead I'd felt my new state of being doing what it'd done to Rhonda. I started to feed on his mending soul. The heart monitors had detected a drop in blood pressure, agitation.

And so I'd stayed out of the ICU when OOB. In fact, I hadn't strayed from my body since then. I was too afraid of what I'd do.

The door opened, and Mom and Rhonda came in. They didn't bring Tim or Steve—apparently the ghosts' magnetic fields played havoc with the electronics. And we all wanted Daniel to keep breathing.

"You look worse today," Mom said as she did her usual checkup on Daniel. Was she talking to me, or to Daniel? She grabbed his chart, did her own scan, and made some inane comment. I guess I looked bad. I had no makeup, wore sweats and a tee shirt. I'd kept my bothersome hair back in a ponytail most of the time—except for that white shock that kept escaping. I wasn't even sure I'd washed it this week.

"But the white hair's growing on me," she said with a half smile.

I smelled the biscuits, and my stomach growled. Even though I wasn't supposed to indulge in too many breads, I usually snagged at least one biscuit.

Rhonda looked well rested. Her hair was up in pigtails today, and her nails were a fresh black. Her kohl-rimmed eyes smiled at me as she pulled her skull-adorned book bag up and handed me my iBook. "Here—I figured you should check your client list and e-mail. I've been tagging a lot of them and set an autoresponse to tell them you'd been on vacation."

Yeah. Some vacation. But I took the iBook and stood.

The hospital wasn't wireless in ICU, so I'd have to hoof it to the visitor's lounge or the cafeteria. I opted for the cafeteria, so I could snag a cup of that oh-so-good swill they called java.

I wanted a Starbucks White Mocha sooooo bad.

Yay! And watch my blood sugar beat the next shuttle launch as it broke orbit too.

The cafeteria was set up as serve yourself. So I grabbed a cup of coffee, dumped a load of sugar and cream in. The guy behind the checkout line—Charles on his tag—had gotten so used to seeing me he just waved me on through to the dining area.

Blue walls, soft muted upholstery on the bench cushions and booths. A prelighted Christmas tree sat in the corner and twinkled colorfully at me as I passed by. Silver and blue garlands hung in waves along the walls, over the backs of the wood dividers of seats. There weren't too many people there. A few men and women in white coats, a single woman in pink scrubs reading a book. Christmas music piped in softly.

Nope, not in the jolly mood.

I walked to the "outside" area. It really wasn't out in the December cold, but the roof was made of glass, like a large sunroom. I picked a warm spot near the back and popped open the iBook.

Two seconds and it'd found the network.

Holy shit!

Two thousand and forty-three messages?

And I was sure there were thousands more that had dumped into the other account. Panic disappeared when I realized a good bulk of them were spam.

I had backtracked to November and started cleaning them out when I ran across one that ran cold shivers down my spine.

Maharba@maharba.com.

The subject line read "We Are Watching." I felt my spine grow cold.

"Dear Miss Martinique—it has come to our attention that you did not fulfill your contract with us on the nature of the meeting between Detective Frasier and Koba

Hirokumi. And now Mr. Hirokumi is dead. We are very disappointed and have suspended accounts with you while we evaluate your position. We feel the relationship between us must change. We will be watching you, and your activities, and we will contact you again to collect on your debt, at a later time."

We? Us? Always I'd thought this was a single person. But this e-mail read as though they were a committee. And a very pissed committee. I'd fully intended to report back to them after the e-mail on my phone that night, but then I'd been kidnapped, and everything had gone to hell since then.

And they were watching me.

Did they know what it was I could do? Did they know I could do even more now? Did they know about Wraiths? And Phantasms? And sexy, spooky Symbionts?

Who the hell *were* they?

Paranoia had arrived and set up house.

I closed the e-mail then and searched for any others, but there hadn't been any. I also checked my bank accounts— the money had never been withdrawn either.

Yeah, I'd owe them. By rights.

I gulped down my coffee, letting it burn the roof of my mouth.

First off, there was a Phantasm out there that had my name, a Symbiont that I'd spared but still wanted pieces of me. I had this really oogy feeling I'd totally screwed myself up by taking TC's offer and somehow I'd damned my own soul, just as they said Rai had damned his. I still didn't have a clue who this mysterious Joe was. And now there was some secretive group that watched me and would call on my services one day.

Okay—that's it—I'm putting my life on e-Bay and shopping for a new one.

Too much coffee propelled me out of the cafeteria and

into the hallway where the restrooms were. I sat the laptop on the sink counter and pushed open the first door I came to, not bothering to check to see if it was occupied.

Imagine my surprise when I found myself staring face-to-face with Dags the Fadó's bartender and Nancy the nurse. Both were naked. And it appeared they were in a heated race to see who could suck the other one's lungs up through their throat first.

My heart pounded against my chest as Dags turned and looked at me, his eyes wide with recognition. "You . . ." he gasped out.

The girl disengaged herself and bounced out of the stall, muttering under her breath.

Dags stood to the left of the toilet with his pants at his ankles.

I smiled.

There is nothing more defenseless than a naked man.